Caladrius Dreams

Book One of
The Queenmaker Saga

Sunlit Publishing
Cheney, WA
Visit our website at sunlitpublishing.com

First edition: July 2016

ISBN 978-0-9977998-1-1

Cover design by James Powers

Printed in the United States of America

CALADRIUS
DREAMS

Erin Ann McCarter

Sunlit Publishing
Cheney, WA

To God,
who has given me all that was needed.

A bone to the dog is not charity. Charity is the bone shared with the dog, when you are just as hungry as the dog.

—Jack London

1

Hunger

The air was heavy with the scent of burning things. I found that fear trapped me, hidden in the closet where Auntie had set me and told me to stay. Fear had made me motionless, but now heat was making me move. The shouts and thundering of hooves had long since faded away. All I could hear now was the crackling of fire.

"Auntie Margaret?" I untangled myself slowly from the clothes I had burrowed into on the floor. There was no answer. I called a little louder. Nothing. "Auntie? Uncle? I'm scared." My voice warbled and tears spilled down my cheeks, cold against the heat on my skin. I was still too small—my fingers couldn't reach the doorknob—but when I pushed, the door swung open. It hadn't been shut all the way. Black dust stuck to the bottoms of my feet as I wandered out into the living room. I paused between the juncture of the kitchen and the living room, wide eyes searching while my feet made trembling, backwards steps towards the door.

"Auntie? I—" My voice trailed off as something bumped gently into the back of my head. My hands came up and closed around the object, suspended at the level of my nose. I turned around. Uncle Barry's boots were hanging from the rafters, dangling in a way that suggested they were attached to something. My heel traced a tentative step backward. Slowly, I lifted my gaze...

I was upright and tense at the perceived threat before I could even register what was going on. Reality came swiftly, like a plunge through cold water; my unconscious mind had abandoned the dream before it could travel my memory's path any further. That day wasn't something I wanted to relive—the day the only family I had ever known died. Auntie Margaret and Uncle Barry weren't really my aunt and uncle—those titles were only terms of endearment—but they were the people who had found me and taken me in when I had been abandoned by my parents as a baby.

For a moment, the memory of fire warmed me, but as my body adjusted, the cold crept in. Somewhere in the back of my mind I noted that there wasn't much difference between heat and cold. The burning sensation worn into the sides of my arms and the tops of my thighs was the same, and I could see my breath coming in puffs which reminded me hauntingly of smoke. The smell of smoke lingered, but it wasn't from the air around me.

For as long as I could remember, the dreams had been there, waiting just outside of consciousness and ready to ensnare. They were always the same, as real and solid as the world around me— so similar in fact that at times I had difficulty telling the difference. Most of the time, I couldn't make sense of them. They were chaos, shadows and screaming, bits of thoughts, and memories that didn't seem to be my own.

But sometimes my dreams were coherent, and those were always the worst. On those nights, I relived my worst memories; the day Auntie Margaret and Uncle Barry died, my first night on the streets, days of hunger and cold, infected wounds, and fear—I forced the dreams out of my mind. It wouldn't do to dwell on them now. I pulled my knees into my chest and pushed away a scrap of garbage which I had used to hide myself from unfriendly eyes. My cheek had been braised by a rough cobblestone in my sleep and I pressed it against a shoulder to numb the pain. After a moment of wiggling my toes to move the blood back into them, I stood. The most important thing now was food.

Out on the corner, at the edge of the town buildings and near the King's Park, I lifted my eyes to the sky. The midmorning fog made it difficult to see, but my eyes soon found what they were looking for. A raven's silhouette, dark body blending perfectly with the clouds above, circled lazy loops overhead. I pursed my lips and let out a low whistle. He descended and dropped a crust of bread at my feet. I opened my mind, and let in his thoughts.

"Thank you, Hookbeak." Crouching, I gathered the crust in a hand. It was hardly bigger than my palm, but it would be enough for now. I pulled my cold, cracked lips into a smile. "This helps me more then you know."

"Don't worry about it...sorry I couldn't get more...not much out there...not much at all." He examined me with an intelligent eye, but there was a fuzziness to the edge of his thoughts—like a child speaking burble—that I could barely make out. With a sharp nod, he took off and disappeared again into the clouds. I let out a long, slow breath and lifted the crust towards my lips.

The crunch of gravel to my left made me freeze. Someone was behind me. "Hey Carrot!" A voice called out. The hairs on the back of my neck rose. I knew that voice.

I turned slowly, balling the crust into a hand and guarding it behind my back. It wouldn't be safe to eat it here, not with him standing right in front of me. He would probably see it as an act of defiance and an excuse to pick a fight. Already, he wore a calculating smile.

He glanced to his right and his left. Two other boys appeared from the shadows of the nearest building. They came like hyenas, their gaunt faces stretched bone tight, their hands as starved as mine.

"What's that you have, bird-girl?" the middle one said. I set my face so they couldn't see my fear, and ignored the shudder that ran down my spine.

"How about you hand it over?" said the boy to his left.

"We promise it won't hurt...for long."

Their voices were like echoes of the night. Joe-Boy, Sammuel, and McAllen. Joe-Boy, the biggest, was their leader. His blonde hair grew in patches and an ugly scar ate up the right side of his face.

Sammuel, to his left, was his brother—or so they claimed—and was only a little smaller. He looked the way Joe-Boy might if his hair had grown in and his face were smooth.

On Joe-Boy's right was McAllen, the newest member of the group. He was small and walked with an awkward slump that suggested his bones hadn't grown quite right. Poor nutrition, probably.

All three of them were kids, forced to live on the streets for lack of family, or a home. Just like me. But unlike myself, they stole to get their fill. I backed up slowly. I didn't stand a chance fighting them—it would be a battle I could not afford. They were older than I. Larger. Stronger. But they had forgotten one crucial ingredient. I was faster.

"Girl..." Joe-Boy's voice was threatening. I quivered as he stepped closer still. And then, before he could even think to grab me, I ran. I ran across the street, splashing through muddy puddles. Leaping over cobblestone holes. I didn't glance back to see if they'd followed. My only goal, my only thought, was to get away and have a crust of my own. One crust could mean the difference between living and starving in the night.

I turned right at Court Street, bumping through pedestrians and sidestepping a horse and cart. A woman selling flowers from a basket on the corner had to jump out of my way, leaving roses crushed and soggy on the wet street. I didn't stop to apologize. I could hear them behind me. Faster. I had to go faster. Up ahead was an old alleyway, partially hidden by rubble and a couple trees. I weaved into the merchants surrounding it and used the crowd as cover. Squeezing past a hawker's cart, I threw myself into the alleyway and paused, letting my breath catch up with me. Running footsteps pounded closer, and then faded away. I was safe.

I turned around, pressing my back against the dingy wall and sliding exhausted into the dirt. Then I unclenched my fist and glanced down at the crust in my palm. It was slightly smashed, but still edible.

My eyes found the street. It was clear. Still, I didn't know how long it would take them to find me. It would be best to eat now, and slip through the alley the back way. Maybe I could find somewhere warm to hide and spend the next few hours conserving energy. I glanced to the road again, and then over my shoulder into the alley. My eyes came to a halt at a shape hidden several feet from me behind a pile of junk. A pair of large eyes blinked at me, just barely shining in the low light.

Tucked against the wall was a woman. A baby lay wrapped in her arms. Her shoulders quivered in a way which suggested she was afraid of me. A feeling grew in the pit of my stomach and I glanced at the crust in my fist. She needed it more than I did. I held out my hand, crust still firmly clenched in my fingertips. The woman shook her head. Her eyes found the ground. "Please take it...?" Before she could refuse, I forced the crust into her palm and walked away.

I found a dry niche under the eave of a deserted storefront and curled myself under it. I would have to find more food soon, but here I could wait out the rain. The pinch of hunger gradually faded, and I welcomed the relief. When the rain was gone and I no longer ran the risk of wetness bringing on a cold, I would venture out and begin again. The ravens wouldn't have anymore food today, but if I could last until the rain stopped, I still had a chance.

* * *

"Hey Carrot!" The voice belonged to Joe-Boy, I recognized it without turning around. I was sitting in a sun patch on the west side of town, a grey woolen hat pulled over my ears and a yard of moth eaten linen draped over my shoulders like a cloak. "Did you enjoy your crust?" It was hard to ignore him when his words carried such a sting.

Disgruntled, I tucked my red hair up under my hat and out of his sight. I hated being called "carrot" or any other term that referenced my hair. The mention of my red hair was an insult—it marked me as belonging to the lower class—and Joe-Boy never failed to remind me of that fact. "Look what I have!" he said. "It's a beauty isn't it?"

Crouching just behind me, he waved a loaf of bread near my face. I winced when a slight breeze brought the scent across my nose. It was warm still. I could feel the heat coming off of it. My eyes flickered shut. I could almost taste the crumbs. A low breath shuddered through my chest and my parched throat convulsed. "Please go away." My voice was strained, but I kept the tone flat. I couldn't let him see weakness. This was a game to him, and I refused to play it. I turned my back and hoped he would leave. He didn't.

"Where'd you get this little treasure?" Suddenly my shoulders ached with cold. He had taken my scrap of cloth. I could see him out of the corner of my eye, running it through his hands and then tossing it up over his shoulder. The upper portion of my back tensed, and I buried my fingers into my skirt. I didn't answer him. "It doesn't matter, it's mine now." I didn't need to see the smirk on his face to visualize it.

Only my pride kept me from shivering. I stood and ignored him, walking away and wrapping my arms around my narrow shoulders when I knew he was out of sight. He didn't follow.

The street was shiny from rain and I padded across it, avoiding the puddles that pooled between the cobblestones. My bare feet were nearly numb. I couldn't feel the roughness of the road, but my steps were cautious anyway. Even a small cut could lead to an infection, and out here, infections often ended in death.

I rounded the outskirts of the city, following the road which I knew would lead me to its center. For a moment I paused, watching the mist which clung to the trees. It would be winter soon. The ice in the air and the colors on the trees made me sure of it. Winter was the worst time of year, for obvious reasons. The cold air smelled of death.

The world around me changed as I walked. It seemed almost as if the poverty that filled the streets could somehow remind the people that life wasn't as cheery as they tried to pretend. So they erased it. The waste piled by the buildings disappeared. So did the dirt. The grime. There was food here. Food and paint. Paint which decorated walls and faces, hiding the tight emptiness from view.

An old, toothless man sat on the elevated edge of a storefront, a bandage over his eyes and a crutch lying on the stone steps. He was like me, a pile of rags and dirt who was desperate enough to sit at a street corner where he did not belong. The stone beneath him was recently swept. Dust fell off his sleeves and dirtied the ground. He rattled his can at me, blind hands searching. "I'm sorry," I whispered and continued to walk. I had nothing to give.

I skirted Main Street, walking down a back alley until I found a street that wasn't as crowded. Once I found a suitable corner, I pressed myself into a painted wall. well out of the way of the carriages which jostled down the street.

It was a long time before I was noticed by anyone. Most simply went around me, not looking up from the ground as they walked. Others carefully held their eyes away as if I were a disease that could be caught just by looking. A few noticed me, and crossed to the other side of the street. I hunched my shoulders, trying to look as inconspicuous and, simultaneously, pitiful as possible. A large woman stood by me, carefully looking over my head and into the shop windows that lay behind. After a moment of hesitation, I approached her.

"Excuse me?" She looked the other way like she could not hear. "M'lady?" Unlike Joe-Boy and his gang, I would never steal. But, in desperate times, I could be driven to beg. "M'lady... please—" I dropped my eyes to stare at her sturdy boots and reached out to touch the edge of her ruffled hem. She looked down at me then. I could feel my cheeks heat under her stare. I peeked up to view her face.

The way her eyes caught mine made me realize I would win nothing from the woman. She drew herself to her full height—several heads taller than myself—and her face became very red. She looked like she wanted to slap me, but seemed to be hesitating. To react would be to admit she had noticed. To react, would mean she had let *scum* distract her from her day. Her gloved hands groped for her heavy skirts and, lifting them, she moved past me. I had to stumble backwards to keep out of her way. My foot slid on an uneven stone, and I tumbled into the street.

"Hey you! Get out of the way!" I could barely hear the coachman's voice over the grind of carriage wheels, slicing air next to my ear. Mud splashed from the spokes, showering my back. I rolled onto my side and out of the way.

For a moment, all I could hear was the sound of my panting and the quick flutter of my heart. Then my head cleared, and I forced myself to my knees. The sound of footsteps punctuated the air. Slowly, I raised my gaze. A pair of feet had stopped in front of me. I didn't quite trust what would happen if I looked, but my eyes darted upwards before I could stop myself. A hand was extended above me. For a long moment, all I could do was stare.

"Take it child," a voice prodded, coming from a long way up. I cringed back from the voice, but I took the hand.

2

Notice

He was wearing a dark grey cloak like the ones the heroes wear in stories. For a moment, my mind tried to follow that train of thought. I pulled it away. This man was not a hero. He was simply a kindhearted man who had appeared in the right place, at the right time.

He turned sharply and moved away from me. I followed. A man willing to help me might be willing to give me a piece of copper, or even a silver for some food. He turned back after several strides and halted. His eyes found mine and I stopped too.

"What do you want?" His speech had the rough edge of a voice used too often—or of one used not often enough. I pondered what to say in reply, and then decided to play meek. A man willing to help me was a man who probably liked the feeling of saving people. Playing the part of a starving child would be the best way to win his heart—and his coin. I said nothing and stared at the ground, rolling my shoulders up to my ears and clutching my stomach as if I couldn't decide whether I were more cold, or more hungry. I didn't lie, it was the truth. Sometimes, the truth makes the best act of all. After a long second, I looked up. He was already half a block away.

"Wait!" I ran after him, jogging until I fell in at his side.

"I'm busy," he said, his brusque voice flat. His face made no expression and his eyes stayed fixed ahead. "Whatever you want, I can promise you I don't have the time."

It seemed I had been wrong. He was not kindhearted, and didn't have the least amount of interest in saving anybody. "I can help," I said, dropping the starving child act and pulling myself up to my full height. "All I ask for is a couple of coppers, and I will do anything you need. I can be the cheapest labor you've ever had." A business man, that's what he was. I would talk business.

"No." We had come to a halt again, and his eyes focused on something far behind me.

"Why not, sir? I am a good worker, I know how to keep my mouth shut and—"

"It's dangerous business." His tone made the answer sound final, but that wasn't good enough. I needed him. I forced myself in front of him, blocking his path. My eyes found their way to his face, and when I opened my mouth, the desperation which had gathered in the pit of my stomach leaked into my voice.

"No more dangerous than what will happen to me if I don't get a meal for the fifth night straight."

I cringed when I heard his feet move towards me, my eyes turning down and my body bracing for the backhanded strike that would knock me to the ground. Above me the man sighed heavily, and suddenly his hand was around my wrist. The warmth from the contact made my skin prickle. "Don't you have anyone to look after you? A mother? A brother perhaps?"

"No, sir."

"Stay here." We were outside a bakery, the one on the left corner of the outer edge of Lowell Street, next to the bookstore and behind the marble statue of the dead king's brother. He went into the shop, and my nose twitched as the sweetness of freshly baked bread flooded my senses when he opened the door.

He was gone only minutes, but it felt like hours. When he came back he carried a steaming loaf of bread. The pinch in my stomach became almost nauseating. He leaned against the wall of the shop beside us, and held the loaf out to my trembling hands. The weight of it made my hands dip and I held it like it were made of glass.

I couldn't remember the last time I had touched fresh food. It warmed my palms and crumbled beneath my grasp. I caught the crumbs in a hand and stuck them to my tongue. Then I tore off a small end. I took a bite, and it melted on my tongue. A deep sigh of relief passed through me. The rest of the loaf I tucked under my arm for later. A loaf this size could last me a week, maybe more.

"What's your name, child?

His voice startled me and my eyes snapped towards him; I had nearly forgotten his presence entirely. For a moment, I hesitated, unsure of how to answer. No one had ever asked me that. "I don't know," I said finally. "I don't remember. People call me Scum. Girl. Ugly. Hey you. That's all."

Questions buzzed in my head, but I didn't ask them. Who was this man, and what was he doing here? His appearance didn't quite match the people in the streets around us, and his accent was strange. I allowed myself to examine his face for a moment, something I didn't normally take the time to do. He was ruggedly handsome, possessing that sort of weathered face which made you wonder whether he was young, or old. His caramel colored eyes were a soft brown that seemed at odds with their hawk-like expression. He wasn't looking at me anymore; his eyes had fixed on something behind my head. His hand grabbed my arm.

"Walk," he said gruffly. I didn't like the tone of his voice. It had changed into something harsher, something less caring and more wild. There was a different feeling on the air.

"What? Why?"

"I said walk. Now." He pulled me from the wall and halfway down the street before I could protest. Running was out of the question, his hand was too tight around my arm. I knew there was no chance of my breaking free. I took the only option left to me, and followed him.

We turned a corner and went down a side street. It wasn't long before the crowd thinned and the only sound I could hear was the splash of my feet in puddles and the wet drumming of rain against rooftops. When we turned another corner he stopped suddenly, drawing himself up against a wall and peering into the darkness. I copied him and flattened myself to it, trying to quiet my breaths. I could hear my heart rattling in my chest.

A few seconds passed with nothing but silence. Then the rustle of dried leaves made my eyes snap around to the left. A figure appeared around the corner nearest us. It was tall—a man, judging by the breadth of him—dressed all in black, his face shrouded by a deep hood. He moved towards us with a deliberateness that sent chills through my bones. Another man appeared at the corner across from us.

The thoughts in my head were too confused to make out. I realized suddenly the grey cloaked man beside me no longer held my arm. This wasn't my fight. Breaking from my place beside him, I ran.

Words that sounded like swearing chased me. I could hear heavy footsteps pounding just behind my lighter, shoeless patter. I didn't take the time to see who was following, the man in the grey cloak, or the men in the black. It didn't really matter after all. I wanted nothing to do with any of them. The air had felt like death back there, and survival had always been my only goal. In my hand, I carried what promised me that. Clutching the loaf of bread tighter to my chest I ran faster, my breaths coming in startled gasps.

The grimy, tattered rags of my skirts twisted around my legs as I ran. I didn't notice until it was too late. I tripped, falling hard against the flagstones and skidding across them. My hat tumbled off, leaving my ears noticeably colder and my hair scattered in a tangle down my back. The pavement shredded the skin on my elbows and my loaf of bread smashed into the cold wet ground. It rolled away from me, breaking apart and sinking into the deep mud. With a gasp I reached for it, but before my hands could take hold of any of the crumbs I was hauled to my feet. A fist held the back of my dress. For a brief moment the warm grey fabric of a cloak surrounded me, rippling out in front of me from his sudden momentum change. Then we were running again.

His hand pulled at me down one alley and into another. It ripped me around the corner and then with a suddenness that made me stumble, it threw me to a halt. I was pulled through the door of a small inn. The man in the grey cloak stood beside me. He didn't look at me and for a long time, he did not speak. The black cloaked figures were nowhere in sight. A few bread crumbs still clung to the fabric of my dress. The loaf itself was gone, soaking in a puddle in an alley somewhere. My fingers felt empty without it.

"Foolish child," the man muttered. His breath was so even that I thought perhaps I had only imagined him running beside me. It seemed more likely that he had always been here. Waiting. "They could have, and very likely would have killed you, had they caught you," he said, pulling me away from the window. He hadn't looked at me once. His eyes peered out into the street. "It doesn't matter. They will forget you soon enough. This is a safe house. They cannot come in here. Stay here an hour, and then you can go. It will be like none of this ever happened." He turned to leave, and my voice bubbled suddenly out of my throat.

"Sir?"

"What do you want?" He turned to me suddenly, a rough motion that made me flinch away from him. His eyes caught mine, and then widened slightly. His hand reached out, his fingers wrapping around a strand of my dark red hair and rolling it between them as if he were just noticing something for the first time. He dropped the strand after a moment but his face remained distant. "Come with me."

"Why?" He didn't answer. Instead, he turned abruptly and began to climb the stairs. I hesitated for a moment, and then followed. A girl less desperate than I would have refused, but following him could mean food, and that food was worth anything. I paused at the top of the steps to look back. My feet faltered a moment and I had to tear my eyes away from the door that lay behind. Away from the wind and the rain and the dirt. Something felt different inside of me and I wasn't sure what. Like the wind and the rain and the dirt didn't belong to me anymore, nor I to them. I didn't like the feeling.

A sudden movement caused me to look back. Just outside, a hooded figure disappeared around the window's edge. The man called to me from the top of the stairs, and I hurried to catch up.

3

Revelation

"What's going on? What do you want from me? Why—"

"Did he see you?" he said, cutting me off. "You said you saw a man. Did he see you?" He closed the door behind me and I jumped at the snap.

"I—"

"Did he? This is very important."

I nodded slowly and looked around, wrapping my arms around my chest. The room was mostly bare. A writing desk sat in one corner; a few pieces of worn parchment, a bottle of ink, and a quill decorated its top. The chair was made of sturdy wood. Across from the desk was a low bed, the sheets too white for the room and the blanket a dark cream. An old sack and a pile of clothes lay at its base. A heavily lacquered chair sat at its foot. The chair was out of place in the stark room, with its red velvet cushions and golden arms glinting brightly in the dull candlelight.

The man threw his cloak on a peg. He sat on the lacquered chair, pulling off his boots and digging through his hair with frustrated fingers. I stood awkwardly by the door, biting at my lip. "Who are they?" I asked. After a second, he stood and cleared a place on the floor. There was a high window on the north end of the room. It was growing dark outside.

"Baldassarre's men."

"The dead king's brother?" Baldassarre. The name sent chills down my spine. It wasn't often I heard that name spoken. People around here avoided it not because they feared the name, but because names held honor, something a man who could kill his own brother did not deserve. By denying Baldassarre his name, it was like the people were denying him his humanity, his sense of self. Baldassarre was the "dead king's brother," because no matter how many times he usurped the throne, to the people he would only ever be the brother of a king.

"Yes."

"Why are they following you? Why can't I leave?"

"You ask too many questions. Get some rest. We leave in the morning." When I didn't move, he came towards me. Despite my protests, he lifted me and deposited me on the bed. He made a simple sweeping motion with his hand and the room went dark. My heart thudded to a halt.

Magic. The thought whizzed through my mind, and I suddenly felt rather sick. I peeked at the man. He was lying on the floor now and I couldn't tell if he was asleep or awake. His back was to me, and he made no movement except the slow expansion of his ribcage at each breath. The wind outside the window made a strange sort of banging and I gave a startled jump, pulling the blankets up to my chin before huddling down into them and breathing their warmth. I peered at him again over the edges of my blanket, and then buried myself from sight. Magic.

I had heard of magic before. Of course I had. But I had never actually seen it, and I had never thought I would. Only those of noble blood could do magic. Nobles weren't common in my part of the city—indeed they weren't common in Golg at all.

Golg was the capital of the northern end of Saldor, the end the dead king's brother had seized. Those nobles with any scrap of honor, the ones who hadn't followed Baldassarre in his coup, lived on fiefs throughout the countryside and further south near Saldor's old capital—the so called golden city, Caeyra. Whatever nobles lived here—they weren't heroes. They were part of the deceit, part of the blackness that clung to the land like a disease.

They weren't seen often, and I wasn't sure if I really cared to see any at all. I didn't know anything more about them than what

I had heard on the lips of gossiping strangers, and in the voices of bards who sung stories in the streets, and I didn't want to. This man...if he could do magic, he was a noble.

I buried myself deeper into the blankets and tried to focus on other things, like the feeling of sleeping on a bed. Sleep was a long time in coming.

* * *

The sun hadn't yet risen when he woke me. My eyes snapped open the minute his hand touched my shoulder. Years on the street had taught me to sleep lightly. I rolled over to face him and then sat up, instantly awake. "Here. Change into these," he said gruffly. He tossed a bundle on my lap and then left the room. I stared at the door for a moment and then crawled from the bed, holding the bundle to my chest.

A candle winked dimly in the corner of the room, and I fumbled with the tie of the sack, unable to see the knots clearly. The knot stuck and then slid as it came undone. Slowly, I dumped the contents out onto the bed, not certain what to expect. The glint of a white shirt caught my eye. Clothes. Clean clothes. I hadn't worn anything clean in a very long time.

The lighting in the room was too low to make out the details, but I could tell the fabric was finer than anything I'd ever thought I might wear. I pulled off my ragged dress so quickly I almost fell and stuffed it rather unceremoniously into a corner where it could be disposed of later. I never wanted to see the thing again. I laid the clothes out, piece by piece on the bed. Boy's clothes, all of them, but I hardly cared. I pulled the soft white shirt over my head and let out a deep sigh. The cloth felt good against my skin and the clean scent was almost as good as the smell of freshly baked bread. The breeches were next, and they wrapped my legs in sturdy warmth. I tugged on some stockings, and then a pair of soft leather boots. My eyes flickered shut as I focused on the feeling of leather and wool encasing my toes. I couldn't remember the last time I had worn shoes. I rolled up my sleeves and pulled my hair over a shoulder.

Caladrius Dreams

He came in not five minutes later, carrying something in his hand that I couldn't see, but I could smell. "Here," he said, and tossed it to me. I caught it out of the air on impulse and brought it to the level of my eyes. It was a loaf of rye bread, heavy and dark, and I started eating immediately. I had learned my lesson. This time, I would not be saving any for later. I didn't know what the day before me would bring and I cringed upon remembering my last loaf smashing into the soggy ground. If this man stuck around for long enough maybe I wouldn't even have to worry about later. Even so, the insides of my stomach squirmed uncomfortably. Was hope worth the pain I would feel if it were in vain? I pushed back the thought, and focused instead on eating. I had food now, at this moment; perhaps that was all that mattered. "Stand still," the man commanded, his voice coming from behind me. My mouth was too full to argue so I grunted and stayed put.

As focused on my bread as I was, I didn't notice when he came up beside me, nor did I notice his hands on my hair. What I did notice was the grating sound, close behind my head, like the snapping of a hundred tiny strings. I froze at the noise and my breath stopped. The bread slid through my fingers and dropped with a dull thud onto the floor. Startled, I reached up to the base of my skull. My hands stopped there, curling around the edges of hair which ended much too high, no lower than the lobe of my ear. Tendrils of red hair scattered onto the ground and stuck to my shoulders. I spun where I stood.

The man's expression was unreadable, like rock. A knife was in his right hand, and a fistful of hair in his left. The hair slid from his fingers like sand and landed in long tangles, looking like blood on the ground. Something inside of me tightened, and a feeling began to work its way into my chest. Anger. It swelled, growing like a bubble and pushing out everything else—the hunger, the fear, the deep seated desire to survive. None of that had room inside me. A roaring heat throbbed in my ears, rushing like a flood. It left nothing behind. "What are you doing?" I could barely hear my voice.

"Keeping you alive."

Somehow, the bluntness of his reply made me even angrier. Only last night he had told me that I could stay for a few hours, and then leave. He had told me it would be like none of this had ever happened. Like I had never met him, and never seen the dark cloaked men that had chased us in the streets. Even after he had changed his mind, had called upstairs and told me to stay, he had offered no answers. The man reached around me, trying to open the door. I blocked him. "Why do you need to keep me alive? What's going on?"

He ignored my questions. "If anyone asks, you are a young boy I picked up from town to help me." He shoved a boy's close fitting cap over my ears, effectively covering what remained of my hair.

"Why?"

He picked up the uneaten half of my bread from where it had fallen and forced it into one of my hands. Then he pushed around me easily and opened the door. "You are just like her," he muttered, half to himself. He grabbed me by the arm, dragging me from the room and into the low brown light of the hall. "Stubborn, hot-tempered—"

"Just like who?" He shook his head and continued dragging me. We didn't stop until we had reached the inn's back entrance. I stumbled against him and he shoved me into a dark corner and peered outside. The building—and the street outside—was empty. He grabbed my arm again, and I bristled at the contact. "Just like who?" I asked again. "Who are you anyway? How dare you come marching into my life, not an answer in sight and—"

"My name is Master Arcturus Sheridan," he told me suddenly. "Guardian to the late king." I fell silent abruptly, my mouth working at questions I had no words for. "And you..." he paused for a moment. "You look just like your mother."

4

Portals

A Guardian? The Guardians were the heroes of all the stories, the legends whose names were whispered in the streets. They were nobles, second and third and last born sons of lords and ladies, sent away to join the king's special militia. The king had other armies, of course, but the Guardians were the elite. The privileged. Honored in the commons as second only to the king himself. Truth be told, I should have known. In the stories, the Guardians were always described as wearing a dark grey cloak, precisely the color of the one this man wore. Now that I looked closer, I noticed the detailing that spoke of his rank in the colors of the embroidery which spread over his shoulders and the seal of the Royal Guard engraved into the iron clasp at his throat. Yes, I should have known what he was. But I had never expected to see one. Not here.

That was the least of my concerns, however. It was his final admission that had drawn my stomach into a hard, cold pit. "You know her? My mother—you know her?" The words didn't sound right coming out of my mouth. The cold pit in my stomach seemed to have ruptured, and was now emptying out over my thighs and spreading up to my chest and my arms. It felt like the rest of me was going to rupture too, and I wrapped my arms around my body to try and hold it together. Auntie Margaret had never told me why my mother had abandoned me when I was barely old enough to walk. My shoulders began to shake, but I trained them to stillness and dropped my arms to my side. This was no place for brokenness.

Arcturus Sheridan paused for a second, still in the darkness of the shadows. "We've met," he answered stiffly. There was a tightness to the tone of his voice, and I guessed that his opinion of her was no higher than my own. That didn't surprise me. What kind of woman would abandon her own child?

"What is she like?"

He ignored me, walking past the corner's edge so his figure was illuminated by a street lamp's flickering light. I followed him with my eyes, and held my tongue. Something about the darkness of the street begged for silence. The questions in my head remained, but I didn't speak them. At his gesture, I went to stand by his side. "We will go through the Golg Portal," he told me as I got close. "It's about three blocks away from here. Do not stop. Do not speak with anyone."

I nodded numbly in response.

His face disappeared within his hood. "Stay close." His rough voice held no emotion.

Daylight rimmed the tops of the buildings, but it did not reach the streets. There, mist swirled through the half-light like a venomous gas. Overhead the sky was clear, but storm clouds bubbled on the horizon, threatening to bring rain. No one looked at us, and he did not look at them. I kept my face straight, copying his emotionless mask. I had always been aware of the delicate fragility of life, but somehow, suddenly, the world seemed much more dangerous. Demons leered at us from the dark. Monsters seemed to lurk behind every corner.

An old woman with the face of a crag pawed at my arm. "Take an apple poor child, you're skinny as a bone." My stomach twisted and growled, food wasn't something I was used to refusing. I held out a hand and took what she offered. The apple felt warm and smooth. I wrapped it in my fingers.

Before I could pocket the gift, Arcturus snatched it away. I watched as he tossed it, a swift movement that tore it to pieces when it smashed into the street ten feet away. It wasn't until we were well past the woman that he spoke. "What did I tell you?"

Caladrius Dreams

"My apple..." the pit of my stomach moaned in despair.

"What did I tell you?"

"I didn't talk to her...or do anything you told me not to do, for that matter." Frustration prickled over the tops of my shoulders. My tone was sharp.

"That apple was poisoned," Arcturus said after several steps of silence. "One bite of that fruit and you would have been dead before you hit the ground."

I felt a shudder pass through my spine. That was not something I would have expected. For a moment my irritation was smoothed by gratitude—until wariness took its place. "How did you know?"

"I placed a ward on you before we left. Undetectable. Useless against any serious magic, but enough to let me know if anyone is trying anything."

More magic then. More than I could ever desire to mix with in one lifetime. This man made me almost as uneasy as the black cloaked men who had chased us last night. Almost was the key word, however. "Was she with them?"

"I don't know." His answer unnerved me, and my mind spun until he shoved me down behind a bush that clung to the edges of an old building. "Wait here." Before I could stop him or call him back, he had left. His grey cloak swirled around his ankles until it faded into the buildings and shadows around him. The air felt cold and rain began to fall from the heavy sky. I shivered and wrapped my fingers around the thorny branches of the bush. Master Arcturus Sheridan was nowhere in sight.

The seconds drug on like hours. Rainwater ran down my face like a flood, dripping into my eyes and off my nose. It wasn't drizzling anymore—the rain had progressed into a veritable downpour. The ground beneath me was turning to mud.

After a while, I began to wonder if he had forgotten me. Maybe this was all a joke. Maybe he had left me here in this bush and wasn't intending on coming back. I glanced around the empty streets, and indecision stole into my veins. My whole being teetered on a precipice. I could leave now. Being near this man felt dangerous—more dangerous even than the streets. My instincts

21

told me not to get mixed up with him and his magic. There was nothing he could do to stop me—his strong hands weren't here to hold me back. All I had to do was stand up and walk away. He could pay his fare and pass through the Portal back wherever he had come from and I could forget I had ever seen his face.

My legs turned to coils beneath me. I made to rise, and then sunk back down onto the wet earth. Another, more pressing thought swayed my indecision. If I left now, would I regret it forever? I had no way to leave Golg without him, would I regret not taking this ticket out? If what I had heard was correct, the Portals could take you anywhere—to the far side of Saldor and maybe even beyond. I had never seen the lands beyond this region.

Suddenly I could feel a strange sort of curiosity light inside me like the plague. What if I could leave here? What if things could be different? I couldn't shake the thought, and suddenly I found myself pondering other ways to exit the city. I couldn't travel so far on foot without food. Even if I had enough coin to pay my way through the gates, I wouldn't be allowed to pass through the Portal itself. I didn't look near as wretched in the new clothes the man had given me, but the gauntness of my face and the dirt beneath my nails meant I could only pass as a peasant—at best. A peasant would never be allowed to travel through the Portals. Not alone. That luxury belonged only to those important enough to afford it.

A dark figure appeared beside me so suddenly I almost screamed. It was him. My moment had passed; the decision had been made for me. Was this really what I wanted? I forced away the queasiness in my stomach. Deep inside, I knew that I would have run if I'd really wanted no part in this.

"The Portal is blocked," he whispered, his rough voice so quiet it was almost inaudible. A sudden movement in front of us made him force my head down so we were more completely hidden by the bush's thorny branches.

A man walked out of the opening to the building that lay ahead. His black cloak marked him for who he was—one of Baldassarre's men. Over his head a muddy sign swung back and forth, squealing in the wind. "The Golg Portal," the sign said in large gold lettering. A street lamp stood near the entrance, flickering wildly like the flame inside was about to go out. Mud squelched beneath the man's feet and he peered through the rain right over our heads. I could just barely see the edge of his hawk shaped nose, illuminated under the cowl of his black hood. The man turned and went back inside.

"We have to go through another way," Master Sheridan whispered when the man was out of sight. "They know we are here, and they know I will be wanting go through. They mean to make sure I don't. With any luck we can beat them to Helmsberg and go through the Portal there."

"And if we don't?"

"We will worry about that when it happens." He ducked out from behind the bush and pulled me out with him. We made several turns through the dark streets, past tall buildings whose tops I could barely see and through dark alleys so black I felt I could become lost in them. I had lived in this city for almost as long as I could remember, but I lost my sense of direction after his third or fourth turn. The hawkers' carts that crowded the roadways were empty, vacated because of the rain.

The white shirt I wore was not warm, and I found myself suddenly wishing for my old coat again. Rain made trenches down my face, drenching my cap and matting my shorn hair against my cheeks. Maybe it was better where he was taking me. Maybe it wasn't. Maybe it was worse. We paused at a store and Arcturus left me for a moment to go inside. When he came back, a fresh loaf of bread was in his hand. He handed it to me and then we were walking again. I could see steam rising off the loaf and I nibbled at its end, half afraid it would disappear if I blinked too fast or looked away. Maybe the place he was taking me wasn't any better...but there was food right here, right now, and the future felt very far away. I was steered onto a larger road and we entered the general throng of traffic. The city hummed around me until I realized it was fading into the background and we were surrounded by other travelers just as wet as us, leaving and headed for some distant future out of the city.

* * *

It was midday and still raining. I had long since finished my loaf, and any strength I had gained from it was beginning to ebb away. It felt like we had been walking for miles—indeed we probably had. Hedges and stone walls lined the narrow roadway and I stumbled over the puddle filled ruts made by wagon wheels which ran down the center. My happiness at being fed was quickly dissipating. Irritation seeped into its place.

"Why are we walking?" A man on horseback headed in the opposite direction splashed mud up on my face as he passed. I glared after him, frowning and shrugging my shoulders against the cold. My feet hurt. I was used to walking, but not this far. Not down a cold, muddy road, rutted and filled with dirt and sharp stones.

"Walking will gain us less notice and if we need to hide, it is easier to do so without a horse." He didn't seem to mind the walk at all. His face was as impassive as always, matching the careless yet somehow deadly slouch of his walk. I could feel annoyance coursing through me, difficult to control and harder yet to quash. All the questions which had earlier plagued my mind were coming back.

"What—" I froze mid sentence, my eyes resting on a figure in the distance, visible just over his left shoulder. There was a person walking towards us. Several people, in fact. I could see their shapes separating out from each other against the horizon. Something seemed dangerous about the way they moved and as they grew closer I realized I recognized the black cloaks that fluttered around their forms. Arcturus glanced in the direction of my gaze, and then he froze too. The way he stood reminded me of a wolf, motionless at the first sight of prey. He put himself in front of me, his hands hanging calmly by his sides.

"They are trying to surround us," he said. Even his whisper was deadly. The men were closing in, coming down the road in a long line that blocked our advances. There were six of them. Soon, they were so close I could almost see their faces beneath their hoods. Arcturus drew the sword hanging at his belt. Its metal flashed in the low light. "Run."

24

I responded to his whispered command before I was even fully aware of what he had said. My feet moved without permission and suddenly I was stumbling, sprinting down the road as fast as I could manage. Puddles splashed up in my face. Rain pounded at my back. My breath was ragged.

There was a rough patch on the ground and I stumbled over it, falling to my knees and then onto my chest. Mud crusted my white shirt, splattering up like brown blood on my front and running down the sides of my face. My fingers dug into the dirt, scraping at the ground as I tried to pull myself up.

"Headed somewhere, Princess?" I couldn't move. My body was frozen, and there was nothing I could do about it. It was like some invisible force held me in place, like a wall made of air had crystallized around me. I was paralyzed. I couldn't even scream. "Roll over. I want to see your face." The invisible wall flipped me, and suddenly I was slammed onto my back, staring up at the man who stood above me. He laughed. "I have to admit," he told me coldly, "I was skeptical when the others told me he had found you. That man—" he shook his head and laughed more, crouching down to peer closer at my face. "He has trailed after so many red herrings I simply stopped listening when they told me he had found another one."

His fingers traced the line of my jaw—almost a caress—and stopped at my chin. Grasping my chin before his thumb and forefinger, he forcibly turned my face up to examine it. "The resemblance is uncanny..." he pulled his hand away and straightened again, climbing to his feet so he once again towered above me. "Arcturus Sheridan has always been a fool, but the fact that he thought he could hide that face with a haircut and some boy's clothing—never mind. It doesn't matter. In a few short minutes this will all be over. If you scream nice and loud, I promise I'll make it quick."

Suddenly his hand was over me and pain tore across my skin like the scorching of flames. I convulsed, writhing on the ground until I couldn't tell if the water that ran down my face was rain or sweat. I screamed, and collapsed into sobs. "Louder," he hissed.

His voice drilled into my skull, a snarl I knew I would never forget—if I lived to remember it. "Scream louder. I want him to hear it." And then I was screaming again. Screaming like my life depended on it—screaming and sobbing while something invisible lashed across my back and it felt like all my bones were grating against each other. The man's hand loomed above me, covered by a swirling blackness that twisted over his wrist and past his sleeve, climbing till it was out of sight.

I didn't even hear his footsteps when he arrived. All I heard were my own screams, broken suddenly by the clashing of metal. I forced my head to turn to the side, and that is when I saw him. His grey cloak swirled around the silhouette of his form, seeming to absorb the grayness of the sky.

Arcturus Sheridan fell upon the man in black like a falcon at the climax of his stoop, wielding a two-handed broadsword with a single hand better than most men can with two. The men collided and the pain that beat me ended so abruptly that I fell against the muddy ground, sobbing and gasping for breath. They danced above me, a dance of death where the black cloaked man's hand-and-a-half blade came ripping out of its sheath to catch Arcturus's twisting attack.

It was the man's distraction that had released me from my invisible bonds. When I realized this freedom I scrambled through the mud on my hands and knees until I was pressed against the bushes that lined the road.

Mud splashed around them as they fought, and for a moment neither seemed to gain any advantage. It was evident however, that the black cloaked man was becoming tired. He spun to block an attack from the left and his foot slipped in the mud. Arcturus didn't lose his chance. In a movement too fast for the eye to see, Arcturus's sword swung up and caught the other man across the cheek. The man spun with the blow, dodging just enough to prevent serious injury. For a moment I could see the blood which ran down his face, and then, before Arcturus could continue his attack, he ran. For a second Arcturus hesitated, and then let the man go. His black cloak faded into the dark and I could hear his footsteps running away. Arcturus moved forward, and dropped to his knees in front of me.

"Are you hurt?"

"I..." and suddenly it occurred to me I wasn't sure how to answer. "I don't know," I whispered. Arcturus said nothing. He took my head between his hands, and suddenly my body was filled with trembling shivers. He moved away, and I felt as if I had just awoken from a good night's sleep. None of that however, could erase the memories. I could still feel the invisible whips in my mind. I could still hear the man's cold voice. "Are they gone?" I asked. Arcturus nodded.

I turned my face towards the direction the black cloaked man had disappeared. Nothing but darkness was there now. Suddenly a thought occurred to me, a chilling thought. I wasn't sure I wanted an answer. "Did you kill them?"

"They retreated, though several carry marks that will keep them from soon forgetting the encounter. Don't worry, they will not come back. They will need more than six men to overtake me—and it will take them several days to find recruitments. By then we will be long gone." I nodded and my breathing slowed. It was night now. If we moved fast, we would be at Helmsberg by morning.

"What were they after? The black cloaked men, I mean?"

Arcturus ignored me. Instead, he cast his face to the darkening skyline. He stood and offered me a hand. "Let's go. The larger a lead we have on them, the better."

I shook my head. I wasn't going to let him brush it off anymore. "No."

"No?" His voice was dangerous, but I didn't waver. I knew danger now. Somehow, I knew he would not harm me. Not the way the other man had. That fact gave me courage.

"I'm not going anywhere until you give me answers."

"Now is not the time to give them."

Something within me cracked. The look on the black cloaked man's face as he tortured me...the tone in his voice—I couldn't look the other way and pretend it had meant nothing. I could feel my cheeks heat, anger swelling from my pumping heart, through my limbs, to my head. It was only with great effort that I kept composure. "This isn't a game anymore," I said, my voice cracking beneath the restraint of holding it even. "I was nearly killed. I'm not going to continue following a man I just met to my death, with no clue why I'm doing so. You owe me answers." He ignored me and made to walk off down the road. I pushed myself to my feet and stopped in front of him, blocking his way.

"Later, Princess," he said. I recognized the word. It didn't make any sense in my head, but I stopped him anyway, dogging his steps as he tried to move around me.

"Why are those men following us? He said you found something—found me. I don't understand what's going on, and I swear I won't go another step with you until you give me answers. Who am I? Why me—?"

To my surprise, he cut me off with a sharp nod and a grunt. "Come." I followed him off the road and through the bushes that lined it. He stopped when we were on the other side of them and turned, digging a hole into the backside of the hedge. Unclasping his cloak, he swung it across the branches where it settled as makeshift roof. Then, on his hands and knees, he crawled into the shelter he had created.

I followed him, pulling myself through the dirt until I was under his cloak and hidden within the bush. It was drier in here, though not more comfortable, or any warmer. Clasping his hands together, he spread them like pulling wool, and a flame ignited between his palms. I watched wide-eyed, but I did not move or speak. He settled the flame into a dug out bowl in the ground and broke off twigs from the brush surrounding us to feed his fire. I huddled my knees to my chest, and waited. He didn't speak for a long time.

"I have devoted my entire life to the search," he started at last. His words were cryptic, remote. They hung hauntingly over the fire between us, causing a rush of shivers to creep up my spine. "When others told me I was wasting my time, that there was no way on earth the child was still alive, I refused to believe.

I have scoured the world, looking. I have pressed on, even when accused of believing in the impossible."

"I don't think I understand."

"I'll show you." His hands hovered above the fire for a moment, looking almost like a potter's hands above his wheel. The fire changed. Shapes formed. Figures. People. Immediately it occurred to me that I was unsure whether his magic was working on the fire itself, or on my mind. Was I hallucinating? Did it matter? Either way, I was seeing what he wanted me to see.

A figure appeared in the flames—a young, eighteen year old version of Arcturus. I wasn't sure how I knew that. The information I needed to know had simply sprung forth into my mind, feeling like my own thoughts. I knew they weren't.

Fourteen other boys stood with the young Arcturus, stiffly erect and forming a long straight line. An older, burly man walked down the line—Master Julius Heidel, I suddenly knew, though I'd never heard the name in my life. The man was the current King's Guard—Arcturus's predecessor. As I watched, another thing became immediately apparent to me. This was a Selection ceremony.

Master Heidel stopped in front of Arcturus, who immediately dropped to a knee—head bowed and forearm across his chest. Around them, the other boys left one by one. The fire gave a loud crack and the images burst apart, swirling into tongues of flame until they settled on a new scene.

Arcturus and Master Heidel were dancing, except not quite. They were training—dancing with swords. Their intricate footwork brought them together and apart, flowing like water—like fire. The flames licked and flickered. Their figures swelled and then ebbed. It was evident that time was passing. Arcturus was growing better. Stronger. Their blades connected and the resulting spark sent out a shockwave which leveled the scene. A new one developed in its place.

An old man lay motionless in a bed. The people gathered around him were weeping. The man, I realized, was the king. I was witnessing the moment of his death. A woman closed his eyes with a forefinger and her thumb and—CRACK!—the scene changed in a flurry of sparks.

A young prince stood high before a throne. It was Coronation day. A few steps below him stood Arcturus, beginning his duties as the next King's Guard. CRACK! The prince—now king—stood in the same spot with Arcturus just below, but it was a different day. A young woman with a head-full of glossy mahogany hair stood by the king's side, wearing a wedding dress. Suddenly the scene was very different. Darker somehow. Glowing over the embers.

The king stood by his wife. A tiny baby was in her arms—the same mahogany hair on its head. Arcturus's voice broke through the scene, echoing dully on top of it. I didn't lift my eyes when he spoke, but rather watched the figures in the fire.

"The queen gave birth a couple years after the start of the war. The king and I were the only ones in attendance. The girl was a perfect little picture of her mother. The same tiny features, and the same green eyes."

"What was her name?" I asked, suddenly compelled to know.

"Callista," Arcturus answered softly. Then he went on. "I had some unfinished business to attend to, so I left shortly after. It was an action I will regret for the rest of my life." Suddenly, the images in the fire dissolved into flames.

"That night, the spot in which the Royal Family had been hiding was found. An assassin murdered the king and queen both, and kidnapped the newborn princess. I arrived moments too late. I tracked them for hours, but it was useless. She was gone.

"Not long after that I learned from some private eyes and ears that the assassination had been an order from the king's youngest brother, Baldassarre. In an attempt to take over the kingdom he had arranged for the death of the king. No word came to us about what had happened to the young princess. Apparently she had been dropped in the escape and lost in the darkness. We never found her.

"At that moment a kingdom which had been whole for the last 200 years, was split. The First War dwindled and died—just three short years after its start. The king's other brother, the High Lord Alastair, has managed to hold the South End—the Royal Castle and Caeyra around it—but it is like being locked in exile in our own land. We hold it only because Baldassarre lets us. The old kingdom exists only under his aid.

"For the past thirteen years I have been searching for our princess. I have been seeking the hope our kingdom needs to revive. I never gave up searching, and at long last my search has led me here." He paused, and then did something startling. He picked up one of my hands in his, and pressed it to his lips. "You look just like your mother," he whispered.

I didn't answer. Instead, I turned my face away, hiding the tear which was tracing its way down my cheek. The truth was, I couldn't speak. My throat had closed up on itself, and my mind was far away in thought. The parents who I thought had left me, had wanted me all along.

* * *

The sun had just begun to peek over the edges of the distant hills when we climbed from of our shelter and back onto the road. The rain had stopped, replaced by a light drizzle that was more mist than rain. The world was dew-struck. It glittered in the silver light of the morning. Arcturus pulled his cloak from the bushes, shaking it off and throwing it up over his shoulders. It was dry.

As we walked, houses and farms began to appear, sprinkled across the countryside in a rough geometric pattern. Soon, the houses clustered and the farms dwindled. We reached the outskirts of the city, and then at midmorning, we reached the city itself. I had never been to Helmsberg before. It was only twenty or so miles from Golg, but I had never had a reason to make the trip.

It was smaller than Golg. The tiny houses were white walled, built of mud and straw and roofed with baked clay tiles. A single butte rose flat-topped nearby, rising high out of the grasslands and shaped like the helmet of a warrior. The sun rose behind it, throwing the city under shadow. A few tradesmen were up, working in their shops. The ring of a hammer against an anvil shattered the air. The pleasant hum of women restocking their wares seemed to make the morning brighter. None of them looked at us—strangers were common so close to Golg—and we passed through uncontested.

It surprised me how easy this step was. It shocked me that all we had to do was walk up to the guards—dressed in brown military cloaks—hand them a few silvers, and take a pair of stones. One stone from the soil of our destination to draw us there, and the other from this city to bring the stones back. Half of me expected someone to chase us down. To yell at us to stop or to jump out from behind a neatly trimmed garden hedge. None of that happened. Baldassarre's men were nowhere in sight. Arcturus had been right. They needed recruitments, something they wouldn't find for a few days at least, and by then we'd be long gone. We were almost gone already.

"Arcturus?"

"Master Sheridan," he corrected. I ignored him.

"Where we're going...what is it like there?"

He took me by the hand and pulled me through the guards. They saluted to him, standing upright and looking straight ahead. It drove home the fact that this man was someone important. I would soon be someone important too, but I tried not to think of that. I shrank close to his side. It was impossible. I was nobody. A girl from off the streets whose biggest concern was food and perhaps a dry bit of shelter. That was all I would ever be. All I could be. All I wanted to be. My heart seemed to flutter right out of my chest. "It is different," he said at last.

I wasn't sure I liked his answer. I clutched my stones close to my heart and moved forward with him. A high stone archway stood in front of us. The draft which seemed to blow out of it caused the hair at the back of my neck to raise. I shivered.

This was it, my final chance. I could run away now...his hands were not on me and if I moved fast enough, I felt I could make it. Somehow, I found I did not want to. Despite the fear, despite the strange welling up in my chest. As I stepped through the archway,

Caladrius Dreams

I took one last look back. Back at my world. The world where I belonged. Leaving it was simple, too simple. One step was all it took, and like the blink of an eye, my world was gone. I stepped through the Portal and darkness surrounded me. I took one final step, and a new world lay before me.

5

Home

It was dark. We were on the opposite side of Saldor now, and the sun hadn't quite reached us. Even without the sun, however, I could tell that it was green.

It seemed we were in the bottom of a valley. Trees stretched out in every direction, tall evergreens that reached so high I could barely see their tops. I shivered. I was used to buildings and open land; I felt suffocated here.

We were in the mountains, and the air was thinner and colder than I was used to. A set of red-uniformed guards held the Portal gates, carefully monitoring who came in and who went out. They stopped in a salute as we came through. "Master Sheridan," one of them muttered with a nod. Arcturus grunted and nodded back.

We handed our stones to the man and as he took them his eyes moved quickly from Arcturus to me, his gaze slowing over my hair and my face. I ducked my head and tried to ignore him, focusing instead on following Arcturus down a steep path that disappeared into the trees. I could feel his eyes on my back until we rounded the corner and continued out of sight.

"It's so cold here..." I murmured, half to myself. I stumbled over a tree root in the dark, and folded my hands into my sleeves. There was a shuffling beside me, and suddenly Arcturus's dark grey cloak swaddled my shoulders. I glanced up at him, but his face was distant. His mouth was drawn in a hard straight line.

The path was set on a slow curve that seemed it might be a circle if we walked long enough. Everything looked the same—trees stood in every direction. I felt certain that I would become lost if I stumbled even steps from the path. I shivered again and pulled Arcturus's cloak tighter around my shoulders. Becoming lost in such a forest didn't sound like a pleasing prospect. My eyes darted towards the trees, and then above them. Maybe if I concentrated on the sky ahead, the trees wouldn't feel so ominous. So monstrous. I stumbled again over a dip in the ground, and kept walking.

So fixed on the sky was my gaze, I didn't notice at first that the forest had thinned. The sky was brightening ahead of me, now the color of blue that comes just after black. A few stars still twinkled against the horizon as if trying to compete with the coming sun. Our walk slowed, and suddenly I realized we were standing in place. "Welcome home, Princess," Arcturus said beside me. I pulled my eyes away from the sky to follow his gaze.

In front of us was a lake—a large lake that shimmered a reflection of the lightening sky. I could just see the sunrise bursting over the edges of a knoll that fell into the lake's farthest shore. Atop the knoll, silhouetted against the joyous sky, was a castle. I felt my breath surge suddenly into my lungs in a gasp that was halfway between a laugh, and a sob. The castle's white turrets reached high above me, the tallest almost seeming to touch the fading stars. "Home," I murmured. Arcturus continued walking. I followed him along the lake's edge and over a small bridge that reached across a stream which fed into the lake's smooth waters. *Home*. The word had never felt so strange.

The knoll on which the castle sat was very steep, and my calves burned by the time we had reached the top of the rocky stairs. Arcturus waited as I stopped to catch my breath, his stance grounded in a way that suggested he belonged here, but his eyes shifting in a way that did not. I thought perhaps the place seemed too grand for him, and he too wild for it. He wrapped calloused fingers around my hand, and led me forward.

In front of us was a gatehouse, manned by two lines of pikemen dressed in the same deep red uniform as the guards down by the Portal, and a couple other men dressed like Arcturus. Unlike Arcturus who wore his cloak over plain traveling clothes, the two grey cloaked men before us stood in full uniform, varnished breastplates over grey tunics and grey breeches, and soft leather boots toed in steel. Their weapons seemed almost part of them, but the longer I watched them, the longer I became aware of the subtle differences between Arcturus and these grey cloaked men.

Other than the colors on the shoulders of their cloaks—Arcturus's cloak was embroidered red, theirs green— the differences weren't apparent. Watching the way they responded to him as he spoke, however, solidified the differences in my mind. They seemed part hatred, part jealousy, and part awe.

Their nods were respectful as we passed through the dark gatehouse and into the court. Sunlight fell upon my face, and I had to squint in the sudden brightness. My eyes stretched wider than I thought they could go; I could not seem to remember to close my mouth. The gravel beneath my feet turned to smooth marble flagstone as we walked and I found myself suddenly wishing that I had a million pairs of eyes, so I could look every which way at once.

The courtyard was open roofed, walled by the castle itself. There were narrow walkways on each side, framed and shaded by arches built back into the castle wall. Delicate lanterns hung from the apex of each archway, lit by tiny flames so steady I knew at once that magic was involved. On the far right was a delicately forged iron gate. Behind the gate I could see the trees and flowers of a garden, greener than seemed possible for late autumn. We moved in a slight circle around the fountain that stood in the court's center, and then straight forward to the main entrance. Giant wooden double doors, bound together by three bands of iron, towered above me. They opened without a touch as we neared them and I threw a suspicious glance to Arcturus. He gave no sign of having lifted a finger. We mounted a set of stairs and entered.

The interior of the castle was dark, and yet somehow brighter than I had expected. It was lit by the light of a thousand candles, some hanging from iron trellises on the walls, others as large in diameter as I and free standing on the floor, and still others hanging from the ceiling on elaborate chandeliers. Torches hugged the pillars in iron cups and the windows with their thick glass panes allowed sunlight to spill through the hall in patches. The air felt like the breath of a cold-blooded dragon. It hit me in a cool gust that came from within the castle's maw. The light scent of rose petals was on the air, mixed with something spicier I couldn't quite identify. We turned off of the Main Hall, to the right and up a broad set of stairs made of cold white marble. Up two flights and then down a second hall—smaller but no less grand—we continued our march. Near the end of the hall, Arcturus stopped.

"Wait here." He dropped me by a door and went inside, leaving me to stare at the rough dark wood. I shifted uncomfortably as a pair of girls, dressed in blue and yellow silk, walked giggling by. Both gave me a hard stare, and then continued their giggling around the corner.

I had never been in a place so regal. The floors were carpeted in a thick red velvet, and where carpet was lacking, marble tiles stood in its place. Tapestries dressed the walls, along with thick draperies and paintings whose prices I was certain could feed a village for month. A year, even.

"Master Sheridan. Please sit." My eyes widened and I pressed my ear close to the door's frame. Muffled voices drifted to me from within. "What is the nature of this visit?" The man who spoke had a soft voice, thickened with formality. I could almost picture what his face must look like in my head. Tall, dark haired, and gentle featured. Perhaps with the grey-blue eyes that were so common in this region.

Arcturus's voice sounded rougher than normal in contrast to the man's gentle one. "I've found her," he said. "I—"

"Arcturus..." the man cut him off abruptly. The formality was gone now. He sounded tired and perhaps more than a bit frustrated. "We have been through this before."

"I'm sure of it this time."

"Sure enough to risk it? How many poor girls do we have to go through before you drop this foolish notion? It is not worth it, Arcturus. Give it up."

"At least let me show her to you—"

"Why? So you can bring to me another girl who looks roughly like she could be my brother's daughter? I don't have time for this. Neither do you."

"It's different this time, my Lord. I was actively looking when I found the other girls. Looking for all the wrong things. This child I stumbled upon by chance and I swear to you she's it. I swear it on my life."

There was a long pause, broken only by the distant ringing of the triple stroked bell. The bell repeated three times and as its hum faded, the man within spoke. "It is a hard oath you make, Master Sheridan. I would hate to be forced to hold you to it." The formality was back.

"I will take any oath I must if it will make you trust me enough to see the girl. I will hold you to it myself if it is not her."

There was a low sigh, followed by several beats of silence. "What choice do you give me? Several lords have arrived today for the Council Meeting next month. I will be busy with them tonight, and several more are due to arrive tomorrow. I cannot spare time for you. Relations are strained as it is, and I mean this to be a peaceful meeting. Bring her to me at the start of next week and we will decide what foolish trouble you have gotten yourself into this time."

"My Lord, I—"

"Next week, Arcturus. I do not have time now. Until then you can keep her with one of the ladies so she does not lack for company. I believe young Lady Emalea has been requesting a roommate."

"My Lord."

"You are excused."

A scuffling like the scraping of chairs came from within the room, and I jumped away from the door. "Arcturus?" His eyes flashed towards me, and then away. He turned and left down the hall, moving faster than necessary. I had to jog to keep up. We moved up a flight of stairs and into the north wing of the castle. He stopped suddenly in front of a small wooden door, arched on top and bound together with iron. Panting, I caught up with him. "There's a chance I'm not the one you've been looking for?" He turned to look at me.

"What did you hear?"

"Everything."

His eyes softened and he knelt in front of me until his height was equal with my own. "You are her."

"There have been other girls, and you probably said the same thing to them—"

"I did not, and I have never been so certain." He took his cloak from my shoulders and moved it back to clasp around his own.

"If I'm not the one, I'll have to go back..." No matter how reluctant I had been to leave Golg, I was suddenly frightened at the prospect of returning.

He chuckled, the sound seeming strange coming from his throat. It sounded younger than him, unused and forgotten. "I bet my life on you, Princess." He stood then, looking away as if that one statement solved everything. "Keep your head down. Try to fit in. I don't want you starting any rumors that I will have to dispel later. Do you think you can manage?"

"I know how to put on an act," I told him stonily.

He nodded. "It's more dangerous here then you know." His face was dark. I could not read its expression. His hand lifted and he knocked on the door before us.

"One moment!" After a second, a girl no older than myself opened the door. There was an excited, almost frantic look to her sparkling grey eyes and the rosiness in her cheeks seemed like a perpetual blush. She smiled at me gently and then turned to scowl at Arcturus. He didn't notice.

"I will be back for you at the start of next week," he said. Then, without a single explanation to the starry-eyed girl before us, he turned and walked away. I shifted nervously on my feet.

"Despicable man," the girl muttered, and then brightened immediately. "Come inside. The servants have started a fire—the first one of the year!—and breakfast just came up. You can share some of mine." She dragged me inside before I could refuse, and

39

shut the door. "I've never been alone with a boy before, and I've certainly never had one in my room!" She turned her excited eyes on me, her blushing cheeks seeming almost frenzied.

I could feel my face turning five shades of red and with a groan I remembered my clothes and too-short hair.

My mouth opened to explain, but before I could get a single word out, a single hand flew to her delicate mouth and her brows shot up in concern. It seemed she had recognized her error. "I'm so sorry...I truly am. I just—" Her voice was tremulous, quavering in a way that mimicked the tears which were welling up in her eyes.

"It's understandable," I told her quickly, hoping to heal the embarrassment on both sides. "It's my fault for dressing in a way that would confuse you." There was a long beat of silence, and awkwardly I pressed on in an attempt to answer the questions I could see on her face. I couldn't think of a good answer, so I stuck to the truth. "I was in disguise."

It seemed a good enough answer, because her questions faded and she grabbed my hand. She began to talk very quickly and I soon lost track of her words. She didn't seem to care that I was a stranger whom she had never seen before. She was warm and friendly and steered me to a well-padded armchair by the fire. Her talking never stopped. As soon as I was seated, she brought over another chair, made of wood and standing next to a writing desk on the far side of the room. She sat on it as if afraid it might break under her full weight, and waved a small gloved hand at a pair of white-clad women in the corner.

"I've never had a guest before!" she squealed to me, clapping her hands as one of the women set a platter between us. "I've only been here a few weeks," she whispered excitedly. "I turned fourteen last month and my mother decided it was time for me to go to court and join society. I was ever so pleased when she told me. The Royal Court is the best place for young women to learn to become ladies."

She leaned forward with a conspiring giggle. "I heard that next month during Winterfest important families from all over the country will be here, and most of the lords will be bringing their eldest sons. Imagine! Young lords all over this place, and a Ball to top it off!"

She paused to take a breath, and then hurried on. "But I'm being rude," she said, a shocked look crossing her face. "I haven't even introduced myself yet! I'm Emalea. You can call me Ema."

I glanced down. One of the white-clad women had set a pot of tea and two cups on the small table between us. The other had set out plates and a little dish full of something that looked rather like small, glazed, triangular slices of bread. I had to stop myself from lunging at them. My stomach clenched in painful knots. I watched Ema lift one bread slice delicately to her mouth, and tried to copy her gesture. I nibbled on one end, and then began to methodically force the entire slice into my mouth. She stared at me wide-eyed. "Sorry," I muttered meekly, giving a little jump when I noticed her gaze. I pried my fingers from the slice, wincing as it thudded onto the plate. Carefully, I folded my hands in my lap.

"No, no, eat. It's rude of me to stare...I should be the one apologizing to you. I'm not being a very good host. Not at all." Her eyes glowed suddenly and she sat up straighter, taking a tiny sip of tea and then placing her cup back in the saucer before she spoke. "Did you give me your name?" she asked. "Because if you did I'm quite afraid I did not catch it."

I hesitated. We were nearing murky water, and I wasn't sure the truth was the best answer anymore. What had Arcturus said? It's more dangerous here than you know. I felt myself stiffen. It was the truth. I didn't have an idea of the political climate of the region...telling the wrong person the wrong thing could be sending myself to an early grave. I didn't know what her leanings were—I didn't know anything about the girl, other than she was sweet and genteel and seemed honest enough. Above all, I found I simply wanted to be her friend...to be normal, perhaps. I had never had either, and both would be nigh impossible if I told her the truth. Remembering the name Arcturus had given me, I shortened it. "Calli." It would have to work. I put on a forced smile, and Ema smiled back.

"Are you of noble blood? I don't know all of the families, but I have met most and you don't look familiar. I've never seen hair like yours except on a commoner, if you don't mind me noting."

I did mind her noting, but I didn't mention the fact. "I'm not from around here." It wasn't a lie, but not the whole truth either.

"Another country then?"

"Arusae," I said, answering with the name of the only other country I knew of other than my own.

Her expression heightened immediately. "I've never been there, but I have heard of it," she said.

I had never been there either, but as long as I had my neck stretched across the chopping block, I figured I might as well get into a more comfortable position. "I'm a refugee," I told her, praying silently that the civil war in Arusae was more than just rumor. "My parents were killed and I was forced to flee the country."

"I'm sorry to hear it." She paused momentarily, and then her eyes lit up. "Is red hair common among nobles in Arusae?"

"Yes, quite." To be honest, I didn't have the slightest idea. Obviously Ema didn't either, because she nodded ecstatically.

"How exotic," she murmured in praise.

"Thank you." Shifting a bit in my seat, I glanced at her out of the corner of my eye, and then decided to take the leap. "Master Sheridan was kind enough to bring me here but if you do not want me, I can leave. I don't want to cause you any trouble…" I lowered my eyes and frowned a little. I would have to play her emotions if I wanted anything out of the girl, and information was something I needed desperately. I shifted a bit in my seat as if uncomfortable and gave her a weak smile. It worked.

"No! It isn't any trouble at all. I have been wanting a roommate dearly, and I am so very pleased to have one."

"As you are to be my roommate then," I began carefully, "it only makes sense to ask you. You see, I am not accustomed to the manners of this region. Would it be too much to ask, if you could acquaint me with them?" I eyed her hopefully. Unaccustomed was a severe understatement. I would be eaten alive if I did not learn how to blend in. Finding a tutor was an absolute essential.

Acting as a refugee from another country was the perfect guise to cover any slip ups until then, but my slip ups were apt to be larger than those of a simple foreigner. I needed to adapt, and I needed Ema's help to do so.

"Of course! It must be such a culture shock, you coming all the way from Arusae."

I smiled at her delicately and tried to copy her way of folding her hands in her lap. For a moment, I focused my attention on the bread in front of me. Bringing it to my mouth in any manner other than haste, seemed impossible. I nibbled on an end, ignoring the painful way my stomach squirmed. As delicately as possible, I set the bread back on the plate. I tilted my head from the smell and, desiring a distraction, I decided it was time for a new question. "What do you know about Master Sheridan?"

"No more than anyone else, I suppose. I know that he is a terrible man, and that he used to be very deep into dark magic. Apparently, he served Baldassarre before the First War and before he became King's Guard. Master Heidel pulled him out, and he has served the Royal Family's true heir ever since. Even so, I do not trust the man."

I winced. Such information was disturbing, but it didn't surprise me. In any case, it wasn't what I was looking for. I pressed on. "I met him outside the city, in Golg. As the King's Guard, what business could he have there?" The question was bold, but Ema face remained steady and unsuspicious.

"He was probably searching for the Royal Family's true heir. She disappeared when the king and queen were murdered, and no-one has heard from her since. Master Sheridan has been searching for her since their death, but no one actually believes he will find anything. Being from out of the country, I don't suppose you would know much about it."

"I have heard a fair bit."

"Apparently, he has not brought in anyone for a while, but there was a period where he brought a new girl every few months—so I've heard." Suddenly her eyes widened. "He is the one who brought you in, is he not?" She asked me very quickly, as if the thought had only just occurred to her. I froze.

43

I could feel myself tensing. My fingers wanted to twitch and I clenched them anxiously in my lap. I forced myself to meet her eyes. "Yes."

"I suppose it makes sense that you would be curious. I have never met one of his girls, but of course I know all about it. Everyone does."

I shifted uncomfortably in my seat, but Ema appeared oblivious. After a beat of silence, I picked up the thread of conversation again, more carefully this time. "What happens to them? The girls I mean?"

Ema shrugged delicately. "They disappear. He brings them back to wherever they came from, and we never hear from any of them again. Don't worry...it isn't likely they die, they just go elsewhere."

"Do you think he will ever find her?"

"I will not say it's impossible, but Master Sheridan has been wrong before. He's been searching for almost fourteen years now, and the likelihood that the princess is alive has never been very good. She was a newborn the day she was lost. Nothing short of a miracle could have kept her alive till now."

I put my teacup down and tried to straighten in my seat. "You must have had a long trip," she said, her voice soft and sympathetic. "Why don't I find you something to wear? I cannot imagine you would want to stay in those dirty things any longer." She smiled suddenly, and stood with an almost giddy excitement. "Oh Calli, we are going to be great friends, I can sense it already!"

Something tightened inside my chest at her words. "Really?" Unbidden, a grin swept across my face. No matter how hard I tried, I couldn't stop smiling.

* * *

The noontide bell had rung near an hour ago and I was settled rather uncomfortably next to Ema on a stiff wooden bench in the arboretum. A pair of large, slender dogs lounged in the sun nearby. A bird was hopping across the grass, pulling up worms from the ground.

It was cool where we sat—I would have argued it quite cold—in the shade of the castle that loomed behind us like a smooth sentry made of a strange white stone I could not place.

Ema held a fan in her hand despite the weather, insisting we appear proper for "propriety's sake." I had told her we had no fans in Arusae. She had laughed, and told me I ought to learn. I held my fan awkwardly in a fist, and tried to hide my face with it.

"Sit up straighter," Ema hissed, wiggling her fan and batting her eyes at a boy who was passing through the garden on our left. I wasn't sure I *could* sit straighter, and I really wasn't sure it was possible to call my posture a slouch. The ribbed corset she had wrenched on me dug into my sides and made anything but a stick straight back impossible. I fought the urge to roll my eyes again, and twisted till my shoulder blades nearly overlapped.

She only grunted at my effort, standing the way I imagined a swan would, had it been seated on a chair. I copied her motion, and then fell back onto the bench when she forced me down. "You slouch like a commoner and you stand even worse," she snapped irritably. "Try again. Don't lean forward when you stand up...bend your knees and keep your back straight! I don't know how it is in Arusae, but a Salcorian lady must always have a straight back..." I lost track of her words after the first few sentences and stood again. Apparently my motion was passable, because she sighed and we moved on. Her words didn't stop—or even falter—as we walked. She continued on like an excited bird, flapping her delicate hands in gestures as she spoke.

We left the castle gardens after a slow round along their outer edge. Ema hooked her arm with mine, whispering in my ear as if she had something of great importance to tell. I tried to pay attention, but the green lusciousness of the gardens distracted me, and I soon found myself pausing to smell a rose. Ema frowned and pulled me on. We continued to the courtyard, passing several ladies who giggled and paid us no heed.

A tension I hadn't known I carried left me. It seemed, suddenly, that I was part of them. They had no way to tell that I was not, standing next to Ema and dressed in her silks, and for the first time in my life, I felt normal. When Ema pulled me towards the ladies, however, I resisted, leaning back and pulling against her arm. I didn't want to get close enough to them for them to see that I was different. They'd know soon enough. "I want to see the lake," I whispered as an excuse. She nodded after a moment and we turned, leaving the courtyard to pass through the gate-house and climbing as quickly as our heavy skirts would allow down the steps to the lake.

She would only walk with me to the closest edge, proclaiming it improper to continue any farther without escort. "Ladies should not wander alone in the woods," she sighed slowly, sounding grateful of the fact. Pausing at the hillside I gathered my skirts around me and sat with my knees pulled up to my chest in the grass. Ema copied my motion after a moment of hesitation, muttering something about insects and the sun and freckles. Glancing at her from the corner of my eye, I saw her holding up her fan anxiously, as if trying to block the sun from her face. I laughed and, ignoring her questioning gaze, fastened my eyes on the blue waters of the lake.

"How do they ever get goods up to the castle?" I questioned after a moment, genuinely curious. "I can barely make it up these steps, I can't imagine a carriage ever would." I shaded my eyes with a hand and glanced at her over my shoulder. She frowned for a moment and then shrugged.

"The servants come down to the base and carry them up. And if the things are too large to be carried, someone usually magicks them back."

"Why don't they just build a road?" I dropped onto my back, and stared up at the sky. After a minute of carefully adjusting her skirts and hair, Ema lay down beside me, her fan still open to shade her face.

"The location and the lack of a road is one of the best protections we have against assault. Why, had there been a road to the castle, Baldassarre could have come right up during the First War and knocked down our door. As it is, we managed to hold the castle against him, and the city too. Caeyra's too difficult to get to for a frontal attack. Baldassarre may have the rest of the country in his grasp, but not Caeyra. He could never take the capital, and he never will."

"So your family supports the dead king then?" I asked her innocently. She nodded, dropping her fan with disgust and rolling to her side to face me.

"Yes. My family is loyal to the kingdom's rightful heir, as anyone should be who has even a drop of honor. That murderer and all his rats—not a one of them deserves to be a part of this kingdom. My mother would never say it, but she didn't just send me here to join society. She sent me here because it is safe—safer than anywhere else at least. We control a small fief on the west side of Saldor. Baldassarre took our lands when he came through." She sighed, leaning towards me and pulling a piece of grass from my hair. "He took everyone's lands."

A noise in the distance made me sit up, and beside me, Ema sat up too. My eyes followed the edge of the lake until they rested on a small trail. The trail led into the forested region along the lake's edge, and out of sight. I could see movement near the trail's furthest visible point. A second later, they broke through the trees, and into plain sight.

A horde of young boys, ages eighteen down to eight were tramping up the trail like legends. "Who are they?" I asked. Their carousing laughter shattered the air. I had never seen anyone so carelessly happy. Dirty white shirts were tucked into breeches and I noticed with a start that most of them carried cloaks the same color of storm grey as the one Arcturus wore, though the colors around the edgings were different.

"Master McDunnon's boys," Ema snapped irritably. "Let's go before they see us." She tugged on my sleeve and her face wrinkled in distaste.

"Why?"

"They are feral dogs, every last one of them. Come on, Calli, let's go." I followed her reluctantly, walking backwards until the boys turned the corner and were out of sight.

"Why haven't I seen them before?" I pulled my skirts up till my feet were free and jogged to catch her hurried walk. "You said everyone comes for mealtimes."

"They eat at different times from us, thank God. Forget about them, Calli. That is not the sort you want to associate with."

"Why not? Who are they? What—"

Ema laughed, pulling me up the hill towards the castle until we reached the courtyard. She sat on a marble bench, pulling me down beside her with her back to the other ladies who flocked in a corner. "You are curious about all the wrong things, Calli. I just cannot work you out." She gave me a smile that could only be called affectionate, and laced her hands with mine. "I do not know what the place you came from was like, but our world I can assure you is very different. We have many rules here. Rules you cannot afford to ignore. I will help you learn them, but only if you let me teach you."

"I will."

"Here, you must learn to always do what is proper and good. Those boys are neither proper, nor good. We of higher ranking cannot and do not associate with them. They are considered lower class. Beneath you and I. Speaking with one of them would almost be like speaking with a commoner." Her eyes were very wide.

"But who are they?"

"I already told you they are Master McDunnon's boys," she muttered exasperatedly. "Novices and Apprentices mostly, in training with Master McDunnon to become Guardians."

My breath caught and my eyes widened. "I can't speak to them?" I whispered. Ema nodded.

"Not if you can help it. There will be times when you must, of course. But you must always remember your rank. They are subservient. My brother is one. I never speak to him anymore. I never see him either. That is simply the way it is." She shrugged as if she accepted the fact entirely. "Come on," she whispered, dragging me to my feet. "Let us have tea with the ladies." She pulled at me until there was nothing I could do but nod and follow. We hurried through the now empty court, and back inside.

6

The Boat Ride

Leaning my cheek against the palm of my hand I sighed, my eyes sliding out of focus as I watched the light creep across the floor. I was bored. I could hardly keep my eyes open and my stomach seemed on the verge of letting out a roar that would be less than appropriate for my current situation. I shifted in my seat uncomfortably, letting my finger trace a shape on the tabletop. The room wasn't empty, not even close. Ladies, several my age and a handful older, clumped around little tables with porcelain teacups in their hands. Ema was at my elbow, perched as delicately as any of them and nibbling on the end of a crumpet too small to truly be called food.

I didn't like the way they were eyeing me. It was like they were cats, and I the mouse. I was nothing but a game to them. Something new with which they could take up time. Ema kept glancing at me from over the top of her teacup. My left knee seemed to want to dance the jig and though I tried to focus more heavily on the steaming cup of tea between my hands, even that didn't seem enough to distract me.

"You are from Arusae, you said?"

"Yes."

"Is your family very wealthy?"

"*Were* they? They aren't anything anymore, but yes, I suppose they were." I could feel myself coloring, and my knuckles were whitening around my cup. So many eyes. So many questions.

I could handle one person easily—though perhaps not much more comfortably—with shrewd questions, snapping comments and veiled defense. My life had equipped me for that. It hadn't equipped me for a pack of civil queens. They sat stiffly on their cooly gilded chairs, adders that envenomed with a glance, that poisoned with a word.

"Oh." She seemed slightly put off that I wasn't responding to her queries with giddy conversation. Shrugging my shoulders up to my ears, I buried my nose in my teacup. They seemed to lose interest after several awkward moments, and began throwing chatter over my head the way two boys throw rocks over a stream. I felt my lips tug down at the corner.

"Ema."

She peeked up at me over the edge of her teacup, eyes widening with pretended disinterest. Her head cocked ever so slightly, and her lips pursed. "Hmm?"

I couldn't take it anymore. This stuffy room. Their off-handed remarks. The way I felt uncertain whether hunger or boredom would kill me first. I stood, and felt all eyes turn in my direction.

"I've had a long day. I think I'm going to go upstairs and take a nap." It was the only excuse I could think of; the only thing that wouldn't make her complain. Propriety was everything to Ema—and the other girls as well, it seemed. Wandering the castle searching for scraps of food didn't seem an action she would approve of. But she didn't need to know. I took her slow smile as a yes, and hurried out the door before she could inquire any further—or offer to come with.

The hallway was cool and a good bit darker than the sunroom—where the ladies took their tea—with its many windows that soaked in the light, baking anyone unlucky enough to be forced to sit inside. The hollow rap of my slippered feet sounded loud against the silence. Other than white-clad servants, silent as shadows—and nearly as invisible—I was alone. The scent of food wafted to me from some distant place. I followed my nose, hurrying downstairs where the food scent grew stronger and into the Great Room where I had taken supper earlier that day.

Caladrius Dreams

I froze at the door.

Master McDunnon's boys filled the room—the same I had seen earlier coming up from the lake. They laughed carelessly, tossing food at each other from across the tables and acting every bit the pigs Ema had accused them to be. Most of them clustered near the back of the room, well away from another smaller group composed of boys who were almost men. It was like a pack of coyotes feasting next to a pack of wolves, and the way they looked at each other from across the room proved the accuracy of the analogy.

I could remember distantly what Ema had told me about them, and I knew she wouldn't approve of what I was about to do. I couldn't help it. The loudness of their laughter drew me; I had never heard anything like it. Laughter wasn't commonplace in Golg. Only the rich could afford it, and they, it seemed, had better things to do with their time. A sudden idea flew into my mind. Turning, I ran from the room and upstairs.

I found what I was looking for tucked behind my bed—the boy's clothing that Arcturus had given me that night in the inn. Shaking the dust from the garments, I smiled. The guise had tricked Ema, perhaps it would fool others as well.

Struggling with my hands behind me, I tugged at the strings of my silken dress. When it pooled to the floor, I stepped out of it. The smooth grey breeches and white shirt felt more natural to me than Ema's silks ever could. Excitement made my fingers tremble and my cheeks burn. With any luck, the boys would still be eating downstairs. With any luck—and my costume as an aide—I would get close enough to learn what their carefree laughter was all about.

The boys were still in the Great Room when I arrived, though they seemed to have finished eating. They stood as I approached, milling about like a beehive and muttering to each other in groans that no longer sounded nearly as happy. A boy smirked at me as I drew near, rolling his eyes until I blushed.

"Master McDunnon will give you an ear-full for slacking," he taunted. "Are you new here?" My tension eased. He hadn't guessed my disguise.

"Yes," I answered. It was more or less the truth. The boy nodded as if he really couldn't care less, and made to move away. I caught him by the arm. "What's going on?"

"It's time for our next lesson." He rolled his eyes at me again and, shaking off my hand, disappeared into the pack.

The whole group was shifting slowly now, moving like slugs towards the door. I grabbed a fruit off the plate nearest me and hurried after them. Whatever they were doing, I felt certain it would be more interesting than tea parties.

No one looked at me as I joined with the edge of the group. We made our way out the Main Entrance and around the edge of the castle wall. There was a little door there I hadn't seen before. Only a couple of guards manned it, and they nodded us through when we approached. The door brought us to a path, and the path led us down to the edges of the trees which flanked the lake. A man waited at the point where the forest and the lake conjoined. We stopped in front of him.

Master McDunnon stood silently at the edge of Glass Lake. He was an older man, with dark hair that faded into white, and steel grey eyes that seemed much softer than their color suggested. His old face was hard, yet gentle. Behind him, a small fleet of boats drifted on the quiet waters.

"Master McDunnon...what's the point of this again?" A small, mouse-haired boy asked, squinting up at him. The boy's mouth was shaped into an obstinate 'o'.

"To teach you to calm your mind, child. Magic is only possible through a quiet mind." His voice was gentle, the low bass of a man who had been through many years, and was bothered by little.

The boy opened his mouth farther, but seemed to have nothing more to say. Master McDunnon scanned the group with quiet eyes, and then stepped into the nearest boat. "Four per boat," he called. Then he pushed the boat from the edge and, without the aide of paddles, drifted away.

Chaos broke loose the minute Master McDunnon's boat left the shore. I moved myself towards the first boat I fixed my eyes on, a small, unpainted paddleboat near the center of the boat cluster. A throng of shouting, shoving boys stood between it and me.

Luckily, I was smaller than they were. Slipping between them was an easy matter. I dodged to the left to avoid a boy hurtling to his right, slid through a tiny gap between two bodies and came slamming up against a force that knocked me to the ground.

"Watch where you're going!" The loud snap of a voice washed over me, and I pulled my gaze up and away from the ground. My eyes widened. A boy stood over me, arms crossed and dark eyes glaring. Even the way in which the sun glinted off his golden brown hair seemed angry. Hiding my embarrassment, I glared back.

"Avery! Hurry up! There are only a few boats left!" a boy standing near the shoreline was shouting. A quick glance showed he spoke the truth. Most of the group was already paddling their boats after Master McDunnon.

Avery, the boy in front of me, snapped his head up and towards the youth who addressed him. "Calm down, will you? I'm coming!" Then the golden haired boy focused his attention back on me. "Just watch it next time," he snapped. "You have eyes for a reason you know." He turned, and joined the others.

My eyes once again found my boat, still empty and bouncing slightly on the waves that lapped the shore, and I pulled myself to my feet before hurrying towards it. Once beside the boat I paused, fingers wrapping around the rough wood to steady it so I could climb inside. Another hand came into my vision. My eyes flickered up. It was *him*.

"Oh sorry, I'm afraid I didn't see you there. My friends and I were about to take this boat, if you don't mind." His sarcasm made my teeth clench and my stomach roll.

"Apology accepted," I grunted, my voice just barely even. "Just try not to make the same mistake again. You *do* have eyes for a reason, you know."

His face hardened. I could tell he was preparing a new retort, but the boy behind him cut it off. "Just get in both of you. It's the last boat left and McDunnon will have our hides if we take any longer."

The boy was right. It was the last boat. I threw one last glare at Avery and pulled myself in before he could make another comment. I pushed myself back into the stern of the boat, making room for the three boys who clambered in after me.

Avery sat at the seat furthest from me, looking sullen. The other two boys grabbed paddles and began to steer us towards Master McDunnon and the rest of the fleet. "My name's Canter by the way," the boy who had rebuked Avery told me. "Brutus Canter." He had a long face, framed by rather dark hair. His eyes were Caeyrean grey and blinked at me as he nodded to the boy beside him. "That's Tom Avery. He doesn't get along with anybody. Don't take it personally." Beside him, Avery grunted.

I turned my gaze to the third boy and it occurred to me suddenly that he hadn't yet spoken a word. He was smaller than the other two, long-bodied and awkwardly put together, like a young colt in the middle of a growth spurt. His near-black hair seemed rather carelessly groomed. Brutus followed my glance. "That's Thurman," he told me. "He doesn't talk much."

I gave a sharp nod, muttering something like "it's nice to meet you all," under my breath. My eyes fixated on a hang nail creeping at the corner of my thumb. A heavy silence fell over our boat, broken only by the slap of paddles against the dark water.

Eventually we pulled up to the edge of the fleet. We were too far away from Master McDunnon and I couldn't hear him clearly. Avery and Brutus had begun to bicker across the boat and eventually I gave up trying to pay attention to the lesson altogether. My fingers tapped out a rhythm against the edge of the boat. Still better than that tea party, I told myself solemnly. At least the air was clean out here. At least I was free to watch the sky and the clouds and the mountains instead of the cracks of stony walls.

"You're not a boy." I gave a little jump, and turned to the voice that addressed me. It was Thurman. He was watching me now, and I realized abruptly that his eyes weren't the same grey as most everyone else's. They were startlingly blue.

The conversation between Brutus and Avery ended abruptly. Both swung their heads in my direction. I ignored them, my eyes narrowing as I watched Thurman. He shrugged it off, but my mind was not so easily satisfied. How did he do it? I felt my brows knit in confusion, and after a moment, I broke my gaze. With one glance, that boy had looked through a guise even Ema had been fooled by. But how? I couldn't think of an answer.

"You know, I think he's right. You aren't a boy at all, which means you certainly don't belong here." Avery said, sneering. "What do you propose we do with her?"

"Give it a rest, Avery." It was Thurman again. I wasn't sure I would ever get used to him speaking. The others seemed surprised too. Surprised or not, Avery ignored him.

"I didn't catch your name, *girl,*" Avery continued, sounding like he couldn't care less. I wanted to tell him it was because he hadn't asked, but I decided to try to remain civil.

"Calli."

"Calli what?"

I froze, trying to remember the name I had given Ema. Suddenly I realized I hadn't given her one at all. I made it up off the top of my head. "Thompson."

"Thompson? It doesn't sound familiar. There aren't too many red-heads around here, Miss Thompson. Are you a commoner? T'would be a shame. A pretty face like yours shouldn't belong to a commoner."

"No." I scowled at him, trying to remember how to sit straight and properly the way Ema had told me. I wiggled in my seat and lifted my chin. It's *auburn,* the voice in the back of my mind snarled.

"Well, that's a relief. I really don't believe they should be allowed. Do you? I mean, this is a castle, not a cottage. Even if they can do magic every now and then, it's not as if we have any use for them."

"The queen was a commoner," Thurman said suddenly. A lump began to form in my throat.

"The queen was queen by marriage, not by right. In my opinion, that hardly made her queen at all."

I glared at Avery one last time and turned my back. Behind me, I could hear Brutus snickering. I ignored him, peering instead through the rising mist to watch Master McDunnon. If I strained my ears, I could just make out his voice drifting across to me, soft and clear.

"Clear your minds now," Master McDunnon was saying. "Focus on your center. Feel it. Hear the beating of your heart. Count your breaths..."

Already bored, I tuned him out and leaned over the edge of the boat. Letting my fingers trail in the icy water, I watched the shimmers and wakes of my finger tips and the shimmers and wakes of the boat combine. Entranced and alone in my frost bitten world, time seemed to slip away.

I didn't notice when they began to rock the boat. I didn't even hear the shouts of Avery, or the scolding of Brutus. Nor did I hear the laughter of Thurman, as he joined in the rocking. What I did notice, at last, was how when I reached out to tap a floating feather with a fingertip, my whole arm instead was plunged into the water by the rapidly tilting boat. It was too late. The boat tipped up, and then down.

A wall of icy water hit me. One gasp was like daggers that suffocated my lungs. The water fed numbness and a dreamy stupor through my veins. There wasn't even time to panic.

*I can't swim...*the thought drifted to me through a void, seeming very far away. I couldn't feel anything. I was blank. I was nothing. I was drifting downward into the depths of icy black death. My mind was fading away. My eyelids fluttered shut.

Don't give up. The thought came to me slowly, shattering through the empty hollow of my mind. I forced my eyes open and turned my face towards the boat's fading bottom.

An arm reached into the water, the refraction of the light giving it a ghostly, greenish glow. *Don't give up.* I stretched my hands towards the arm. I gave a feeble kick. *Don't give up. You've come this far. Are you going to lose it all now? Think of it. Think of what you have to lose.* I felt my mind grow fuzzy. Blank. Nothing. *No! Think! You have a life! You could have friends. You have a family ... a real family. Don't give up. Not now. Not yet.*

I kicked my legs. A little harder. A little stronger. They were so cold—the movement felt as if they were breaking. Breaking into a million icy shards. Breaking and drifting away into the nothingness of endless water.

The arm grew closer. And then my numb, cold fingers brushed the tips of its fingers. I felt them slip away, but the fingers were strong and they curled tight around mine. They did not let go. Soon, I had a grasp of its slippery wrist, and it was warm and beckoned me to life. Another arm grasped my elbow. My head broke surface, and air came screaming into my lungs. Ripping, tearing into my lungs. I gasped, trying to drink as much of the fiery air as I could. Sunlight shattered the glass lake like dew drops. Its breath tore at my skin.

"I've got you Calli. Hold on. I've got you." It was an angel's voice. It came from above. It adjusted its hold on my body, and pulled me aboard.

Laying on the floor of the boat, I shivered. The slight breeze chilled my wet body. Tom Avery and Brutus Canter sat at the bow, looking unruffled and vaguely disinterested.

I sat up stiffly. My hair clung frozen to my face, and my teeth chattered. Someone was wrapping a cloak around my shoulders. "Here," he whispered. He placed it gently over me and when I protested, only shook his head. "You need it more than I do. You must be freezing." He smiled then, his blue eyes warmer than I had remembered. "I don't think we were properly introduced. You can call me Leo."

7

Rats

"What do you think you are doing?" Master McDunnon's calm voice wasn't calm anymore. It seemed as if he *could* be bothered.

"She fell into the lake." Avery pointed an accusing finger at me.

"We were rocking the boat, Master. It really wasn't her fault—"

"That's enough from you, Thurman. I do not stand for disturbances during lessons. You, of all people, should know that by now. I expect to see the four of you in the castle armory before the end of the first hour tomorrow morning."

"Master McDunnon—" I began, and then broke off mid sentence when he raised an eyebrow at me.

"I don't have time for you, girl. I will expect you in the morning with the rest of them, for your part in this." I opened my mouth, and he stopped me. "And I don't want to see you in my classes again." I felt my face coloring, suddenly aware that he probably thought I was nothing more than a common flirt. I cleared my throat to object, but he had already turned away. "Class is dismissed. Novices, I will expect you in the training field tomorrow morning. Be there with the sun."

When the boats reached the shore, I stood and stumbled out. Leo steadied me with a hand. "Are you okay?"

"I've been better."

He smiled ruefully and lifted a hand to my cheek. "You're freezing. You'll catch cold if we don't get inside soon." He hesitated a moment before grabbing my arm and dragging me with him. "Come on."

My cold limbs didn't want to make it easily up the slope and we soon fell behind the others. His demeanor changed as we left the group. His shoulders relaxed and when he spoke, his voice was even. "You're not from around here, are you?"

I threw a half glance behind me, and then back towards his face. "How did you know?"

"I've been here awhile."

I didn't answer, and he didn't push. In truth, I wasn't really sure what to tell him. He had seen so easily through my guise to-day...would he believe me if I told him what I had told the others, that I was a refugee from Arusae? But what else could I tell him? Certainly not the truth. Doubtless, he'd laugh—or believe me. I wasn't sure which was worse. Silence followed us up the hill. I let it chase me, and lost myself in my thoughts.

* * *

"Calli!" A voice called from behind me. "I've been looking for you everywhere! We are going to miss dinner." It was Ema. Her face was brighter than normal, her cheeks a frantic shade of strawberry. Her eyes slid from my face to the boy beside me. I felt my breath catch. "Who's this?"

"Leo Thurman," Leo said promptly, holding out his hand. She didn't take it. Instead, she looked at him with disgust.

"Thurman?" She turned to me. "Believe me, Calli, you don't want to hang out with him. I know his kind."

I scowled at her and crossed my arms over my chest. "He saved my life." Her face visibly tensed.

"That hardly changes anything."

"How does it not?"

"We need to have this conversation upstairs." She grabbed my wrist in a hand and before I could even pause to say good bye, she drug me away. I almost had to jog to keep up and when she shoved me into the room, I stumbled across the floor. She shut the door with a snap and rounded on me. "Explain yourself."

I groaned. This was going to be a long conversation. What was I going to say, I pretended to be a Novice, and ran off to take a lesson with McDunnon's boys—the nasty ones you told me never to speak with?

Unfortunately, this is exactly what I chose to tell her—except with more words and good deal less eloquence. She was beginning to look quite dangerous. "I told you he saved my life, Ema. I fell into the lake and he pulled me out. Don't I owe him my gratitude?"

"Gratitude, perhaps, but not so much as to make you like him. A simple 'thank you' would suffice."

"Why, because he's one of those boys you warned me about? Maybe all of them aren't like that. Avery was awful, yes, but that doesn't mean they all are—"

"He is more than just one of the boys. You do not know anything, do you?"

"What is there to know? Why can't I be friends with anyone I wish?"

"Because he's a *rat.*"

Silence filled the room. It suffocated me, punctuating Ema's statement like a stinging nettle. I stared at her, uncertain. Her eyes did not soften. "What?"

"I said, he's a rat. A dirty traitor. I would have discouraged you had you tried to make friends with any of McDunnon's boys—they are so far below our station, it wouldn't be fitting—but you had to go and choose that one. His family is no good, Calli. Murderers, the lot of them. They were one of the first to cross over during the First War. His father is Baldassarre's right-hand man. There are a half dozen families I would have warned you to stay away from, and you had to jump right in with the worst."

"Traitors?" My voice squeaked up a notch.

"Yes. Don't you understand now, Calli? Don't you see why you cannot speak with him?"

"Just because his family are traitors, doesn't make him one..."

"Calli—"

"I like him, Ema. Whether you say so or not, I'm going to give him a chance."

"Don't be stupid."

"I will be exactly as stupid as I wish to be."

Ema opened her mouth to argue, and then closed it with a snap. "You are all wet," she muttered finally. "Let's get ready for dinner and go down. Then we can go to bed. It's been a long day. We will find out how stupid you are in the morning." I nodded slowly and allowed her to help me change into some drier clothing.

"Ema? Why does the High Lord Alastair allow traitors here in the castle?"

Ema let out a deep sigh. "Because he did not have a choice," she said. "It was written into the Treaty when his brother stormed the country. We could keep Caeyra if we allowed Baldassarre's men to remain within the city walls. To keep an eye on things, I suppose."

I dropped Leo's cloak onto a chair, and shrugged into a clean silk dress. The corset and the dress combined chafed at me, restricting my movements. Behind me, Ema pulled at the lacing till I could scarcely breathe.

Had a lady told me a week ago when I was in rags, I wouldn't have believed silk could be so abrasive.

8

The Aviary

"What just happened?"

"You just knocked her right out of the boat, Avery!"

"I wasn't the only one doing the rocking!"

"You started it!"

"Stop it." Brutus Canter snapped. *"Is arguing going to get us anywhere?"*

"No," I muttered sheepishly. Avery didn't say a word, but his scowl clearly indicated that he didn't appreciate Brutus taking charge.

"Obviously, she can't swim." An uncomfortable shiver ran down my spine and into the pit of my stomach. *"What are we going to tell them? The others I mean, when we get to shore?"*

I stared at him for a long moment before his words made sense in my head. Avery was nodding along slowly. I glanced between the two of them, and then, in a sharp flash, rage welled up in my chest. I ground my teeth to suppress it, clenching the wooden sides of the boat until my knuckles whitened. A wave jolted a sliver deep into my palm.

"What do you mean, 'what are we going to tell them?' You make it sound as if you are planning on leaving her!" My voice cracked, but I held my face steady.

Avery's scowl changed immediately to a mocking smirk. *"Looks like little Leo has a soul after all,"* he taunted. *"You can't save everyone, Thurman. Besides, she was quite irritating, don't you think? I doubt anyone will even notice she is gone."*

Irritating? Who in their right mind would think her irritating? A bit abrasive perhaps, but anyone would be abrasive with Avery hounding them like that. She seemed sweet enough. Quiet and shy, certainly, and more than a bit unsure of herself. I glanced at the cold water around us and immediately those flashing green eyes made their way into my head. I groaned. I couldn't just let her drown.

"Looks like Leo's developed a little crush. Isn't that right, Kitty?"

I ignored him. It wasn't true, of course. Avery just liked to jump on any possibility of conflict. I pushed him out of the way and leaned over the edge of the boat. Tossing off my cloak, I threw my arm full-length into the icy water.

I woke with a gasp. The early morning sun was streaming through the windows, tracing gold highlights across the scarlet bedspread. Somewhere nearby I could hear the first bell beginning to toll. A dream flashed through my mind, vivid and strangely clear. My brow furrowed. Normally, my dreams were either completely nonsensical, or perfect snapshots of my past. This had been neither. It had felt as if I were reliving a memory of my own—except it wasn't mine. Probably, my mind had put together bits and pieces of yesterday's events, stringing them up into a logical tale. But why then, had it felt so real?

I shivered and sat up in the bed. It was cold. My right arm felt like it had been plunged into a bucket of ice water, and my palm throbbed faintly. Ema was still in bed, snoring slightly, with her knees drawn up to her chest and her arms tightly embracing more than her share of the blankets. I frowned at her, wrestling myself from the covers and swinging my feet onto the floor. My toes curled when they hit the cold marble.

Winter was coming. There was more than a nip of frost to the air. In the corner, a maidservant stoked the fire. The fire didn't do much to warm the drafty air, but at least it took the edge off. Pulling aside the bed's sheer canopy—the material would be swapped out for a heavier wool soon—I stood. The white clad maidservant jumped to her feet as well.

Before I could argue she had thrown a heavy robe over my shoulders. Despite my embarrassment, I was grateful. The thin chemise I had worn to bed offered little protection from the chill. My bare feet slapped against the cold ground, and I pulled the robe tighter around my shoulders, moving towards the closet to borrow another of Ema's dresses.

I was shivering so much I could barely stand. Eventually, I was forced to let the maid dress me—the clothing here was much too complicated to tie together one's self—and stood stiffly as she tugged the breath right out of my chest. I let out a great cough, and the laces tightened till I could only sip the air back in. I was glad when she was done.

I left the room quickly, and silently. I didn't want Ema to wake and learn where I was going—doubtless, she wouldn't approve of me allowing Master McDunnon to rope me into serving punishment with the boys. Truthfully, it wouldn't have been hard for me to get out of it. But I wanted to go. It would give me an excuse to see Leo again, and to thank him for the previous day.

It didn't take me long to find the Great Room—my mind had been honed from a young age to memorize the locations of food. Down the stairs to the ground floor, through the entrance hall, and to the right. I could already smell the distinct scent of hot buttered rolls. My stomach trembled. I pressed thin hands against it, and hurried inside. The room was near empty, save for a cluster of boys dressed in storm grey who laughed as they tossed food and sarcastic jests across the table. I took a seat at a table across the room from them. A bird I couldn't quite identify was being roasted over an open fire in the room's center; it turned slowly on a spit. I grimaced.

A young woman dressed in white put a plate of steaming food on the table in front of me. She filled my cup, soundless when I thanked her, and departed just as quietly. The rustling of her white skirts as she hurried away seemed startling against her silence. Despite the complaining of my stomach, I found for the first time in my life, that I wasn't hungry. I toyed with the food on my plate, feeling a bit sick to my stomach. I bent over my plate, and focused my attention instead on the gold patterns traced into silver. A loud yell from the boys made me look up.

My eyes locked with a pair of dark blue eyes on the farthest edge of the group. Leo. I saw him glance at the boys behind him, and rather pointedly roll his eyes. They were creating an absolute ruckus, though from over here I couldn't tell what could possibly be so amusing.

With a hand I motioned Leo over. I saw him hesitate, but he stood after a moment, and made his way across the room.

"Morning..." he said as he approached, sounding shyer than I had expected. His shyness seemed to fade as he sat down across from me, but my own was creeping up unannounced. I could feel my cheeks heating and the end of my nose began to burn.

"That's my favorite color you know," I stammered, nodding to the embellishment on his cloak. A stupid statement, really, but I was having trouble coming up with anything more intelligent.

"Blue?"

"No, not blue...dark blue. That color blue." I smiled slowly, and rolled a piece of the fabric between my fingers. "The color of the sky, just before it turns black." I paused, and then remembered suddenly the grey cloak lying balled up on the floor of my room. "I forgot to bring your cloak down," I said.

His eyes smiled, and he shrugged. "I have several. There's no rush."

I watched as he reached for the cup nearest him and then caught his hand on an impulse before he could finish the action. Raising it to my eyes, I examined a bit of red flesh. A sliver was embedded deep in his palm. My thoughts wandered back to my dream from last night, and I shook my head. It was a coincidence. "Where did you get that?" I asked. "You should get rid of it before it gets infected."

In an instant, he was fumbling and awkward again. His face turned red, and he pulled his hand away. "It's nothing. I was careless, that's all." He eyed my toast. "Are you going to eat that?" His tone was cautious, as if unsure whether such a question was too bold. I rolled my eyes.

"Help yourself."

He took a piece and finished it in a single bite. "Are you okay?" he asked after several mouthfuls. "You look really pale."

"I'm fine," I lied. The truth was that I didn't feel quite right. I didn't want him to worry though. It was probably nothing.

The tolling of the bell in the nearby distance made me start, and Leo's face snapped up towards the direction of the sound. I could see him visibly tense. "We're late." A half eaten slice of bread fell to my plate and he stood, eyes wide. "McDunnon's going to kill us."

I looked around. The room was nearly empty; the tables were being cleared. Brutus and Avery were nowhere in sight. "Are the others with Master McDunnon already?"

"Probably." I followed him out of the room, back through the Main Hall, and towards the northern wing of the castle.

It was cold and dark on the north side. The colors were more muted and the windows fewer. Candles fluttered against the dank air, as if fighting for life. Leo nodded to a row of red doors on our right. "That's my room, third door down. I'm with Avery and the rest of the Novices my age. Complete slobs, the lot of them." He made a face.

We hurried down a long hall, turned left and mounted a set of stairs that led us down into a lower room. "Welcome to the castle armory," Leo said with a grimace. He stopped in front of the door, but it was already open. I crowded in behind him on the last step, peering over his shoulder. A very angry Master McDunnon stood inside.

"You're late."

"We..." Leo's voice faded off, and I realized we had both come to the same conclusion. We didn't have an excuse. Master McDunnon's scowl deepened.

"Get to work." Leo scampered through the door, taking as wide a berth around McDunnon's cross armed frame as possible. I followed.

The armory was lighter than the hallways above. On the far end, a door opened to the outside and early morning sunlight spilled through it. The stone walls were supported by wooden poles and weapons of every kind hung in the corners. Torches lined the edges of the room, back where the sunlight from the door couldn't reach. Leo took me to the far corner and pulled a chain mail shirt from its place on the wall. From the way he went to the cleaning supplies and sat down beside Avery and Brutus—both on their knees, scrubbing the rust from the hinges of helmets—I could tell he did this a lot. His movements seemed almost routine. I had to stop myself from laughing—I couldn't help but wonder how often the boy 'disrupted lessons'—and picked up a shield before kneeling beside him. "What do I do?"

"Scrub until your knuckles bleed," Avery said suddenly from his place on the ground near Leo's elbow.

"It's not good enough unless you've blood to prove it," Leo said, in an uncanny imitation of Master McDunnon. He threw back his head and laughed. I couldn't help but chuckle along.

It was well into the day, and I had been scrubbing for hours. Ema was probably thinking I'd died by now. My hands really were beginning to bleed; my skin cracked at the knuckles and the edges of my cuticles were peeling down. A strange sort of dizziness was washing over me, and I suddenly remembered I had eaten nothing this morning. Strangely enough, I still wasn't hungry. My stomach seemed to curdle at the thought of food.

"He should let us off soon," Leo said, as if reading my thoughts. I turned my head to look at him, and the room shifted. My chest tightened and my hands fell to the floor to hold myself steady. I gave my head a small shake. The room between my ears seemed full of jelly. "Calli? Are you okay?" I nodded, blinking to clear my head and pulled my eyes back towards the breast plate I was working on. My fingers curled against the metal, and then slipped off. Suddenly the world was tilting and that space between my ears began to roar. "Calli?" I could barely hear him. The tightness in my chest was getting worse and I was so cold I thought my bones would break apart from shivering. A hand was on my cheek and jerked away. "Calli, you're burning up!" The roaring got worse and the world kept tilting until it was out of control. Darkness clouded my eyes and I found myself vaguely wondering when nighttime had begun.

* * *

"Where...where am I?"

"You are in the Aviary dear." A small woman with soft eyes bent over me. She was dressed in light blue and a chain with a small stone pendant was draped around her neck, falling out of her neckline to hang over me like a swaying pendulum as she hovered. I jerked my eyes away from the stone and fixed them instead on her face.

"What happened?"

"Your friend brought you up. Such a nice boy. One of Mc-Dunnon's novices, I think." I smiled at her weakly. She took my temperature on the back of her wrist, examined me a moment, and looked perplexed. "I am afraid you are going to have to stay here a while. You have caught quite the cold."

My brow creased with worry.

The woman smiled at me kindly, her hand coming up to push the hair from my eyes. "Don't you worry about one thing, dear," she said. "I'll have you fixed up in no time." She gave me one last smile and left my bedside, sliding the long white curtain shut around me as she went.

* * *

It was late. I could see the stars, shining high outside the window. My throat was raw; it burned down the back from bile. I had been throwing up all day. Sweat matted my hair to my forehead and my cheeks.

The curtains which surrounded my bed parted and someone entered. I recognized the blue eyes and crooked smile instantly. "Leo?" I whispered, my voice like gravel.

"Hey."

"What are you doing here?"

"You didn't think I'd leave you up here all by yourself did you?"

I hesitated, and then let my eyes drop to my lap. Honestly, I hadn't expected to see him again. I didn't reply.

Leo laughed softly. "I saved your life didn't I? I might as well finish the deed." I cringed. I should have expected the answer,

68

but it wasn't what I had wanted to hear. He seemed to notice the look on my face because suddenly he was letting out a bark like laugh and moving towards the bedside chair. "It's a joke," he said, still laughing. "I was joking." His eyes sparkled, and his face sobered. "I like you Calli. You're different. Interesting. You're a breath of fresh air in this musty old place." He paused for a moment, and then cautiously took the leap. "Friends?"

"Friends," I agreed. "I like that."

"Good. I brought you food...which would've been awkward had you answered differently." He chuckled and glanced sideways at the bucket beside my bed. "Don't know if you'll be able to hold it down though." He placed a loaded plate on the table beside me. "You really should eat a little something. Here. Take the bread. It will help your stomach. I'll eat the rest."

I ate my bread in silence, feeding myself slowly and hoping each bite would manage to stay down. It did, and Leo had been right. The bread calmed my stomach.

"Leo?" I asked when I had finished.

"Hmm..?"

"Why do they call this the Aviary?" The thought had crossed my mind earlier. I was sure it was because this room was like a birdcage. The long bars on the ceiling reminded me of roosts.

"Because they used to keep birds in here."

"What kind?" I asked, slightly startled.

"Caladrius birds. The queen used to breed them."

"Where did they all go?"

"Nobody knows. They left after the queen died."

I straightened in my bed, suddenly curious. "What did they look like? Why did she keep them here? Why—?"

Leo's chuckle interrupted my stream of questions, and I let them die on my lips as he shook his head. "I really have no idea," he said. "It all happened before I was old enough to remember. I just know the basics."

I sighed, and let it go. Leo leaned back in his chair, making himself more comfortable.

We talked well into the night.

9

Princess

I was running. Running through a field with the sun in my hair. I could just see him at the top of the hill, pausing to wait. The camp was on the other side. He was showing it to me today.

"Come on, Lell, hurry up!"

I laughed, and continued running. The day was too beautiful to be hurried in anything. Once at the top I steadied myself beside him. "Took you long enough," he taunted. I lifted my eyes from the ground, meaning to stick out my tongue at him. I was distracted in the action. The view took my breath away.

"Archer...it's—"

"I know right?"

I shook my head in shock. "Amazing..." I finished. Hundreds of tents lay pitched at the bottom of the hill. Tents fronted with picket lines of horses and surrounded by uniformed men. Guardians. Their grey attire named them. And today—today Archer would bring me right down among them. Right into the camp itself.

"Lell?"

"Hmm?"

"I've been wanting to ask you something. I've been meaning to for a long time but...I dunno. Lell, I wanted to—"

"Calli."

My eyes opened slowly. I could hear birds in the distance and sunlight spilled across my face. I had been dreaming again, though about whom I didn't quite know. It had been so real that, for a moment, I wasn't even aware I was awake. *My name is Calli. I am upstairs in the Aviary, at the castle in Caeyra...*slowly I recited a list of facts which I knew to be true over to myself in my head.

It was morning, and the sun was just cropping the edges of the mountain tops. I could see its cold glow coming in through the high windows of the Aviary.

"You'd much rather come watch my lessons, right?" Leo's grinning face came into focus above me. I blinked. Ema was hovering behind him, scowling deeply.

"Thurman, I already told you—" Ema began.

Leo cut her off. "Come on, Calli. Come watch me at my lessons. There's a wall that you can sit on, and it isn't too cold, I promise. It will be fun!"

It was obvious they had been arguing, though over what, I couldn't quite tell. I pushed myself upright in the bed, hugging my blankets close to my chest. "What's going on?"

Ema opened her mouth to speak, but Leo jumped in and cut her off again. "Lady Dubois says you can leave now, as long as you take it easy for a few days. You are feeling better, right?"

I nodded slowly. I *was* feeling better. In fact, I felt as if I had never been sick. I had been in the Aviary for two days now, under the constant and diligent care of Lady Dubois, the castle healer. Ema had been visiting at least once a day to sit by me and chat. Leo had been coming even more often—whenever he was free, I suspected. Still, it surprised me to see them both here at the same time. "I feel as good as new," I said in answer to Leo's question.

"Which means there is no reason for you to not come," he said. Ema glowered at him.

"Master McDunnon said he didn't want to see me at his lessons again—" I began. Leo cut me off.

"McDunnon's an old bat. He doesn't really care. All bark and no bite."

I hesitated, torn between Leo's badgering and Ema's scandalized looks. It would be fun. More fun than sitting in a stuffy room with Ema all day, to be sure. "I'm supposed to go with Ema..." I muttered weakly, staring at my hands.

Besides, Arcturus would be furious if I drew any more attention towards myself. My stomach gave a sudden lurch at the thought. I would be seeing him today, though I didn't know when. Today was the day that marked the beginning of the end—the end of my old life, or the end of my new adventure. I wasn't sure which was worse. Beside me, Ema gave a satisfied huff.

"Are you really *supposed* to go," Leo persisted, "or is this just another thing she's dragging you to while trying to make you a lady? Come on, Calli. You're hardly a lady. We both know it."

"I—"

"It would be absolutely scandalous, Calli. The training field is no place for you. I don't know how they do things in Arusae, but here it would be completely unacceptable. The girls would not stop talking for weeks! They already gossip about you more than is healthy. Come to tea with me instead. Maybe I'll show you how to embroider."

That settled it. "I think I'll go with Leo," I said quickly, wrinkling my nose. "A little outside air can't hurt." Ema frowned. I stood—perhaps more swiftly than I should have after having been sick—and immediately sat back down. The whole world tilted and swirled.

"Lady Dubois said you will be tired for a while, and that you need to be careful until you regain your strength," Leo said cheerfully. Ema said nothing. She looked too angry to form words. "I'll stand outside while you change."

Grudgingly, Ema tossed the dress she had been holding— made of blood red scarlet cloth—and helped me change. "I love living at Court," she told me distractedly. I gasped as she cinched tight the corset. "There are so many luxuries here that we just could not afford at home. Especially now. This fabric..." she trailed off. Her fingers rubbed the soft draping of the scarlet cloth dress. Then she put on a strained smile and pulled the red dress over my head as I held my arms high. "Red looks absolutely lovely on you, Calli." She finished the bow on the back, kissed my cheek, and left.

It was bright outside, and more than a bit chilly. I shuddered and pulled the thin shawl closer around my shoulders. Scarlet cloth didn't offer much for warmth and the shawl was made to be worn indoors. "You said it would be warm," I snapped at him. He rolled his eyes and laughed.

"I never said that. I said it wouldn't be *too* cold! Moving faster will warm you up. McDunnon will be livid if I take too much longer. That, or think you killed me. Not that you could." He peeked at me from over his shoulder, and then he ran. Huffing, I chased him down the hill and onto the path. It didn't take him long to outstrip me. In a few seconds he was far ahead, laughing and calling me slow and telling me to hurry up. I wasn't used to running. Not this much. I was used to huddling on a corner and conserving as much energy as I could. I was panting when I reached him.

"Took you long enough," he taunted. I wasn't paying attention. I was too busy staring over his shoulder. Too busy listening to the absolute ruckus that filled the air. Leo noticed, glancing over his shoulder and grinning broadly. "Told you you'd like it. You can sit up on that wall over there and watch." He nodded to a low stone wall on the far left of the field. When I didn't move, he grabbed me by the hand and drug me towards it. "Sit here," he told me. Then, with one last laugh at me from over his shoulder, he hurried off to join the other boys.

There were so many of them—so many more than I had expected. Some were Novices, fumbling through mock battles and grunting as their swords clashed. Many more were older boys— Apprentices I assumed—with silver-white embroidered around the edges of their grey cloaks, in place of the Novice's blue. The rest were Guardians, marked by full uniform and ranked—like the boys—by the color on the edges of their cloaks. Watching them was like watching wolves play, or eagles dance. I couldn't take my eyes away.

* * *

I had been sitting on the wall for hours. The sun had hidden itself behind a cloud, and the air was laced with frost. My teeth chattered until I felt sure they would shatter and all fall out. A bird landed next to me on the stone wall, fluffing its feathers and looking entirely too pleased with itself. *"Don't you look happy,"* I snapped, shivering and pulling my shawl closer. The bird didn't answer and, whistling something I assumed to be cheering, flew away.

"I've been looking for you all afternoon." The pit in my stomach which had been there all morning grew. It was Arcturus. I knew why he was here.

"I've been *here* all afternoon, Arcturus."

His face was stone, and when he opened his mouth to speak, I cringed. "You should be inside with Lady Emalea, resting. This is no place for a lady out here."

"I was watching Leo practice," I told him as innocently as I could.

"Who?"

"My friend Leo. Leo Thurman, over there." I nodded in Leo's direction. By the look on Arcturus's face, it became apparent he now knew exactly 'who'.

"That boy is no good—"

I cut him off, surprising myself with the ice in my tone. "So I've heard. I like him." I nodded as if that settled it. To my surprise, Arcturus didn't argue. Instead, he took my arm and pulled me from the wall.

"Just like your mother," he muttered sourly under his breath.

"What do you mean?" I asked. He ignored me, guiding me from the field and back to the castle before I could even wave to Leo goodbye.

"You're going to be late," he said, finally breaking the silence as we reached the top of the hill. "The High Lord does not like to be kept waiting."

We made it upstairs to the High Lord's study faster than I thought possible. Suddenly, the hallways of the castle seemed colder to me. Darker. Less welcoming. I shivered and wrapped my arms around myself, watching as Arcturus grasped the handle of the tall oak door, and drug it open. In less than a second, I was stumbling inside.

"I have brought her, my Lord." The rumble of Arcturus's voice behind me made me jump. I bit at my lip till I was sure it was bloody. I kept my eyes firmly fixed on the floor. Somehow, all my courage had left me. It took all of my strength to remain standing.

"Look at me, child." I don't know how I pulled my eyes up from the ground. Something in his voice gave me strength—made me trust him, and want to obey. My shoulders shook from the force of that voice. My face lifted, and my eyes met those of the High Lord's. They were a warm grey-blue and the minute I found them, I felt my fear leaking away. "Do you know who I am?" I nodded slowly, unable to say a word.

He was a bear of a man, with broad shoulders and arms that reached across his heavy desk like the roots of a tree. His hair was dark and laced with silver, and his face was dressed in a well-groomed beard which lined his granite jaw. His lips smiled, however, and his eyes twinkled from beneath his heavy brow. Being in his presence was like standing before a landslide—and yet knowing somehow that you would be saved. "Arcturus Sheridan is my best man," his voice rumbled, "and he has bet his life on you. I would hate to have to act on the oath, but he had forced my hand. And for a peasant girl? By the looks of you, you are not even that high, are you?"

"I found her on the streets, my Lord."

"'Tis no matter. In a few moments, we will know. Do you still hold to your oath, Master Sheridan? If you do, it is both your lives in jeopardy."

"I do, my Lord. If you would just look at her—"

"I *am* looking, and I do see. It is extraordinary, the resemblance. Those eyes—as green as I remember—I have never seen the like. You have brought me many girls, Master Sheridan, all of whom have looked the part. I would have labeled any of them as possible kin to my brother, but this girl looks as if she were the queen's alone. But never mind that. Looks bear no importance if there is no blood behind them."

He reached behind him and pulled out a round, silken bag. Then he turned and addressed me directly. "Do you know what this is, child?" I shook my head. He placed it on the table before him, and pulled a pair of gloves over his hands. Then he reached into the bag and took out what lay wrapped inside. "This is the crown of the Royal Family," he told me. In his hands was a silver circlet, delicately worked and wrapped in silver vines which grew leaves so detailed they seemed alive. Sapphires hung like dewdrops from the crown's edge. "It is worn by the True Heir to the throne, and by him or her alone. It has been passed down from generation to generation." My eyes grew wide as they fell upon his gloves. Behind me, Arcturus took a step back. The High Lord seemed to notice my gaze. "I am of the Blood," he told me gently. "But if I touch it, it will still cause me extreme pain."

"And if someone not of the Blood touches it...?" I asked.

"It will kill them."

I stumbled backwards, drawing ragged breaths through tightened lungs. Before I could stop myself, I was at the door and the handle was in my hands. No one moved to stop me. I wrenched the door open and threw myself outside, meaning to run and run and never look back. Instead I shut the door behind me and leaned down, hands on knees, with my eyes shut tight. I drew at the air between clenched teeth and tried to steady my breath. Fear made me tremble, but no matter how badly I wanted to flee, I found that I could not.

A thought entered my mind, and though I tried to rid myself of it, it remained persistent. *What happens if I leave? Will I always be wondering?* I knew the truth. If I ran now, I would regret it forever. I had laid my life on the line when I had followed Arcturus and left Golg. I could not give up now. Not when I was so close. Pulling myself as straight as I could, I turned back to the door. The knob was so cold it seemed to burn between my fingertips. I hesitated only a moment. When I let myself in, they were waiting. Something in Arcturus's eyes told me he had known all along that I would come back. "I am ready."

The High Lord nodded, capturing me again with his calming eyes. "There is a strange sort of courage in you, child," he said. He lifted the crown in his gloved hands, and placed it on my head. Its cold metal embraced my temples. I stopped breathing.

Nothing happened. No pain. No sudden darkness. I let go of the breath I had been holding and collapsed to the ground on my knees. "Extraordinary," I heard someone whisper above me. "Impossible. Take her to her chambers, and let her get some rest. She will need it. Then come back here so we can discuss the future."

"Yes, my Lord."

And suddenly, someone's arms were around me. Someone was lifting me off the ground and carrying me out the door. I was crying, I realized. Sobbing uncontrollably with my head buried in his chest. Whose chest? I wasn't sure. It didn't matter. I was asleep before we got back to my room.

10

Poison

"Did you sleep well, your Highness?" *Your Highness?* The address rung through my thoughts, almost paralyzing me. I had to concentrate to keep the emotions from my face.

"I did, my Lord."

"Will you take a seat?"

"Yes, my Lord." I sat in a heavy wooden chair directly across from him. It was the morning after I had been confirmed as the princess—I had been summoned to the High Lord's study almost directly after waking. Distractedly, my hand touched my belt. A satchel hung there, hidden beneath my clothes. Inside, rested the crown which promised death or pain to anyone but myself. Why someone had thought to place such a dreadful curse upon the object was beyond me.

"Call me uncle," the High Lord said, interrupting my thoughts. "We are family after all."

"Yes, uncle."

He bridged his fingers on the table and stared at the papers on his desk for several moments before speaking. "Master Sheridan tells me that you have constructed a story to explain your presence here?"

"Yes, uncle, I have."

"And what have you told them?"

"I've been telling them that I am a refugee from Arusae, that my parents were wealthy nobles who lost their lives in the war."

Where was he going with this? I could feel myself tensing. Surely he didn't mean for me to keep up my lies. Surely he only wished to know so that he could assess if any damage had been done by my tale.

He watched me over his fingers. "It will do," he said after a long silence. "I suppose it would be foolish to try to change the story now. Nobody here—none of the ladies at least—have ever been to Arusae, so I doubt they will know better. Luckily news of the war is all over Caeyra now, so that at least will not appear as a fabrication."

There was a tight feeling of anxiety in my chest and in my arms and legs that I couldn't quite get rid of. I flexed my toes beneath my seat and curled my fingers together to keep them from trembling. "Now that we are certain, we can set the story straight with the truth," I said. "Let me know when and how, and I will keep my silence till then." I didn't like the look on his face, and when he answered, my shoulders shrugged involuntarily up to my ears.

"Not yet, child. Keep your story for now."

"Uncle?" I couldn't hide the discomfort in my voice. Surely, he didn't mean indefinitely. Of course not. A few weeks at most. The lies were already burning in my chest.

"It would be too dangerous, especially now with the Council Meeting so soon and rebel leaders coming here to Caeyra. As long as Baldassarre's men and all those associated with him are here, it will be too dangerous. He will seek your life once he knows about your presence here. This is dangerous information in the wrong ears." His bridged fingers folded and his blue-grey eyes found mine. The lies seemed to burn less, and I found myself nodding in consent.

"What do we do until then?"

"Lay low. Keep up your story, whatever it takes. Make them believe that you are nothing more than a frightened girl, run away from the wars in Arusae. Leave the rest to me. I've been running this country for almost fourteen years. I can handle it for a little while longer."

And then I was on my feet and he was pushing me gently towards the door. He was telling me that I should get rest, that I had had a long few days, and that perhaps I should go take tea with Ema. "Do your very best to blend in, child. The future is riding on it." The door shut behind me and I was standing alone in the hall, feeling more than a bit confused. No matter how hard I tried, I couldn't get rid of the nagging feeling that there was something he wasn't telling me.

* * *

Irritated, I picked out the rose I had been trying to embroider into the edge of a kerchief Ema had given me. This was my fifth attempt, and the result still looked more like an asymmetrical bowl of potage than a flower. When the needle slipped through my fumbling hands and pricked me, I threw it down with a groan. A thick drop of blood beaded at the end of my finger.

"Oh give me that," Ema snapped, pulling the embroidery from me more forcefully than necessary—I would have gladly given it to her—and tucking it at the edge of the table, well out of my reach. "I simply cannot believe that you never learned embroidery in Arusae."

There it was. Guilt. It rushed up like a tidal wave at her words, threatening to overwhelm me. "In Arusae I had others to do my embroidery for me," I told her stiffly, for what seemed like the thousandth time. The lie curdled on my tongue.

Ema rolled her eyes. "You're going to have to learn eventually. And to learn, you need to try." I groaned. "I am sorry if I am too harsh," she said sympathetically, completely misinterpreting my expression. "I can hardly imagine how difficult it must be for you. Our culture is very different here. I promise I will help you in every way I can." She smiled cheerfully and pushed my teacup into my hands. "Take some tea. The herbs will help to calm your nerves."

The tea didn't help, but I pretended like it did. I smiled and laughed and nodded contentedly along with her gossip. In fact, my smile never faltered until my ear caught the hushed whispers of the other girls. Their words caused all my distracted thoughts to fly from my mind. For a moment I forgot about being the princess. I forgot about the lies.

"I've simply never seen anything so hideous," one of the girls remarked in a whisper loud enough that I felt certain I was meant to hear. It was Gisele Heidel, a long haired, catlike girl whom I had keenly disliked the moment Ema had first pointed her out. I didn't like the way she looked at me, down her nose as if there was something she knew that I didn't.

Another girl flounced her hair, twirling it between fingers and looking at it as if it were something disgusting. Then her eyes flicked very pointedly towards me. Another giggled, gathering her own hair behind her head so it looked like a short crop. The whole lot of them burst into peals of laughter.

I felt my cheeks redden and I drained the rest of my tea. Fiddling with my cup, I tried to keep my eyes down. They were mocking me. Next to me, Ema offered a sympathetic smile. "Just ignore them," she told me quietly.

From behind me, a maid approached with a steaming new pot of tea. I smiled at her as she re-filled my cup, and wasn't surprised when she didn't respond.

"The problem is that you've been holding the hoop all wrong," Ema said, breaking through my thoughts. She had re-directed her attention to my embroidery, and I could tell she was trying to steer my attention there as well. Her back was turned to the other girls, and I gave her a weak smile. I knew she was trying to make me feel better. It wasn't working, but I pretended it did. I nodded along with her instructions, and turned my back on the girls as well. I reached for my tea.

Before my fingers could even connect with the cup, it tottered on an edge and fell, splashing hot tea across the table. An audible hissing filled the air, followed by an acrid scent. I glanced down. A deep trench was burned into the table where the tea had spilled. Beside me, Ema seemed oblivious.

I covered the spot with my napkin before anyone could notice. My hands shook. Was that a coincidence? An accident? I looked around. The woman who had served me my tea was gone.

I stood quickly, shaking at the knees. Ema glanced up at the sound of my chair, scraping across the floor. Nearby, the other girls watched as well.

"What happened?" Ema asked.

I shook my head, trying to play it off. "I just spilled my tea," I told her. "It was a silly mistake. I must be tired." The answer seemed to satisfy her; she smiled at me, and turned her eyes back to her embroidery. I pushed my chair in, and hurriedly left the room. Once outside in the hall, I pressed my back to a wall and sunk to the floor.

My heart pounded as I thought over what had happened. There had been poison in that cup—of that much I was certain. Had it been meant for me? Or was it only coincidence that the deadly draught had been poured into my cup? Fervently, I hoped it was the latter, but my gut knew I was lying to myself. That left only one option.

Somebody knew who I was. They knew I was here, in this castle. And they wanted me dead.

Or did they?

The cup had spilled before I had laid a finger on it. *Magic.* I felt certain that some sort of magic had been involved. My cup hadn't spilled on accident—in fact, I had never been meant to drink it. Someone was toying with me. They were letting me know that they were here, and what they were capable of. The hair on the back of my neck prickled. All alone in the hall, I felt surrounded by enemies.

"As long as Baldassarre's men and all those associated with him are here, it will be too dangerous. He will seek your life once he knows about your presence here." My uncle's words from this morning rung in my ears. My breathing had slowed. I stood, suddenly determined. I had to do something. I needed to be able to protect myself. No matter what.

The first door on the right after the stairs on the third floor. That was where Arcturus's study was, so I had been told. Hurrying up the stairs, I tried to ignore the way the torches lit the hall. There were fewer windows up here, leaving the halls drafty and dark. The sallow light gave me goosebumps, and the shadows which danced in the corners made me jump. When I reached the top of the third floor, my heart jumped into my throat. Arcturus's door was cracked; a stream of light pierced the darkness.

"Sit." A voice came from within the moment my hand rested on the brass knob of the door. I took the first seat I saw in the room. I wasn't sure if it was the eery lighting or the man who sat in front of me, but suddenly my hands would not stop twitching. My heart fluttered somewhere in the pit of my stomach. There was a palpable tension in the room. I straightened in my seat and tried to hold his gaze. I had never been afraid of the man before, why should I start now? Because Ema said he is not a good man, the voice in the back of my head tried to tell me. She said he used to support Baldassarre. I pushed the voice away. I was being foolish.

"What do you need?" The question came out as more of a demand, and I fixed my face to match the tone.

"I want you to train me." His face darkened. I shivered at the intensity of his gaze, but I didn't back down. "I need to be able to protect myself."

"What happened?"

His question caught me off guard. I had expected him to refuse, and I had prepared myself to convince him. Instead, he stared me down with caramel eyes, and waited for my answer. Quickly, and in a hushed voice, I explained what had happened. "Someone knows who I am," I said.

"I suspected as much." He stood abruptly. "The only way to get started is to begin. We might as well do so now."

He steered me to the back of the study towards a small red door. He had to stoop to walk through it. I followed him through, and looked around. We were in a large room—empty for the most part—roughly the size of a ballroom. The domed ceiling caused echoes to erupt around us as I padded across the polished marble floor.

The only furniture to be seen was a large, two door cabinet that stood on the right-hand side of the room. To this, Arcturus brought me. Large and made of a glossy maple, the cabinet stood a good seven feet tall—nearly a head higher than Arcturus himself. I was only barely eye level with the tiny gold handles. These Arcturus grasped and opened the cabinet wide. The inside was so deep I could not see its back.

"This cabinet contains whatever I need it to provide," he muttered, half to himself. "I got it for a more than handsome price from a cabinet maker in Cambria. These cabinets are his specialty, he is the only man alive today who remembers how to make them." Reaching into the back he pulled out a pair of practice swords, wooden and rather eloquently carved. He tossed one at me in one swift fluid motion, a little harder than was perhaps necessary. I reached out my hands to catch it. It fell to the ground.

"I'm not an athlete—"

"Then you'd better learn. In this world, men live and die by the sword. This is not a game. If you cannot learn, you will die. I can promise you that."

"I don't know what to do."

"First, you must pick your sword up off the ground." He bent, and grasped the rough wooden end in his calloused hand. Then, standing behind me, he wrapped the fingers of both my hands around the hilt. "This is your grasp. Hold it tightly. Do not deviate from it for now" I squeezed the hilt until my fingers throbbed. "Stand sideways to your opponent. You have more strength from this angle, and you will be better protected from attack." He stepped away a few strides and lifted his own sword. "Hold your weapon upright. Always let your opponent attack first."

What if he decides I'm not good enough? What if he decides this is a waste of time, and sends me away? He lunged towards me before I was able to clear my thoughts. His weapon crashed against mine with a dull thud. The practice sword danced through my distracted fingers and shivered to the ground. I watched it fall, abashed. Arcturus's voice brought me back to reality. His shortness made my toes curl. "Try again."

* * *

By the time he had finished with me, it was late into the night. My fingers were almost bloody and the muscles in my back had corded tight. My vision was murky, my legs wobbled when I walked. The man had not been gentle.

"I want you here at the same time tomorrow."

"Yes, sir." Even speaking hurt. Though I could not see it, I could feel the bruise that was spotting its way across my jaw—a souvenir which had taught me quickly how to duck.

"Stand still." He moved towards me and his hand reached for my head. I shook him off, tensing. The last time he had come near my face, my hair had been cut off.

"What are you doing?"

He sighed and took a step back. "Healing you. It will raise questions if they see you wandering around the castle covered head to toe in bruises. It is not right for a lady to learn to fight."

"If it is not right, then why did you agree to teach me?"

"Because you are not a lady," he answered. "You are a princess. And one day, you will be the queen. Now stand still." His voice was hard again.

His hand reached for my head, and this time I did not brush him off. For a second he closed his eyes, and then my body burst into a million shivers that itched like a hundred bruises, all healing at once. Which was exactly what had happened, I realized. When I raised my hand, the bruises were gone. All that was left was a bit of dried blood at the edge of my smallest finger. The cut that had once been there was gone, healed over with new pink skin. I turned to thank him, but he had already left. The door beside me slammed shut in my face.

I lost myself in my thoughts on the way back to my room. There was almost too much to think about, so much that my mind spun in endless circles that never quite touched on any of the topics it spiraled around. I was a distracted mess by the time I reached my door. It took me a second to realize there was a shape in the shadows.

"Hello?" I took a few steps forward, peering at it with decided worry. "Who's there?" My voice rose up an octave and I took another step forward. The shadow moved. I screamed and jumped back, away from the figure that was shrouded in the night.

"It's just me." The figure stood, rising to a height only slightly above my own. I recognized the lanky frame, and when he stepped forward into the light, I heaved a sigh of relief.

"Leo. Why are you here?"

"Ema told me you weren't here. She didn't know where you had gone, so I decided to wait for you."

"It's nearly midnight!"

A careless grin appeared on his face. "Take a walk with me?"

I nodded enthusiastically. A walk sounded perfect. Anything to take my mind off of Arcturus and the hundred other things that swirled endlessly through my thoughts. "Definitely," I told him. I took his arm and let him steer me down the hall.

Leo didn't say much as we wandered. The torches gave off just enough light for me to see his face and that his normal smile had tightened into a frown. He seemed distracted. I could feel the tension in him. Something wasn't quite right.

We were near the side entrance to the castle. I could hear the rain that hammered rhythmically on the rooftops. A sudden thought made me grin. I didn't feel like being boring. I wanted excitement. Something Arcturus wouldn't approve of. And maybe, just maybe, I could distract the boy from whatever was on his mind. "Want to go outside?"

"It's raining."

"Exactly!" I danced to the edge of the doorway and gave a quick glance outside. "Please?"

"No." He tried to smile, but his voice still sounded wrong.

"Why not?"

"I'll get wet."

"Please Leo?" For most of my life, I had dreaded the rain. Rain meant cold and sickness. Now, however, for the first time in my life, I didn't have to worry about such things. Most things weren't simple, but I wanted this to be. All I wanted was to enjoy the rain.

"Maybe..." I darted outside before he could refuse, running to the grass and letting the cold rain wash down my face. It felt almost as if—if I stood here long enough—all of my worries would be swept away by the downfall. In spite of myself, I smiled at the sky. Nearby, Leo stood in the archway, watching and clearly amused.

"Come on!" I called.

He shook his head. "I'll just wait here."

Overcome with a sudden impish inspiration, I ran back to the archway and pulled him out into the grass. "Isn't this great?" I kicked off my shoes and squished my toes into the mud.

"I guess..."

I laughed and blinked happily at the grey sky. Running a few feet away from him I twirled, arms spread wide. I closed my eyes and let the rain soak in. I could hear peals of my laughter, echoing off the castle's stone walls. "Don't just stand there!"

"What else am I supposed to do?"

I grinned. "Dance!" I grabbed for his hands.

"No...really. I'm having fun just watching you..."

"Please?"

It wasn't really dancing, but after a moment he was laughing too. The pain in his face had lessened and after a while of spinning, I tumbled to the ground. The wet grass squished beneath me. Beside me, Leo dropped to the ground as well. "See? Wasn't that fun?" His face was glowing. Deftly, he reached forward and tucked a strand of rain soaked hair behind my ear. I could feel the water that dripped down my nose. More drops clung to my lashes. He wiped them away, laughing. Then something shifted in his eyes. The laughter fell away.

"Leo? What's wrong?"

"Nothing."

"Please tell me."

He sat up straight, moving away from me as if he thought distance could hide his emotion. "It's nothing Calli. Please don't worry about it."

"But I *do* worry about it. I worry about you, Leo. Isn't that what friends are supposed to do?" I placed a hand on his arm, tentative. I could see him cracking. His face was tense in the moonlight, shadows creasing under his eyes and running across his forehead. He waved a hand as if to brush away the rain.

"My father arrived this morning, for the Council Meeting," he said slowly. "He is one of the Elder members this year, so he was required to come."

"That's wonderful. I bet you haven't seen him in a while."

"I haven't." His face had tightened into a frown again.

"Leo?"

"I've never been the favorite. I'm the youngest son, how could I be?" He was talking half to himself now, a hushed whisper that I had to lean in to hear. "Not good enough except to be a Guardian someday, and serve in the King's Army. And I'm not even very good at that.

"Everything is always my fault. He never talks to me. Just yells. And he rarely even does that. Sometimes he just looks at me, without saying a word. Most of the time he doesn't even acknowledge I exist. He would kill me, you know. If he didn't think he could use me."

I didn't know what to say, so I leaned forward and pulled him into a hug. Head buried in his chest, I whispered to him. "You're going to be just fine. I promise."

We sat together, there on the grass in the pouring rain. I cradled his head in my arms and tried to calm his tears. The sky bled his pain.

11

Master McDunnon's Boys

"Archer..." I tugged anxiously at his sleeve. "Archer!"

"Lell?"

"What are you thinking about?"

"Nothing." The words left his mouth a bit too quickly, but I ignored my curiosity. Pushing never worked with Archer. I'd just have to wait till he told me on his own. "Do you want to walk out to the fountain? It's getting hot in here." He tugged on the neck of his coat for effect.

I shrugged. I didn't think it was too hot and it was snowing in the courtyard, but I didn't argue. Arguing always seemed to make things worse, lately. "Sure, whatever." Whatever would take his mind off of what had it so fixated. I didn't like the way his eyes glazed over when he thought. It made me nervous.

"Great." He pulled me by the hand out into the night air, but his lack of concentration did not waver. He was more distracted than usual this evening.

He stood at the edge of the fountain, his eyes staring out somewhere beyond the castle wall. A giggling couple passed us, the girl's satin ball gown shivering in the breeze. I looked down at my own gown and sighed. The light wool fabric was well cut, but it wasn't as beautiful nor as expensive as the satin and silk that clothed the ladies. Fingering the yellow knit, I sighed again and brought my attention away from it. Wishing would get me nowhere.

Beside me Archer shifted uneasily, his dark grey cloak swinging as he moved. Abruptly he sat, bringing me down beside him. Something like anxiety hung on his brow.

"Arch? Really, what's up?" He ignored me, his eyes tracing the edges of my face. The intensity of his gaze caused me to shift my attention elsewhere. I pulled my shawl closer and watched the stars that peeked out between the clouds. Snowflakes landed lightly on my lashes. I blinked them away. "Leslie?"

I turned back to face him and was surprised to find his face so close to mine. My eyes widened. "What is it Arch?" I could feel my voice shaking. "I..."

I woke slowly, my eyes opening as if from mid-blink. It took me several seconds to push myself upright in the bed. Ema still slept beside me, snoring slightly. The room was colder than normal; a glance outside showed frost lacing the edges of each window pane. A fur lined robe hung beside the bed and I pulled it over my sleeping chemise before standing and moving closer to the hearth. A quick look told me I was alone in the room, except for a sleeping Ema. Somehow I felt as alone as I ever had on the streets.

My dream pressed itself against my thoughts, but I swatted it away like a persistent fly. There were more important things to think about. *I am the princess.* That thought had not left me for days; it rung through my head like the resounding of a gong. It was too disturbing to think of, so I pushed it away, just like the dream.

"It's getting cold already," I muttered to myself, pulling the robe closer around my shoulders and kneeling to grasp the handles of a pair of bellows. Working it with my arms, I fanned the coals in the hearth. A small flame burst into life, flickering into being by the breeze of the bellows—and went out. I dropped the bellows with a sigh. I had no skill in coaxing fires. Whatever skills I had, they weren't needed here in the Court.

I had been in Caeyra a little over a month now—a fact which seemed scarcely believable. A month. So long, and yet such a short time for such a radical change.

Suddenly, a maid appeared through a side door in the room, so silently, I almost didn't recognize her presence. The instant I noticed her, an idea sparked in my mind.

Something had been bothering me, recently. Trust was not part of my nature—my past had eaten it out of me—and lately the sensation of mistrust hand become almost unbearable.

I trusted Ema, to a point. She was too silly for ulterior motives. I trusted Leo completely. My heart simply knew that somehow, I could. Arcturus I had never trusted completely—and that in itself was comforting. I knew where I stood with him, insofar as I knew that I could never know. My uncle, on the other hand—something about him made me uncomfortable. He seemed nice enough. And that was exactly what made me worry. He was *too* nice. Too perfect. He had a strange way of filling up a room with his presence, and instantly calming anyone in it. He made me feel safe...and I hated it.

I understood his reasoning behind me keeping my identity secret. When I sat down and thought about it, it made sense. But it also made me uncomfortable. If no-one but Arcturus and the High Lord knew who I was, it would be too easy to get rid of me if I became a nuisance.

The truth of the matter, was that someone already knew who I was. The poison the other day had made that much clear. And if someone knew, then both Baldassarre and my uncle had the upper hand. I needed to take it back. I dropped my head to my knees and pretended not to notice the maid now cleaning somewhere in the back corner of the room.

"What am I doing here?" I wondered aloud, pretending to talk to myself in a voice loud enough for her to hear. "A throne is no place for a street rat like me. I am the princess but—" A sharp squeak to my left broke off my verbalized thought. Slowly, I lifted my head from my knees and turned in the direction of the sound. "Who's there?" My voice came out harder than I had intended.

The girl who came out from around the corner of the bathing chambers was a tiny thing, holding a duster in one hand and a rag in the other. Her eyes traced the ground. "I was not eavesdropping, milady—" suddenly her little hand flew to her mouth. "Your Highness," she corrected, and collapsed in a deep curtsy before me. "I was simply cleaning the shelves," she mumbled into her skirts. Suddenly I realized she was sobbing.

My heart went out to her. I stood silently and moved to her side. Once there, I knelt beside her. "Will you swear to tell no one?" I took a deep breath, and waited for her answer.

Slowly she lifted her face, still refusing to meet my eyes. Tear stains drenched her face, but the tears themselves had gone. "Who would ever speak with a serving maid, Your Highness? Who would I ever tell?" I smiled at her and reached out to squeeze her hands. It was several seconds before she relaxed into the contact.

"Swear it." I was careful to keep my voice very gentle.

"I swear on the Throne of Saldor and on the Crown of the Golden City."

The Crown of the Golden City. That was an address I had not heard before. Caeyra was the Golden City, a poetic name taken from some of the old stories, and the Crown...? *That would be me,* a little voice said in the back of my head. I shuddered, and tried to forget.

The girl's eyes were very wide now. I could see her lip trembling and she leaned back from me, as if I were contagious. She was as delicate as a bird and I found myself wondering her age. "You are the lost princess?" she asked. Even her voice was bird-like. She spoke in a whispering treble, but there was something new on her face. Hope.

"Yes."

Suddenly she was all movement. Her hands pulled from mine and she moved away from me in a rush, scraping with her hands to pull her white skirts with her. Her eyes had filled with fear. It was me she was afraid of, I realized suddenly. It was the same fear I had felt on my face and in my heart, back when I had lived on the streets. "Your Highness—"

"Please! Stop!" I followed her with my hands, trying to still her. "Don't be frightened." My voice trembled every bit as much as hers had. Leaning towards her, I caught her hands. "It hurts me to see you like this." I could see the bones of her hands. Her cheeks looked pinched. Her dark hair fell from its pins in a tangled mess.

I bent my head to catch her gaze. Her eyes were the grey blue of the region and in them I could see Ema and every other girl I had met here. Only a title separated them. "I know what it feels like to be considered less than nothing," I whispered. "Someday I will be the queen and I swear I will do everything in my power to change the way things are."

Her eyes were almost brimming over with tears now. I could feel her shaking. Suddenly, she was leaning forward and, before I could react, her cold lips were on my cheek. "Thank you." She pulled herself to her feet, hurried out the door, and was gone.

I collapsed into the chair by the fire and pressed my face into a hand. Hopefully, this would have the effect I had wanted. I had made the girl swear to keep silent, but I knew better. The news that I was here, in this castle, would spread. First, it would proliferate amongst the servants. And then, eventually, word would get out. Someone from the castle would go home to their families, and share. Before long, every commoner within a ten mile radius of the castle would know. My seed was planted. Hopefully, with the people behind me, I had a chance of winning the game.

Unbidden, another thought rose up from my subconscious to haunt me. The dreams. I shook my head roughly and focused my attention on the sound of rain outside. Only a dream. Nothing more. The knowledge changed nothing. I could still feel the cold snowflakes that fell gently on my lashes.

* * *

It was the last week before the winter months. A glance outside showed only a few leaves still clinging to the autumn-struck trees. Gold and orange, they blanketed the ground. The lake gleamed from outside the window, reflecting the cloudy sky. A heavy mist hung in the air.

The Great Room was full today, the air thick with loud chatter. Though I had woken first, Ema had made her way downstairs more quickly than I. After the maid had left, I had drawn myself a bath and soaked until the water had grown cold. I had hoped the water would soak away the dream the way it soothes sore muscles. My nerves had been calmed, but the dream was still there. I found Ema sitting at the edge of a group of giggling ladies and took a seat on the bench beside her. The ladies around her fell silent, their chatter extinguished like a gust of wind had blown out the flame of their gossip. I could feel their eyes turn on me.

"Come ladies," Gisele Heidel said, standing primly. "Let us migrate to more elegant company." She didn't look at me, but the lack of acknowledgement spoke more than any glance or word could. I was different, and that was a fault she could never forgive. The ladies left, leaving Ema and I alone at the table.

"Ignore her, Calli," Ema whispered in my ear. "She likes to think she is better than the rest of us, but she isn't. She outranks most of the ladies here, but her family is respectable only because her uncle was the King's Guard before Master Sheridan."

I grunted at her words, but only half my mind was on her. The other half was still turning endless circles over questions I couldn't quite grasp.

"Calli? Are you okay?"

"Of course." I gave her a weak smile. "I just had a weird dream. That's all."

She nodded quickly, as if eager to move on to another more important subject. "Today Lady Canter is going to give a class on dancing, if you would like to come. It is open to anyone who is interested."

I barely heard her. "Not today, Ema. I'm sorry." I pushed my plate away and stood. "I'm going to go outside and watch the boys practice. The sun is out, and it is reasonably warm. Who knows how much longer such weather will last?"

By the set of her lips I could tell she did not approve. Ema never approved of me running off to watch the boys practice or to speak with Leo, but she had given up complaining. "You haven't eaten," was all she said.

Caladrius Dreams

"I'm not hungry." I left Ema frowning behind me. Two servants at the entrance of the Great Room curtsied rather deeply as I passed, whispering something in my direction that I didn't try to hear. I dodged around them and all but threw myself out the door. I needed outside air. I needed the cool, crisp scent of rain and a cold breeze to clear my head.

Leo was at the practice field, as expected. He gave a distracted half-wave as I approached. I smiled in response and made my way over to my usual perch on the low wall.

The stone was wet from the rain and I dug through the leafy matter on the ground until I found a pocket of dry leaves. These I spread on the top of the wall as a barrier between my woolen dress and the wetness. Then, wiggling my way onto the wall, I shoved my hands beneath my arms and shrugged my shoulders up to my ears. I could see my breath, fog-like in the early morning sun, and my teeth chattered rhythms against the methodical clash of wooden practice swords. For a moment I watched them—their attacks and their defense, the flaws and intricacies of their footwork, the way they swept from one form to another—and all the while I heard Arcturus's steady voice in my thoughts. He had been teaching me daily for several weeks now, and though he told me frequently how hopeless I was, I knew was progressing. I could finally hold a sword without dropping it, and I came to the end of practices with one or two less bruises than I had at the start.

Eventually my mind drifted away from Arcturus and his lessons, and the boys practicing in front of me. I was rather innocently listening in on a conversation between two redbirds when my distracted thoughts drifted in another direction entirely. A direction I had come out here specifically to avoid.

What were these dreams? No matter how many times I told myself to forget them—that they were simple dreams and nothing more—the strange feeling that something wasn't quite right kept buzzing in the back of my head. Never in my life had I had full dreams from anyone's perspective but my own. I had never met the people who often populated them, but they seemed as real to me as Leo and the boys in front of me. Who were they? The names were foreign. Leslie. My dream's eyes. And Archer. The boy at her side. Their names and others floated dizzy circles in my head. Unanswered, they mumbled questions in my ear.

"Hey! Thurman!"

My thoughts were broken by the shout. Leo was in the corner of the practice field nearest me—well away from the rest of the boys in the field—leaning up against a tree and waiting for Avery to return from wherever he had run off to. He was being approached by a pair of burly boys whom I had never seen before. The boys weren't dressed in the Guardian's grey. They wore fine silk shirts under brightly colored coats with golden buttons and gold embroidered sleeves. The swords on their hips looked out of place, but there was something superior in their manner. "Anderson." Leo's greeting and nod was formal at best. "What do you want?"

"Just coming to observe a traitor practice. You never know, I might have to put you in your place someday." From my location at the wall, Leo's back was to me. I couldn't see his expression. "I never understood why the High Lord let *rats* stay here in Caeyra. We are practically training the enemy."

"It's a provision of the Treaty, Anderson. Even you would know that."

"You think that means I wouldn't hurt you? It would only help everyone if I did. If I *killed* you. One less rat in the world wouldn't damage things too much."

My nails were digging into the cracks in the stone wall. I glanced toward Master McDunnon. He was on the far side of the field, working with a pair of younger Novices. "You wouldn't dare." Leo's voice was shaking, but I agreed. The boy, whoever he thought he was, was clearly bluffing.

"Dare what? Kill you? No. I would not. Not because I can't. Because I won't. I'm not a traitor like you."

"I've never killed anyone Anderson. You should know that."

"Your parents have. Your father is Baldassarre's right hand man; he practically killed the king with his own hands."

Before I knew what I was doing, I was sliding from my place on the wall. Before I could censor my judgement, I was between the pair of them. "Leave him alone!" My face was hot, and my nails were drawing blood from the palms of my hands. Behind me I felt Leo grab for my shoulder. I shook him off. Anderson seemed rather taken aback. He regained his composure quickly and a sly grin swept his face.

"You'll have to introduce me to your green-eyed friend here, Thurman. I don't believe we have met." I didn't like the tone in his voice. One hand was rested jauntily on the hilt of his sword, the other smoothed back his brown hair.

I drew myself to my full height and tried to imitate the icy stare Ema often threw Leo's way. I tilted my chin up and tried to ignore that he was still several heads taller than I. "You had no right saying those things," I said cooly.

"I had every right in the world, because every word of it is true. You'd agree if you backed the king." The sly grin changed to a sneer. "Pity, a face like that shouldn't belong on a traitor."

My teeth clenched until my jaw hurt. I had to hiss to get my voice out. "I'm no traitor."

"She's from Arusae." Leo said suddenly from behind me. "She hasn't been here long enough to take sides."

"Is that so? Just some advice, girl. Taking his side is the last thing you want to be doing. It could get you in trouble."

"Leo's no more of a traitor than I am."

The boy who had come with Anderson—he hadn't spoken a word and I'd completely forgotten about him—leaned toward him to whisper something I couldn't hear in his ear. He was grabbing at Anderson's arm and by his gestures I could tell he was trying to convince the boy to give it up. After a moment of strained hesitation, Anderson nodded. "Yeah, let's get out of here. You aren't worth my time, Thurman."

"One of these days I'm going to teach them a lesson," Leo grumbled at their backs. "They think that just because they're their daddy's little first born sons that they are somehow better than the rest of us. I'll show them..." I could feel him tensing beside me, and I put a hand on his shoulder.

"Leave them be. He said it himself. It isn't worth it." His fists unclenched and he nodded regretfully.

"You know..." I looked up. Anderson had paused in his retreat, apparently incapable of holding back one last remark. "Every word of what I said is true. The time will come, and they will ask you to join them. You won't refuse will you? We both know what they'd do to you if you did. You are going to turn out just like your father and you know what? That makes you every bit the traitor they are."

The hurt that lashed across Leo's face struck a nerve. Suddenly blood was boiling in my ears. "Leo, give me your sword."

"What?"

"Your sword. Give it to me." I took it from his outstretched hand before he could refuse and weighed the rough wooden handle in a fist. The sword was larger and less balanced than the ones with which Arcturus and I practiced, but it would do.

"Calli, what are you doing?"

"Anderson!" There was something emotionless in my voice. Cold almost. My whole body was on fire and the blood which had boiled in my ears roared now. I took the stance Arcturus and I had practiced.

Anderson stopped and turned. There was an amused look on his face, and an open laugh rolled from his companion. "You want to fight me?" I nodded. "Have you ever held a sword in your life?" I didn't answer that. *"Tell your opponent as little as possible. If you can keep him guessing you will have the upper hand."* Arcturus's words echoed in my head, lessons pounded into my subconscious so they played on repeat until it would be more effort to forget than to remember. Anderson chuckled and drew the sword from his belt. It was clear by his expression that he was simply trying to humor me. His sword glinted in the sunlight and for a second it occurred to me that his blade was real, made of steel, tempered and sharpened. Mine was a roughly cut, wooden practice sword. I pushed the observation out of my mind. A pointless detail. I was too angry to have time for logic.

"Calli, this is crazy." Behind me, Leo sounded concerned. I ignored him like I ignored the steel of Anderson's blade.

I was quivering as I watched Anderson before me, squaring his feet. Raising his sword arm. Sinking into his knees, a wolf waiting for the right time to spring. He still hadn't wiped the amused smirk from his face. "What are you waiting for?" He taunted. "Change your mind?" Before he could finish his remark, I lunged at him.

"Perhaps the largest mistake you can make with any opponent is losing your patience. Always, always, always let your opponent attack first! How many times do I have to tell you this, Princess?" Arcturus's voice grated clearly through my mind, and I cringed at the mistake. Arcturus had told me the same thing often enough that I was certain what he'd say about it now. Admittedly, I shouldn't have lost my temper, but Anderson's stupid grin was nauseating. His sword swung around, easily blocking my ill-planned attack. The moment his blade connected with mine, it was evident he far outmatched me in strength. My foot slipped and the flat of Anderson's blade made a loud crack as it connected with my shin.

"Give up?"

I gritted my teeth. "Not yet."

My hands tightened on the hilt until my fingers began to sweat and my knuckles turned white. I reassumed a ready position. This time I waited. I was ready when he came. *"Concentrate,"* Arcturus had said during our lessons. He was always telling me to concentrate. *"Don't forget, your opponent may be stronger, but you are faster. Finesse and skill can save you against pure strength."* My blade whipped around to meet the side of his leg before he could react. I blocked his next attack as I spun to the right, and then rolled away from him before he could power through and force my sword from my hands. *"He cannot win if he cannot catch you. Use his strength against him, Princess."* He turned to meet me from behind, but I was standing too close for his long arms and clumsy blade to manage. *"Stay in close. A man's best fighting comes at a distance. He will have the advantage then, with his arms and the length of his sword, he will be able to catch you on his blade when you cannot even reach him. Stay close, and his lack of maneuverability will be your advantage.*" One twisting turn and I caught the tip of my blade up under his hand guard and spun the hilt from his hands. The sword shivered onto the frozen ground.

I grinned at him. "Give up?" The look on his face was laughable. I tipped my chin into the air and tried to arrange my expression to look as though none of this had been quite so big of an effort after all. Nose in the air I turned from him and back toward Leo behind me. I froze. Leo wasn't the only one standing there. Half of McDunnon's boys had flocked around us, drawn to the fight like a moth to flame. It wasn't their laughter or their jeers that held my attention, however. In the middle of them stood Arcturus, looking angrier than I ever cared to see him. My carefully planned expression slid from my face. "Arc—Master Sheridan," I corrected myself quickly. I would be regretting it for weeks if I ignored his title in public. "What are you doing here?"

"Master McDunnon asked me to come and observe the progress of his Novices today," he told me. There was ice in his voice and even more of it in his eyes. My eyes found the ground and the wooden practice sword I had proudly held in a hand dropped to my feet. "Come here, girl." I shuffled toward him, suddenly realizing the dilemma my rash thinking had put us into. It jeopardized every one of the secrets I was supposed to be holding. The pit of my stomach seemed to want to come up into my chest and maybe further. I pushed it down stubbornly, and when I halted before him I brought my eyes up to meet his.

"Yes, sir?"

"A lady's place is not here. Get where you belong." I cringed. His next words were quieter, whispered for my ears alone. "Go up to the Aviary and tell Lady Dubois to look after whatever bruises you may have obtained in your little...skirmish. We will discuss this tonight." He turned from me abruptly, his grey cloak sweeping a circle around him as he went. With a few sharp words he sent every one of the Novices back to work, running like their lives depended on it. Leo was too wide-eyed to say anything much, but he nodded to me awkwardly before taking up the sword I had dropped and hurrying off to join Avery. In only a few minutes I was alone.

* * *

I was sitting on a mat well away from the rest of Lady Dubois's patients while the Lady herself hovered over me, that stone pendant of hers swinging above me and her brow creased as if she was trying to recall something with some difficulty. I tried to adjust my focus beyond her and onto the vaulted ceilings above, but when I realized all those vertical bars were actually perches for some bizarre bird that had apparently disappeared ages ago, I jerked my eyes back to her face. The place made me think of a cage. I didn't like to be reminded that it really was.

"Be more careful next time," Lady Dubois was telling me. I had told her my bruises were due to a fall down the stairs. I don't know if she believed me. After several moments of hovering, she let me go. I bolted for the door.

I found Ema downstairs in the tearoom. She didn't notice me when I entered, and I didn't make myself obvious. For several moments I stood in the corner, watching. Her rosy cheeks were bunched in a smile, and her eyes danced at the stories told by the ladies closest to her. I found myself envying the carefree quality of her laugh, the way it bubbled like a brook, and the way it made everyone near her smile. Sitting there in her silks with a porcelain teacup in her perfectly gloved hand, she reminded me of a painting. A painting in which everything was perfect and everything belonged. I smiled uncertainly and took a step forward. The painting shattered.

"Well, look who's here. Out playing with the dogs this morning were you, foreign girl?" I cringed away from Gisele's stare and tried to make my way over to an empty seat near Ema. They were all staring at me—giggling behind hands and whispering things I couldn't and didn't want to hear. "Perhaps you haven't realized, but you are really gaining yourself quite the reputation, hanging out with such...friends." Her eyes locked with mine, and for a moment I couldn't break away. Ema's hands found my own and I gave a little start at the contact.

"Your dress..." she whispered as she pulled me into a chair beside her. I glanced down. There was a large dirt stain down my front and the edge of the hem was torn, dragging on the ground and catching on snags as I moved. "Where have you been?" Her voice was half consoling, half scathing. She rubbed a spot of dirt from my cheek and pulled her fingers through my short hair.

"Watching Leo like I told you." She arched a brow at the defensiveness in my tone, but I didn't elaborate.

Across the room, Gisele broke in. It was like she seemed to think this was her business. It really wasn't. "If hanging out with Guardians is not bad enough, at least you could watch what kind of background your 'friends' have. Associating with a traitor is not going over so well. You cannot afford to make enemies." She examined me through pale blue eyes, like a cat examining a bird in a bird cage, and flicked a strand of dark hair over her shoulder. "No one quite knows who's side you are on, foreign girl. And around here, that is a very important question."

"I would not be talking that way if I were you, Gisele," a small voice said suddenly. It was Emily Dubois, a girl whom I had spoken with once or twice, and I was surprised to hear her speak now. Tiny and mouse-like, she rarely made herself known in any situation. "It is not as if your family has any better of a reputation." Her voice was wavering, and I threw her a grateful smile.

"Master Heidel is my uncle. Guardian to the old king, if I recall correctly. Master Sheridan apprenticed under him. I would not question where his loyalty lay, would you?" Her voice was sickly sweet.

"That is only one man. You know as well as I that the rest of your family is no good." Emily's voice was tight, her little chin held high in the air and her back very rigid.

"That is a hard claim to place, I think. Dangerous even. I would be careful with whom you accuse."

Emily's mouth opened but no sound came out. Her big eyes widened so far I thought they might pop, and dropped to her lap where her fingers lay curled against the satin of her deep green gown. Pink tinged the top of her cheeks.

Gisele laughed, a low sound I almost missed entirely, and turned her eyes back on me. "It's no wonder you have no friends. Just look at you. Red hair, cropped up so short I almost had to wonder if you even had any, dirt under your nails, hem half torn off...I'm shocked that dress is even still on. I heard they bred savages in Arusae, but I would have never believed it was this bad."

I opened my mouth to speak but she cut me off before I could get in a word. "Why don't you just leave, foreign girl? You are not wanted here, is that not obvious?" Several of the girls around me snickered. I looked at Erna sitting beside me. Her eyes were wide and avoided my gaze. She didn't speak a word.

My lip trembled and suddenly there was a pressure behind my eyes, like all the hurt in my heart was trying to escape. I was shaking and my chest felt so tight I could hardly breath. I turned my back to them before they could see the tear that had forced its way down my cheek. I ignored it, keeping my hands at my side, and stiffly walked from the room. I could hear them laughing behind me. Once out of their sight, I ran.

I was back in my room before I even knew where my feet were headed. It was empty. The fire glowed dully in the hearth, only embers now. Shutting the door behind me, I threw myself upon the bed. I wanted to shut out the world, and I didn't want to think about my problems. Not any of them. Not who I was, or who I was pretending to be. I pulled a pillow over my head, shut my eyes, and cried myself to sleep.

* * *

It was late when I woke, feeling so cold I could have sworn I had been lying in a bed of snow and ice. I was face down against the covers, my fingers curled into the edges of a wool throw and the remnants of tears burning on my cheeks.

A dream sat uncomfortably in the back of my mind, as if waiting for me to notice it. Determinedly, I pushed it away. The fire was crackling happily now and a servant was dusting the ends of the mantle with a long feathered brush. Coldness filled the room despite the fire, and I pulled my arms around myself as I stood.

Ema was not back from tea yet. She had probably gone straight to the Great Room for supper. I grimaced. She would not be back until long after I had left to practice with Arcturus, and would be in bed long before I returned. If she was avoiding me—well, it didn't matter. I didn't want to see her either.

The servant near the fire dropped an unnecessarily low curtsy as I past, murmuring something under her breath I couldn't quite catch. The air in the bathing chambers was like ice—the warmth of the fire had yet to reach them—and I cringed as my feet touched the marble floor, hopping back and forth as I scrubbed the sleep from my face with a perfume scented cloth. The thin slippers which wrapped my feet did a poor job protecting them from the cold. It would be time to change to leather or wooden bottomed shoes soon. My feet were used to being cold, but in these few months I had stayed at the castle, already I was growing soft. Out in the main room I heard the door open and a small, young voice call my name.

"I'm here!" I shouted, hoping he could hear me through the wall. I lurched for the door of the bathing chambers, leaning into the frame while I surveyed the room for who had called. A young boy, one of McDunnon's younger Novices by the color on the edges of his cloak, waited by the door.

His wide eyes caused me to recognize my mistake. Haste and yelling was never ladylike. The expectation was to remain in my chambers and allowed the maidservant to fetch me when the boy called. I felt my face grow red. My eyes dropped to the floor. It seemed as if I was always making mistakes here. Will I ever fit in? I pushed the thought away, but it persisted. Will the manners of the court ever become natural? Or always bizarre?

"Master Sheridan wishes to speak with you." The boy's message brought me from my thoughts.

"Thank you. I—" I looked up. The boy was gone.

I sighed. My question had been answered for me. No. I would never get used to this place.

Behind me I could hear the maid whispering something, her voice birdlike and soft against the crackling of fire and wind that hammered trees against the windows. I turned toward her. A long red dress was draped over her arms. I glanced down at the ruined fabric of the dress I wore and nodded. It would do no good to see Arcturus looking like this. He would probably give me some lecture about needing to blend in—as if I needed the reminder.

The maid's hands were quick and practiced on the ties that held my dress. In no time the old dress had been replaced and tossed into a corner. When I turned to thank her, she crumpled to a curtsy at my feet. The words died in my throat. I left without a sound.

It was cold and dark in the halls. When at last I had made it to the right door, I tensed in preparation. Judging by his voice this morning, he would not be gentle with me tonight.

"Come in." Arcturus's words came snapping towards me before I had even opened the door. I cringed and slipped into the room, shutting the door behind me and pushing myself close to the wall. This would not be pleasant. The worst part, was that I knew I deserved every word he would have to say.

For a long while he did not speak, only sat in his desk facing away from me, writing something on parchment that I could not make out from my position in the room. The silence unnerved me. I knew it would be broken any minute by a deafening crash. Just when I felt certain I could bear the suspense no longer, he stood.

"What are you waiting for, Princess? You know where the practice room is." He sounded tired, but the anger I had expected was not present in his voice. "We don't have all night."

I didn't wait for him to tell me again. I hurried toward the red door in the corner of his study as quickly as I could and entered into the marble floored practice room immediately. I didn't trust his strange calmness, and I didn't want to test how far it would hold. He followed me in, saying nothing and shutting the door behind us as he came to my side.

I heard his footsteps pass me and I waited, eyes tracing patterns on the floor, to hear the rough squeak of the wooden cabinet near the door and the clunk of him drawing out weapons with which to practice. I heard none of this. His footsteps had stopped. I looked up slowly, and found him standing in front of me, one hand rested on the hilt of his sword and the other hanging by his side. "You said you wanted to talk to me?" I asked stiffly. "About today? You said this morning that you would want to talk to me about what happened today."

To my surprise, he didn't drop his calm expression and when he spoke there was no anger in his voice. "It is taken care of. I have told my men to speak to no one about what happened. Even Master McDunnon is bound to obey me. They will not speak. Do not let it happen again. Next time I won't cover for you."

"And the boy I fought?"

"He will tell no one. Unless I am mistaken, that boy will hope the incident is forgotten perhaps more than we do." I nodded and tried not to look too pleased. "Don't let it go to your head, Princess. Bettering a lord in swordplay is no feat. Those boys are worse than freshly started Novices." His voice was snapping and curt again. Any note of gentleness had left it.

"What are you teaching me tonight?"

"Disarming."

"With a sword?" I reached toward him, waiting for him to place one of the wooden practice swords in my hands. We had practiced disarming techniques perhaps a hundred times, I wasn't certain why he felt the need to go over it again.

"Weaponless disarming." My eyes flew to the sword at his hip. My hands were still empty. "It would be hardly proper for you to carry a sword around the court. And not in the least bit conducive to keeping attention from yourself—not that you were ever any good at that. You must learn to defend yourself when only your enemy carries a weapon." I blinked stupidly and stepped away from him. His expression never changed. In one fluid motion he drew the sword which hung from his belt. "Begin."

Caladrius Dreams

Still aching despite the healing Arcturus had given me after our lesson, I made my way back to my room. I was snarling by the time I reached my door, so much so that maid waiting in the room seemed frightened to come near me. Her fingers leapt as she worked on the back of my dress and undergarments. Her hands shook as she pulled a thicker chemise—wool now because of the changing weather—over my head. She was away from me just as quickly.

Ema was asleep already, but I was not careful as I pulled the covers away and forced myself into them. Arcturus had not been gentle tonight—not that he ever was—and I hadn't once succeeded in disarming him. I knew we would continue the same routine night after night until I got it right. I groaned and pulled a pillow over my head, stuffing out the sounds of tree branches slapping against the castle walls. In the time it took to draw three breaths, I was asleep.

"Leslie! Leslie come inside! You're going to catch a cold, it's wet out there!"

"Yes Momma." I wiggled myself through the panels of the door, dancing on the dirt floor of the hut and shaking rainwater from my hair like a dog. *"Momma?"*

"Yes Leslie darling?"

"Momma I'm hungry." As if in an exclamation of my plea, my stomach gave a loud grumble.

"Dinner will be up in a bit."

I danced on my tiptoes and pulled my mother's red braid. "Dinner! Yay!" These days, dinner was a special treat. Little Alec, my youngest brother, played sticks on the floor. I lifted him and twirled him around. *"Is Daddy gonna be home for dinner, Momma?"*

"I don't know dear. I don't know." She turned her back to me, though I knew I had seen a tear running down her face. I pushed myself under her arm, giving the best impression of a 'grown-up face' that I could.

"Everything will be all right, Momma. You'll see. Why..." I paused for a second, thinking hard of something to say. Something that would cheer her. *"Why...when I'm grown, I'm gonna be rich! And then we'll eat*

dinner every night! Won't we Momma?" She smiled and drew me close, her arms tight and warm. She opened her mouth to say something, and then closed it and continued with dinner.

It wasn't yet morning when I woke. Slowly I sat, combing my hair straight and trying to even my breaths. These dreams— they were collecting in my memory as if they belonged. I shivered and pushed them to the back of my mind. Only dreams. Nothing more. I forced myself to lie down and closed my eyes. Only dreams. It was a long time before I drifted back to sleep.

12

Winterfest

The sun shone cold in the sky, but despite the wind and rain, preparations had not stopped. Master McDunnon had cast a protective ward around the festival area in the courtyard—apparently it was not possible to use magic to control the weather; to try would take too much energy and result in possible death—and the rain tapped against the air as if met by a solid wall of glass.

It was the first day of Winterfest, a little over a week since the incident with Gisele. Ema and I had not spoken of it, the morning after Ema had awoken and acted as if nothing at all had gone wrong between us. She had acted the same every day since. I had decided to let it be. If she wasn't going to bring it up, neither would I. No matter how strained things were now. Stubbornly I set my jaw. *If she wants to be like that, let her. It's her problem, not mine.* Still, her lack of apology irked me.

I could feel the strain even now, though of course neither of us mentioned it. Currently, I sat cross-legged on the floor of my room, talking animatedly to Ema and Leo as I pulled flowers from my short hair. I had just come in from outside, where I had watched as several ladies decorated the courtyard with exotic blooms I couldn't name. Ema sat beside me in the fireside chair, stiffly and with her back turned towards me a bit more than necessary, her knitting on her lap and her eyes focused intently at the boy who leaned head on wrist, elbow on knee. Leo was listening to my speech with uncanny intensity, ignoring Ema's glares. They were little more than a fly's buzz to him.

"I had to Leo, who else would I have asked?"

"You know people won't like it..."

"And I don't care. You are my best friend. Of course I'm going to ask you to the Rose Ball. And dinner tonight, if you'll go with me." I peered at him and swatted away Ema's mumbled protests. "Ema wouldn't leave me alone until I chose a date," I made a face to express how clearly I disliked the term, "and I choose you. It will be a good deal less awkward than spending all night with some random lord with whom I have never spoken." Here I sent a glare in Ema's direction. That was exactly what she had wanted. Doubtless she would rather have me go alone then with Leo. But she had asked me to make a choice, and she really couldn't pretend she hadn't seen it coming. "Please Leo?"

"Novices never attend...even the Guardians rarely go."

"Exactly what I have been trying to tell her!" Ema exclaimed. Her knitting lay forgotten and she leaned forward, both hands on her knees.

"I hardly think that matters," I said, giving him a smile. The way he fidgeted with his hands told me he was breaking.

"And then there's my family," he mumbled. "You can't pretend you haven't noticed, Calli. It puts people on edge, seeing you with me. They don't know which side you support, and they dislike being uncertain." Leo's eyes were serious. Beside him, Ema nodded enthusiastically.

"Then let them be uncertain. It's not as if they would like me any better if they knew." I made a face and tried to block Gisele's curdling voice from my memory.

He opened his mouth to argue, then closed it quickly again, shaking his head. "Fine. But this better not get me in trouble. If I hear even one complaint I swear I'll—"

"Swear you'll what?" I smiled innocently and leaned forward till we were a breath apart. "Swear you'll never talk to me again?"

He hesitated and melted with a groan. "You know I could never do that." I giggled quietly and sat straight again, leaning my back against the fireplace. "But I won't talk to you for an entire week. Word of honor."

"An entire week? That *is* a long time." I rolled my eyes. "I don't think I could bear it."

He didn't respond, shifting away from me and staring moodily at the floor. The silence lasted long enough for Ema to get a word in. "I think this is a very bad idea," she said with an excited scowl. "You are both going to get in trouble—and probably a lot of negative attention as well. Why, I bet you will not even get to enjoy festival week, because they will hassle you so much. I bet—"

"We'll discuss this later," I told her, cutting her off before she had a chance to get started. Standing, I grabbed for her arm and pushed her back towards the bathing chambers. "It will take you longer to get ready then I, so you'd best get started." A maid who was dusting cabinets in a corner, intercepted the girl for me. Ema nodded vaguely and allowed the maid to pull her away.

Tonight there was a great feast and tomorrow the Rose Ball. I groaned. A Ball was the last thing I wanted to attend, and a perfect situation for me to make a complete fool of myself. It was the second day of the Winterfest, and perhaps the most anticipated event of the year. So I had heard at least. This is why I had asked Leo. Perhaps his presence could take off some of the pain of attending. "I don't want to go either," I told him, "but I'm grateful that you'll come." I smiled weakly.

Leo grinned, and quickly changed the subject. "The Ball is no fun, and the feast tonight will be stuffy at best, but it's worth it. The rest of the week is worth any of the pain tonight and tomorrow might hold."

I shrugged. To be honest, I didn't really know what Winterfest entailed. "Sure? I don't know. I'm not from around here, remember?"

"They didn't have Winterfest where you are from?"

I winced. That insatiable need, that overwhelming desire, was back. I was tired of hiding things. Where I was from, people didn't have much reason to celebrate anything, much less the coming of winter and the end of autumn harvests. Winter was a time of death, and a time of escaping that death one more year. I glanced out a nearby window covered in hoarfrost and shuddered. "We didn't really have winter in Arusae," I lied weakly. The tightness in my stomach increased. I avoided his eyes.

"It's great, Calli! I know you'll enjoy it. It starts with the feast of course, on the first day of winter. That's tonight. Tomorrow is the Rose Ball, which lasts all day. The women spent all last week preparing for it, cutting the last of the flowers from the gardens to make garlands and bouquets. After that, there are the festival days when peddlers come in from the city to sell wool and other things that people will need for the winter. During the days, women sing and dance, and string up berries and leaves all over the courtyard. And every night, there's a bonfire with stories and music." He gave me a satisfied grin, and then paused as if realizing he had forgotten something. "And the Council Meeting begins on the last day," he added.

"The Council Meeting? That's why all those lords are here, right?"

"Of course." He gave an exasperated sigh and spoke as he would to a child. "One from every region in the kingdom."

"What do they do during the meeting?"

"I don't know. I've never paid too much attention. Not that anyone would tell me if I asked. I'm training to become a Guardian, remember? Lords don't wander around giving out precious inside information to people like me. It's all politics, I assume. All I know is that the Council consists of the Lord of each region, with the King's brothers at its head. Baldassarre went crazy, so that just leaves Alastair."

From the back of the room I could hear a muffled sound, like someone calling to me through the walls. I grunted. "That will be Ema. She's probably done and ready to start torturing me. Meet me here later?" Leo gave a sharp nod. I nodded back and stood to go as swiftly as I could towards the sound of Ema's voice. She sounded impatient. Ema was already waiting for me, her hair up in curls, and dressed in a pale blue gown. The perfect picture of what a lady should be.

"You have barely time to get ready," Ema said, shoving a bundle into my hands.

"We still have an hour—"

"Only barely an hour. Hopefully it will be long enough."

I made a face, wrinkling my nose at her and sticking out my tongue when she turned her back. "Gosh, let's hope," I muttered. She ignored me. I untangled the bundle in my arms. It was a dress in creamy off-white and decorated with a deep red. Red circled the waist, corded the sleeves, and traced the neckline. Embroidered patterns of leaves and roses wove up the sides and across the full skirt. It was finer than anything I had ever worn, finer than anything I could have thought would ever exist. Looking at it, I gave a sharp grunt.

When I had pulled it on, and Ema had done up the laces, I went to the bathing chambers to find a mirror. What I saw made me scowl.

"What is that face for?"

Somehow, the dress made me look childish, and at the same time, ridiculously grown up. "This dress makes me look like a china doll," I groaned. Ema stifled a laugh, hiding it behind a delicately gloved hand. When she had controlled herself, she smiled and moved to tie the bow at my back.

"You are too hard on yourself, Calli. You look lovely." She paused for a moment, and stepped back. "And I'm not just saying that to make you feel better," she added after taking in the look on my face. I didn't believe her, but I nodded anyway. There was no use arguing. "Now we must decide what to do with your hair. It has grown a little since you came here, but not enough to really make a difference."

She heated a round tool in the fire, and with a deftness I hadn't fathomed possible, rolled the tool through my hair, making sleek curls that fit tight to my head like a cap. When she stepped back to appraise her work, I lifted my hands to feel it.

Ema gave me a look that could have stopped a lion in its tracks. "Don't touch it," she snapped. "You'll ruin it, and it won't hold. Is that what you want?" I had to bite my lip to hold back the incriminating reply that I didn't care in the least. Dropping my eyes to the ground to avoid rolling them, I shook my head quickly. "Good. Now hold still—"

A knock on the door and the bustling sound of someone entering the main room interrupted her. I leapt to my feet at the noise, jerking a curl from her fingers and causing it to stand lopsided on my head. I pushed myself around her and out of the bathing chambers, back into the main part of our room. A young boy, dressed in castle livery, swept a deep bow before muttering some message so softly I had to move closer to hear.

"The High Lord Alastair would like a word with you," he stammered. Before I could get another word out of him, he turned and fled out the door. I frowned after him. Some servants, it seemed, were as timid as sheep. I half expected to hear him bleating as he left.

"I wonder what he could want," Ema wondered, appearing at my elbow so silently I jumped. "At least let me finish—" her hands reached for my hair but I pushed her off.

"The High Lord probably doesn't like to be kept waiting." It was as good an excuse as any to get her to stop fussing over me. I shook my head a little in an attempt to sweep the lopsided curl from my eyes and, before she could complain further, hurried out the door.

I slowed as I reached a branch in the corridor, and turned down the left side. My mind spun nervous circles as I walked. What did he want? When I reached the familiar oaken door, I knocked. A voice came from within, too muffled to understand. Sliding the door open a crack, I peeked my head through, then my shoulder, then my feet. Uncle Alastair was in the far corner, buried behind a stack of books. He nodded distractedly at my entrance. I sat at the edge of a cushioned chair, waiting patiently for him to speak. When I felt I had sat in silence long enough, I raised my voice.

"You called for me? Do you have something you would like to say?" The question was edging on impertinence, but I somehow managed to keep the quake out of my voice. I fixed him with a steady gaze.

"Yes, yes. One moment. I...here it is." My uncle turned his blue eyes to me with a smile. "I wanted to speak with you about an Oath."

"An Oath?"

"As a sit in for the king, it is my duty to do what is best for my people. For your people. You will be their queen one day, but until your 16th birthday and coronation, your allegiance to us is not binding. I must have complete assurance that you will be here for this kingdom when it needs you, and that you will give your all for the people. An Oath will bind you to them, it will ensure that you do your best to serve. I hate to impose such a burden on a child, but for the people it must be done."

I could feel myself stiffening, and my eyes darted around the room. It was empty except for my uncle and I. "Doesn't someone need to be here...as a witness, or something?" I stumbled at forming my words, I was guessing at thoughts, but the idea in my head sounded right. I frowned.

"Who here could be a witness? No one in this castle knows of you."

"Master Sheridan?"

"Master Sheridan is busy, child. He does not have time to sit in on meetings of politics." There was a snap in his voice that hadn't been there before. His eyes hardened, and then softened again. "Our people have known defeat. They have stared it in the face and known that Baldassarre would eventually seize the entire kingdom. To live under the rule of Baldassarre would mean slavery, poverty, and the worst kinds of torture. My brother does not understand what it means to spare a life. These people have stood at the edge of the darkness, and have not backed down. They have not given up. With you, there is hope now. The people need a princess and a queen to win the war. Will you be there for them? Will you accept them as your own? A great burden has been laid before you. The question is, will you pick it up?"

I trembled silently at his words. I understood his meaning. I looked behind the mask of his voice, and delved out what he was trying to say. I stared at my hands, unsure what to say. Unsure what to do. *I never wanted this.* It was an idle thought. "Why now? Why have you never mentioned this before? Why can't it wait?"

"I did not want to tell you when so much pressure had already been forced upon you. It seemed too much to ask all at once. But this must be done, and soon. I wish to have it completed before the coming meeting. I must be certain I have you behind me before I face the Council."

I bit my lip, and suddenly the answer became clear to me. And for a split moment, I had the courage to do it. "I will accept the burden, if only because there is no one else to do so. I shall do as you say, uncle."

"To pledge yourself to the people is an honorable thing," he said. "But once you do, there is no turning back. Are you prepared for what must come?" I nodded. He stood, towering over me and forcing me to look up. Taking my shoulders in his hands, he beckoned me from my chair. "Kneel before me and repeat the words I say." I knelt. "I understand fully my actions and I am prepared. I am ready to give my life, my strength, and my heart to my country."

"I understand fully my actions, and I am prepared. I am ready to give my life, my strength, and my heart to my country." It took effort to steady my voice.

"I swear on my life to serve the people, no matter the cost." There was something ominous about his voice. I peeked up at him, and squared my shoulders.

Taking a deep breath, I repeated his words. "I swear on my life to serve the people, no matter the cost."

"I bind you, Princess Callista Williams, in the name of your country, in the name of your people and in the name of your late father, the king, to serve and protect to the death this country." His hands rested briefly on my head, and I was surrounded by a sudden white light. I felt a strength go out of me, and for a moment it was all I could do to stay upright. "It is done. You may rise, your Highness. You are bound now to the people. With your honor and life, you must serve."

I stood, determined not to shake or tremble. I set my face into a mask and waited.

"Go. Enjoy this week of festival. The time has not yet come to worry." His hands were on my shoulders again, and he steered me toward the door. "I am sorry," he said, his voice softer now and almost a whisper, "It is not right for a child to be forced to grow to adulthood so soon. It is not right, but there was nothing I could do. It cannot be helped." There was something tired sounding in his voice, something worn, and as it faded from the air it sent shivers down my spine.

The door shut behind me with a click, and I was alone in the corridor. For a moment I wanted to cry, to break down in the hall and not move till I had finished. But I pushed away the longing and pushed away the fear. Instead, I hurried back to my room and buried all those feelings deep inside in a place where it could never get out. When they asked where I had been and what had happened, I would lie, of course. And I would not shed a single tear. A princess must be strong.

* * *

The feast was grand. Breads, cheeses, and meats adorned the table. Apples and spiced pears sat in bowls with other colorful fruits I couldn't even name. The heavy scent of wine hung in a drowsy stupor over the room.

While trying to force a buttered slab of crusty bread into my mouth as daintily as possible, I let my eyes scrape the room once more. Like some sort of nervous tick, it was a motion I couldn't stop myself from indulging in every few minutes. The way the room bubbled with laughter, the way the firelight flickered across smiles, the way the music of the minstrel trilled, the brightness of the ladies' dresses, the shining faces of lords whom I had never met—these things entranced me.

With a loud cry, the minstrel jumped onto the long table at the room's head. Plates and bowls clattered as his feet struck them and my uncle had to hurriedly shift his seat away. After a moment of muffled astonishment, the room burst into the roar of applause and laughter. With a flourish of his cloak and a dramatic clearing of his throat, the minstrel began a tale.

"Deep within the forests and mountains that surround this city, resting hidden in mist, is a valley unlike any other. Its circular edges are carved from white-faced cliffs which surround the valley floor. At its center lies a lake, crystal blue and deeper than any man could swim unaided. The lake, like the valley in which it resides, is round—a perfect reflection of the moon.

"The waters of Vision Lake, it is said, carry powerful magic. A single draught can cause hallucinations which last for days. A plunge within the lake itself, would cause the swimmer to enter into a manifestation of their own psyche. If a man with a dark mind were to bathe in its depths, the waters would spawn monsters so real, they could kill.

"Some say that no-one has ever seen the Valley Shrouded in Mist. Tonight, I will tell you a tale of an old woman who once did."

Several minutes into the tale, I found myself distracted. I had heard this one many times before, from the wandering minstrels who walked the streets of Golg. It was about an old woman who had stumbled into the Valley Shrouded in Mist—a place supposedly hidden within the mountains about Caeyra—and had to do battle with her deepest nightmares within the waters of Vision Lake. If I recalled correctly, the woman died. I shivered. It wasn't a story I wanted to hear again. I let my attention wander instead to the people seated around me.

At my left, Ema was caught up in some bit of gossip with the ladies that had taken their seats near her. Her back was edged towards me, proclaiming with her body that she wanted no association with the boy on my right.

Leo seemed fully occupied by the plate in front of him. I watched him finish off the last of his roasted pheasant—I cringed at the sound of tender meat being smashed between his teeth— and a boiled potato. I hadn't touched the pheasant on my plate, and I honestly couldn't understand why he would eat it either. How anyone could stomach bird meat was a mystery to me. It was hard to have an appetite for an animal you held conversations with. Instead I picked at the leg meat of a wild boar and layered more cheese on my bread.

I frowned when Leo's arm reached across my view, nearly knocking my water over and groping for a distant roll his fingers couldn't quite reach. Beside me Ema gave a rather loud sniff, and after several seconds of stretching, he sat back with a sigh. Grumbling, I reached for the roll; he shook his head to stop me and his face stretched wide with a grin. His hand came up in front of him, as if waiting to catch an imaginary ball. He sat like this for a few seconds until suddenly the roll zoomed into his outstretched fingers.

I nearly choked on my breath as I inhaled. Leo rolled his eyes at me, leaning back in his seat and laughing. When he began to speak of some aspect of the festival, my mind didn't follow him. It was still lost, spinning circles around the magic he had performed and connecting dots to possibilities I had never considered.

* * *

"Arc—"

He cut me off with a sharp look. We had finished lessons for the night—Arcturus had informed me that I would be practicing every night, despite the festival—and were standing in his study. The look on his face bore no patience for the questions I had to ask. He almost looked angry. In fact, he had been acting strangely angry all night. "What do you think you were doing?"

"Doing? I don't know what you mean—"

"Taking that Oath," he spat. The anger was evident in his eyes now. It vibrated through every strand of his body, making his stance rough and tense. It appeared on his face as a blank slate, wiping away the emotion he never had and made him appear, to all eyes, a stone. I knew better. I could see the storm brewing behind his granite wall. I cringed inwardly, bracing myself and trying to copy the coldness of his stare. How he had found out so quickly, I hadn't the slightest clue. "You had no right. Of all the stupid, half-brained, irresponsible ideas—"

"What?" His anger confused me. Uncle Alastair had informed me that such an action was necessary. Surely Arcturus would support that. "I did what I had to. My uncle informed me of my duty. He said the people needed me. And there is no one else to do it, is there?"

"That's not my point, girl."

His uncooperative attitude annoyed me. "Is there?" I asked, demanding an answer.

"I suppose not."

"Then why am I being irresponsible? I understand the seriousness of the Oath I took. I understand that I am bound to this country now, and to serving the people. But, Oath or no, I would have been bound. Can you expect me to sit by the side lines and do nothing? In any case, the Oath will have no real power over me until I'm older," I reasoned. "For now, the Oath is just words, nothing more. I had to prove I wasn't going to run away."

"You don't understand, do you?" His voice was harsh. "This Oath binds you now as strongly as it will when you are older. Don't underestimate what you have done. We are entering into a war, perhaps not officially, but a war nonetheless. Even now, there are men dying in the street from Baldassarre's assassins. Men fighting for their lives. Because of this Oath," he said the word like a curse, "the High Lord can send you anywhere he wishes. He can ask you do anything, in service of the people. He could send you to battle tomorrow, and you wouldn't even be able to say no. Because of this Oath, you no longer have a choice as to which direction your life will take. You are in this for the long haul now, Princess. Expect to die for the cause."

"I didn't have a choice."

"Was anyone present? Besides the High Lord and yourself, was anyone there?"

"How could someone be? My uncle and you are the only ones who know who I am."

"It is unlawful to take a binding oath without a witness." He spun from me, half speaking to himself now, and muttering so vehemently I could see spit spraying out from his lips. "Was there magic involved?"

"I think so."

"Then it was binding." The anger on his face cracked and for a moment I could almost see some form of emotion in the crevices of his brow. A hand flew through his hair and the tenseness of his body dropped from him like a hundred pounds. "There is nothing we can do now, but move forward."

There was a long pause, and in his silence I could see it was time for me to leave. It was my last chance. A question sputtered to my lips, one I had longed to ask from the moment I had first seen him this night. "Will you teach me magic?" Silence filled the room, so dense I felt like I could touch it and so deadly I felt I might die if I tried. He turned away from me, his hand reaching for the knob on the door.

"No."

"But I can do it, can't I?"

"Magic runs through your veins. You have as much capability as any of noble blood."

"So you'll teach me?" I asked again.

He didn't answer. Instead he turned from me and, before I could think up another word, the door had slammed behind him and he was gone.

13

The Rose Ball

There were men in the village. Men I had never seen before. Mother said they were Guardians of the king. Soldiers. The thought sent waves of excitement through me. Guardians! To think that I, a poor peasant girl, would have the chance to see them! Pushing myself through a low bush, I crouched silently. Mother had warned me not to get too close, but I couldn't help it. Curiosity pricked like thorns, driving me forward. I swept my red hair over a single shoulder and crept closer still.

Most of the men were old and grizzled, with sun hardened faces and grey in their beards. They sat by tents or on their proud horses with stern looks stretched across their faces. I was almost to the edge of the far corner of the camp when I saw a small cluster of men around the tent nearest me. They were only boys! Some looked to be no more than a year or so older than myself. Boys, in soldiers' uniforms. Someone close to me spoke and I shuffled backwards, deeper into the bushes where I was hidden from sight. "Get some water for the horses, boy," the voice said. Footsteps came in my direction and I backed further away, coiling to run.

The footsteps slowed and came around to my back. There was a well behind me, and I turned around as silently as I could to watch the boy who filled his bucket with its water. He was in that awkward stage of youth—small and rather scraggly, but his light brown eyes were gentle and an easy, carefree look was on his open face. He finished filling the bucket and turned to leave.

I followed, crouching through the brush and watching his progress with my eyes. Then, just as he was about to disappear from sight, a stick snapped beneath my feet. The boy whipped in my direction. His soft brown eyes met mine.

Slowly, he set the bucket on the ground, approaching me as one would approach a wild animal. "Hello?"

I backed away. The bush was at my back and I found quickly that I couldn't go far. "My momma says I'm not to talk to strange boys."

His face cracked into a challenging grin. "What are you, three?"

"I'm eleven," I told him fiercely. An angry heat rose in my cheeks and I pushed out my chin.

"Me too," he answered, and then added rather hastily, "but almost twelve."

I made a face, mocking him with my eyes. "Shouldn't you be bringing that bucket back? You wouldn't want to get in trouble."

"I get in trouble all the time," he said. "Once more won't hurt." He didn't budge an inch. He only stood, regarding me with those curious eyes.

That was when the oddity of the situation struck me. I, who had never left the village once in my entire life; I, who was a nobody, was speaking with a Guardian! Or a boy that would be one someday, anyway. Someone born of Noble blood, at the very least. I felt my cheeks color again, though it wasn't from anger this time. "Why risk it? You have better things to do, I'm sure." I tried to sound as demanding as possible, though I could see by the odd way he held his face that he didn't take the bait.

"You're interesting," he answered. And then his brows lowered, and he began to laugh. Laugh! The anger was back. I scowled.

"Well, I have better things to do. The only reason I was sitting in this bush was because I was trying to retrieve a basket I left here yesterday," I told him haughtily. "Now, I have to go." I turned on my heel and began to leave.

"People call me Archer," he told me. He paused, waiting for my reply.

"Leslie," I told him over my shoulder. "My name's Leslie." I hesitated, and then added rather hastily, "but most people call me Lell."

"Meet me here after dinner...Lell?" The way he posed the words was not proper for one asking a question. It was closer to a demand. I said nothing, and continued walking.

I sat up slowly, rubbing my head with the heel of my palm. I dreamt every night now. Each one was different, and yet the same. Sometimes, my dreams were just like they used to be, filled with memories of my own—memories so real if felt as if I were reliving them.

All the dreams were like that. Every last one was accompanied by that same dreadful feeling of reality. Of solidness. I shivered, forcing myself out of bed. Breakfast would be well underway now, and Ema would chide me for sleeping in. We had preparing to do.

* * *

"You can look now."

Ema had spent the last hour working on me—yanking strings, tightening cinches, and threatening hair which wouldn't quite lay the direction she desired. I tried to keep my mouth shut and my misery to myself. A few quips in the beginning taught me that complaints only made the torture worse. I cringed as she pushed me towards the mirror, sure that I would feel happier without the knowledge of how she had made me look. Despite myself, I peeked anyway, if only to make her happy. With all her sighs and giggles, you would have thought she'd made a piece of art.

To my complete shock, I didn't look bad. She had chosen a dress from our shared closet, a pale green ball gown which Ema told me "brought out the color of my eyes." I had never worn it before. Its silk fabric was much too fine for everyday wear. The sleeves, neckline, and waist of the dress were embroidered with a green satin ribbon. The skirt hung loosely, though it fluttered and swirled when I moved. It was a modest dress and I gave Ema a satisfied shrug.

"What do you think?"

"I think I look like a lady," I told her honestly. I pushed at one of the pins in my hair and forced a smile.

Her giggle, like the tinkling of little bells, told me that she had taken my smile as genuine. She swept to the closet, her blue dress—of the same cut and design as mine—fluttering around her as she moved. Ema looked almost like a princess in her blue.

Standing beside her left me feeling a little better than plain. The comparison was good, I tried to tell myself. It meant less attention. Less curiosity towards the new girl with the funny hair at a celebration meant only for those in the Court. Ema took a pair of shawls from a drawer and shrugged one over her shoulders. The other she handed to me.

From nearby the bells in the clock tower tolled. Ema turned quickly toward the sound, her fingers pulling at the shawl around her neck. "We are going to be late!" Without another word she turned on her heels and hurried out the door, skirts lifted to free her slippered feet and pearl woven hair bouncing delightedly as she ran. I followed, though not as quickly. This was an event I wouldn't be upset to miss.

I froze at the entrance of the Great Room, forgetting Ema beside me. She swept inside, smiling radiantly and looking prepared to take on the world. I hesitated. I had never seen a room look so grand.

Flowers draped the walls and sat on the tables in ornate bouquets. Enchanted rose petals drifted endlessly from the ceiling in a sort of mystic rain. The air smelt heavily of roses; petals smeared under my feet as I took my first step into the room. There was something odd and yet magical about the contrast between the flowers and the snow that had just begun to fall outside the windows. Harp music and the trilling of a pipe sang from the far corner of the room. The tables had been pushed aside, and somehow the fire pit was gone as well. In its place, tapping slippered feet against cool marble, were dancers.

Making a face in their general direction, I shrunk back and made my way into the far corner. Somewhere I wouldn't be noticed—and therefore, not asked to dance—was the best place for me. The magic of the setting was wearing off, and my starry eyes had disappeared with a disgruntled roll. The grandeur of the event, the excess, sickened me. I tried very hard not to think what all of this might have cost, and of how many people even a third of this could feed. Grumbling, I settled myself into a corner behind the punch bowl.

When I saw someone making their way toward the punch I ducked out of view, pushing myself backward and behind a banner which hung from the ceiling. Something warm and slightly squishy collided with my elbow. I froze.

"Although it is nice to see you here, I wish you'd watch where you threw those elbows of yours," a voice said, sounding more amused than annoyed. I rolled my eyes and turned to face the slightly disgruntled boy standing behind me.

"Leo, what are you doing back here?"

"The same thing as you, I suspect." There was that smile. Something in the way his eyes sparkled suggested a sort of mischief brewing. I wasn't sure I wanted to know what it was.

Letting out a sigh, I pressed my back against the wall. "I just don't feel like I fit in here. All those silks, and the dancing, and—" I shuddered and let my sentence hang.

"Don't tell me my Lady doesn't know how to dance?" His tone was sarcastic, but honest curiosity sat behind his eyes.

"We don't have dances in Arusae," I answered stiffly. "At least, not like the ones you have here." Avoiding his eyes, I picked at a loose thread on the back of the banner. I expected him to push further, but he let my statement go.

"Calli?" A few minutes of awkward silence, and his eyes were sparkling again. "Want to do something fun?" I didn't like the sound of "fun" and wasn't entirely sure his idea of the word equaled mine. I grunted, and hoped he wouldn't continue. The last thing I needed was some hare-brained adventure to draw attention to myself. "I promise it will be better than sitting in this stuffy old room." His whispered hissing—as if he thought someone could hear or that they cared enough to listen—was beginning to grate on my nerves.

"What do you have in mind?" I asked cautiously. He obviously wasn't going to let it go until I heard him out.

"Come on," he hissed. The hissing was for dramatics. I could tell that now. His facial expression and the way he leaned close to my ear was entirely unnecessary. "Let's go outside. We can talk better there." And then, in an odd hunched over walk that jested at being sneaking, he ducked from behind the banner and, tip-toeing, disappeared from sight.

I wasn't sure whether to be irritated, or to give in to the feeling of laughter doubling up inside my chest. Going out into the courtyard wasn't a crime and there would be fewer people because of the snow, so I decided to humor him. I stepped out from behind the banner. Leo had paused by the door and motioned for me to follow. When I did, he waved his arms and shook his head until I imitated his hunch and tip-toed after him. We were both in hysterics by the time we reached the exit.

"You are ridiculous," I muttered when we had hurried out the door. Taking a deep breath, I composed myself as quickly as I could and brushed the snow from my hair.

"But you're having fun, aren't you?"

"Of course not." The twitching of my lips betrayed me. He raised an eyebrow, clearly unconvinced. "What did you want to tell me?"

"I wanted to propose an adventure, of sorts," he said. It was my turn to be skeptical, and I crossed my arms in front of my chest. "Have you ever seen the city?"

"Caeyra?" I hadn't. The only city I had ever seen was Golg—my brief experience of Helmsberg had been just long enough to assure me it was a town, not a city—and I wasn't sure I ever cared to see another. From my experience of cities, they were not the types of places one visited for "fun". Riddled in deceit, starved, decrepit—no, a city was not the sort of place I cared to be. "No, I have never been there."

But it would be good to know the layout of the land here, and to experience the city I now belonged to and understand its quirks. Doubtless my uncle or Arcturus would never allow me into Caeyra, and Leo's blind excitement was already seeping into my blood. The boy had a way of persuading me to do things I might not have otherwise. After a moment of hesitation, I nodded. "Okay. Let's do it."

The air was sharp and crisp in the courtyard. I blinked at the snowflakes gathering on my lashes. Leo grinned and gave a shout of joy, laughing aloud. "This is going to be so much fun!" he proclaimed. I swallowed the urge to stick my tongue out at him.

"How do we start?"

Leo opened his mouth to reply, but was interrupted by a sudden voice behind us. "Calli!" I turned to see who called.

"Looks like the fun's over," Leo mumbled beside me. Ema was coming towards us. Leo shifted as she approached, nodding respectfully and forcing a tight smile. "I'll take you to the city sometime before the end of this festival. I promise," he whispered in my ear.

I grunted in response. "She probably saw us and is coming out to make me come back in," I sighed. Then, in a louder voice that she could hear, I greeted the girl who approached. "Ema!" Snow rested in her dark hair, turning her beauty into that of an angel. Her shawl was pulled tightly around her shoulders. An older boy, a young lord I presumed, trailed after her, his hand on the small of her back. I smiled at him warmly. He was well-tanned and of a darker complexion than most. His teeth glistened white when he smiled back.

"People have been asking for you," she told me as soon as she approached, sounding breathless and more than a bit excited.

"People?" I raised an eyebrow at her. "Why?"

"To dance," she replied as if by those two words she could explain everything.

"Who?" The question was out of my mouth before I could stop it. I didn't really want to know. I cringed as her face lit up. She opened her mouth to say it outright, and then seemed to change her mind.

"Who do you think, silly?"

I rolled my eyes at her. I wasn't really in the mood for listening to her gossip, or playing her game. "I don't know." Her excitement diminished, the disappointment of my lack of interest showing plainly on her face.

"Robby."

"Robby?" I didn't have a clue who she was talking about, and I wasn't certain I cared.

"Robert Anderson."

For a moment, all I could do was stare at her. "Anderson?" Beside me, Leo shifted uncomfortably. I glanced at Leo and he nodded. It was the boy I was thinking of. I could feel my face heat. Ema seemed to take my blush the wrong way, clapping her hands and squirming where she stood like a small child. "Why?"

"Does it matter? His family is the most well to do family in the kingdom, besides perhaps the McDunnons and the Royal Family themselves. He is a very proper and well brought up boy, and one day he will inherit his father's fortune. His family supports the king. The *true* king."

"Oh I *know*," I told her before I could censor my words. "Robby" had made the fact of his parentage and their support of the king very obvious during our last meeting. But Ema didn't know about the incident at the training field. I wasn't planning on telling her.

It was Ema's turn to be surprised. "What do you mean?"

Leo was so tense beside me I could feel him shaking. "I just assumed," I told her, as casually as I could. I glanced at her, at Leo, and then back again. She nodded slowly, agreeing with the point I was only pretending to make. "I figured you wouldn't be so excited if they didn't."

We sat in silence for some time before her date motioned to the castle. "It's getting late," he said softly, a dove's whisper against the quiet. "Why don't we go back inside? It's cold out here now." Ema nodded as if she had never heard a better idea in her life. I didn't relish the thought of returning indoors—it was so beautiful out here now—but I turned with the rest of them and wandered inside. Leo followed, clinging close beside me like a shadow and saying nothing.

The excitement had not died indoors. If anything, it was even higher. Rose petals still drifted eternally from the ceiling and the flowers that lay crushed on the floor released an intoxicating scent. The air felt hot and sticky against my throat as I breathed. I tried not to think of the mugginess as evaporated sweat from bodies. Instead I focused on the footwork of the dancers, spinning to a particularly rambunctious rendition of *Swing Around the Ladies*.

The spinning of the dancers on the floor happened so quickly I could hardly track them with my eyes. Following their motions made me sick with nausea, so I turned away. My eyes stopped in their tracks when I recognized the face approaching behind me. "Anderson." The name sounded harsh on my tongue. I didn't have time for him.

"May I have this dance, my Lady?" The music changed, slower now but still sickeningly quick when I thought of dancing to it. My eyes narrowed as they met his. A glance over his shoulder showed Ema far away by the punch bowl. Somehow she had managed to drag Leo with her and for a moment I began to wonder what exactly they were bickering over. I jerked my thoughts to the present and brought my eyes back to the boy before me.

"I was just getting ready to leave," I told him stiffly.

"One dance is all I ask. Besides, you can't dance with the same boy all night." There was warmth in his tone, but the way his eyes flashed in Leo's direction provided all the insult he had neglected to assume.

"I *prefer* to take my dances with *gentlemen*." I hadn't danced a single dance that night, and certainly none with Leo, but he didn't need to know that. I made to move around him, but he blocked my path.

"One dance," he pressed.

And suddenly, it occurred to me that making allies wasn't as silly as I had thought. I needed to make friends here. It was necessary to my survival. Continuing to ignore the rules, the titles, the alliances, the treaties—these ignorances would get me nowhere but in a coffin three-feet below ground. If I wanted to survive in their world, I would need to play their game. His outstretched hand beckoned me. I took it.

The steps of the dance were slower than I had expected, now that I was in it. The people on the outside only watched, and when watching it had been impossible to imagine how easy it could be. How easy it was to follow the footsteps, the gestures, the smiles, the sighs. Anderson was smiling at me. Across the room I could feel my uncle's eyes; I could feel his approval. And I felt beautiful. Powerful. Trapped in a game of gestures where I was on top, where other girls envied me, where Ema smiled and the slap of slippered feet pounded like a drum beat in my heart. And then the people faded away. I forgot about Leo, about my uncle and Anderson and all the others. It was just me and the footwork, and the empty gestures, mixing in an enchantment that left me breathless. The music stopped too soon.

Anderson was standing before me, his breath matching the rhythm of the music. "Why me?" I asked him suddenly before he had a chance to leave. "Why did you want that dance?" After our meeting on the training field, the last thing I expected Robert Anderson to wish for was a dance with me.

"Because you are different," is all he said. He left before I could ask him what he meant.

* * *

It wasn't long before Leo reached me, and shortly after, a crooning Ema. "Isn't he dreamy?" She murmured softly. She continued like this for several minutes before Leo, looking uncomfortable, shifted on his feet and began to back away. "I'm going to go get some cider, anyone want some?"

I nodded in acquiescence and beside me, Ema squealed with delight. "How about one of those cakes they just brought over?" Leo didn't argue, only nodded and wandered off towards the table at the back of the room.

"Where's your date?" I asked Ema after realizing the boy was nowhere in sight.

"Dancing with a few girls closer to his age," she muttered smugly. "It seems he decided I was too young for him." I snorted. Why it had taken him this long to come to such a conclusion escaped me, and the fact that Ema saw no such issues, was simply absurd. "I want to go over there and talk to some of the ladies," she whispered to me, gesturing towards a giggling knot of girls. "Come with me?" The question was posed so carefully I couldn't say no, and moments later I was standing with Ema, listening politely to the latest gossip.

It wasn't long before my mind wandered. Bored, I found myself drifting towards a nearby table to smell a delicately arranged vase of roses. Ema was so deep in her conversation she didn't notice. For a moment, I considered making a dash towards the door. My feet turned in that direction.

"Excuse me, my Lady." My shoulder collided with the shoulder of a man I hadn't noticed. His hand caught my upper arm, a steadying motion that held me upright.

"I am sorry, my Lord. I was not watching where I was walking." I made to move around him, but his hand on my arm locked me in place, an iron grip I could not break.

"I would be more careful if I were you, *Princess.*" The hairs on the back of my neck stood on end. His voice was barely audible, but I recognized it. It was a voice I had sworn I would never forget. *The man from the road.* The one who had tortured me. The one whom Arcturus had fought. I realized with a start that a slim scar traced his cheek, red and shiny like new skin. His hook nose was strong in the light.

His hand broke contact with my shoulder and he turned away from me, to all eyes only steadying me from our brief run-in. He paused in his step when he saw the boy who was approaching from behind us, carrying three glasses of cider and a small cake in his hands. "Leo. Come with me." The man's voice was curt and unforgiving.

Leo's eyes went wide. The cider and cake clattered to the table beside which I stood. "Yes, father." Together, the two of them left the room.

14

A Visit to Caeyra

It was midday, and the scent of flowers, beer, and sweet spices filled the air. I sat bundled in a thick nest of snow, waiting for Leo. The first snow of winter had passed, leaving a deep blanket of powder white on the ground. The sun was high in the cloudless sky. Even so, a frosty bite clutched the air.

I sat at the west end of the King's Gardens, the end nearest the castle itself. Through the open gateway I could see performers in the courtyard tumbling, blowing fire, and juggling knives. Such things were a novelty to me. Even in the main city Golg, laughter and performances were hard to come by. I shook back the memories that threatened to overtake my mind. This was not the thing I wanted to think of.

I hadn't seen Leo since he had left the night before, trailing the heels of the man with the scar like a wounded dog. Lord Thurman. His father. Ema had supplied the name for me, scowling after the pair as if her frowns could make them disappear. "They don't belong here," she had told me. "None of them do. They have picked their side, and it isn't the right one. The only reason we have to allow them to stay here is because of the Treaty."

Her scowl had increased then, and her hand had gripped my arm till her nails dug into my flesh. "Do you believe me now? Do you understand why you can't hang out with him?" I had shaken her off then, and stormed upstairs. But not before stopping a liveried servant to request a message be sent to the boy I called my best friend. The problem, was that I didn't know the answer to Ema's question. My mind was playing a war inside my head. To survive, I needed to play their game. To play their game, I needed to hold true to their views. Something deep inside of me screamed out against that, whispered in my ear about the wrongness that went on in Court. I couldn't turn my back on Leo. Could I?

When I had come away from Golg to this den of snakes, the only thing for which I had hoped, was survival. That was the only game I could afford to play.

The crunch of footsteps in the snow caused me to look up. "You sent for me, your Highness?" The contents of my stomach curdled. Leo Thurman was sweeping a deep bow in front of me, half mockery, and none of his playful jest.

"You got my message?"

"It came very promptly."

"Leo—"

He cut me off. There was no patience in his voice, but no anger either. Only a dull sort of hollowness that cut as well as any anger ever could. "The only reason I came was because I promised you I would take you to the city and I won't go back on a promise. I'm not a liar."

That last bit stung. An indignant heat rushed to my face, but after opening my mouth with a retort, I realized there was nothing I could say. I had held the information back because I had to, not because I had wanted to. *Did you? Or were you just protecting yourself, afraid he would judge you? Afraid he would run away?* I pushed the voice out of my head. I *had* been protecting myself, but not out of selfish fear. "I wanted to tell you, Leo. I really did. But both Arcturus and my uncle agreed that the castle is dangerous. Too much information in the wrong hands could be deadly."

"And you couldn't trust your best friend with it."

"Leo...please." I could trust him. I could. I did what I had to.

"No. I get it. My father's a traitor. How could you ever trust a boy like me? You know what hurts the worst, though? Not your not telling, not the lies, not your distrust...no. I can understand those things. I don't like them, but they make sense. What hurts the worst is that I had to learn from my father. I had to learn from the very snake you were trying to protect yourself against. I had to listen to an hour of lecture, followed by another hour of him trying to use me to get to you. So excuse me if I'm a bit short today, your Highness."

"Leo. I'm sorry..."

He shook his head. The apology wasn't enough. But he bent over anyway and offered his hand to pull me up. "Just stand up, Calli. I told you I get it. Let's just go down to Caeyra and not talk about it anymore." He sounded tired, only the dull ring of common courtesy and the final threads of loyalty to a dying friendship echoed in his voice. I examined his proffered hand for a long while before accepting it and allowing him to pull me to my feet. It felt like the closing of an unhappy deal.

He tried to crack jokes as we left the gardens and made our way into the courtyard, talking in a way that almost made me feel as if nothing had gone amiss. But the strain was real; I could feel it in every syllable. His laughter wasn't easy and each joke seemed to come at a price. I could tell he was only trying to make me enjoy this day, trying with every bit of courage he had to honor our friendship before uttering those final, fatal words of goodbye. He would after today. I could see it in his face that his mind had been made up, though whether out of pain from my betrayal or protection from what he hinted his father was trying to make him do, I couldn't tell. Perhaps both. Perhaps it didn't matter. Either way, the result was the same. I would be getting what I wanted in the end—the ability to play the game of the Court perfectly; to follow their rules. To survive. That had been what I wanted. Wasn't it? I couldn't remember anymore.

We made our way quickly through the courtyard, bumping through the crowd which had gathered there with hastily murmured apologies. People moved as we pushed through them, glancing at us with startled faces and muttering at the disturbance. Vendors sold wares in the carts around the courtyard's edge. Dispersed throughout were various forms of entertainment.

We passed a juggler juggling eight knives, a bard telling stories, and a minstrel singing a song about a rose with a harp in his hands and a flute at his feet. In the middle of the courtyard brightly dressed acrobats did flips above the crowd. I paused to watch all of this. Leo pulled me on. "This will be here tomorrow," he told me quietly. "The best time to go to Caeyra is today."

We were reaching the outer edge of the crowd when suddenly, like an itch, a feeling grew inside me. I was being watched. My skin crawled and my eyes snapped up to scan the crowd. Nothing seemed out of place. I couldn't locate the source of the stare.

My eyes scraped the crowd again, and then with a jolt snapped back in the direction of a figure at the corner of my vision. There was no one there. Even so, I couldn't deny what I had seen. A figure, dressed entirely in black, hood pulled up to shroud its face. But no matter how hard I searched, the person was nowhere to be seen. And that feeling of being watched, the itching suspicion that crawled through my skin, was gone as well.

"Leo?" I hurried to follow him closer and glanced nervously behind us. "Leo."

"Shh." We were mingling with the edges of the crowd near the east side of the courtyard. "Not now."

He pointed to the castle's outer wall, next to the side gate by the back of the gardens. A tiny door stood there, covered in ivy to the point of near invisibility. I scanned the area quickly. No one was looking our way.

"Shouldn't there be guards in front of that door?" I whispered. Leo gave me a long sideways glance before sighing and answering in a voice as quiet as my own.

"You forget the very nature of a festival. Everyone gathered in one place. Everyone. All of our best warriors, gathered together just inside the walls. No one with half a brain would choose to attack at such a moment. The Guardians are so paranoid, I don't think anything could ever take them by surprise— even in the middle of a festival—so it wouldn't be a good strategy even in that light."

"But Leo..."

"Shh. Do you want us to be caught?"

My skin was still crawling. No guards at the little door, and no one looking the least bit concerned. That black cloaked figure, wherever it was now, it didn't belong here. I shifted anxiously, and tried to push the feeling away. Maybe I had been imagining things.

"It will be less suspicious if we don't go together," Leo whispered slowly. I nodded. "I'll go first and make sure the other side is clear. Count to three and if I don't come back, follow me." After a quick glance around to see that no one was watching, he turned, stole out of the door, and shut it softly behind.

"One..." I began with an uncomfortable sigh. My eyes slid through the crowd, and back to the door. "Two..." I whispered, half expecting the black cloaked figure to suddenly appear. No one was paying me the least amount of attention. I turned to walk to the door. A twig snapped behind me; a man was lingering at the edge of the crowd. His eyes caught on me and his sudden movement made me throw myself at the door though the third second had not fully passed. The door was small and narrow and I had to double over in order to pass through it. Brass knob in hand, I threw the door shut behind me and collapsed against its blue wooden panels.

"That was quick—" Leo began. I cut him off.

"Someone saw me."

Before I could even blink, Leo had hold of my arm and was dragging me away, off the path and into the bushes. We crouched behind a pile of bushes by the edge of the path, sitting silently with bated breath. "He probably just thinks we are some children from town, making trouble and trying to slip in for a peek of the festival. If that's the case, he won't look for us long."

It seemed Leo was right. Footsteps came from above us at the door, echoing eerily off the castle's high walls. They stopped only feet from our hiding pace, and then receded back up the path where they faded behind the closing of the door. We waited a few moments longer, but he did not return.

Eventually Leo grabbed my arm, dragging me back onto the path. "The longer we sit here, the larger the chance that he will come back, and with reinforcements. If that happens, I would rather be long hidden within the city. Caeyra is large, they'll never find us among so many people." There was a long silence, as if both of us had just remembered the circumstances in which we had come together today. For a moment, Leo only stared at his hand on my arm. Then his hand dropped to his side and he turned away. "Let's get going." I couldn't tell what sort of emotion was hidden in his voice.

It was a steep descent, rocky and treacherous even with dry ground. Today, the path was slick with ice and snow. When Leo stopped, it was without warning, and he was nearly trampled in effect. I slammed into his back, unable to quell my momentum so quickly. We stumbled forward a few feet before coming to a panting halt. "More warning next time would be nice," I grumbled. He didn't respond to my comment, only looked forward and gestured to what stood before us.

I looked in the direction of his pointing hand and nearly bit my tongue from shock. I hadn't been watching where we were headed; my eyes had been too trained to the ground, watching the slick footing. Directly in front of us, behind the stony walls that surrounded it, was a city. It was even larger than Golg. Between us and the city itself stood a small gatehouse, identical to the one that stood at the castle's front entrance, yet in miniature. Steely eyed soldiers watched us from its peak. A man with a pike came to meet us, his eyes as cold and hard as the rest.

"Where are you from?" he asked roughly, as if bored from the routine. He barely looked at us, and Leo shuffled himself in front of me to speak with him.

"The castle," Leo replied with a politeness is his voice I wouldn't have thought him capable of.

"What is your business?"

"We came to see the city."

The man gave him a level-eyed stare. "From the looks of you, you are a student. One of McDunnon's Novices I presume." Leo gave a stiff nod, and the man continued. "Novices are not allowed within the city without supervision," he said coldly. I felt certain he didn't care one way or another, though he perhaps took pleasure in denying us. I gave Leo a sidelong look.

"Nice plan," I muttered sarcastically. I pulled him aside, out of earshot from the steely eyed guards. "How did you get by the last time?"

"Last time?" he questioned innocently. I gave him a rude scowl.

"Leo..." I threatened. He lowered his eyes, scraping his toe against the snowy ground and into the dirt below. "Don't tell me you've never been here before."

"Well...I have. I've been to the city. It's just..."

"What?"

"Maybe I came with Master McDunnon?" he replied rather sheepishly.

"You thought we'd just walk in? Of course they aren't going to let us through, we aren't allowed! Why would you even think it would be that simple? This plan of yours—" I stopped myself and turned away. It was easy to be angry when things felt so strained between us.

Now was not the time for anger or frustration about anything either Leo or I had done, however. Now was the time for a plan—a new plan, better than the hare-brained one Leo had come up with.

Reaching my fingers up to the edge of my hood, I drew back the warm, fur-lined fabric and let it drop back against my neck. Then I turned back to the guard, pulled my shoulders up to my ears and made my eyes as large as they could get—almost to the point of tears. It was a trick I had learned on the streets, making myself look as innocent and pitiful as possible, and then pleading with a soft voice and trembling lip.

The guard did not look at me as I approached. He held his eyes straight ahead, firmly ignoring both Leo and myself. "Sir?" I asked gently. He looked at me then, and his expression changed. It was not, however, what I had expected. Before I could move or speak another word, he fell to his knees before me.

"My sister was right, when she said you looked just like your mother."

"Your sister—?"

"She is a maid at the castle, your Highness. If I may—" and slowly his face rose to meet my own, "may I ask you, was what she has told me the truth? Are you are our lost princess?"

I opened my mouth, and then closed it. I smiled slightly, letting the curve of my lips offset the elevating of my chin and the firmness of my gaze. If I was going to make this claim, I might as well look the part. I pulled myself straighter and tried to stand more gracefully. "I am," I told him softly. There was nothing else I could say.

The man's demeanor changed so quickly I could not follow the expressions that crossed his face. He opened his mouth, stuttered, and shut it again. He blushed, he wiggled in his shoes. "I had heard, but I did not believe. I—" and suddenly his face dropped from mine and turned toward the ground. "Your Highness. My deepest and most humble apologies. If I had known... I...I wouldn't have acted in such a deplorable manner."

The man was sweating, I realized, the sickly pallor of fear etched deep in his face. Something in the core of my stomach grew sick. The airs I had put on to act "like a princess" wavered. I struggled to maintain my mask. I tipped my chin up higher and moved to look down on him. In doing so, I caught a glimpse of his face. It was the face of a broken man, and suddenly that sick feeling became overwhelming. Moved to pity, my guise shattered. I fell to my knees beside him, the velvet of my dress growing soggy in the snow as I reached to touch his arm.

"Please stand," I pleaded softly. "There is no need for you to bow to me." Holding his elbows, I guided him to his feet. The man straightened slowly, though he did not remove his eyes from the ground. "What is your name?" I had to look up at him, now that he was standing. He was a big man, muscular and stocky, and I felt like a child's doll standing next to him.

"Gareth Hartfield," he replied in a low tone. His face raised hesitantly to mine, and for a moment I was able to hold his eyes with my own.

"There is no reason for you to be afraid, Sir Hartfield. It was not your fault you did not know." His expression didn't change so I placed my hand on his shoulder. "You did well," I told him gently. "I could ask for no better. You do your job well, Sir Hartfield."

What could have passed as a smile flickered across his face. "Thank you, your Highness. Your words gladden my heart."

I smiled at him and settled my hood more neatly against my back. "Can you keep this to yourself, Sir? The High Lord Alastair thinks it wouldn't be a good idea for me to reveal myself yet. It would be too dangerous."

"I will keep your secret, your Highness," he said loyally. "I swear it on the Throne of Saldor, and on my life. If I could but provide a member of the Guard to keep you safe—"

"That will not be necessary," I answered quickly. An amused laugh tugged at my lips. "I trust this city is secure, and I have a young Guardian at my side. Besides," I added with a wry smile, "I have been learning to take care of myself. Should trouble make itself known, I will be well prepared." Lifting my hands, I pulled the hood of my cloak up to hide my face. "Fear not, Good-sir," I told him carefully. "No one here will even know me."

The man nodded, and stepped aside to let us pass. I hesitated a second before passing him. "Your sister," I asked suddenly. "What is her name?"

"Amelia."

I nodded, and continued through the gate into the city. The men behind him bowed in unison, their knees touching the ground with a hand at the breast and the other swept behind. Head down, I hurried past them. I was well into the city before I stopped.

It took Leo a moment to catch up—he had become tangled in the crowds—and when he did, he stopped in front of me. It was a while before he spoke. Instead he only looked at me, an odd expression on his face. When at last he did speak, it was in a low voice. For the first time today, his eyes fully met mine. "You will make a good queen," was all he said.

The shops that lined the streets amazed me, drawing my attention like a gnat to a flame. The streets were clean and the buildings scrubbed to immaculacy. The walls of the shops were painted in bright hues—reds, royal blues, and all tones of golds, greens, and browns. The windows were glossy, not a single pane was broken. The things behind those windows were artfully displayed and nearly as fine as anything within the castle itself.

People crowded the streets, filing in slow straight lines like drones. There was no poverty here. Merchants and the upper middle class donned cloaks, tunics, and dresses only slightly lesser in quality than my own. Even the mass majority, whom I assumed to be lower middle class, wore clothes that were nothing close to rags. Every face looked well-fed, if tired. I wonder how these people can remain so well fed when there is so little food? I wonder how they can bear it when people are starving only streets away?

* * *

Nearly an hour later Leo and I walked out of the last shop of the row, a pair of new fur lined gloves on my fingers and a small bird carved out of gold in my hands. I had cooed over the bird for a full fifteen minutes—too cheap to buy it—before Leo had plucked it from my hands and bought it himself. The tension had died between us, and though neither him nor I spoke, it felt almost as if everything were back to normal. But the air had a feeling of ending in it; no matter how hard I tried to pretend the day was just as it always had been, I knew that Leo's smiles were his goodbyes, that we were silent not because of anger or of hurt, but because neither of us had the right words to fill the void. Speaking would ruin the illusion of normalcy. I pulled my fur lined hood close against my cheeks, as if by better shrouding myself against the cold, I could hide from the feelings and thoughts that threatened my consciousness. The last few coins my uncle had given me clinked in my pocket as I walked.

As we turned a corner, I suddenly realized where we were. Caeyra was laid out in roughly the same order as Golg, and I could tell by the subtle changes in the streets that we were nearing a different section of town. I had not seen poverty since Arcturus had taken me from it just a short time ago. It felt like an eternity, though I knew it had only been several months. My stomach did a strangled flip and I slowed to a stop. "Leo." It was time to break that quiet barrier. He needed to know, and I needed a chance to face the past.

"What is it?"

"As long as you know the main parts, I guess you might as well know the rest of the story. I've never set foot in Arusae."

"I know." When my eyebrows shot up in surprise, he merely shrugged and let loose a small laugh. "The accent's not quite right."

"You knew all along? Why didn't you say anything?" I hadn't expected this. I had assumed his father had told him the bare basics, that I was the princess, but not where I had come from or that not a single part of my story had ever been true. I certainly didn't expect that he had suspected my lies all along.

"I always knew there was something you weren't telling me, Calli. I just assumed you would tell me when the time was right."

I didn't have an answer for that. To distract myself from the guilt that had welled in my chest, I pressed onward with the story. "I grew up in Golg," I told him. "On the streets. I was a street rat—an urchin. That is where Arcturus found me, lying on the sidewalk begging for bread."

"And you want to go see that life again?" No judgement, no questions, only quiet understanding. I nodded, and suddenly I found myself wishing I had told him long ago. But it was too late for that now. Wishing would get me nowhere.

"Yes." To see a place so like my home, to see the condition in which I had been, to see what I had been...I could hardly bear the thought. For a moment, I wasn't ready for the reminder. "Yes, I do. I need to." I needed to see it, because I couldn't let myself forget.

His hand was on my elbow. "Let's go then."

I found where I was going without his help. It didn't matter that I had never been to Caeyra. I could read the streets like a book. I knew their stories. I knew how to follow their paths.

When we passed a large brick building, Leo pointed it out to me saying, "That's the Soldier's Academy. All boys of a certain age born of commoners are sent there. It's the same sort of training I go through, except without the magic. When they finish their training they are sent around the kingdom, to serve in the main body of the army. They are the real protectors of the kingdom. There are probably a hundred of them to every ten of the Guardians." We paused in front of the iron gates to examine the building for several moments.

"Have you ever spoken with them?" I asked him curiously.

"We train with them from time to time. Master McDunnon has brought us here once or twice. I wasn't lying when I said I'd been to the city before. That part was true." He gave me a wry grin.

We moved past the building and it was as if we had walked through a portal, and into another land. The streets were dirty here; weeds grew in the cracks. Most of the shops were closed, with bashed in windows, and graffiti which decorated the chipped and fading walls. I shivered. This was home.

There were no people in the street until we rounded a corner. A woman stood in the middle of the cobblestone street, dressed in rags and rattling a can. Disgust and fear roiled through me and I turned, frozen in place. My whole body trembled, and for a moment Leo's hand rested on my shoulder, steadying me. It was all I could do to stand.

This place, that woman, they filled me with emotions I could hardly handle. Disgust, not of the place or of the woman, but of what had created them. Fear, not of the dirt or the poverty, but of what I myself had been. Fear of memories, and of their pain. It was several moments before I could go on.

There were more people the further we went. Soon the streets were full again, but with a different kind of crowd. These people were dressed in rags. Their faces were dirty and gaunt, filled with a kind of hopelessness that tore at my heart. *I used to look like this*, I thought.

My nose led me to a bakery down the street, like being in this place triggered old habits I no longer remembered I had. I hesitated at the door. The place was run down, the inside smelled like mold and wet dogs. Then Leo's hand was on my shoulder again, his voice was quiet in my ear. "It's okay," he whispered. "Go on." He knew I needed this as much as I.

Slowly, I crossed the threshold. The baker seemed surprised to see me. At first I was unsure why until I remembered I no longer belonged in a place like this. My clothes were too fine. My health, too good. Even my manner, I felt sure, was out of place. I walked up to the counter anyway, pointing to a thick loaf of bread. "I'd like to buy that, please." He took it out, wrapping the loaf with care and glancing smugly at my gloved hands when I reached for the package.

"That would be...three crowns," he told me. The price was undoubtedly higher than it should have been, but I didn't argue and pushed the coins to him across the table. His face slowly turned upwards into a grin. After a second of thought, I placed the rest of what my uncle had given me on the table by way of a tip. The man's eyes widened, and his smile increased. He would be able to buy food for his family for a week with that much. I gave him a half smile and turned without a word. Leo followed me out.

I nibbled at the end of the loaf as we continued down the street. Neither of us said a word, but it was a very different sort of silence this time. After traveling for several minutes, I decided it was time to get away and calm myself. I wasn't ready to leave, but I couldn't stay. We turned into an empty street, where I leaned against a wall and took several shallow breaths. This isn't right. People shouldn't have to live like this. Not when others live so well. It was all I could do to keep from crying.

When I straightened at last, my gaze fell on something that made me quiver more than anything else ever had. A girl—about my age or a perhaps few years younger—crouching on the sidewalk with a moldy blanket over her shoulders. She was shivering and bone thin. Snow and ice crusted her sleeves. For a moment her eyes met mine. They were frightened and dark. "One minute," I said, turning to Leo behind me. "There is something I have to do."

I approached her cautiously, kneeling in the snow before her when I got close. Her dark eyes were wide, and I could see them dart to the loaf beneath my arm. She leaned away from me but did not run.

"Hi," I said softly. "My name is Calli. What's yours?" Comfort grew in her eyes, and she settled more easily before me. Curiosity burned in her face.

"Shadow," she whispered with soft intensity. It was a nickname, I was certain. Derived probably from her dark eyes, and inky black hair. Doubtless, the girl didn't know her real name. Perhaps she didn't even have one.

Taking the loaf from under my arm, I held it forward and placed it into her eager hands. "Don't eat it all at once," I cautioned. "You'll make yourself sick."

"I won't," she told me wisely. Her eyes found mine. The curiosity was stronger. "Who are you?" she asked after a moment.

I smiled. The simplest and best answer, perhaps, was the truth. "I'm a princess," I told her softly. Wonder and awe pierced her face like sunshine.

"Really?"

Reaching into my pocket, I pulled out the crown and settled it on my head. "Really. But I used to be just like you."

"Like me?"

"I grew up in a city just like this one, on a street the same as this."

"What happened?"

I smiled, pondering for a moment how to answer. "I dreamed and I hoped," I told her. "And then one day my dreams came true. And luck of course. A good portion of luck."

Hope appeared on her face, and though I felt guilty, I treasured it. Though the hope could prove unfounded, I knew it would pull her through more than a few dark days. Her eyes sneaked a glance at my gloves. It was an admiring glance, not an expectant one, but without hesitation I drew them from my fingers and placed them in her hands. "These should keep you warm for a while," I whispered. Then, standing and brushing the dirty snow from my cloak and dress, I walked back to Leo, who waited patiently a few steps away. His eyes were watching me.

When I turned back to the girl, she was gone, vanished around the next corner. "I'm ready to go now," I told him. I removed the silver circlet from my head and placed it back in my pocket. We turned together and walked back down the street. Behind us, poverty shrank forgotten. *I will never forget,* I told myself silently. *And if it takes a million years, I will end this. I will help them. I must.*

* * *

It was almost dark when we made it back into the wealthy section of town. The shadows had grown long on the clean, white snow and the perfect streets. There were fewer people out now than there had been. Only a handful of carriages drifted through the streets, their wheels rattling and screeching against the ice and snow. Several small parades drifted through the streets, the final celebrations of Winterfest for the day. In a square by the gates, a small cluster of vendors sat shivering in the snow, hawking their wares to the last few stragglers coming in from the festivities. The square was strewn with streamers and the ends of meat kabobs, evidence of earlier activity. I was surprised I hadn't noticed all the celebration going on in town earlier, though I supposed I had been too overwhelmed to notice much other than the brightly colored shops and the people's fine clothing. I laughed at myself and wandered over to a vendor, intending to examine their wares.

A sudden prickling feeling at my back, and I turned toward the emptying streets. No one was there. I turned back to the wares, and the feeling reappeared. Leo was several tables back, looking over a set of knives. I shifted uncomfortably, willing the feeling to go away. I was being watched. I felt sure of it.

I scanned the area again, more slowly this time. Nonchalantly, I drug my eyes over the streets, letting my gaze sink into every nook and cranny. Still, I saw no one. I turned to the vendors and began to examine those near me. At first I saw nothing, and then my eyes jarred as if drug over a bump in a rough road. A person stood in the shadows between two vendors, hardly feet away. A black cloak hung from its shoulders. A black hood hid its face. *The person I saw in the courtyard.* With a sudden chill, I remembered the black cloaked figures in Golg.

I shook my head. It couldn't be the same. This one was shorter, only a bit taller than myself.

The person began to move away and with a shout, I ran. The person ran too. I don't know what spurred me to chase it—perhaps overconfidence in Arcturus's teaching or the inability to handle any more questions and unsolved riddles—but I dodged through the vendors after it, despite the poor logic of such a decision. "Wait!" I called. "Come back!"

We turned a sharp corner. I was gaining on it. I pushed myself faster, anxiety and adrenaline pulsing through my blood. We took another turn, and time slowed down. The person's distance from me increased, and my foot caught on the rough edge of a rock. For a moment, time stood still, and then resumed its usual pace with unfortunate rapidity. I plunged to the ground face first and when I looked up, the man had gone.

"Calli?" Leo appeared beside me, panting, and with worry creased across his forehead. "What was that? What do you think you were doing?"

"You didn't see him?"

"No..." Leo hesitated. "All I saw was you running. What or whom you were running after was already long gone when I had looked up."

"There was someone watching me." I told him slowly, spitting out the words with deliberation. "I saw him earlier today, in the courtyard."

Leo frowned, rubbing his forehead as he sat beside me in the snow. "That's odd..." he muttered softly, almost to himself. "And I don't like it. Do you remember what he looked like? Maybe if you described him I—"

"I never saw his face. He wore a black cloak, with his hood pulled up way over his eyes."

"Then how do you know it was the same person?"

I thought for a second, and then shook my head. "I just know." Leo nodded as if to accept my answer, and then frowned.

"He was wearing a black cloak?"

"Yes, why?"

His face creased with worry. "Haven't you ever noticed there is no black in your closet? Shortly after Baldassarre left the castle, black was banned from being worn. The only people in Caeyra who wear black now, are those who support him. And those going to a funeral," he added with a quick grin. "Though I suppose the two are synonymous."

With a frustrated sigh I pulled myself off my knees and sat heavily back with my legs stretched out before me. "I just wish I could have gotten close enough to see who it was," I muttered.

"Just be glad you didn't. In fact, I pray you never see him again." I tried to stand, but before I could regain my feet, Leo stopped me with an arm.

"Your dress is wet," he said suddenly, pointing to a section of my green dress that peeked through the flaps of my cloak.

"I have been sitting in the snow," I told him pointedly. I tried to push his arm away, but he was surprisingly strong. He shook his head quickly, and gave me a serious look.

"Let me look."

"I'm fine," I told him defensively. He ignored me and repeated the query. No. Not a query. It was closer to a demand.

When I refused he did the act himself, pulling up the edge of my skirts and baring my leg to the knee. A dark stain soaked the stocking of my left leg. With deft fingers, he pulled that down as well.

A deep gash ran the length of an inch down my leg. Its edges were ragged and it bled profusely. In all honesty it was only a scratch. Something requiring attention perhaps, but nothing to worry about. I shrugged it off, but Leo's eyes remained concerned.

"It's just a scratch, nothing more. I'll be fine." I told him stubbornly.

"We need to get you up to the Aviary, to see Lady Dubois," he said quickly, sounding like he thought it was an urgent, life or death matter.

"Leo, I'll be fine, really," I repeated. His concern did not fade, and his eyes locked on my own. "I just scraped it when I fell...probably on a rock or something. That's all."

He nodded and tore a long strip of fabric from the bottom of my petticoat. "You didn't need this, right?" he joked. "Seriously though, stay still. I need to wrap your leg to slow the bleeding."

I held my leg out to him, and stayed put.

Once he had finished, Leo swept his arm beneath my knees, lifting me as he would a baby or a bride. I snarled at him and pounded his shoulder with my fists, but he only grinned. "Keep that up," he laughed, "and I'll be forced to make Sir Hartfield take you." I wrinkled my face in disgust. Trust Leo to find humor in every situation. Glancing sideways at the look on my face, his grin broadened, and he laughed even harder.

* * *

By the time we had made it back up the path and through the door in the castle wall, I had paled considerably. Despite the bandage Leo had made, my wound was producing a lot of blood, and the pain had become numbing. Leo's jokes and laughs had subsided.

We hurried through a side door to avoid the crowd and unneeded questions. Once we were inside however, Leo set me on my feet. There was no doubt we would meet people in here, and gossip would be spread if anyone saw him carrying me. I stumbled when my feet touched the ground, but I pushed his hand away when he tried to steady me. I could make the walk myself.

When at last we arrived, I had lost a fair amount of blood. The room was dim around me, spinning in dizzying swirls. Somewhere in the back of my mind I made the observation that this room reminded me of a giant birdcage. Somewhere deeper in my mind, I felt sure I had made this observation once before. I smiled weakly at Lady Dubois as she scuttled over to us.

Lady Dubois's eyes grew wide as she reached me. "What happened?" she asked when she had reached us.

"She fell and cut her knee," Leo said simply, pushing me over to the bed.

"How long ago?"

"Probably a bit more than half an hour ago, Milady," He took the chair nearest the bed.

"And did you bandage the wound?"

"I did."

She nodded, and sat in a second chair to examine my wound more closely. I clenched my teeth as she undid the bandages, which stuck to the wound like adhesive. A sharp pain ripped its way through my leg. "Go get me some rags and warm water," she told Leo sharply. I had to bite back a laugh. Leo jumped, stood, and ran from the room quicker than I had ever seen him move before. In a moment he was back, a sloshing bowl in one hand and a handful of clean rags in the other.

Lady Dubois took the things from him without a word, and bent to clean my wound. Grinding my teeth and clenching the edges of the bed, I turned my face skyward and tried to ignore what she was doing. It was no use. The towel she wiped along my leg was like a knife, and the water she poured into it like fire.

"Why do you have to clean it first?" Leo asked her curiously. "Why not just heal it?"

"If I just heal it, there will still be dirt trapped inside," Lady Dubois answered quickly. She did not look up, and the ripping of my skin never faltered.

"Can't you just make the dirt disappear?"

"Foolish boy," Lady Dubois snapped. The ripping stopped now, and she turned to stare Leo down, bloody rag waving like a red banner in her hand. "You can't just make something disappear! Haven't you been paying attention to your lessons? I ought to have a talk with Master McDunnon, see what he thinks about you asking such foolhardy questions. Nothing can be done to break the laws of nature, boy. You can no more make something vanish than you can create it from thin air Move something from one place to another, yes. But vanish them?" She scowled, and the ripping resumed.

"Then why don't you just move it all with magic?"

"More trouble than it's worth, boy. It takes much less energy to clean it the common way." Her tone had a finality to it that said she would tolerate no more questions.

After what seemed like ages, the burning stopped and Lady Dubois dropped a pile of bloody rags to the ground beside her. Then, grabbing a jar from the table, she opened it and poured the contents on the wound. It burned, and I sucked in my breath. "What is that?" I gasped.

"A potion for sterilization," she explained. I could see in her face her irritation at all the questions, and I fell silent. She closed her eyes, and placed a hand over my leg. When she removed it, the wound was gone. I let my head fall against the pillow. Exhaustion was seeping into my veins. "Good as new," she told me.

"Can I leave now?"

She laughed. "Leave? Heaven's child, of course not. Healing a wound that large caused you to lose a good deal of energy. You'll have to rest a bit while your body replenishes it." She stood, and glanced out the window. It was dark outside. Only the winter moon shone coldly through the trees, casting shadows against the windows. "It's late, and high time you go to bed," she said, turning to Leo. Then, holding her arms wide like a mother hen, she herded him to the door. For a moment he looked about to say something, but she stopped him. "You can come back and visit her tomorrow," she told him. "For now, she needs to rest." The door swung shut behind him, and he was gone. *Tomorrow.* Suddenly it occurred to me that today had been my goodbye.

Lady Dubois interrupted my thoughts. "I suggest you go to sleep now, child. Do you need a potion to help?"

"I'll be fine my Lady," I told her politely. "Thank you." She left the room then. The torches snuffed out as she went, leaving the room pitch black. Pitch black, and deadly quiet.

Exhausted, I leaned back on the pillow and shut my eyes. I forced my mind to clear. Darkness surrounded me.

...and the day was as warm and crystal clear as it had been the first time I had come to this place. There was a flash of white, and the whistle of feathers that broke through the air. Some sort of bird, exploding into flight in front of my face. I smiled—

Caladrius Dreams

With a gasp I drug myself from sleep. I could feel the hot sun beating on my back. I could even almost smell the verdant flowers blooming against the grass. I shivered. These dreams were driving me crazy. With everything else I had to worry about, I didn't have the time for them too. I needed to put an end to them. Soon.

15

Remedy

It was early afternoon when I woke, shaking myself from an unhappy sleep. Panting, I sat up straight in bed and stared moodily at the walls. Despite my best efforts, the dreams had chased me into the darkness of sleep, and had not relinquished their grasp until I woke. Mostly they had been garble, though that was all my dreams usually ever were. Words floating through the dark. A white bird, flying through the trees. Two people arguing. The pounding of running feet. Even so, each little dream, each glimpse—for a glimpse was what it felt like—was filled with that same awful solidity. That feeling of reality that quaked me to my bones. I shivered involuntarily and watched as Lady Dubois bustled into the room.

"My Lady!" I cried as she reached me. I was ready to leave this room. I was ready to leave and never come back. "Can I go now?"

Her eyes closed for half a second, and then she shook her head, the curls of her hair bouncing with the shake. "You'll have to stay here for today. Do you think that much energy will replenish itself over night?"

I wasn't certain what she meant by my 'energy replenishing,' but I was sure that I didn't want to be cooped up here while there was a festival going on outside. "But my Lady—"

"I'm sorry child, but no means no," she told me firmly. Then she turned and left the room before I could make a reply.

Caladrius Dreams

Being stuck up here, alone in this room was the last thing I wanted. The sound of someone snoring drifted to me from a nearby cot. I groaned and threw myself sideways in my bed, pulling the stark white blankets up to my ears. With an arm I propped myself up so I could see out the nearest window. Music, just barely audible, played from the festival below. Snow fell outside, drifting past the window like small white feathers in the air. Some flakes fell through the open panes, piling in a crusty white ridge along the window sill. I watched the snow fall a moment longer, and then leaned back into my pillow with a sigh. I was tired. I could feel it now. Cautiously, I closed my eyes and let sleep take me. Before drifting off I squeezed my hands together, praying for the absence of the dreams.

At first, there was only darkness. Darkness that swirled around me like the opening of a black pit. No dreams lay in wait for me here. I could feel my consciousness relax...

It was a hazy morning. A few bright stars still burst like pinpoints in the sky. I clutched the edge of the gate, glancing down at my hands with a grimace. They hadn't always looked like this. I used to be young.

"My Lady!" A man approached, his silhouette dark with the morning sun at his back. It was the High Lord. I gave him a small curtsy and smiled in reply to his greeting. I watched him as he neared me. His black hair, streaked with silver at the temple. His bright eyes, calming and soft. The smoothness in his gait. I could not deny it. The High Lord was a handsome man.

"Why, might I ask, are you here today, my Lord?"

"To ask a favor of you, of course." For the first time, I noticed the bird on his shoulder. A white bird. It regarded me with a clever eye and then turned away in disinterest, preening its feathers with care. "Are you still doing healing here, in this small town?"

I nodded slowly, turning back to glance at my house. This town was all I had. Ever since my husband had died...I jerked from my thoughts and turned my attention back to the man in front of me. "I am still healing here, my Lord. I love this town very much."

"I am glad of it, my Lady," he said with a smile.

"What is your favor?"

"I was wondering, Lady, if you would ever consider being a healer at the castle?" He said it as if the statement were simple enough, but I stared at him with wide eyes.

"The castle!" I exclaimed. "I haven't been there since Thomas died! I—"

"We need you Mary. We really do." My eyes widened and I shook my head. When he continued that expectant gaze I broke eye contact and turned to run from him, swinging—

A hand shook me awake, pulling me from the dream. It felt somehow as if I were being pulled out of reality. I opened my eyes, blinking in the sunlight that poured into the room. The creak of a swinging gate followed me into wakefulness. It rang dully in my ears.

"I figured you would be hungry."

It was Ema. I had to focus on not letting out a sigh of disappointment. I had been hoping she was someone else. I choked back my sorrow, however, and gave her a welcoming smile. "I'm glad you came."

"Thurman told me you slipped in the snow and hurt yourself. He said he did not think Lady Dubois would let you out today. You are missing so much! There's—"

"I know, a bonfire, and stories..."

"And there are going to be fireworks tonight!" she squealed, clapping her hands and laughing. "Can you believe it? I have not seen fireworks since I was very little!"

I had never seen fireworks, but I wasn't going to tell her that. "I suppose I'll be able to see them through the window," I answered. I took a loaf of bread from the plate she held, slathered it with butter, and proceeded to tear into it with my teeth. I was hungry. Almost as hungry as I had ever been. But only almost.

As I ate, Ema told me about the day's events. Of course, the things she told me were the events of purpose in her eyes. Most of it consisted of boys and gossip. I soon found my mind wandering until my attention lapsed entirely and my sole focus was the food on my tray.

The tray was filled with more food and more variety than I could have ever hoped to eat at once. Roast duck—which I promptly pushed to the side—venison, beef, and fish. Several thick slices of crusty bread, their innards warm and steaming. A stick of butter. A bowl of marmalade. Cinnamon apples, pears, strawberries, and melon. A dozen mushrooms sautéed in oil, spinach leaves, tomato and something that resembled a squash. A thick cut of blue veined cheese. Mulled cider and a glass of water. Smells wafted from the food and my mouth watered with delicious anticipation. I ate all of it.

Ema was done with her stories by the time I had finished eating. "And that's about it," she told me resolutely. I didn't let on to the fact that I had heard not a word of her speech. I only nodded and grunted in pretended interest, wiping my face with the back of my hand and licking my fingers like a cat.

It wasn't long before Lady Dubois hurried over and hustled Ema from the room. "She still needs her rest. She's talked long enough," Lady Dubois told the girl. Secretly, I was glad. Listening to Ema's gossip was exhausting. When Lady Dubois pulled the curtains around my bed, I collapsed with a sigh of relief. Sleep overtook me before I could fight it and for the third time in one day, I dreamed.

I was running. Running as fast as I could. "Get back here, Kitty!" a voice snarled behind me. I skid to the left and took off down the hall. Behind me, the smashing of glass tinkled through the room. I ran faster still.

It was gloomy in the house. I could hear him screaming. Down the stairs and through the kitchen. I slid across the immaculate tile floor, and fled through the door. I didn't slow to shut it. Instead, I embraced the wind that cooled my face, and made for the trees. Quincy was close on my heels.

Somehow I managed to lose him in the wood. A cluster of trees blocked our chase. I darted one way, and he the other. He was gone now. I hid myself in a bush and crouched, sick with fear. Silently, my stomach upheaved itself and I lost my breakfast in the grass. Bile was like acid on my tongue. I wiped my mouth with the back of a trembling hand and peered out from my hiding place. Quincy appeared just ahead and to the left.

"I know you're out here, Kitty," he said with a sneer. There was something cruel about the way his features mixed. Something disgusting about the smile on his face. He walked in front of me, his footsteps thudding dully on the cold ground. He disappeared around a corner, and out of sight.

A moment of silence, and I relaxed with a heavy sigh and leaned back against a tree trunk. I closed my eyes for a brief moment. A hand rested on my shoulder. Jerking straight I turned and—

With a scream I sat straight up, my eyes already twitching to examine my surroundings. It took a moment before I realized was awake.

Silence filled the empty room. I couldn't see beyond the white curtains pulled around my bed, so I curled to my side and stared at the ceiling. The hum of songs carried through the walls. Outside, musicians played *Pretty Ladies* and *To be a Gentleman*. The clap of hands provided a gentle beat, a sound which thrummed like a heart and eased my trembling. I relaxed into the bed and pulled the covers tight around my shoulders. But, despite the exhaustion that seeped through my mind, I did not sleep.

* * *

"Calli?" It was almost dark outside now. Through a gap in my curtain I could see a handful of stars, winking in the lavender sky. "Calli?" It was Leo. His voice was soft and cautious, but I recognized it all the same. My breath caught in my throat.

"Yes?" The word sounded strangled and I had to swallow hard after it.

"Can I come in?"

"Yes."

A head peeked around the curtain's edge. His wide eyes were careful. "Lady Dubois said you might be sleeping." I almost laughed at that. I hadn't slept since morning.

I shook my head. "Nope. No sleep. I've been having night-mares." He came all the way in then, pulling the curtain back just enough so I could see the sky in its entirety. He didn't sit in a chair, but rather, on the edge of the bed.

"I'm sorry," he whispered mutely. "Is there anything I can do?" I shook my head. "I bought you some candy," he said, as if trying to distract me with happier topics. Digging his hands into his pockets, he emptied several fistfuls of paper wrapped chocolate on the bed before me. "They had vendors today, down in the courtyard. The stuff is even better then what they had in town."

He paused awkwardly, fiddling with the wrapper on one of the candies and looking uncertain. "Why did you come up here?" I asked suddenly.

His brow furrowed. Then at length, he ran a hand through his hair and sighed. "I couldn't do it," he whispered to me. "I couldn't say goodbye."

"What do you mean?" My heart was fluttering a hopeful little beat that I tried to subdue. I couldn't hope, not just yet.

"I meant for yesterday to be the last time I saw you, Calli."

"Because you were angry?"

He shook his head. "I don't even know what I was. Angry. Hurt. Disappointed. It hurt me that you couldn't trust me. It hurt that you lied, and it hurt because I suddenly felt that I didn't know you at all."

"But that changed?" I couldn't keep the hope out of my voice now.

"When I saw you in the city—when I saw the way you treated that guard and the way you treated that little girl, I was proud to know you. I wasn't exaggerating when I said you will make a good queen. Perhaps you lied about your title, but I realized you weren't lying about who you were. Who you are. You are different from the rest of them, Calli, and I am proud to be able to call myself your friend."

I could see there was more to it in his eyes. He was holding back. "But that's not all?" I pressured gently. He sighed again and shook his head.

"The hurt wasn't really enough to make me go away, or even to make me consider it. Once I got past my pride and realized people aren't perfect and that you are allowed to mess up too, I realized that it was only a matter of forgiving you. It wasn't hard. I had already begun to forgive you a bit when I saw you speaking with Sir Hartfield. Which only hurt worse, because my mind had already been made up.

"My father wants to use me. At first, he was only angry. He spoke to me for about an hour about how I was letting the family down, being friends with you, about how he was ashamed of me and about how I was failing him. He didn't yell—he never does—but he is the kind of man that just doesn't need to.

"After he was done telling me how I was no good, he started telling me about his plans. He told me who you were then. He is the only one of Baldassarre's men who knows about you and he won't tell anyone else. He means to bring you to Baldassarre himself—'alive and screaming' were his exact words—so that he can have all the credit. Baldassarre is generous to those who help him, that is part of why so many chose to follow him, and I think my father believes he will receive a more than generous reward. Which is likely. He wants to use me and my friendship with you to get what he wants. He gave me two options. Double-cross you, or never speak to you again."

My breath was tight in my chest. "And which did you choose?"

He laughed a little, looking up from his hands towards the dark blue sky that mirrored the color of his eyes. "I chose option number three," he whispered. "Double-cross *him.*"

"What if he suspects you?"

"He won't. He doesn't think I'd have the courage. Honestly, until just a few moments ago when I came up here, I didn't think I had the courage either. But I want you as my friend, Calli. If you'll have me."

There was a sickening pause when something inside me hesitated. *Hadn't you wanted him to go away?* A nasty little voice whispered in my ear. *Hadn't you wanted to leave him, so you could play the game?* I hadn't wanted him to go away. I wanted to survive. I wanted to play the game of the Court, a game based on allies and who knew who. I hadn't wanted him to go. I hadn't.

Another little voice spoke in my head, nastier than the first. *He knows now. Having him anywhere but on your side could be dangerous. He is willing to double-cross his father for you, double-cross the man more dangerous than any except perhaps Baldassarre himself. You could use him.* "Of course I'll have you, Leo. You're my best friend. Why would I ever want it any other way?" He was my friend. That was all. The only reason.

It was completely dark now, and I pointed this out to him, waving my hand in the direction of the windows. "Shouldn't you be going?" I asked. "The fireworks will be starting soon; you don't want to miss them."

To my surprise, instead of leaving, he swung his legs up on the bed and leaned back on the pillows beside me. "I wouldn't miss them for the world," he whispered. He pointed towards the window, and I followed his gesture on impulse. Bright in the darkening sky a firework exploded, perfectly framed by the window's edges.

A thrill rose within me, and I couldn't stop the smile that leapt to my lips. Leo leaned in to me and whispered, "I told them they should aim for the west windows." Then, with a satisfied smile on his face, he settled back against the pillows once more, his eyes trained on the fountains of fire in front of us. I smiled too, and silently we watched the fireworks that danced through the midnight sky.

* * *

It was late when the fireworks ended. The room had long since gone dark. Leo stood to leave when suddenly, unexpectedly, my stomach twisted with fear. "Stay?" I pleaded, and my voice shook. "Just for a little bit. Please?"

He stared at me for a long second, and then realization dawned in his eyes. "The nightmares?" he asked. I nodded. "I didn't realize they were bothering you so much." He settled back down beside me, taking the bedside chair instead of the bed.

"I can't sleep," I told him slowly. Painfully. My lip quivered and his hand pressed against my forehead.

"Just try. Whatever waits for you in those nightmares of yours, I'll be here to fight them off." He gave me a quick smile and shifted in his chair, leaning with his elbows against the edge of the bed. "I'm not going anywhere."

"Thanks," I turned to smile up into his face. "You're the best friend anyone could ever have," I told him solemnly.

"I know," he answered with a short grin that reminded me of his old self. "Now get some sleep."

After one last long look, I closed my eyes. Fear fluttered through my heart, and then faded. Concentrating on low, deep breaths, I felt myself drift to sleep. And for the first time in a long time, I slept deeply. Dreamlessly.

16

Council Meeting

"I'm so glad to be out of that room!" I told Ema as I sat myself in the armchair by the fire. It was somewhere around midday, several hours past breakfast and one or two before lunch. Lady Dubois had released me about half an hour ago, allowing me to leave the Aviary with the promise that I would be careful. I smiled at nothing in particular. Freedom was sweet.

"It's too bad you had to miss everything yesterday," Ema told me sorrowfully. "They're breaking down now, and there is really nothing happening at all today." She sighed, running another brush stroke through her long dark hair before collapsing back on the bed, slippered toes kicking over the edge in exclamation of her frustration. "I am just so *bored,*" she said. "I wish life could always be a festival."

"You mean there's nothing at all happening today?" I asked. "I really do have the worst luck."

"The Council Meeting does begin today, but that doesn't concern anyone other than the High Lord and some of the lords." The pounding of thunder came from outside and Ema glanced toward the rain lashed window with a groan. "And now I cannot even go outside. The ladies and I were going to go out and ice skate—the fountain in the gardens has frozen over and it's the perfect size—but now it's raining and worse. It's so *dreary.*"

"I'm going down to eat," I cut in, interrupting her laments.

"You should stay. Lunch doesn't start for an hour, and it's a perfect day for meals in bed. One of the maidservants should be up any minute with milk and crackers. She might bring honey too, if we ask nicely. You're hardly ever up here, Calli, and it will be so lonely without you."

I shook my head. "I need to talk to Leo," I told her.

She grunted in unveiled disgust, but didn't comment when I stood and left the room.

* * *

The Guardians took their lunch before us, of course, a fact of which I was quite glad. I really wasn't interested in food, but mealtime meant I would know where to find him.

Leo was exactly where I had expected him to be. In the Great Room, waiting for lunch to be set out on the table. "Leo?" His back was facing me, but he turned at the sound of his name.

I have never seen a boy's face light up as fast as Leo's did now. His eyebrows raised, his blue eyes widened, and his quirky grin flashed ear to ear. "I've gotta go," he muttered to Avery and another boy whom I recognized to be Master McDunnon's young nephew, Jasper. The boys both made non-committal grunts, but their brows twitched in amusement.

"You look as if you didn't expect me," I told him as I pulled him away from the table.

He grinned. "I half forgot I'd ever see you again." That was the only allusion either of us made to what had happened since the Ball. I led him out into the hall and stopped, spinning to face him. Excitement burned under my skin. An idea had formed in my mind while talking with Ema, and I couldn't put it away. "What's up?" Leo asked.

"We are going to spy on the Council Meeting."

Leo's face paled. "Are you crazy?" he hissed. "We'd get ourselves killed!"

"They wouldn't kill us," I answered skeptically. I rolled my eyes and crossed my arms, waiting for him to calm down enough to consider the suggestion. He was overreacting.

"They might not kill you, but they would certainly kill me."

"Come on Leo, they aren't going to find out."

"No."

"If you won't come, I'll just have to do it myself." Risky or not, this was something I needed to do. If my uncle wouldn't tell me what was going on—and I knew there was no point in asking—I would find out on my own. I needed to know what my uncle and the lords played at behind closed doors. I told Leo as much. There was no need for secrets between us now.

For a second I paused, watching his face and waiting for him to react. When he didn't respond, I turned and headed to the stairs. The meeting would be in the Throne Room, a long hall surrounded by seats of different heights. It was the place, I had been told, where the king or queen took visitors to the castle, where peasants came to petition, and where commoners and nobility alike were brought to be heard. The Throne Room was also where all formal meetings were held, so it seemed only natural to me that it was were the Council would meet as well.

It wasn't long before Leo had caught up with me, muttering something about how it would be my neck, if we were caught.

"When do they start?" I asked him casually.

"Earlier this morning. But don't worry," he added quickly, "it usually lasts several days, so we probably haven't missed much."

We had almost reached the second floor when, slightly ahead of me, Leo slowed to a halt.

"What—"

"Shh. Whisper," he hissed, throwing up an arm to stop me. "Do you want to get us caught?"

"I *am* whispering."

"Oh? You whisper like a bear."

"You whisper like a bear," I mimicked. "I don't even know what that's supposed to mean."

"It means, if you don't keep your mouth shut, somebody is going to hear you."

"And nobody is going to hear you?" If he wanted to complain about my whispering he needed to take a second and listen to his own. I scowled at him.

Leo made a face, and then turned from me to examine the hall. "They have guards blocking the entrance," he said. "There's no possible way we can get around them, short of confrontation. We are going to have to go up by another route. Let's go before they see us." Before I could complain he had pulled me back down the stairwell.

He didn't slow until we reached the first floor. Then, walking as casually as possible, I followed him to the northern end of the castle. "Where are we going?" I asked once I could be certain no one would overhear.

"There's another stairway that leads out behind my room. Not many people know about it, so I doubt they'd have it blocked."

"A secret staircase?" Leo glanced at me askance when the pitch of my voice rose a notch.

"Not exactly secret. Just old. Master McDunnon says they built around it when add-ons to the castle were made. It's hard to get to, so new staircases were made throughout the rest of the castle. I found it my first week here." There was a proud sort of gleam in his eye that I didn't fail to notice.

We rounded a corner, and Leo slowed. Before us was a cluster of red doors. "That one's mine," he said, pointing to a door on the right. "The stairs are around back."

He hadn't been exaggerating when he said the stairs were hard to get to. When we next stopped, I was certain it was in front of a solid wall. Then he pulled me to the side and through a crack where two walls had failed to be joined properly.

We were behind the rooms now and when I turned, I saw a narrow stairwell turning its way up the wall. In front was a pile of rubble, like someone had been building and then failed to clear up afterward. We had to scramble over the dingy stone to get to the stairs. Once we'd made it to the bottom step, we slowly climbed our way up.

It was cold in the stairwell, cold enough that the edges of the sharp air stung my lungs when I breathed. The steps and walls blended together in a haunting sameness. There was no gold or satin here.

After several minutes of steady climbing, the hum of voices filtered through the silence. Leo stopped. "It seems we were luckier than I dared hope," he whispered, drawing my ear close. "The Throne Room is right on the other side of this wall."

Creeping to his side, I pressed an ear against the wall. It was cold and stunk of mildew. "In there?" I whispered. He nodded.

"If we can just find a crack or a hole..." he trailed off, searching.

I searched behind him and below, reaching the lower areas where he had not thought to look. A few minutes of silence had passed when I let out a strangled cry.

"What?"

"I just found a hole, that's all."

Leo scowled. "I thought you were dying or something down there," he muttered darkly. Getting down on his hands and knees, he crouched beside me.

The crack ran the length of three to five stones and was about the width of my fist. When pressed against it, I had a clear view of the room. Voices swirled eerily, seeping like thick mucus through the crevice. "I just don't think you're handling the situation right. I—" The urgent voices faded as I moved to make room for Leo. We locked eyes for a second and then turned together to press our faces into the scene before us.

The people in the room were seated in a long hall at high desks raised to a height slightly lower than those at the far end. Uncle Alastair sat at one of the higher seats. The other three were empty. The emptiness seemed strange. After a moment of hesitation, I turned to Leo and asked him about it. He raised a brow, and then turned to whisper back.

"The one next to your uncle, is the king's chair, and the one next to that, belongs to the queen." My stomach felt slightly sick.

"And the last?"

"The last belonged to Baldassarre." For a long moment I said nothing, pondering his words. When I opened my mouth to speak again, Leo cut me off.

"Do you remember what I said about your whispering?"

I frowned at him and wrinkled my nose. "I just wanted to know what Baldassarre's role was. My father was the first born, so he's king. My uncle is the High Lord, but what did he do? What did Baldassarre do?"

Leo sighed and pulled me away from the crack. "I can't believe no one's told you any of this yet," he whispered sourly. "The High Lord has traditionally been the second eldest—Alastair in this case. He is the head of the Council. Baldassarre is the youngest of the three. The third born has the right to the throne if the king dies and has no heir to succeed him." A sudden chill ran through my bones.

"So that means..."

"He can't just kill you, if that's what you're getting at. It's a lot more complicated then that. First, there's—"

"Shh," I interrupted. "I think they're saying something important." An uproar had seeped through the walls. It rumbled ominously through the air like the brewing of a storm. Scrambling back to the edge of the crack, I pressed my face against it, trying to make out what was going on.

"—such an act would break the Treaty, my Lord—"

"I am perfectly aware of the consequences of my actions, Lord Anderson. And I assure you my words are not without thought." My uncle looked very stern in his seat. He bridged his fingers and looked through them at the lords seated below him. "We have all taken sides. Let us not pretend any longer that we have not. Anyone who does not declare alliance to the True Heir is an enemy of the state, and I will no longer tolerate their presence in this court. To anyone who decides to take such path, I expect you gone when the roads clear in spring."

A man stood from the chair closest to Leo and myself. I could not see his face, but when he spoke, there was something familiar in his voice. "The king is dead. There is no True Heir. Baldassarre holds the right to the throne. It is law."

"Sit down, Lord Sheridan. Unless you have forgotten, I still run this Council. As for my brother, he lost his right to the throne when he committed treason against the king. Anyone who chooses to follow him will be accused of the same crime."

Turning from the wall, I whispered again in Leo's ear. "Is he—?"

Leo nodded. "That's Master Sheridan's elder brother. Master Sheridan is the only member of his family who claimed support to the king."

Another man was standing now, rage painted clearly on his face. "Do not forget that it was your master who killed the rightful king, Lord Sheridan," the man spat. "Therefore, neither you nor any of the others can claim innocence to the issue that now sets itself before us."

Lord Sheridan growled—an angry sound that seemed to rip from deep within his throat. "The king deserved to die."

At that simple statement, an uproar swept through the room. The room surged like the roar of an angry sea. I could no longer make out words. Black and terrible, the tirade swept along until—

"Enough!" High Lord Alastair stood, his voice thundering through the room. "I will not stand for this foolishness. Not when our nation is on the brink of war."

"We passed that brink when you made your decision, Alastair Williams. Let us not pretend and call this anything but what it is." It was the first time I had heard him speak and his voice sent shivers down my spine. Beside me, Leo stiffened. Lord Thurman walked up swiftly to the High Lord's desk, and spat on the ground before him. "I take my leave."

"Will any of you follow him?" Alastair asked sharply.

"I have already stated where my alliances lie," Lord Sheridan said.

"Then you may leave this room as well," the High Lord answered, his voiced echoing with a deadly coldness.

Lord Sheridan stiffened, and then slowly made his way to my uncle's desk. Copying Lord Thurman's gesture, he spat on the ground and left the room.

Four other men followed. By the end, six families had been tossed without preamble to the other side. I let out a breath I hadn't known I had been holding.

"I do not choose to take sides, my Lord, if such choice will keep my family safe," a man to Alastair's left stated.

"A wise choice, Lord Dubois. I would do the same, were it not my position to choose. You may remain here after the others leave in the spring, but can no longer take any part in this meeting. My best wishes to you and your family.

"Does anyone else wish to follow Lord Dubois? I will not force any family to take sides, only know that now is your last chance. Who else wishes to follow this man? I must know now."

Two other men stood, firmly if a bit hesitant. Lord Mubarak, and Lord Ivanov, Leo identified them in my ear. Both men from the far south, and far north of the kingdom, respectively. The three men bowed respectfully, and quietly left the room. Uncle Alastair addressed those who remained slowly and painfully. "Six families have turned against us. Thurman, Sheridan, Avery, Canter, Heidel, and Black. Three, have refused to take sides. Only four remain."

One of the remaining men spoke up. "My Lord, you know what this means?"

"I do," my uncle replied. "It means we are at war."

Some dust fell from the molding of the room's interior, and drifted out through the crack. Explosively and violently, Leo sneezed. I froze, staring at him. "If they heard you..." I warned.

"They didn't," Leo whispered back. "Look, not one of them has even flinched."

It was true. The room was quiet now, and I had trouble making out their words. The remaining four families had gathered together in a clump. Only disembodied words and phrases managed to make their way to my ears. "Yes, Arcturus, you may," Uncle Alastair said loudly and suddenly. There was a shuffle in the far corner of the room.

My heart stopped when a pair of strong fingers caught me suddenly by the ear. Beside me, Leo was caught in a similar fashion. His eyes were wide and round. Behind us, was Arcturus Sheridan.

"What do you think you are doing?" he snapped. "Do you not realize what might happen if the wrong person had found you out here?"

"Master Sheridan, she only—"

Arcturus cut him off. "You—of all people—should know better, Thurman."

"Yes, sir."

"And you!" he snarled, turning on me. "I thought taking that Oath was a hare-brained idea, but I hoped that perhaps it would keep you from having more. Now it seems you are full of them, my Lady." I didn't bother correct the false title. Now did not seem the best time to let him know that Leo—the son of Baldassarre's most adamant supporter—knew the truth.

"I'm sorry, sir." I bent my head and lowered my eyes to the ground. I felt repentant, but only for a moment. A moment later, the adventure of what we had done thrilled through me once more, and I had to work to hide my smile.

"Go downstairs," he said fiercely. I winced at his tone.

"Yes sir."

"You too, Thurman. I'm sure your father will want to see you tonight. You would act surprised and not tell him about this, if you have any sense in you."

"I will sir." Leo had assumed the same position as I—head bent and eyes grounded—but his shoulders were tense and his hands flexed at his side.

Arcturus held my gaze for a moment and then turned away, cloak swirling as he stalked back up the hall. "Just a pair of children, lost on the way to lunch," he said, his muffled voice drifting quietly through the wall. Then, more quietly he added, "There's a two inch crack in the lower portion of the molding, my Lord. I suggest you have it sealed."

"Thank you Arcturus. I—" their voices faded as Leo pulled me out of earshot.

"Well, I'm glad it was only Arcturus who caught us," I mumbled as we walked further down the hall.

"Arcturus? Since when are you on first name basis with Master Sheridan?"

I rolled my eyes at him, as if it were obvious. "Since he found me, of course. He has been giving me lessons for a while, self-defense in case I might need it. A body guard following some simple girl from Arusae would look suspicious, after all."

"That explains a lot," Leo muttered. When we had traveled a decent distance from the room, he paused and sunk back against a wall. "I told you that was a bad idea." His face was paler than normal.

"You had as much fun as I did, don't try to pretend you didn't."

He shook his head for a minute, and then shrugged at last. "Fine," he muttered. "I won't lie. But that doesn't make it any less stupid. We could've been killed."

"But we weren't, and neither were we caught."

His eyebrows raised. "I wouldn't exactly call that not being caught. Master Sheridan—"

"Arcturus doesn't count," I said patiently. "He likes to talk, and he likes to yell even better, but he won't rat us out. And neither will he kill us. I hope." I leaned next to him against the wall. Suddenly I was very aware of feeling weak. My heart pounded in my chest.

It was several moments before I spoke again. The excitement of the adventure had worn off, and all that was left was cold realization of we had overheard. "We are at war," I whispered. "We are at war, and it is my fault."

"You can't blame yourself, Calli."

"You heard my uncle. Whoever does not support the True Heir, will be declared an enemy of the state. He was talking about me, Leo. He would have never made the decision to break the Treaty if it weren't for me. That's what the Oath was about. He needed to know I backed him before he made such a choice." I was talking more to myself now. Leo took my arm.

"You haven't eaten yet today. There is no point worrying about this yet. There's nothing we can do."

"Leo? You are going to have to leave now, won't you?"

He avoided my eyes. "I don't know," he said, his voice catching.

I followed him back to the Great Room. We ate in silence, but no matter how much hot cider I drank, the cold pit in my stomach would not go away.

17

Nightmare

It was quiet in the house. I was lying on the couch, resting. A baby, just a few hours old, slept in my arms. Amal was in the back room.

Master Sheridan had left hours ago, and he'd said he'd be back soon. I could hardly wait. I felt lonely, and cut off from the world. Master Sheridan could bring us news. A war was raging over us, just outside our hidden circle of ground. It made me nervous not knowing what was going on.

Our friends couldn't even come over anymore. I hadn't seen them for months. Master Sheridan and Derek had said we couldn't know who to trust. I suppose they're right. Soon though. Soon this war would be over. I glanced at the child in my arms. With the war over, she could grow up. She could grow up happy and fearless. She would be safe. They would be safe.

"I love you." A pair of arms snaked around my neck. I looked up at him.

"I love you too," I whispered.

"How are you, my darling rose?"

"Worried." I couldn't be anything but truthful.

"Everything will be alright, Lell. You'll see." He took a seat on the couch beside me.

"But what about our friends? They're still out there, fighting against your fool of a brother."

He winced, but his hand reached up to stroke my cheek. "They can take care of themselves."

"What if they can't? Katie and Greg...they're planning on getting married in a few weeks. What if they don't make it? What if—?"

"Shh...Gregory will be fine. And Kate? She's not exactly helpless."

"What about Jeremy? Even Arcturus! If anything happened to any of them...I don't know what I'd do." My eyes welled up with tears. I hated thinking about it. But it was just so hard not to. "And Lady Rachel... She's such an innocent little thing. She doesn't belong out there. She—"

"The others will take care of her. Don't worry."

"I just feel so selfish! Locked up in here, all safe, while everyone else is out there fighting. Dying. All for us."

"Let's not think about it, darling. Please? We are lucky to be alive ourselves, and we will do more good to our friends and the rest of the people alive then dead. Please don't think about it now. I want to be happy tonight."

A weak smile was my only answer. When his lips closed on top of mine, all my worries floated away. I kissed him back, careful not to smash the baby huddled against my chest.

A few minutes later, Derek pulled away abruptly.

"What is it?"

"Someone's knocking. It must be Arcturus." He gave me one last kiss and made his way to the door.

"Derek?" He paused halfway. Something inside of me didn't feel quite right. Something inside of me didn't want him to open the door. But that was silly. "Never mind."

I watched as he opened the door, wondering what had taken Master Sheridan so long. It startled me when Derek's breath caught.

"Leslie run! They've found us!"

The chill that overtook my body happened so fast, it left me breathless. Adrenaline sent my nerves quivering, and the hairs on the back of my neck stood on end. It took me a moment to calculate his words—I didn't truly understand them until Derek fell to the ground, and a man cloaked in black came bursting in. It wasn't Baldassarre himself. Of that much I was certain. Baldassarre had never been good with magic. Had it been him, we would have had a chance.

Shock was all I could feel. My mind seemed to be drifting somewhere above me, a spectator, while my body moved without it. Somehow I managed to get off the couch. I stumbled across the room blindly, towards the back room. I placed the baby on the floor inside and shut the door.

With the door shut and the baby safe, my world came flooding back into focus. I would not run. How could I? I couldn't leave him. I couldn't let him stay here. *Stay here to die. I wouldn't let it happen. Derek. He was my life. My love. My heart and soul. My everything.*

He was more important than me anyway. He was the king—I was only queen by marriage. The people needed him. They needed the life that lay in the room behind me. They didn't need me. I forced myself forward, and stepped between the man in black and my husband.

"Bravery won't get you far in life, my darling Queen," the man sneered.

"Leave my family alone."

"Move, girl. My master doesn't care if you live, it's your husband he wants."

"I won't." *My panicked voice sounded braver than I felt.*

I didn't notice the pain when he hit me. All I knew was that suddenly, I was on the floor looking up at him. "Don't give me lip," the man snarled. "If you weren't the queen, you'd be nothing but a nasty commoner. Something you'll be again in a few minutes. Let's practice, shall we?" *Foot on my chest, he pressed me into the floor. I could barely breathe; it felt like my ribcage was breaking.*

"Leave her alone." *Derek had regained his senses. He pushed himself to his feet and stood over me like a wall, forcing the man to back away from me. An unspoken battle raged between them; I could tell by the sweat that lined Derek's forehead. Derek had always been strong in magic, but this man, this assassin, was stronger.*

Before I could even move, the man's hand had caught Derek's shoulder. All it took was a thought. A single thought to stop his heart forever. I heard the sound of his body drop lifeless to the floor long before I registered the sight before me.

"DEREK!" *I was screaming. Hot tears ran down my cheeks.*

He was gone...gone forever. And there was nothing I could do about it.

"DEREK!" *I was sobbing hysterically now.*

The noise of a frightened baby sounded behind me and my courage strengthened. In that room, lay all that was left of me. All that could ever hold my heart. I wouldn't let him hurt them. I'd die first.

"Be quiet, woman," the man snapped.

I screamed like my life depended on it. Sobs choked me. I couldn't breathe. "You killed him," I sobbed.

I backed up, on my knees. The man stood before me, his dark hood filled with all the malice in the world. "Move girl," he snarled. "You do not have to die. Move aside."

"I will not."

The man didn't even flinch. In fact, he said nothing.

"Calli? Calli, wake up!" Someone's hands were on my shoulders.

The man grasped my arm in an iron grip. "Foolish girl," he spat. "You didn't have to die, though I'm sure my master won't see it as a loss." I tried to stand, but he shoved me back on my knees, his hood falling so I could see his face. The sickening thud of my heart said I knew the man.

"Kill me, do anything just—"

"Calli? Calli, it's just a dream. Wake up!"

His hand reached out and touched my shoulder, and then nothing. Nothing but darkness, and Derek's arms flying me quickly to heaven.

"DEREK!" I woke screaming. Tears blinded my vision.

"I'm here, Calli. Everything's okay. It was just a dream."

Just a dream. Somehow, the words didn't seem to fit quite right in my head. Just a dream. Then why had it seemed so real?

I blinked slowly. Above me, Ema's face was creased with worry. I wanted to cry.

"You were having a nightmare of some sort," Ema said, stroking back the sweat matted hair from my forehead. "It was horrible." I sat up slowly and looked around the room. I was in my bed, in my sleeping chemise. The covers were twisted as if I had been thrashing. A glance out the window told me it was still late at night.

"Master McDunnon was passing our room and he heard you. He went up to the Aviary to get Lady Dubois. She is going to bring you a sleeping potion, I think."

"I...I..." I couldn't find any words. Instead, I fell apart. I collapsed into desperate sobs. Ema pulled herself into the bed, and curled up beside me.

"Lady Dubois should be here soon," she whispered, stroking my hair and holding my head to her chest.

I nodded weakly, but said nothing. I could hardly control myself. My shoulders shook. It had been so real. As solid a reality as the bed that now sat beneath me.

"What happened?" It was the healer. She on the edge of the bed and ran a worried hand over my forehead.

"She had a bad dream, my Lady. I think she'll be alright now." Ema's fingers wrapped around mine. I clung to them for dear life. Maybe, just maybe, they would hold me in reality.

"What kind of dream? A nightmare? Do you remember what it was about, child? It could be important."

"They're...they...they're dead." The words came out as scarcely more than a whisper. I couldn't say more. My voice wouldn't work. The tears returned to my eyes.

"Who's dead?" Lady Dubois asked, sounding slightly perturbed.

"Please Lady, she doesn't want to talk about it now. I'm sure she can tell you tomorrow." Ema's hand tightened around my own, and for a moment a flash of gratitude ran through me. Ema had never spoken up against an adult. Ever. I squeezed her hand weakly in reply and leaned into her touch as she stroked my hair.

Lady Dubois sighed in an exasperated sort of way. Then, patting my head, she stood. "Very well then. I brought some sleeping potion for you. It will let you sleep dreamlessly for the rest of the night." She placed a small vial filled with a blue sort of liquid on the table. "I'll leave it here for you to take when you are ready. Don't stay up too late," she added with a sharp look at Ema. Then she left, leaving Ema and I alone in the room and shutting the door softly behind her.

"Are you sure you're okay?" Ema whispered as she stood.

"I'll be fine, I think." I gave the vial a quick glance, and shuddered. I did not welcome the darkness of sleep. "It was so real, Ema. It wasn't like a dream. Not a normal one, anyway. It was...different." I curled myself into a ball and tried to forget the other dreams that weren't quite dreams. They were as impossible to forget as reality itself.

"It was just a dream." Ema told me firmly. "Nothing more." I tried to smile at her, but something in the muscles of my face wouldn't work quite right. I settled on a hopeful looking frown. "Get some sleep," she whispered. "Lady Dubois's potion will keep you from dreaming any more. Sleep, Calli. You need it." She smiled gently and pulled herself back under the blankets beside me.

"Here goes nothing," I muttered as I picked up the potion. The vial fit neatly in the palm of my hand, and I downed it in one swig. It tasted like old water from a fish bowl and burned on the way down. Sweeping my hair off tear stained cheeks, I turned and buried my face into the pillows.

I felt numb. Emotionless. And yet, somehow, more frightened than I had ever been in my entire life. I didn't know what was happening to me anymore. I could hardly tell the difference between reality and dream. I felt as if I were living two lives. The room was very dark.

Already, I felt drowsy. The room blurred out of focus, distorting even further my sense of reality. Frightened, I huddled deep into the blankets, burying myself away until I was wrapped at last in the safe cloak of a dreamless sleep.

* * *

It was midmorning when I woke. Ema had already gone, likely to the Great Room for breakfast. My stomach rumbled at the thought.

Shivering slightly as the cold castle air brushed my skin, I rolled the blankets back and swung my feet to the floor. The room was empty, so I pulled a thick fur robe over top of my chemise and stood. There was no way that I could get into one of Ema's complicated dresses myself, so it would have to do. The people who dotted the halls eyed me askance, but I ignored them. Their looks weren't worth my time.

Nothing seemed different in the Great Room. The cold ending of the Council Meeting had not yet seeped to the rest of the court. Doubtless, no one even knew that their kingdom had just begun the second war of this decade. Perhaps they wouldn't know for a while. I wasn't about to tell anyone. If my uncle had decided to keep the news a secret, he obviously had a good reason to do so.

Ema sat in her usual spot, and when she saw me she gestured me over to the table. I scanned the room for Leo. He was nowhere to be seen. He and the other Novices were all probably sweating at the training field by now. Shifting my robe around my shoulders, I slid across the rough wooden bench and took a plate.

"How are you?" Ema asked when I sat.

"Well enough," I told her. Last night's dream was still vividly imprinted in my memory.

"Did you sleep well?"

"That potion Lady Dubois gave me worked wonders. Not a dream in sight." I smiled at her weakly.

With the festival officially over, the hall was normal again. The only thing that remained was the ghostly scent of roses which clung to the air. A lone harper stood in the corner of the room, strumming a lonely song and singing in quiet tones about the cold winds of winter. Feather light snow fell outside the windows.

"I think I'm going to go down and watch the boys practice for a while," I told Ema after a moment of silence. "Would you like to come?" She glanced outside and shuddered.

"I would rather be up in the library listening to one of Lady Canter's lectures on civil theory than go out in that snow," she told me dramatically. "Besides, I have embroidery with the girls today. You are welcome to attend. It will be warm, and there will be tea." I shook my head. I needed a distraction, and sitting around embroidering with Ema and the girls would not be the distraction I sought. It would only drive me into the safety of my thoughts—a place that currently, was not very safe at all.

Between yesterday's meeting and last night's dream, my thoughts were spinning circles that made my head ache. A dull sort of pressure had gathered behind my eyes. I pushed away my plate, and stood. Perhaps I wasn't hungry after all.

Ema's eyes followed me for a moment, her brow creased with faint worry. "You will be okay, won't you?" she whispered.

Okay? Okay didn't seem the correct word in such a situation. I was far from okay. But, to spare her the worry and anxiety, I turned my frown into a smile and shrugged her statement off. "I'm fine." I told her gently. Ignoring her searching look, I turned and walked away.

It was warmer than I had expected outside—or perhaps my robe protected me from the cold far better than I had hoped. The ground was covered in a foot of white down and the distant treetops were laced with winter's white breath. I followed the paved road that led out the main gate for several minutes before turning to the right and making my own path by the lake. Guards stood at attention and followed me with searching eyes as I passed through the gatehouse. A few men moved as if to follow me, but I shook my head and waved them away. Then, at long last, I was free.

The sharpness of the cool winter air allowed for a clarity of thinking that I had not come across in a long time. I paused for a moment at the edge of Glass Lake and watched the ripples that danced over its mirror like surface. A flock of geese passed overhead, murmurs fading as they disappeared into the far distance. I shivered and dug a toe into the snow. Then, pulling my robe higher to cover my ears, I continued my walk, tracing a path for myself along the lake's smooth edge.

It wasn't until I rounded the edge of the western watchtower that my thoughts turned in a rather unpleasant direction. The dreams. I had known I wouldn't have been able to avoid them forever, but I had hoped. Last night's dream had rent a particularly gruesome gap into my psyche. Just thinking of the event made me want to collapse into the ground sobbing. With delicacy I restrained myself, but only barely.

The people who had populated last night's dream were familiar to me. It took me only moments to realize that I had dreamed of the girl—my narrator—before. I could tell her by the way she presented her thoughts and by the way I felt when I moved in her body. I could tell by the tiny bird hands that fluttered into my vision. Yes, I had dreamed of this girl before. In fact, my dreams of her were more common than those of anyone else. The fact made no sense to me, but I knew it to be the truth. The mind of the girl in last night's dream had become as understandable to me as my own. It was a paralyzing thought.

No matter how I tried, I couldn't get the girl out of my head. Who was she? Why had she died? I paused for a moment in my walk to drag the details to the front of my mind. The girl. Her name...it was Leslie. A common name, but it felt somehow familiar on my tongue. And the boy. The man. The one who had died with her, who had died *for* her. His name was Derek. With a sudden gasp, my feet froze in the ground. The wheels of my mind whirled in sudden motion.

The man. Derek. He was a king. And that made the girl... for a moment my thoughts raced with such turmoil I could no longer decipher them. My brain was foggy. Overcome with a sudden wave of dizziness, I pressed myself against a nearby tree. Leslie and Derek. Why had I not made the connection before? The names rung like a gong in my mind. And the baby in her arms...my heart thudded to a sudden, screeching halt. My nails dug deep into the bark of the tree to which I clung. My breath came in gasping sobs. Leslie. The girl in my dreams.

She was my mother.

* * *

"Calli!"

I was still trembling when I reached the training fields. My mind spun in endless circles. It was hard to smile at the boy who was now coming to a halt in front of me. "Leo," I murmured quietly. My mind was elsewhere.

"Are you okay? Ema told me about last night..."

I smiled slowly at him and replied with an obvious lie. Yes, I was fine. I had never been better. He wasn't convinced, though I hadn't expected him to be. Regardless, he said nothing, only nodded, and gave me a quick hug before hurrying back out onto the field.

I watched him go and wandered to the old wall at the edge of the field. Pulling myself to the top of it, I wiggled a spot for myself amongst the snow. There, perched like a redbird a top a fir tree, I could see the entire field. I watched them spar with calculating eyes, trying to distract myself from my discovery. I tried to imagine Arcturus's guiding words. I tried to hear him spell out each step as the boys swept across the field, but I couldn't. I simply couldn't. Instead, my eyes drifted to the snowy horizon and I lost myself in my thoughts. My father's eyes, glazed in the embrace of death, loomed over me. My mother's cries rung shrilly in my ears.

"Calli?" Leo's voice surprised me, and I teetered on the edge of the wall. "Would you like to come to lunch with me? Master McDunnon's let us off for an hour." I smiled at him and pushed myself from the wall's top. He caught me on the way down, lowering me gently to the ground like a small child. *Is it really that late already?* I thought distantly. A quick glance at the sky confirmed the fact. The sun squinted brightly through a mass of grey clouds at about midpoint in the sky. That meant I had been here, sitting on this wall, for more than a couple hours. I frowned, trying to figure out where the time had gone. The image of my father's dying face flashed up before my eyes and I winced, shutting off my thoughts entirely.

"Are you sure you're okay?" Leo asked me. We were walking now, though I hadn't noticed, and his arm was wrapped tightly around my waist. Distantly, I realized that if he let go, I would probably no longer be standing.

"I..." I shook my head. The fogginess of my brain had increased ten-fold.

"Calli? What's wrong?" The pitch of his voice had taken on the stinging edge of panic.

Images flashed before my eyes. Colors. Faces. Dreams.

"Calli?" The panic was no longer only an edge now. His voice ripped through my mind, but I was trapped. I could not answer.

Light colored eyes stared back at me, covered by a head of honey colored...

...and a bird took flight from its perch in a tree high above me. A bird as white as...

"DEREK!!"

Somebody was screaming. The jabber. The voices. The flashes of scenes. They swirled around me in a fog of nothingness. A deep consuming fog that...

"NO! Please! Kill me, do anything just—"

"Calli!"

"Calli!"

He was my...

"NOOOO!!!!!"

Caladrius Dreams

The world floated delicately around the edge of my vision, and a blurry pair of blue eyes peered anxiously down at me. It took me a second to realize where I was; that I was on my knees in the snow at the edge of the training field, my hands pressed over my ears and my head cradled to my chest. "What happened?" My voice was weak.

"I don't know," Leo said, and suddenly he was on his knees beside me, prying my hands away from my face and pulling me into his chest. "Are you okay?"

I had lost track of how many times I had heard that question. There was no point in lying anymore, either to him, or to myself. "No," I whispered in response. "Not at all."

18

Magic

"Calli, I really don't think you should be practicing tonight."
Leo sounded concerned, but I shook him off. Dreams or no, Arcturus would expect me to be in his study. I ignored Leo's protests and kept walking. "You practically blacked out this morning," he reminded me.

I paused for a second, glancing at him over my shoulder. "That was several hours ago," I told him. "I've been fine since."

It was true. After the strange glimpses—or whatever the phenomena I had experienced on the practice field had been—the pressure in my head had largely subsided, like a valve somewhere had been released. Leo had forced me to relax for the rest of the day, but now it was time to meet with Arcturus, and I was sick of resting. Besides, when I was resting, I couldn't stop my thoughts from returning to last night's nightmare. And that was something I wanted to avoid at all costs. Watching Leo practice this morning had failed at being distracting. But maybe, just maybe, practicing myself with Arcturus would force more focus.

Leo sighed at my answer. "At least let me walk you there," he said. I hesitated, opening my mouth to refuse him. But there was a note of finality to his tone, and after a moment I decided arguing wasn't worth the time. I gave Leo a short nod, and began to walk. He followed, grabbing my arm and leading me down the hall.

We were in front of Arcturus's door in a few short minutes. "You can go now," I told Leo softly. He shrugged.

"I'll go once you're inside." I only nodded, and turned to knock on the door.

The door burst open while my hand was still hovering, about to knock. A man came through, his face showing more than a little irritation. His shoulder collided with mine, nearly knocking me from my feet. He paused his stride long enough to catch me—his cold hand wrapping around my bare forearm in a vice-grip—and continued walking. I stared after him.

"Master Julius Heidel," Leo told me. "The old King's Guard, before Arcturus. For your grandfather." he added after a second. "Don't worry about him, he's gotten moody as he's aged." Leo grinned and shrugged. I turned back to the door, swinging partly open.

"Arcturus?" I called to the inside. There was no answer. "Arcturus?"

The sound of rustling drifted to my ear and then his voice came, gruff and short. "Come in." I gave Leo a half smile and slid inside, closing the door behind me.

He was rifling through paperwork when I entered and glanced up for only a second when the door clicked shut. He stood and walked to the door in the back of his room. Then, without a word, he disappeared into the practice room. I followed him inside.

He was waiting for me in the middle of the room, his arms crossed and his feet square. His face told me nothing of his thoughts; his mouth sat in a hard straight line, and his eyes watched me with the slow calculating gaze of someone so used to watching and calculating that it was no longer even an occurrence of thought.

"Sit." Even his voice was hard. Arguing wasn't worth the time—I was here to learn not complain—so I did as I was told and sat cross-legged on the cold, hard floor. Immediately he turned and moved away from me. Across the room he rummaged through the old wood cabinet. When he came back he held an object small enough to be concealed entirely in a single fist. He stopped several paces in front of me. He didn't bother to stoop or kneel down to my level, but instead stood above me, looking down while I sat on the floor. "Magic," he began, and suddenly a sharp shudder ran its way through my spine, "is not a game. It can kill you in a second. Do not forget that, princess."

"Yes, sir."

"You must never, ever practice it on your own. You must never work ahead, and you must always do just as I say. Do you understand?" I nodded quickly, half afraid he would change his mind about teaching me altogether.

He looked satisfied with my nod and, bending so his hand brushed the ground, set the object in his fist before me. My stomach sunk a bit when his hand uncovered it. A simple river stone. I looked at it a second and turned my eyes back up to his. He was standing several paces away from me again, his arms crossed once more and his face set in that ever impassive gaze. "If nothing ever touches that rock, will it move?"

I felt as if he were asking a trick question. Of course it would not. It was a rock. I frowned. "No?"

"Be more confident in your answer, princess." His voice was the crack of a whip. Setting my face like his, I did not flinch.

"No."

"An object needs to be acted on to move. Magic works in a similar manner. In order to move that rock, some sort of energy must be put into it. Correct?"

"Yes."

"Nothing happens without energy. And energy cannot be created. It must be taken from a source that is already filled with it. Energy can be transferred, but never created or destroyed. Remember that."

"Yes, sir."

"When magic is used, the energy needed to cause the re-action is provided by your own body. You provide the energy, princess. The act of lifting that rock with your mind takes as much energy as lifting it with your hand. Perhaps more."

"So," I wondered aloud, "if you do something with magic that requires more energy then you have...what happens?"

"You die."

I shuddered, but I didn't allow the emotion to pass to my face. "What is magic?" I asked. "Where does it come from?"

Arcturus paused for a brief moment, his brow creasing between his eyes. "We aren't sure," he said at last. "Anyone of noble blood is capable of magic, though not all ever learn to use it proficiently. Some never learn at all. Magic is the opening of your mind; it is seeing possibility in the impossible. It is your imagination. It is your wildest dreams. A friend of mine once said it like this—'Magic is when you believe in something so much, it comes true.' Close your eyes." I hesitated for only a moment before I shut them. "Hear your heart beating. Listen to your breaths. Count them. Focus your whole mind, your whole soul, your whole world, on the space inside of you. Do not allow any unwanted thoughts to cross your mind.

"When you are ready, turn your thoughts to the stone. Think of it. Think of every curve, every crack. Feel it. Know it." He had placed the pebble in my hand now. I rolled it like dough in my fingers. "Now, imagine. Imagine the stone, hovering above your hand. Picture it in your mind. The clearer your image, the more steady it will be." I held my hand flat and did not open my eyes. In my mind I pictured the rock, I imagined that it was hovering, floating. I imagined it was a feather, held above my hand by the dancing of a breath. A few seconds passed. The seconds turned into minutes. The rock rolled over.

With a gasp my eyes flew open and my startled hand leapt, causing the rock to tumble onto the floor. The clack of it against the tile was sharp and metallic. I glanced up at Arcturus, expecting to see pride. Nothing but cool blandness showed on his face.

"Try again." His words were harder than the rock I had held in my hand. I picked the rock up once more, allowing my eyes to slide closed. Listen to your breaths, his words echoed in my mind, count them. One...two...three...I was tired. I could feel my head nodding. My attention sliding away. Four...five...six...seven...

"Foolish girl. You didn't have to die, though I'm sure my master won't see it as a loss." I forced the girl to her knees, down where she belonged. The motion dropped my hood from my head, but I didn't bother adjust it. It didn't matter if she knew me now.

"Kill me, do anything just—"

"You choose to seal your fate." A single thought was all it took to stop her heart. Her body collapsed on the floor, down and away from my now empty hands. The black vein corded further up my arm, knotting muscles as it went. I ignored it. With my foot I kicked the body. It was stone cold.

"What do you want me to do with the evidence?" asked one of my men, who had just entered the house. He gestured to the bodies on the floor.

"Burn it. All of it."

The rock burst into flames in my grip and I dropped it with a cry. My eyes snapped open. I couldn't breathe. The air seemed like sandpaper, it ripped my lungs when I drew for breath. Something warm rolled down my hand. I glanced down. It was blood. My skin was charred, black like the burnt side of a fire log. The pain came as I noticed the hand, sharp and intense. I bit my lip to hold back the whimpers collecting in my throat.

"What happened?" Arcturus was on his knees beside me. He covered my burned fist in both hands. After a moment the pain subsided. When he brought his hands away, all that was left was blood. The skin beneath was supple and smooth.

"I don't know," I answered truthfully. "I just have a lot on my mind."

"You cannot afford distractions. I told you magic was dangerous. This is minor compared to what could have happened." I didn't answer him, but gave a sharp nod and turned my face away. He didn't understand. It wasn't as if I wanted the distraction. It would make me glad, were the dreams to disappear and never come back. "Did something happen?" I cringed at his question. Arcturus was more perceptive than I gave him credit for. I nodded slowly.

"Last night I had the nightmare—I've had other dreams before, but none this bad—and Lady Dubois gave me a potion to let me sleep without dreams." *Dreamless.* What a sweet thought.

"And today?"

"I was fine this morning, I went down to watch Leo practice with the other Novices. It happened when we were walking back up to the castle later. I couldn't think straight and then suddenly all I could see and hear were flashes, like bits of dreams or memories all smashed up together. It felt almost like they *had* to come out. Like something had been holding them back and my head would have exploded if they hadn't come out once that something was gone." I had crouched myself into a tight ball on the floor. My arms were wrapped around my knees and my muscles were corded tight. I couldn't remember how I had gotten there, into such a position. I buried my head into my knees, and waited for his judgement. It never came.

"What happened today, they were like dreams, you said?" When I looked up, he appeared deep in thought. His face seemed softer, though no more readable.

"Yes."

"And you said you've had other dreams?

"Yes."

"For how long?"

I shifted uncomfortably. "As long as I can remember."

"And you never thought to tell anyone?"

I hesitated. "No."

He paced the floor a little ways away from me, and then stopped. "Have they all been the same dream?" he asked.

"No. Different dreams. Different dreams, and yet they are the same. I don't even always know what they are about. Sometimes they are just scenes, voices, thoughts, all garbled together. But sometimes, it's like I'm watching a story unfold itself."

He resumed his pacing. "The same?" he asked after a length.

"They're all so real. Everything is tangible in them. I can hear everything. Smell everything. Taste everything. It's as if I'm reliving a memory. I can hardly be sure when I'm awake and when I'm dreaming anymore. They aren't merely realistic. They aren't merely my dreaming mind being tricked to perceive reality. They *are* reality. And I can remember every moment of them, as if they had actually happened."

"But the one last night was worse than the others," he said, stating it as a fact rather than a question. I nodded. A lump had formed in my throat. "What was it about?"

His question caught me off guard. For awhile I said nothing, staring into my knees and wondering why all this was happening. A choke ripped through me, and tears threatened to overwhelm me, but I held them back. "It was about the death of my parents." My voice sounded cold and dead. I raised my head to look at him. "I watched it through my mother's eyes. Every gory second. And no matter how hard I try, I can't erase the scene from my mind."

Arcturus's pacing had halted. I couldn't really place the expression that crossed his face, but it was something close to sadness. Perhaps regret. He broke his gaze from me roughly, and resumed his pacing. When he stopped again, it was to address me. "You may go." Any emotion his face had shown was gone. "There will be no more lessons fvor tonight." Then, turning on his heel, he left the room.

I sat for a long time, staring off into nothing. The room grew dark around me, and the clock struck many notes before I moved. When I did move at last, I hurried off to my room as if chased by a specter. Safe in my bed I stared at the shadows that danced across the ceiling. I watched the moon play with the stars. I watched the gentle fingers of trees, dragging across the window. I watched all these things, and more. But I did not sleep.

19

S t u d y

Early the next morning, I drug myself from bed. I hadn't slept. Swinging my feet to the ground I dropped my toes onto the cold marble, wiggling them for a moment before heading off to the bath. A nice warm bath would help to wake me up. I couldn't afford to be tired today. I had things to do.

The bath water was already warm and after filling the tub, I sunk into it with a sigh of relief. The tiredness didn't wash away, but under the drowsy relief of warm water and scented oils, my worries eased. Nothing could bother me when the world was this good. Nothing. Not even dreams.

After soaking for several minutes and washing my hair— now just past chin length—I stood and drained the tub. Then I wrapped a fluffy towel around myself, and left the room. As I exited the steamy warmth of the bathing room, so too did I exit the careless comfort that had drifted over me like a thick blanket of fog. As I entered the chill of the bedroom, my problems slammed back upon my shoulders. I staggered across the floor.

Ema was just beginning to awaken when I entered the room. She was sitting up in bed, hair mussed past recognition. She sighed sleepily at my entrance, but the look in her eyes said she was still more than half asleep. I didn't answer her grunts. Instead I ignored her and pulled on the first bunch of clothes my fingers came in contact with, standing impatiently as a maid laced me up.

I made my way to the Great Room out of habit, but once there, I found I wasn't hungry. Leo was seated at the other side of the hall, in the center of a clump of Novices. When he saw me, he moved from his spot. I let my head fall to the table and watched him from the corner of my eye. He slid onto the bench beside me, and said nothing.

Somewhere near my head, a plate slid across the rough grain of the table. It made a scraping sound as it rested beside my ear. Prying fingers poked at the side of my face and eventually I rolled my head to the side to glare at them. The look on Leo's face almost made me smile, but I stubbornly held back my grin. Right now, I was determined to be miserable.

"Calli, come on. You've got to eat something," he goaded.

"I'm not hungry."

"You'll starve."

"I've starved before," I muttered sarcastically. "Besides, I won't starve from one missed meal. I'm not hungry."

The poking resumed, more vigorous than ever. I groaned and sat up to look at him. "Eat," he commanded. Arguing was too much effort. I picked up a slice of toast, and nibbled on an end. A glass of orange juice slid my way. "You look terrible," Leo commented after several moments of silence.

"I feel fine."

His hand slipped beneath my chin and forced my face up to his. He gazed at me intently, and then released his grasp. "You need to rest," he said.

"I did." It was a lie. But just a little one. I didn't want him to worry. I lifted the glass of orange juice, and forced a few gulps down my throat.

"Calli, your hair looks like it hasn't been brushed in weeks, your eyes are sunken and you have dark circles a corpse would envy. Your clothes aren't even on straight. Or matching," he added after a moment of thought. "You can't tell me this is rested. I know better."

"I'm fine," I repeated.

He looked worried, but if such was the truth, he said nothing. "Eat your food," he told me, pointing to my plate. Then he turned and joined the other boys. He dissolved into a mass of swirling grey, and disappeared around the corner.

I toyed with my food a moment longer before dropping it to the plate and pulling myself from the table. Standing, I surveyed the room. Now that the young Guardians had left, the room was nearly empty.

Somewhere around half an hour later I was seated in a side corner of the library at a large, empty table. Here, within these walls, lay my answer. I was going to find out about the dreams. I was going to learn about them. I *would* discover what was happening to me. I needed to. A stack of books as high as I was tall balanced perilously in front of me.

The books were a rather eclectic mix—the only thing that tied the collection together, was the listing of the word "dreams" on the cover. The first book—a large brown one with a molding leather spine—I tossed aside almost immediately. More followed it in quick succession.

"Dreams, are often thought to have symbolic meaning. There have been many studies on the talents of dreamers, though that will not be discussed in depth here. In this book, it is our focus to explain those symbols which often permeate dreams. In this volume—"

I shut the book with distaste. I didn't care about the symbols. What I cared about was the talent itself, and how to get rid of it. Of one thing, I was certain. These dreams were anything but normal.

* * *

The next few weeks passed in a rough hurry of days. They were the kind of weeks that, when looking back, I found that I could not remember a single moment of them. The days were a terror I could not keep up with. The nights were worse.

I wasn't ignoring Leo or Ema. It was just that my mind had become so consumed, there was no room for anything else. I threw myself to the books. Something in my attitude and thoughts began to feel deranged. The dreams became my obsession. Researching them was both an analgesic, and a drug.

I was listless in public. At mealtimes I remained only long enough to gather a handful of biscuits to carry back up to the library. My days consisted of research, and my nights of practice with Arcturus. I didn't sleep until late, when the dreams would at last overtake me. When I did sleep, it was restless. I was sure people noticed, or at least, that someone did. But I didn't care. Instead I had buried myself into a deep hole, both to hide, and to escape. It was a long time before somebody at last pulled me out.

* * *

"Calli?"

I grunted and pushed back the mass of hair which obscured my face like a choppy red bush. Raising tired eyes to meet his, I dropped the book in my hand. "Where have you been?" The question was accusing and harsh. It ripped from my mouth like a whip, and I immediately regretted it. He stood beside me, his eyes ashamedly seeking mine. He looked almost as tired as I did.

"You've been avoiding me," he explained slowly. There was some sort of relief hidden in his face, a relief so strong it gushed unbidden to the surface. His voice crackled with it. "I didn't even know where you were until just now. I finally managed to corner Ema, and she told me you've been up here. Says you've been obsessing over something like a slave under the lash. I'm worried about you Calli. I've been trying to talk to you for weeks. Please stop this."

"What took you so long?" I asked in no more than a whisper. I'd been thinking he had abandoned me. I'd been thinking he hadn't cared. I knew, somewhere in the back of my head that it was *I* who had been ignoring *him*. But somehow, through all of it, something deep in my heart had been crying out to be noticed. To be saved.

"I miss you," I told him. Then, even more quietly, "I'm sorry."

A smile spread itself across his face, slow and grateful. "I missed you too." For a moment he fell silent, and flipped through the book in his hand in a distracted sort of haze. When he spoke again, his tone was questioning. "Dreams?" he asked me. A second passed with only bewildered amusement on his face. Then suddenly, like the passing of a tendril of wind, the pieces began to fly together behind his eyes. "Your nightmares. Is that why you've been up here all this time?"

I looked over him long before answering. My nightmares were between me, and me alone. The fact that Arcturus knew was an accident. It wasn't something I wanted to discuss with anyone else. Not even Leo. He'd think I was crazy. Or something worse. "Maybe...?"

"The dream you had that night, what was it about?" His question struck me to the core, reverberating unexpectedly throughout my entire being. It amazed me that he had somehow managed to immediately grasp at the very center of my desperation. It astounded me that he somehow knew the exact question that needed to be asked. It terrified me the way his eyes seemed instantly to know my heart. To know my fears and my troubles, and to understand them. And if not understand, then accept.

I couldn't deny him an answer. Suddenly, I was filled with an overwhelming desire to tell him everything. I stuttered a bit when speaking, but eventually answered, "It was about my parents. Their death, to be more exact." Leo nodded, and somehow I knew, without explanation, he understood. "I'm always watching from someone else's point of view, in my dreams," I told him slowly. "Usually, I don't know who the person is, but I'm beginning to be able to differentiate between individuals. I've had dreams of this one girl, over and over again. I didn't know who she was, until that night. I've been dreaming about my mother, and I didn't even know it." There was a slight pitch in my voice, a slight upward turn at the end of my sentences. Leo noticed. His eyes flashed with concern, and without a word, he sat down.

"I guess we'd better get to work then," he said. That was it. No questions. No doubts. Only acceptance. It surprised me that I didn't mind sharing my research with him. My research had been private, and intensely personal. I had expected to feel some sort of jealousy, some sort of apprehension at the idea of sharing it. I didn't. All I felt was the joy of not being alone.

20

Raçe

For the first time in forever, I found myself at the practice field again, dangling like a shadow at Leo's side. He had promised to help me find out more about the dreams, as long as I swore to stop locking myself away. I had been more than happy to oblige. And the time that I spent with Leo not researching, was more than made up for by the increase of efficiency when two people researched side-by-side. I went to his lessons with him, more for the company than for anything else, and we took our meals together in the library, where we could research relentlessly.

We were clustered at the edge of the training field now, in a large, sprawled out group which crowded around Master Mc-Dunnon like a flock of hungry birds. "This is a very rare plant," Master McDunnon said, leaning over a small flower that was blooming in the snow. "It is *Saldoria Molbi Latori,* which means—more or less—Saldorian Torch Bearer." He knelt beside the plant's delicate flower and bent to stroke a leaf. "This plant is one of only a few with confirmed magical properties. Can anyone tell me what it is used for?" The boys said nothing.

Master McDunnon looked rather disappointed. "This plant," he said at last, "was discovered only a few decades ago. Its value in magic is, for the most part, unknown. We have, however, discovered a few of its uses. For example, one berry—of which the plant will produce three of in its lifetime—if chewed will allow for control over a person's dreams. The leaves of this plant can also be distilled into a very powerful sleeping draught."

Caladrius Dreams

My attention had been caught. Scooting forward several inches, I peered at the plant with an intensity I had neglected earlier. Before, it had been only a plant. Now...I stared with longing at the cream petals that pierced the white snow. The flower was lily shaped, the color of butter with a crimson throat, and its honey colored stamen was tipped with a midnight blue anther. It was like a tongue of flame opening from the snow. A shadow passed above it, and for a moment I could have sworn I saw the flower glow.

"Due to its power over a sleeper's dreams, the plant is more commonly known as the Dreamer's Elysium." Master McDunnon stood, brushing the snow from his knees as he did so. "This particular specimen is almost near the end of its life. At this stage of its development, all parts of the plant are highly toxic and would be of no use to anyone, except as a very powerful poison. Even a whiff of the steam from a drink with this plant brewed in it would be powerful enough to place the victim into a permanent state of dream filled sleep. One sip of the same potion, would be instant death. There are no known antidotes."

We moved further from the field, following him off of the trail, and into the forest's black depths. As we walked he pointed to plants and spoke loudly of their virtues—or deadly propensities. A moss lichen growing yellow and green on a rock could be brewed into a tea that healed sore throats. A star daisy—peeking its snowy eyes out from around the edges of a tree—could be ground into a deadly and undetectable poison. A mash of needles and bark from a Harper's Pine could sterilize a wound and keep off flies and rot. A milkwort could be boiled into a cup to ease the effects of respiratory illness. The list went on and on.

It was lunch time when we trudged our way out of the forest and into the sparkling light of day. Leo and I separated ourselves from the others, hanging back until they were well along on the trail to the castle. Now that Master McDunnon wasn't here, their glares and words were capable of becoming nasty.

If I were to be completely honest with myself, I'd admit to the fact that things really hadn't gotten better now that I had begun to hang out with Leo all the time. In fact, things were worse. The anger that had been directed at Leo for being a "rat" was now directed at me. The anger that had been directed at me for being an outsider whom no one wanted was now directed towards Leo. Neither group accepted us. Neither wanted us. But, once again being completely honest, I didn't care. It's often better to stand against the wrath of a million with a good friend at your back, than to stand against the wrath of one all alone.

We took our lunch in the library, just like always. And, also just like always, Lady Rachel the librarian skirted around us, squawking like an angry bird about food on the books. We ignored her. Had I been researching anything less urgent, I would have listened, but the dreams were eating me up inside. I had to do this, squawking Lady Rachel or no. After several minutes, she accepted my apologies and promises. She left us, though I felt certain I could still feel her eyes watching from between the shelves.

I stood, and a few moments later returned with a stack of books—some that we simply hadn't gotten to yet, others that were new, and a few that held useful information—and piled them onto the table before sitting down. Leo parceled the stack out between us—an act which had become almost custom. Bending over my first title, I got to work.

It was slow going, and other than a few excited proclamations—all immediately confirmed as false alarms—we made no progress and spoke little. Somewhere near three hours had passed when I at last threw down a book and collapsed against the back of my chair. "This is pointless," I grumbled. "There's nothing in here. That, or we are simply looking for the wrong thing." I tossed aside a copy of *Lucid Dreaming*, and another book titled *Dreams and Your Psyche*.

"I'm sure we'll find something," Leo murmured in reply.

I stood and threw a handful of books into a bag for later. Taking another book in hand, I eyed it for a moment before tossing it in the ever growing stack of books deemed worthless. "I mean, *Dreaming About the Future? Dream Images from Your Daily Life?* What does any of this have to do with me? These dreams aren't images...or even symbols. And they certainly aren't about the future. Over half of them are about my mother, so how could they be? I don't know what to do, and I don't know where to look. Let's just face it, Leo. This is useless."

He stayed seated for a moment, watching me with thoughtful eyes. "It's not pointless," he said patiently. "We'll figure this out. We'll figure it out if I have to sit up here all day and reckon with Master McDunnon's wrath. I promise. Just don't give up, okay?"

His words settled me, and though I did not sit down, I sank more comfortably into my stance and sighed. "Fine. I won't give up, I promise." He stood with me and I gave him a weak smile. Draping an arm around my shoulder, he steered me from the room.

"Good. But for now," he said, "I have lessons to go to. And you promised Ema tea."

I grumbled at that but nodded slowly to him. Leo had been insistent that I tried my best to heal the discord which was growing between Ema—and all those in support of the rightful heir—and myself. I didn't like it, but I had to admit he was right. I was that rightful heir after all, even if they didn't know it. It wouldn't do to make enemies of people whom I would be needing desperately in the future. Not that my attempts at peace did much good. I nodded slowly, promising to meet up with him again later for dinner and more books.

* * *

"I really don't think it's wise for you to be hanging out with him anymore, Calli. Everyone notices. Why can't you see?" We had just entered the Great Room after an afternoon of tea and embroidery. With a quiet nod of farewell, I had separated myself from Ema's side to make my way over to where Leo was waiting. To my surprise, Ema stopped herself dead in front of me. Ema had never tried to hide how she felt about my friendship with Leo, but she had never forced the issue. Now, hands on hips, she stared me down.

"You don't think it's wise?" I challenged. The girl had been bothering me lately, speaking little—even at night in the room— and passing me with many humphs and snotty glances. My temper was tied tight and I narrowed my eyes threateningly at her advances. "I can hang out with whomever I like. What right do you have to tell me what to do?" My voice raised several decibels.

"I'm your friend, Calli—"

"And so is he!" I exclaimed, moving towards her and raising my hands emphatically. She didn't seem to hear me.

"I've been here longer than you...I know how this world works. And it's my job to help keep you safe—"

I cut her off, too angry to wait and hear what she had to say. "Keep me *safe?*" I asked. I was shouting now. My voice rose incredulously. My plate dropped down on the table with a clatter. "Who are you, my self-appointed bodyguard?" I shook my head and backed away from her. "You have no idea. No idea at all." She didn't. Ema Chevalier had no idea what she was up against, no idea what she *really* needed to protect me from. I almost laughed. The room was dead silent around us. The music that normally filled it had halted, and the chatter that hissed around its edges was gone. I could feel all eyes turn towards us.

"I just don't want him putting his slimy hands all over you!" Now we were both yelling.

"What are you suggesting?" I growled dangerously.

"I'm suggesting that he's a rat and cannot be trusted!"

I shook my head at this, backing up several steps before stopping. For a moment, all I could do was stare. "You're kidding right?" I asked, dumbfounded. "Can't be trusted? I don't know where you've been, Ema, but Leo's the most trustworthy person I know. He would never hurt me, if that's what you think. You can't judge people by their family. It's not right."

"You don't know what you're talking about," she persisted. Somehow, by the tone of her voice, I could tell she actually thought she was doing the right thing. It irritated me. "I've grown up around these people. I know how this world works. You don't, Calli. You just don't. If you'd been here long enough you'd know that family names don't lie—"

I cut her off, enraged. "Have you actually taken the time to get to know him?" I shouted. "Have you? He's my best friend, Ema. I don't care what you—or anyone—has to say about it. If you really were as good a friend as you pretend to be, you'd have stopped to give him a chance. If you had, you'd realize that he's nothing like his family. Maybe you're right. Maybe family names *don't* lie. But there are always exceptions to the rule..." I was pleading now, though I didn't like it. Ema remained unmoved.

"Do you really think I'm going to let you hang out with him? This is social suicide, Calli—"

"Social suicide?" I scoffed. "Yeah, because I really care about ruining what I have right now."

"It can get worse," Ema cautioned slowly, her voice echoing in the sort of tone you would use while scolding a three year old. "And I can't let that happen."

"Let?" My voice was cracking in a million places. The anger was back. "Who do you think you are, my mother? Sorry to break it to you, but I don't have one of those. I've had to learn to do without. I can take care of myself. I've done it all these years haven't I? I don't need you, or anyone else, to tell me what I can and cannot do."

"Please...I just want to help..."

"Then help by being my friend. By being a real friend." Angry tears blurred my vision.

"Calli! Wait..." She reached forward and grabbed my wrist, but I wrenched it from her grasp.

"Leave me alone." I turned to leave.

"You're going to get burned one of these days, you know!" she called after me. I kept walking.

* * *

I didn't see Ema again until late that night when I made my way back to our room. She was lying in the bed when I walked through the door—a dark hump that neither moved nor spoke. The fire glowed dimly in the fireplace and the candles were all snuffed out. I didn't bother relighting one. Instead, I dressed in the dark and then climbed into bed.

By her breathing, I could tell she wasn't asleep. Still angry, I rolled over, cramming my head into a pillow and facing my back towards her. Neither of us said a word.

Calli and I had just entered the Great Room after tea. We were just talking, just like normal. All in all, everything was normal. Or at least for the most part. Things had been breaking down between her and I.

There had always been discord between the families, according to my mother. This used to be normal competition. The normal struggle of class and rank. Now though...now the accusations were true. They really were traitors. They had left us. Left us, and their rightful king to follow a murderer.

From beside me, Calli drew herself away. That was when I saw him. Leo Thurman, the son of the worst traitor of all, patiently waiting at the far edge of the table. Perhaps that is what made me break. I have never been shy in showing my dislike for Thurman, but since she obviously refused to hear my complaints, I had settled for subtle disdain. Now however, was not the time to consort with a "rat". Something was different in the castle, something intimately tied to the alliances within the court. No one had spoken of it, but there was a strange sort of tension in the air. Calli was giving people all the wrong signals, and the conclusions they were making about her were downright dangerous.

Gritting my teeth, I blocked her path. It was time to put an end to this. I would make her see what she was doing. I had to.

Stopping in front of her I turned and opened my mouth. "Calli...I really don't think it's wise for you to be hanging out with him anymore. Everyone notices. Why can't you see?" Bluntness was perhaps the best approach. Hands on hips, I watched her, waiting for an answer.

"You don't think it's wise?" she answered. There was a stubborn sort of fire in her voice. "I can hang out with whomever I like. What right do you have to tell me what to do?" Her voice raised to an irritating pitch. I lifted an eyebrow at her and crossed my arms in front of my chest. Shouting was never ladylike.

Putting on my best face, I tried to answer her as patiently as I could. It was like dealing with a child. "I'm your friend, Calli—"

"And so is he!" Would she never learn? Why could she not see, why could she not understand what people were thinking about her? In the end, it didn't matter whether he was different or not. All that mattered was that she continued to blindly oppose those who made the rules.

"I've been here longer than you," I began, my original patience wearing a bit thin. "I know how this world works. And it's my—

Caladrius Dreams

I woke with a jolt, sitting upright in bed and pulling the covers tight around me. "Sorry," Ema muttered coldly, her legs swinging over the edge of the bed as she pulled a robe over her shoulders. It was late morning. "I didn't mean to wake you."

I didn't respond. My mind spun like the roiling of hot water, making it hard to think straight. It took a second for me to process this last dream, but when I did my eyes widened and I pulled the covers up around the bottom half of my face. I remained seated like that long after Ema had exited the room, frozen. One thing was clear. The dreams were real.

21

Memories

"You need to concentrate more, princess."

I didn't know what it was, but something in his voice irritated me. "I *am* trying," I snapped back. Lifting my bow, arrow nocked and ready, I drew the string taut to my cheek. My hand shook in the release, and I missed the target. Again.

"Trying isn't good enough."

Arcturus's callous voice seemed cutting. I barely noticed. My mind was reeling, trying to catch hold of something half-realized. Something hidden in my peripherals, known but just out of sight. "I'm sorry," I replied. My voice was rougher than I meant, but the statement was true. I was sorry. And I was trying. The reeling of my mind seemed to be getting out of hand. I groaned and pulled another arrow from my quiver. *Concentrate. Just concentrate.*

His granite face had softened considerably, if a rock could ever be called soft. His hand caught me as I drew my bow, causing me to stop. My arms dropped to my side; my face went blank. My eyes focused on something in the distance, something unseen to everyone but me.

"Are you having nightmares again?" Arcturus's voice snapped me back to reality. It surprised me how perceptive the man was. The only other person I knew who could pick up on my moods so well was Leo. My lips tugged down in the corners, and I avoided his eyes. It was impossible to lie to Arcturus. I nodded, not trusting my voice. It was true that the man had guessed the cause of my distraction...but he didn't know the half of it. I wasn't about to let him in on the whole story. I had nightmares every night. But he didn't need to know that.

To my surprise, Arcturus took the bow from my hand—as easily as I would have taken a toy from an infant, despite my white knuckled grip—and the quiver from my back. Without a word he brought them to the cabinet and placed them back inside. "You've practiced enough for today," he told me finally. "Go get some sleep." I could tell he was attempting to be congenial, but the attempt was poor. His words sounded more like an order and carried a harshness that would have made anyone who knew him less turn and run. I smiled weakly though, recognizing his attempt and watched as he strode from the room, turning out the lights behind him with a single movement of his hand.

I stood in the room for a long time after he left. It was dark and empty. I could hear my breathing echo off the cold walls. The buzzing of my mind hadn't slowed. In fact, it had picked up the moment he had left. The dreams were real. I hadn't been able to stop thinking about them all day.

I hadn't spoken to or seen Ema since morning. For a moment, I considered that maybe, just maybe, my dream about her last night had been a coincidence. Maybe, after our fight, my tired mind had conjured up a replica of what Ema might have thought. Somehow though, I didn't think that was the case.

What if—and the thought made something in my heart tremor excitedly—what if the dreams were memories? Certainly, I dreamt often enough of my own memories to suggest such a fact. But what if, somehow, my dreams were also filled with the memories of other people? I sat up straighter. My mind seemed suddenly closer to grasping that thought which had danced in my peripherals.

My stomach squirmed uncomfortably. It was a strange thought. Adrenaline shot through my veins like fire. If I was right—if these dreams were memories—then how was I getting other people's? Memories of my own I could understand. But

Ema's, Leo's, my mother's, and those of countless others whom I didn't even know danced in my head. Where had they come from? All at once, everything snapped into place. The thought in my peripherals zoomed suddenly into focus, so clear I wondered instantly why I had reached for it so long.

What if—? I stood and began walking down the hall quickly as possible. There was only one way I could be sure.

* * *

The door opened at my knock. It was Avery who greeted me. For a moment, the surprise on Avery's face had dislodged his usual disdain. For a moment, he simply looked like an innocent child. Innocent, and vulnerable. The illusion vanished as soon as he regained his composure, the sneer re-appearing on his face so quickly I thought maybe I had only imagined his expression moments before. "What do you want?" That tone was properly disrespectful. It made me much more comfortable. I had enough mysteries and questions to deal with without trying to judge Avery's character too.

"Is Leo in here?"

"Maybe. Why?"

"I need to speak with him."

For a moment, Avery did nothing. Then, with a curt nod he closed the door, vanishing inside.

It was several minutes before Leo appeared at the door. "Calli...it's almost midnight." Clearly, I had woken him. His eyes were unfocused and his hair so disheveled that it covered half his face. He yawned and brushed the hair back with a hand, a motion which cleared it from his face but didn't do much to improve his overall appearance. I cupped my hand in front of my mouth to hide the twitching of my lips.

"Walk with me?" My eyes darted nervously to the door cracked open behind him. I didn't want to talk here. Not where someone could overhear.

Something in my voice must have sounded urgent because his eyes widened and he nodded without hesitation. I took him by the arm and pulled him down the dark hallway, looking for somewhere quiet to sit. He followed without a complaint, but with several long yawns. Pushing open a door, we entered into a dark room. It was empty, and I took a seat near the back door. Leo waved his hand—a gesture I had seen Arcturus make dozens of times—and a few lights came on in the corner. Leo took a seat in a chair across from me, examining my face with tired eyes. "What's up?"

"The dreams are memories," I told him with a certainty I didn't remember from my previous thoughts.

"That's impossible."

"Is it?" I walked him through my dream about my fight with Ema. He frowned, his face tight and thoughtful.

"How?" His brows furrowed further. I shook my head.

"I'm not sure exactly, but I'm working on developing a theory." Leo let out a low chuckle, as if he thought something was funny. "What?" I snapped. It was late and I was tired and running low on patience. I hadn't brought him here to laugh at me.

"You're crazy..." he said, his chuckle a full laugh now. He shook his head and clutched at his sides.

"Well, thanks for being such a great listener," I grumbled sarcastically. This only made him laugh harder. I stood to leave, and he sobered.

"Stay. It was a joke, Calli. I didn't mean any harm," he said quickly. I sighed, but sat. "What else are you thinking? There's more. I can tell. Something is eating you up inside." He flashed me another grin, which faded at my frown.

"Yesterday, after my fight with Ema, she grabbed my wrist." I told him my voice dropping to an even quieter whisper. "She was pretty amped up, and I doubt much else was on her mind at that precise moment."

"What does that have to do with anything?" Leo asked. I grumbled at his interruption, but continued.

"Give me your hand." It was meant to be a request, but the words came out more like a demand. Maybe I had been spending too much time with Arcturus. He held his hand out to me, and I wrapped my fingers around his. "Now think about something very hard. A memory I wouldn't know otherwise." For a moment his eyes were wide, but then he nodded once and closed them, appearing deep in thought. His face twitched a few times, and I couldn't help but wonder suddenly what it was that he was remembering. When his eyes opened at last, they looked strained.

"That should do..." he muttered hoarsely. He threw me a grin, but it was forced. "What exactly are we doing?" For his sake, I suddenly hoped this worked. His face was pained, and I didn't want to put my friend through pain for no reason at all. He seemed to pick up on my anxiety, because he muttered softly, "It's fine. Don't worry about me." He gave me another weak smile that was a little more believable.

I released some tension I hadn't known I had been holding, and withdrew my hand from his. "If I'm right," I said softly, "this should prove it." I squirmed a bit in my seat, and continued. "I have a theory. What if, somehow, I am getting memories from people through direct contact?"

"Like the flu?"

I rolled my eyes. "Sure."

"So basically," Leo said, "you're catching memories like viruses."

"And maybe people are most 'infectious' if they are thinking about something really hard. When their mind is completely and utterly engaged on something, perhaps that makes it easier for me to pick it up."

Leo nodded slowly, though I could tell something was still on his mind. "It makes sense," he said at last. "But how?"

That part of the question I hadn't solved yet. It weighed heavily on my mind. Knowing that the dreams were real—that they consisted of actual events—in no way helped me get rid of them. I shook my head and shrugged. "I don't know," I whispered back to him. I stood and he followed. Once at the door we bid each other goodnight and I turned, walking slowly back to my room alone. His question rang dully in my ears. His question, followed by one of my own. *But how? Why?* The difference seemed subtle, but distinct.

Once in my bed, I fell asleep almost immediately. The moment my eyes closed, they came. Dreams.

"*Quincy...please. I'm sorry.*"

"*I'm gonna tell Father, and he'll kill you.*" *His eyes told me this wasn't an exaggeration. I believed him. Fear almost made me sick. I was on my knees, begging. Begging it seemed, for my life. My brother didn't seem all that sympathetic.*

It didn't matter that it was Quincy's fault anyway. It was always my fault in the end. Whether Quincy had accidentally broken mother's best vase, or lied to father through his teeth, it somehow always turned out to be my fault. Quincy was the eldest, and therefore, always right. The shattered glass from whatever Quincy had thrown at me earlier littered the floor with its broken shards. It had been something valuable, I remembered, but I wasn't sure what. Quincy stared at the glass between us and I knew he was working out how to use it to wound me, even though he hadn't managed to hit me. I heard steps coming from upstairs and shivered involuntarily. "Quincy...don't do this. Please..."

"*Father?*" *I froze and the blood drained from my face.*

A few minutes later and our father stood before us, his face ashen. I hadn't seen the man in months. He had been gone—though where to, I couldn't have said. For a moment, all I wanted to do was run and hug him...laughing like a normal child. For a moment, I was glad to see him. He was my father after all. And didn't I have to love my father? Such thoughts fled when I saw his face. When I remembered again what fear felt like.

His eyes scraped the room, tracing the lines of glass scattered across the floor. He didn't ask any questions. In the end, Quincy didn't have to tell him anything. His eyes flew to me. There was rage behind his glare. "Leo." The way he said my name made it sound like an insult.

A few steps my way—he didn't have to take many, my father was a big man—and suddenly my left cheek stung and my ears were ringing. I staggered to the ground. The only thing in line with my spotty vision was his fist, clenched and hanging by his side. I struggled to my feet. He would hit me again if I appeared weak.

But when I stood, I realized my father wasn't even looking at me. He wasn't even looking at the glass on the ground. His boots crushed it, like whatever lay broken there carried no value. "Come upstairs, Quince," was all he said. He took my brother by the arm, and together they climbed the stairs and disappeared. My stomach curdled. The truth of it was...the fear wasn't the worst part.

I was quivering when I woke. It was morning, and very cold, though I felt warm enough beneath my blankets. I didn't move for a long time. I just lay in bed, and stared at the ceiling.

* * *

It had been a slow day. I had been with Ema for most of it, though she had pretended I didn't exist. We had sat up with the girls, knitting and embroidering silk with satin. For once, I hadn't minded. Knitting was a mindless task, and my brain was reeling too much for anything that needed much thought. Arcturus had called off our lesson for tonight. He had something important to do, though what exactly I wasn't sure. I hadn't seen Leo since last night.

Evening found me lying on a chair in the sunroom, gazing out of the large windows to watch the sunset. It provided a perfect view of the mountains, the sunset, and the stars. The sunroom was always empty this time of day—who would use it when there was no sun? Just me, I supposed. Curling beneath my shawl, I watched the view in front of me, and tried very hard not to think.

I was startled when behind me, the door opened. Footsteps echoed in the empty room. I turned, wondering who it would be. Leo. Of course. Only he would know that this was where to find me right after dinner, and right before my lessons.

"Calli?" His voice shook, and the look on his face made me realize that something was wrong. Very wrong. I sat up. Suddenly, I was worried for my friend. I gestured for him to come sit. He didn't move. "I was talking with my father today," he said, each word punching out like he had trouble forming it.

I took a sharp breath. "What happened?"

"I think he suspects something." His face quivered suddenly. Quivered like it was trying to split in two. "He informed me that he has eyes all over this castle. He was threatening me."

"What are you going to do?"

"Nothing. Be more careful." He stared past me, seeming at a loss for words. I noticed suddenly that a bruise was forming above his left eye. Gently, I placed my hand on his, and rested my forehead against his own.

Caladrius Dreams

For a moment I could think of nothing to say. "It worked," I told him finally. "The dream worked. I saw your brother and the shattered glass." Leo let out a long, slow breath. "I'm scared..." he whispered at last.

"I know," I answered, and my hand tightened over his. "I know."

22

Contagion

The air smelled wet and heavy with the scent of late fall. The yellow light of the day's end sparkled against the west window. I shifted a bit so I could see my needlework more clearly.

"Leslie, they're back." I jumped a little, my needle sliding so it pricked my finger. For a moment, I couldn't understand her words. They're back? Then, with a squeak unbecoming of a queen, I shot out of my chair. My work dropped forgotten to the floor.

"Derek." The word sounded foreign to me. I hadn't used it in so long. But something in my heart stirred, reminding me it had been my favorite word. My favorite word before it had run off with the soldiers to fight in this cursed war.

Running to tthe window, I leaned over the ledge and pressed my cheek against the glass, up near the top where it was thinner and I could see through more clearly. Off in the distance, in two lines as straight as an arrow, I could see men marching like ants. Tiny grey cloaks blurred their figures into the dusky light. But their presence could not be doubted. They were there. They were back. "Derek." I murmured again. A little louder this time. A little more breathlessly.

Turning from the window, I picked up my skirts and ran. With my dress hitched to bare my feet, I raced down the three flights of stairs, not caring who saw. I ran through the Main Hall and past the Great Room. Ignoring the guards who bowed and scraped and the ladies who whispered in the corners, I flung myself out the doors and paused at the top of the entrance steps, panting heavily. I wrapped my arms around a stone *pillar and peered through the waning light, trying desperately to see. And then, when my eyes could strain no longer, I saw him.*

He was seated on top of that big white stallion of his—the one I called a brute and he adored—with his arm wrapped up in a sling. I couldn't tell from here, but his face seemed bandaged too. It didn't matter. He was alive. Wonderfully, deliciously alive. Forgetting propriety, I loosed my hands from the pillar, picked up my skirts once more, and ran down the steps as quickly as I could to meet him. My silks rustled against the wet ground. The patter of my slippered feet seemed to ring with joy. Off in the distance I saw him dismount, and then he was running too. His face...

I woke with a lurch, clutching to my blankets and panting heavily as if I had just run a mile. Sweat creased my brow. Slowly, I relaxed into the pillows, counting heart beats until reality sunk back into focus. *My name is Calli. I'm in my bed, in the castle at Caeyra.* No mattter how long I continued recounting the facts, my heart didn't seem to want to slow its desperate hammering.

* * *

"Any dreams last night?"

I rolled my eyes at the boy squaring off in front of me, wooden broadsword in hand. "I saw another of my mother's memories," I told him matter-of-factly. Asking me whether I had dreamt was like asking if I had eaten this morning, or taken a breath last night. I was never without dreams these days.

We were in the far corner of the training field, well away from prying eyes. I had been begging Leo to let me practice with him for weeks, and he had finally caved. Doubtless, Master McDunnon wouldn't approve. Arcturus probably wouldn't either. But there was no reason he needed to know.

Most of the older Novices and Apprentices had already started. I could hear the clanking of swords off to my right, pierced by the occasional twang of a bowstring. "You ready?" Leo asked, both hands gripping the long pommel of his practice sword. He looked nervous, probably uncomfortable with the idea of fighting a girl.

I raised my eyebrow at him before pulling off my gloves and stowing them carefully in my cloak's deep pocket. "It's just practice Leo, don't look so uncomfortable."

"I might hurt you..." he muttered slowly, rolling the words over in his mouth as if he had trouble even thinking them.

"You don't have to partner me," I snapped back. "Go with Avery. I can find someone else. I just wanted to find someone other than Arcturus to spar with for a change."

The look he gave me was a strange cross of shame and shock. I wanted to pull the point of my sword up from the ground and hit him with the flat of it. He thought I couldn't take care of myself, did he? I'd show him. He shook his head slowly. "I don't want you with someone else," he groaned, looking genuinely stressed. "Who knows what they'll do?"

"I doubt they'll *do* much of anything." I answered bluntly. "Nothing worse than what Arcturus does on a daily basis anyway." I lifted my sword and turned as if to find another partner. Leo stopped me.

"No. I'll partner you. I said I would, didn't I?"

I turned back to face him, took my sword in one tightened hand, and stood on guard. "Good." I paused, and then added, "I wouldn't be so proud as to presume that *you'll* be the one to hurt *me.*" With a final grin, I raised my sword.

Despite all his complaining about lessons and school, the boy wasn't half bad. He bested me certainly in strength and was seasoned with several years more of practice. But he hadn't been training with Arcturus the past few months.

Leo lunged, his wooden blade reaching to make a winning blow. I stepped aside lightly, rapping him on the shin and laughing when he stumbled. I whirled and parried his next blow. I backed up several steps, narrowly escaping as he attacked to the left. Then, running through the list of forms Arcturus had taught me in my head, I drove him backward until he was forced to defend himself.

We continued silently for about another half hour before I heard Master McDunnon call out the lunch break. Distracted, I turned to look in his direction. With a whirling thump Leo's blow connected with my side. Giving out a strangled yelp, I crumpled to the ground where I lay, panting. I dug my bare fingers into the snow covered ground. It didn't hurt—much—he had just knocked the wind out of me. Leo's response was dramatic.

"Calli!" His sword dropped from his hands like a snake and he all but flung himself to my side. "Calli, are you okay? I know I shouldn't have been fighting you...I just knew you were going to get hurt...I..." Lifting my head, I silenced him with a rueful glance.

"I'm fine, Leo."

"Did I break anything? Bruises? Blood?" He made to reach for my cloak and I swatted him away. The boy sure could run on.

"Just a bruise I'm sure," I muttered weakly. "Nothing worse than what I've given you." There was a hint of sarcasm in my voice, and I rolled my eyes at him when he continued. "Really Leo. I'm fine." I forced myself to stand to prove it.

I *was* fine. After brushing the snow off of my cloak and dress I shook myself and assessed the damages. No bleeding. Nothing broken. My side was tender where his blow had struck, but nothing more. I took a few deep breaths to regain my lungs, and gave him a brief smile. Leo seemed to be calming, if only slightly. His eyes were still wide, but his face wasn't quite so pale. His shoulders didn't shake when he breathed. I almost laughed at him. Almost. "Let's go," I told him. Taking his arm, I led him back up the path and towards the castle.

We had just crossed the training field when a loud cry sounded behind us. Leo and I turned at the same time, looking back towards the source of the sound. A crowd had gathered on the eastern edge of the field, near the equipment shed. Not waiting to see if Leo was following, I picked up my skirts and ran in their direction.

The jostling heads of Novices were like a wall that was impossible for me to see over. I stood on tiptoes and tried to push my way in, but it was useless. Leo appeared at my shoulder.

"What's going on?" I asked him. He was taller than me by a head—just enough to have a decent view through the crowd.

"I can't tell from here, but it looks like something's happened to Master McDunnon."

Just then, Arcturus appeared, walking the path down from the castle in quick strides. Lady Dubois was close behind him. The sea of bodies gathered around Master McDunnon parted to let them through, and as they did, the scene became visible before me.

Master McDunnon was on the ground, his face ashen and his breathing labored. There was blood in the snow around him. "He started coughing up blood, and then he just collapsed," a Novice was saying, his voice pitched. My heart sped. Living in the streets had given me a lot of experience with sickness. I had seen people drop in the streets like Master McDunnon had. I knew what happened to them.

Before I could stop myself, my feet had turned and I was running. Partially, it was an ingrained response. In my previous life, when you saw evidence of a contagion, you stayed as far away from it as possible. Mostly however, I simply didn't want to stay around to see how this would play out. I was had grown fond of Master McDunnon. I didn't want to watch him die.

Leo caught up to me as I paused by a fir tree to catch my breath. "Calli?"

"He can't die," I whispered. He was so strong. So constant. A person like him couldn't die. "He can't," I said into the rough bark of the fir. I buried my fingers into the wood and closed my eyes.

"He'll be fine." Leo told me gently. "Arcturus and Lady Dubois are bringing him up to the Aviary now. You'll see. A few of Lady Dubois's potions and a bit of magic and he will be as good as new."

I turned my face from the tree to look up at him. His face was sincere, his eyes confident. "You promise?"

"I promise," Leo answered. I nodded, and let him pull me back towards the castle. Still, my heart was sick. I didn't feel so sure.

23

Surprises
and Denial

"Happy birthday, Calli." *Happy birthday? Is she kidding?* I looked around the sunroom. Everyone near me wore the same excited expression. She wasn't joking. After a moment of silent, ridiculous smiles, each member of the group stood primly, hugged me, and left the room. It was almost like they cared. Then I was alone, except for Ema, who was sitting there smiling at me like she had just conquered the world.

I should have been grateful, but the only thing which slipped out was frustrated accusation. "Who told you?" She had no way to know. I hadn't even known. My frown deepened.

The smile that grew on Ema's face said she had expected such a reaction. It also said clearly that she would not, under any circumstance, tell me how she knew. It seemed like a secret she was pleased in keeping. "Today is going to be the best day, Calli. I have all sorts of things planned. First, we can—"

I cut her off, incredulous. "I thought you weren't speaking to me," I snapped. She hadn't spoken a word to me since our fight. And she hadn't apologized. What gave her the right to talk to me now, as if nothing had ever happened?

"It's your birthday, Calli. What kind of friend would I be if I didn't speak to you today?" There it was. Behind her words and her smiles. I could see it now. This was a thinly veiled attempt to be cordial. I smiled and tried to play along. But my heart wasn't in it.

"Don't you think it's odd," she began, "that you were born on the same day as the anniversary of the death of our king and queen?" My eyes widened and I looked up from my food. I *had* known I had been born on the same day as my parent's death, but the thought hadn't occurred to me until she mentioned it. "I do not think it is coincidence at all," Ema confided closely. "I think it is destiny's proof that you were meant to be with us."

Something seemed wrong with my breathing. The tightness of my chest physically hurt. My parents had died the day I was born. Exactly fourteen years ago, that dream—the king of all nightmares—happened. It happened on this day. I was going to be sick. I opened my mouth and spluttered the first thing I could think of. Analyzing it later, I realized it was the truth. "Today's not my birthday," I told her quickly.

Ema looked startled. "Calli..." her tone had lost its playful quality. It now held the hurt defiance of a girl who had been angry, and was trying to play nice for a day. I cringed, and felt guilty. But that did not sway my heart.

"I'm sorry Ema...I don't expect you to understand." I told her, and my voice was a little softer. "I know you say my birthday's today. But I don't want to celebrate my birthday. Not today. I don't want to celebrate anything."

She looked angry and confused. I couldn't blame her. In fact, I pitied the girl. She had no idea what she was saying, no idea what she was doing to me. I'd be angry too, if we had to trade places, but I couldn't help it. The worst part, was that I couldn't even explain it to her. She had no way to understand that if today was my birthday, then I couldn't celebrate. I couldn't.

But why couldn't I tell her just enough? Enough that she could understand, but not enough to betray my secret? "My parents were killed on my birthday," I told her haltingly, as if the words alone had power to destroy me. "I don't want to celebrate that fact. Not when they died *because* of me. It was my fault. And I don't want to celebrate anything on a day when they gave *their* lives to save *mine.*" For a second I held my breath, certain she would put the pieces together. She didn't. No realization dawned on her face, the information I had so painfully given had been taken just the way I'd hoped. She attached it to the fact that I was from "Arusae" and assumed those faraway parents had died there.

Despite my revelation, I could tell she still didn't understand. The fact stung, and I turned away from her. There was nothing more I could safely tell her, but if the death of some pair of imaginary parents in Arusae wasn't enough, would the whole truth be any different? I choked back the urge to tell her more.

"I told you I don't want to talk about it, Ema." I didn't give her a chance to argue. I stood quickly and left the room. Once around the corner, I ran.

* * *

I hid myself in the library for the rest of the day. In truth, the library was the last place I wanted to be. The library, filled with books that seemed to whisper their secrets all around me. Secrets I would never know, and the answer that would explain what was happening to me. That would end the madness. That would let me be, or at least pretend to be, normal. I pushed such thoughts away. The dreams—and what they contained—were the last thing I wanted to think about right now. Especially on a day like today, when the worst of all those dreams had come true. I shivered, and curled up in a window seat between two shelves.

Maybe, if I tried hard enough, I could pretend that none of this had ever happened. I could pretend that I was still crouched in a box, rubbing my hands against the cold winter air. I could pretend that the dreams were nothing but dreams. Meaningless nightmares. But no matter how hard I tried, I couldn't believe it. My mother's fear, my father's dying face, they flashed through my mind as clear as a memory of my own.

I closed my eyes and rested my forehead against the cold window pane. Listening to the wind that moaned outside, I gave up and allowed the memories of my parents' deaths to replay in my mind.

* * *

"Calli?"

From behind me, a hand reached out and touched my shoulder. I groaned and turned my face from the voice. Letting my eyelids flicker open, I watched as my breath fogged up the window's icy glass. It was almost dark outside. The library had grown cold.

"Calli...it's—" I didn't let her finish.

"Yes Ema?" My voice was hoarse. If she was coming to scold, I didn't want to hear it. Slowly I turned my head, meeting her eyes with a level gaze.

"I just wanted to tell you that I'm sorry about this morning... and the other night, if it helps. I know you don't like being put in the spotlight like that. I should have waited until we were alone. For both things." She sat down on the seat beside me, forcing me to move my legs. Her apologies made me sick. She was apologizing for something that wasn't even an issue, and was leaving untouched the true problems that stood between us. I knew she wasn't going to offer a real apology. Not soon anyhow. My stomach sank. I was disappointed in myself for hoping she would.

"Happy birthday, Calli," she whispered, leaning in for a hug. I stiffened as her arms tightened around my shoulder. Looking confused and disgruntled, she pulled back.

"I was serious about what I said earlier, Ema. Today's not my birthday."

Her brows furrowed, and I watched as her full lips turned downwards into an angry pout. "You're being silly, Calli. Today is your birthday. Since last I checked, you can't just randomly change the date."

"Ema..." I replied slowly, biting off each word into chewable chunks. "Please try to understand. I'm grateful to you and everyone else for trying to make me happy today. I really am. I just really don't want to celebrate the day my parents died. I've already told you that."

"These parents of yours, in Arusae, did they die during the wars?" For the first time, I could see her trying to understand. I rewarded her with a smile. "Do you remember much?"

Caladrius Dreams

I shook my head. "I was too young," I told her, not wanting to allude to the fact that those parents had died the day I had been born, not just on my birthday. Too many coincidences could make her put together the pieces which I desperately needed to remain hidden. "Do you remember that nightmare I had several weeks ago? When Lady Dubois brought me the sleeping potion?" She nodded and I continued, stiffly trying my best to make her understand. "That dream was about their death. I watched a man kill my family. I watched my father die, protecting us. My mother could have run—she could have gotten away. But she didn't. She died, standing in front of me, hoping against hope that I wouldn't die with her. Please Ema, try to understand. I don't want a birthday today. I don't deserve one."

Ema's face was white now, and her voice shook more than a little when she spoke. "It was only a dream..." she whispered.

"Yeah. It was only a dream." I stood slowly and left before she could see my tears. A sick knot had formed in the base of my stomach. Only a dream. I had wished all day for that to be the truth. I had pretended I believed it as hard as I could. But no matter how I tried, no amount of wishing could make it true.

* * *

I was on my way back to my room after dinner to lay in my bed early. I wasn't planning on sleeping. All I wanted was to lay down, hidden in the folds of my blankets and rest my weary body. Miraculously, Arcturus had called off our practice for the night. I was free to rest.

To my surprise, Leo was waiting by my door. The smile he gave me was almost infectious. "How was your day?" He asked innocently, blocking my way to the room. He opened his mouth as if to say more, but the words seemed to die in his throat. "What's wrong?"

For a moment all I felt was surprise. How could he have known? I had been sure I was concealing my feelings about the day quite well. But my smile fell as he examined me. He could see behind the fake grin. Leo had never been one to fall for pretended airs.

"I'm having trouble with the dreams today," I told him honestly, unsure of how to begin.

"Then let's not think about them," Leo answered gallantly, taking my arm. "It wouldn't do for my birthday girl to be worried."

His words made me freeze up. I tore my arm from his grasp. "Today's not my birthday." The answer came out automatically now. My stomach twisted and I picked at a bit of lint on my sleeve.

He opened his mouth to argue, and then stopped. His lips formed a silent 'o' and his eyes met mine. Recognition dawned on his face. I didn't need to explain a single word. He already knew. "Ema wasn't happy when you told her that, was she?"

I shook my head.

"I'm sorry," he whispered, and continued hurriedly before I could stop him. "I'm the one that told her. I thought it would be a nice surprise. I wasn't thinking."

Forcing a smile, I joked, "Did you bribe Arcturus to give me a night off as well?"

"Actually, I did. I was planning on—well, it doesn't matter anymore." For a moment, he paused, apparently deep in thought. Then, he smiled and held out a hand. "Walk with me?" I took his hand, and did my very best to smile back.

It was dark in the halls, and we walked through them rather quickly. Leo led me down the stairs and to the right, towards a side door that would lead to the gardens. Once outside, I paused for a second to let the peaceful silence of the falling snow soak in. Then I gave him a nod, and he led me on.

We came to a halt in front of two stone slabs, surrounded and covered by an overgrowth of rose bushes and ivy. "No one's come out here because of the Treaty," Leo said. "It wasn't allowed. But now that the Treaty is broken, well, I thought you'd want to see them."

Reaching out, I brushed the ivy back from the surface of one of the slabs. There was writing carved into the stone, I realized. Names, and dates. They were gravestones. The names belonged to my parents.

"Thank you," I whispered to Leo, who stood several paces behind me. A single rose still bloomed on one of the bushes to my left, hidden under the overgrowth and protected from the snow. Reaching forward, I broke it off its branch, and dropped it at the foot of the grave. A single tear slid down my cheek. I didn't bother to wipe it away.

24

A Perfect Day

"Calli!" Leo was practically skipping towards my spot in the snowy gardens. I rolled my eyes, pretending to ignore him as I patted the snow into the semblance of a snowman. Master McDunnon was still sick, and Leo, of course, was elated at the prospect of having no practice. I shouldn't have been surprised.

"Yes?" His bright expression made me feel like I was talking to a small child. His hands were hidden behind his back and his lips were twisted into that mischievous grin.

"You wouldn't let me celebrate your birthday yesterday, and I completely understand."

"Mmmm..." I didn't like where this was going.

"But, you can't possibly have any good reasons as to why you can't celebrate today." There was a strange sort of sparkle in his eyes. It made me nervous.

"No." I had been right. This really wasn't going anywhere good. I groaned and tried to look away.

"Please?" He put on his best pathetic face.

"Fine." There was no real reason why to deny him his little bit of fun. There was also no real reason why I had to have fun as well.

"Great!" Before I could protest, he had drug me to my feet, effectively smashing the thing I had tried to call a snowman. "I almost forgot," he proclaimed, turning to reach for something he had dropped on the ground. "Happy birthday, Calli." From behind his back he pulled out a small cluster of lilies. And then he kissed me. Kissed me square on the cheek. I'm sure my eyes were as large as saucers.

"Uh..." What else do you say in a moment like this?

"Do you not like them?" He sounded disappointed. "You said they were your favorite."

"Oh...uh...no!" I was stammering. My face felt as if someone had lit a fire under my skin. "I love them. I'm just a little shocked is all. I've never had a birthday before..." I trailed off pathetically. He remembered? Yes, I had said they were my favorite, but I hadn't expected him to *remember*. It was small talk. Not valuable information.

"Well...uh...I'm glad you like them." he mumbled, smiling shyly at the ground. What was up with him today?

"How...uh.." I began, searching for something to say. My throat seemed to stick and my brain wasn't working quite right. "How did you find these?" I asked him, gesturing at the flowers now clumped in my hands. "It's the middle of winter."

Leo laughed, a short bark that seemed to echo off the castle walls. "You're thinking like a commoner, Cali," he answered diplomatically. And then that playful fire whipped into his eyes and spoiled the guise. He grinned at me like a child and pulled at my free hand. "This," he said, patting the flowers, "is what magic is for!" he laughed again and pulled me towards the castle.

* * *

"Close your eyes."

I groaned.

"I said close them!"

"But Leo..."

"No peeking!" He slapped his hands over my face, blocking my sight completely. "Now forward!"

"What—"

"Shh. It's a surprise!" He sounded utterly happy about this. *Too* happy.

"Leo, I can't walk forward if I can't see anything."

"Trust me." There was something in his voice, some emotion I couldn't quite detect. Questioning was only driving me crazy. So, I did the only thing I could do in such a situation. I trusted him. He shoved me forward into a slow walk.

The air was getting colder. My footsteps echoed through the room. "Where—" He cut me off.

"Stairs! And step...now. And now..." his hands guided me down. Somehow, I didn't fall. Not once. "One more time...now. Almost there!"

"Leo..."

"Open your eyes!" His hands came away from my face, and he was smiling. Smiling happily, if a bit too much. I didn't know whether to be pleased, or frightened. I blinked, and stared stupidly at the door in front of me.

"It's a door," I muttered, nonplussed.

Leo's enthusiasm never wavered. "Don't you know where we are?"

It had to be a trick question. It just had to be. We were obviously somewhere lower in the castle. "Somewhere cold?" I suggested casually. How original.

"We are in the servant's quarters!" He laughed as if this were a joke. It wasn't. It really wasn't. His neurotic joy was beginning to grate on my nerves. I rolled my eyes. "Go on, open the door!" I was growing sick of how everything he said seemed noted by an exclamation.

"Fine." What was he showing me in the servant's quarters? Servants? It wasn't as if I had never seen one. What did any of this have to do with this "pretend" birthday idea of his? A loud groan betrayed my frustration. I placed a hand on the knob, and turned it slowly. The door pushed open with a squeak.

The hum of working reached my ears, and a sallow light split through the darkness of the corridor. With a hand on my back, Leo pushed me through the door. I stumbled forward, uncertain of what to expect.

Somewhere in the back of my mind, I had been painting myself the image of a line of white sheeted beds, or of a storage closet rowed in tools. That would have been exactly the sort of thing Leo would have thought to drag me to. Instead, I saw ovens. I saw pots, and pans. Flours, and sugars, and spices, and an assortment of things I couldn't even name. A few dogs laid in the corner, watching for scraps. This wasn't a storage closet. It was a kitchen.

My breath caught as a plump woman found my eye. Without a word she bustled over and with a warm smile she hurried us to a small table in the back of the room. Leo was glowing when I turned to look at him. "Isn't this amazing?" he whispered to me. He was proud of himself. I could see it in his face. But for once, I didn't mind. I just smiled and laughed a little, and let my eyes stray through the room.

My wonderment faded with my smile as I took in the whole of the room. This was not the castle as I knew it. The walls were dirty and grey. The light was not the happy yellow I had come to expect. It was the dusty light of disrepair. The room was tidy and the atmosphere cheery, but I couldn't ignore the stains that dressed the countertops, or the cold that cloaked the air. I couldn't ignore the way my nose ran, or how my fingers turned blue. No, this was not the castle I knew. This was my home on the streets, surrounded by four walls and filled with the drone of work. I stiffened as a maid in white place a mug of cider before me. Shivering, I tucked a strand of hair behind my ear. "Leo," I hissed, watching as he buried his face into his drink.

"Mmm?" his voice was muffled in the bowl of his cup. I continued without waiting for further reply.

"How can they treat them like this?"

"Calli?" his voice was no longer coated with joy. He sounded cautious. Even worried. I could see his face flinch away from my words.

"It's just not fair..." I murmured quietly.

"I know. Believe me, I know. But it's always been like this. There isn't anything even *you* could do about it. It just *is.*"

I took a long sip from my cider, staring at a gash in the table before me. Suddenly, I felt terrible. Leo had been trying to be nice. And I had to go and ruin it all by complaining about something that wasn't in his power to fix. "I'm sorry Leo," I whispered. He smiled at me from over his mug and for a moment, the room didn't seem quite so dreary.

"I'm sorry too...I shouldn't have taken you down here. I just—"

"Don't worry about it. I'd rather know, than be ignorant. The happiness of ignorance is a poor price to pay for this." I gestured to the room with a ruff sweep of my hand, and took another sip of cider.

"I just wanted you to be happy," he whispered. There was something heartbreaking in his voice and in the expression on his face. "I thought you'd be more comfortable down here, than up there with all of that—" With a hand he gestured at the main castle above us. "I know how you feel about the way they treat you. I just wanted you to feel normal for once...just for one day." He gave me a weak sort of smile.

"I *am* happy Leo. Thank you." That was all I needed to say for him to understand. His smile returned.

One of the dogs in the corner—a large wolfhound—trotted over and sat by my side to nuzzle my hand with his slender snout. Awkwardly, I patted his head, and then ran my hand down to bury my fingers into the white fur around his neck. It was warm and soft.

"I think he likes you," Leo chuckled. I smiled in response.

He gestured with a hand and asked one of the women for a cake. His voice was soft and gentle—compassionate. And, were I a sappy romantic—which I would *never* be, especially with my best friend—I would have said there were stars in his eyes.

* * *

"Leo! Stop it!" My words were sharp, but laughter softened them. Leaning over, I bent to shake the snow out of my hair. Trailing us at a distance was the hound from the kitchen. He had followed us up the steps and out into the snow, trotting along like a shadow in the trees. We had gone outside with the intention of walking around the lake. We never got further than three steps into the trees before Leo had declared war.

"Why?" He was smirking in a feigned sort of innocence, but I saw what he held as he casually ducked behind the branches of a dark pine. There was more snow in his hands. His innocence wasn't innocence at all.

I turned away from him, meaning to continue our attempted walk around the lake. It was a mistake I should have never made. The minute my back was turned, a snowball hurtled into it. For a moment the flush of anger rushed to my cheeks, and then I laughed and ducked to grab at the snow.

I had never been in a snowball fight before. It wasn't the sort of thing you wasted precious energy on, back in my previous life. But I had seen kids do it before; laughing kids with food in their bellies and a sparkle in their eyes. I scooped up some snow into my fist, desperate to pack it to fling-able size. Several more clods bounced off my back before I could manage a hand sized ball. Leo's laughter was taunting. It came from somewhere behind a stand of trees.

The next few minutes passed in a blur of snowflakes. All caution was lost, and eventually we found ourselves scrambling across the ground on hands and knees, flinging fistfuls of snow into each other's faces. Giggling, I collapsed on my back and threw several desperate handfuls his direction. The ground gave a muffled thump as he dropped beside me. Snow scattered my hair, falling down the back of my cloak. I smashed a handful of snow into his face with my palm and rolled away, burying my head in my arms. I stayed there on my stomach for several minutes before I turned back to look at him.

He was on his back, his eyes turned upwards to the sky. It was growing dark rather rapidly, and the first stars were beginning to sprinkle the horizon.

"Aren't they beautiful?" I breathed. Out from the trees, the dog came and dropped down beside me. Distractedly, I let a hand run through its brown and white fur.

"Hmm?"

"The stars! Aren't they beautiful?"

"Yeah..." He sounded rather preoccupied. I curled up on my back next to him, and began to trace lines in the sky.

"Sometimes, I think maybe they are the tears of angels, suspended out there in space." I whispered softly. I followed the statement with a sigh, and turned my head to look at him.

"Sometimes, I think maybe you let your imagination run away with you." Shifting, he crossed his arms behind his head, and gestured to the sky with his chin. "Do you know the constellations?"

"Uh...sorta..." I peered into the sky, pretending to see images painting themselves in the sky. Maybe if I squinted hard enough, he would believe me.

"Look there," he told me, pointing to a large cluster somewhere above our heads. "That's the Great Bear. And if you follow the top two stars, there's Polaris. The Guide Star"

"I..." my face flushed suddenly and I found myself glad it was dark. All I saw was a strange mess of dots. "I don't see it."

"There..." he took my hand in his, and pointed it in the direction of a particularly bright star. I saw it.

"That's it?" My voice was a hesitant whisper. I smiled cautiously in the dark.

"Yeah." He laughed softly and pointed to a slightly higher point in the glistening sky. "That's Draco, the dragon. You can see his back wrapping up around the top of Polaris."

I squinted, and I stared, but Draco the constellation just wouldn't show itself to me. "All I see is a bunch of shiny dots," I muttered.

"That's all I saw at first too. See that kite shaped cluster up there?"

"...yeah..."

"That's his head."

"Oh!"

"And if you follow the stars down to the right of Polaris, that's his neck."

"Which stars?"

"There." He pointed.

"I see them!" No sane person should feel this excited about seeing an imaginary picture in the sky. "That's him?" Obviously, I wasn't sane.

"Yes."

I smiled proudly, and carefully scrutinized the sky. "Leo?"

"Yes?"

"Why do you know so much about the stars?" I rolled over to face him, my eyes glittering in the dark.

"My family was into it. Most noble families are. A mark of rank I think. Only the wealthy have the time to sit around and stare at the sky." His face tightened as he stared up into the sky and beside me, his hands clenched. "It's like a tradition I suppose. My parents used to take me out every night and force me to learn the names of every star and constellation."

"How lovely!"

"Yeah...I guess."

I rolled onto my back, and returned my eyes to the sky. "I wish I knew it so well..."

"A lot of families name their kids after stars, you know."

"Really? I never noticed. Is your name a star?"

"A constellation actually. It's not out right now."

"What is it?"

"A lion." His lips tightened, and I immediately felt as if I was nearing a sensitive topic. I fell quiet, and the silence grew around us. Leo didn't point out anymore constellations. Instead, I could feel his attention become lost in the stars above. And as I gazed happily at their beauty I could feel him tense beside me, lost in thoughts I could never know.

* * *

I was with Arcturus late that night. It was as if he was punishing me for being late. Magic was coming easier now but by the time we were done, I was exhausted. I stumbled back to my room, planning to fall asleep the minute I fell into my bed.

It was dark in the room when I entered. Cold, and dark. The fire glowed only faintly and I could hear the soft tick of a clock humming somewhere nearby. The dog had somehow found its way to a spot of carpet by the fire. I smiled and crossed the floor to the closet, planning to fetch my night gown. A figure rose up from the armchair, breaking up the shadows in the dark.

"Calli?"

"Ema."

"I...I'm sorry." For a moment, I couldn't quite take in her words. My hand froze on its way to the silk fabric of a gown.

"Oh. Ema, it's—"

"It's not fine." I loved how she just knew what I was about to say. "I was thinking today...and I think...you're one of my best friends, Calli. I haven't treated you right. Or...Leo." His name was forced, but she said it. I turned to her, smiling slightly. "I think maybe I was wrong. I've complained about him, but he's done more for you than I ever have. I've called him a traitor, but I think maybe I'm the one that betrayed you. Can you forgive me?"

Her words made my heart melt, and I found suddenly that I couldn't be angry any longer. "All's forgiven Ema." I smiled at her, and she smiled back.

"I never got you anything for your birthday," she blurted suddenly. "Leo's idea of celebrating today was a good one. I noticed," she added with a smile. "But I didn't get you anything today or yesterday." Her face twisted with regret.

"Well..." I paused for a moment, thinking. "Sit. Just sit on the bed with me, and we'll talk. That's the only birthday present I need." I pulled her down on the bed beside me and curled comfortably by her side. "We haven't had the chance for a really good talk for quite some time." I smiled into the dark, and as I listened to her speak, a little thought came flooding into my heart. I could tell Ema about the dreams. She would understand, or at least as much as she could. A secret shared between three is a bit easier to shoulder than one borne by two. Leaning my head against her knee I took a deep breath. It had been a perfect day.

25

Tale of the Past

"Sweet girl. Sweet baby girl," the woman cooed, leaning over me. I smiled, letting out a burble of happy giggles. I reached my arms upwards, towards her shining face.

She scooped me into her arms the way a man would carry a bride. Bringing me to the kitchen, she set me down on a chair, and turned her softly wrinkled face to the pantry. My mouth watered at the plate of bread and cheese that she carried as she came back to the table. A glass of thick goat's milk was in her other hand. Both the plate and glass shook the wood beneath my small fingers with a muffled clunk. I smiled the toothy grin of a seven-year-old who hadn't all her teeth. I wiggled in my seat and reached for the thickest slab of cheese. "Thank you Auntie Margaret," I gurgled.

Sweeping a loose strand of snow-white hair behind an ear, she smiled back at me. Her eyes...

There was sunlight streaming in through the curtains, casting the room with the thin, pale sheen of morning. I sat slowly, rubbing the sleep from my eyes. For a moment, I wasn't sure if I was awake, or in another dream. Beside me, the dog—who had been following me around since my pseudo-birthday—yawned and stretched. *The dog's here*, I thought sleepily. He had yet to be in a single one of my dreams. Burying my fingers into his fur, I pulled myself back into reality.

* * *

It was hard to ignore the eerie chill that seemed to cover the room. I was at breakfast late—a half hour or so later than Ema—after having spent a rather sleepless night. Apparently, several Novices had fallen sick—and showed the same symptoms as Master McDunnon. Nervous voices hissed through the room. The illnesses of the winter season were here. I shivered and pushed my food away, hunching deeply in my seat. The sense of the unknown—clinging wispily to the edges of the imagination—was putting everyone on edge.

"Ema, stop that." Her fork rapped erratically on the edge of the table table. She ignored me, and I pulled the fork from her grasp. "You're making me nervous." Now unoccupied, her twitching fingers flew to her mouth. Her teeth bit down on her already too-short nails. I rolled my eyes, and turned away from her. I had other things to think about. I didn't need more complications.

"You're being awfully quiet this morning, Calli," Leo commented suddenly, appearing out of thin air by my side. Like the rest of the Novices, he still had no lessons with Master McDunnon so sick. Where he had been all morning, I had no clue.

"Just thinking." I pushed at an egg on my plate and then dropped my fork. My stomach gave a disappointed sort of groan.

"Thinking about what?" He pulled my plate away when I began to poke at my egg with a finger and gave me a level look.

To avoid his gaze, I glanced over at Ema beside me. Her nails were still in her mouth, her eyes growing wider by the second. The girls sitting beside her flashed Leo dirty looks behind demure lashes. Now that Ema was friendly with the boy, they wouldn't oppose him outright. But not even Alastair himself could change their silent opinions. I turned the corner of my lip in a half attempt of a smile. *Let them think what they like. I don't, and never have, cared.* I copied their guise and hid my thoughts behind batting eyes. A poke at my arm brought me back to the current situation.

"Talk to me."

"I don't really want to." It was an honest answer, but I don't think he liked it. His scowl was proof. "I had a dream, last night." I answered finally.

"A non-normal dream?" His attempt at innocence was failing. I scowled heavily at him.

"Of course a non-normal dream, you half-wit. Look, can we talk about this somewhere else?"

"Library?"

I nodded sharply, and stood. Beside me, Ema shook her head, signaling that she didn't want to come. A small part of me was glad. I appreciated her company and loved her concern, but I was relieved to have a break from her. Ever since I had told her about the dreams, she had been exceedingly, and perhaps obnoxiously, helpful. Whether trying to make up for past months, or trying to one-up Leo, I wasn't sure, but I appreciated the gesture. It was simply the way in which she chose to do it that was mildly annoying, following me around as if she thought I would have another "panic attack" from the dreams, or as if she thought I couldn't take care of myself. I glanced over my shoulder at her quickly, and then followed Leo from the room.

Leo made it to the library faster than I, and when I rounded the second flight, he was there waiting. Going to our table in the far corner, I stopped and rounded on him. This talk wasn't going to be pretty. I wanted it over with.

Taking a deep breath, I tightened my fingers on the edge of the table. "I was a young girl, in the dream..." I started in a whisper.

"Do you know who it was? Who you were, in the dream I mean?" Leo leaned forward, his face expressive. I looked away from him, focusing my eyes on a deep crack in the table. I didn't want him to see the tears that were beginning to cloud my vision. The answer was simple.

"Yes."

"Who then?"

"It was me." The tears were coming faster now. They scraped my cheeks as they fell.

"You?"

I nodded. "It happens sometimes. Before I came here, the only intelligible dreams I *had* were of my own memories. I had other dreams back then too—which I realize now were the memories of other people, just so garbled I couldn't make sense of them."

"Why are you crying? What happened?" His hand caught my chin, forcing my eyes to his.

I pondered his question for a moment. In truth, nothing had happened. Not in the dream at least. But moments after that second in time, something had happened that I had tried to erase from my mind forever—something that had plagued my dreams for years. This was the first happy dream I had ever had of her. I chewed on my lip, and pulled my face from his hand. "Nothing."

"What happened, Calli?" His voice was firm.

"It was a happy dream," I whispered. "From my childhood. I was with Margaret, the woman who practically raised me. She and her husband were like the parents I never had. That memory, the one in my dream, it was the last memory I have of her." I cringed as I spoke. The words weren't entirely true. That hadn't been the *last* memory I had. But close. Close enough. Leo looked thoughtful.

"I thought you grew up on the streets."

"I did grow up on the streets. Since I was about seven anyway. My life before then is hazy." Wiping the tears from my eyes, I allowed myself to become lost in the memories I had kept from myself for so long. "I remember she taught me to read. To write and count. To clean my room, and to dig a garden. Her husband Barry taught me to ride a horse, to pick berries, and to sing. We lived in the country, where it was beautiful and green. I remember that much. And I remember the stories she used to tell me. There was one in particular. She used to say she had found me on her porch when I was an infant, barely old enough to walk. She said one morning there had been a bird in the window. A pure white bird. The bird had flown away, and that she then heard a knock on the door, like the pecking of a woodpecker. She told me she opened the door then, and that there was no bird in sight. Only me." I laughed a little, and buried my face into my shoulder. "Sometimes, it almost seemed like she thought it was the bird that brought me," I whispered into the fabric of my dress.

"What happened?" Leo asked softly. He had been silent through my story, but he now leaned forward solemnly. "What happened that day after the dream's end?"

I opened my mouth to speak, and then my shoulders shook. "I...I" my voice broke. "I don't really know. Everything gets so hazy after that. I've tried so hard not to remember. I remember I was sitting at the table when they burst in. She hid me in the closet just before they got to her. They took her away from me, then. They drug her away screaming and then...and then everything was silent. There was smoke in the air, and flames. Uncle Barry's boots were hanging in the doorway by the rafters. I ducked under them and ran and didn't look back.

"I went back there once. Back to the farm in the trees, with its little garden and the ivy all around. It was a long time ago, when I still believed in hope. The entire farm was burned to the ground. There were two little graves under the apple tree." I pulled my arm clear of Leo's hand, and focused on the tassels at the end of my shawl. I twitched one between two fingers and tried to forget.

"Calli...I'm so sorry."

"Don't be. It was a long time ago."

"Were they Baldassarre's men?"

I shook my head, turning away from him to face the window. "No." I stood and took a few steps from the table before turning back to him. "They were men in dark grey cloaks." Shrugging my shawl closer around my shoulders, I walked away.

"Calli, wait!" Leo ran after me, but I kept walking. I didn't feel like talking about it anymore, especially after that look on his face when I had implicated the Guardians.

"I don't want to talk right now."

"You don't have to talk. Just let me walk with you."

"I want to be alone."

"Are you mad at me?"

Those words made me stop in my tracks. I wasn't mad at him. I couldn't be. The fact that his cloak was grey said nothing of him. He had only been seven too, back then. He had never been to the castle—Novices weren't admitted to the castle until they were nine—or possibly even outside his region, at that time. Nothing of the past could be blamed on him. Leo Thurman would never do something like that. I knew him too well to doubt it. His hand reached in my direction. His eyes seemed tight. "No."

"I'm sorry about what they did."

"Me too. But there's nothing to be done about it now."

"Do you know why?"

It seemed a foolish question. Who really cared? The simple fact was that it had happened. No reason could justify the event. "No. No I don't. But I don't want to know." His hand reached for my arm and rested there. I smiled weakly, and then my face became lined with fierce determination. "Someday, I'm going to be the queen. Someday I'll have the ability to change things like that. I'll be able to control what the Guardians can and can't do...and I can make sure justice is carried out fairly. Even for the poorest of farmers." I pushed my brows together until a crease formed between them and balled my fists by my side. The faces of the forgotten poor flashed before my eyes. "Someday I will be able to change everything. Someday, I swear it."

We were in front of my room now. I pushed open the door and walked in. I sat on my bed with my knees pulled up to my chest and buried my head in my arms. When he came close I pushed my arms at him as if to make him go away, but gave in when he ignored me and sat by my side. Forgetting decorum and any sense of propriety I gave in to my emotions, and cried.

* * *

"Calli!" After a quick rap on the door Ema came flooding into the room. Her eyes were wild with a mixture of excitement and alarm. Her hands seemed to have a mind of their own.

"What happened?" My tears had long since dried, but I raised my head from Leo's chest with trepidation. I did not want her to see the crusty tracks that streaked my face. Ema seemed too frenzied to notice.

"Lady Roselle has taken sick! She was carried up to the Aviary hardly an hour ago. We were all in the sunroom when she simply fell out of her seat!"

Scrubbing at my cheeks, I sat up from the bed and let my feet slide onto the ground. Lady Roselle was the Mistress of the Youth, it was her job to keep track of and help the young ladies—like Ema—who had been sent to the court to be refined and "join society". The pit of my stomach churned and the hairs on the back of my neck stood on end. Something wasn't right. Taking my shawl from its hook, I slipped it over my shoulders. "I'll be back," I told them. And before either could argue, I left them there and hurried from the room. I needed to speak with my uncle.

Uncle Alastair was not in his office, but a servant at the door informed me that he was upstairs in the Aviary. I headed there immediately, my mind reeling.

I was used to sickness. On the streets where I had grown up, illness was a fact of life and death a very real threat. But my knowledge of illness also let me know another fact. Members of the upper class—having full access to magic and medications—rarely became sick. There was no way, here at the Court, that the higher standing members of the nobility—and those of great influence such as Master McDunnon and Lady Roselle—were not powerfully warded against ever becoming ill. It made sense perhaps that the servants, Guardians—including Novices and Apprentices—and even lower ranking lords and ladies might occasionally become ill. For someone like Lady Roselle or Master McDunnon, the probability of illness was so low it was almost nonexistent. The probability of both becoming ill, and in quick succession, was simply zero.

A young Guardian paced in front of the Aviary door. When I had made it clear I meant to pass through, he stopped me. His face was stone. "You aren't allowed in there."

"Said who?"

"The High Lord Alastair, milady."

"Is he inside?"

"Yes, milady."

"Bring him to me."

"Milady, I cannot—"

I put on my most convincing face and squared my shoulders. "I must speak with him immediately." The young Guard did not know I was the princess, but I was still a lady and he a Guardian, and therefore he was outranked. He had to obey.

"Yes, milady." The boy gave a short bow, and disappeared behind the high doors.

It was several moments before my uncle appeared. He looked worn, and there was a hardness about his face. He took my shoulder in a hand and steered me around the corner. Silently, he spread the fingers of one hand and I saw the air around us shimmer. We had been surrounded by a sound barrier, very simple magic from what Arcturus had explained. No one would hear this conversation.

"I expected more from you, child. Imagine my horror when I hear that you, of all people, have come storming up here, demanding to see me even after you have been told that no one is allowed to enter."

"I'm sorry uncle I just—"

"What made you think you were exempt from my orders?"

"As the princess, I assumed my place was to help our people. My Oath binds me to it."

His face softened a bit, but his iron grip on my shoulder didn't loosen. "Do you understand why I am not allowing anyone to enter this room? We don't yet know the nature of this illness. I will risk no more people in that room than I have to. Especially not you. We have placed special warding around the room. It is very complicated magic, and very strong, but I cannot be certain how well it will hold. Do I make myself clear?" His dark brows pulled themselves into what looked like a worried frown. I felt myself waver under his glance, but I pushed on.

"Something isn't right, uncle," I said quickly, explaining my theory. He was backing away from me and I could tell he was not listening. My voice piqued and I urgently tried to force out my thoughts. He didn't seemed concerned, not suspicious in the least. He had to hear me. "Have you considered biological warfare? Perhaps Baldassarre—"

"Your imagination is running away with you, child. Go rest. Have some tea with Lady Ema. I will send a servant up with warm honey and some crackers. A little warmth might do you good."

"But uncle—"

"I am busy. Whatever you have to say, it can wait." Before I could say another word, he broke away. The warding around us shattered and he disappeared around the corner. I heard muffled comments to the young Guardian, the scuffle of feet, and then the creak of the Aviary door. It clicked shut behind him and he was gone. For a moment, all I could do was stand dumbfounded. Then I shook myself and headed back towards my room. The sneaking suspicion that something was not right still haunted me. But if my uncle wouldn't hear me, it seemed there was nothing I could do. I had too many things to think of anyway. It seemed better to trust his judgment. I pushed away my worries stubbornly. My uncle would know what to do.

26

Arcturus's Gift

Tonight was MidWinter night, a feast, Leo told me, that marked the middle of winter and joyfully looked towards the spring which glistened hopefully on the distant horizon. It was early morning, and Leo and I were in the library researching. We were up early to make full use of every little moment of free time we had.

I was sitting at a desk in the far corner, directly across from Leo with a book in both hands. The dog was lying next to me, his hare-like front feet stretched out in front of him, and his long swan neck draped across my foot.

"You really should give him a name," Leo commented. "At this point he's practically your dog."

I glanced at the wolfhound at my feet. "How about Pan?" I suggested. "Because I met him in the kitchen."

Leo laughed. "Pan it is," he said. The dog lifted his head for a half second, and then dropped it back to the ground. For a moment, I felt certain he was laughing with us.

Turning back to the books, I dropped the one I had been scanning into the "read" pile. It had been talking about memories, yes, but memories in normal dreams. Normal wasn't getting me anywhere. These dreams were anything but. I grabbed another book off the top of the endless pile, and flipped it open to a random page.

"Keeping a dream diary is often...."

I slammed the book shut. A dream diary was not something I was interested in right now. Besides, dream diaries were for normal dreams, the kind you forgot minutes after waking. I only wished these dreams were the type which were easily forgotten—but wishing would get me nowhere. I tossed the book into the growing pile of failures and started on yet another. This process repeated itself for a long time.

Several hours later, I sat curled in my seat—legs folded neatly beneath me—absentmindedly going through what seemed like the thousandth book. I ran a hand through my hair and glanced up at Leo. He was sitting on the table now, his feet resting on the seat of his chair. A book lay in his hands and his nose had buried so deep in it I could barely see the tops of his eyebrows. I sighed, running my hand through my hair again and leaning back in my chair.

The book in front of me was snatched suddenly from my hands. "I've been looking for you for hours."

Leo's face had frozen in its frown and was now turned upwards away from his book. I turned quickly to look at the figure looming behind me. I knew that voice. "I've just been in here reading."

"Reading?" Arcturus's normally stoney face seemed like granite laced over with ice. His golden eyes were dark. "Leave, Thurman." He still didn't know that Leo knew who I was. I wasn't going to tell him. One glance from Arcturus, and Leo stood faster than I had thought possible. Once we were properly alone, the man turned his gaze on me. "Your uncle, the High Lord, has ordered me to see to it that you halt any and all association with young Thurman. Your friendship with him is making the people of the court uncomfortable, and your uncle thinks it would not be wise to develop prejudices against you when these people must one day be your allies. You have tonight, and then after that you are not to speak with him any longer."

Something like rage welled up in my chest, and then died down to a simmering dismay. "Arcturus..." I began, for a moment uncertain of what to say.

"I expect to see you in my study, ready for lessons, in an hour." His face never changing in its expression, he turned to leave.

"You are not always so easily persuaded by my uncle's ideas," I said boldly, before he could go. My voice was on the edge of breaking in frustration. "I can't believe you would agree with this. Leo is my best friend, surely you cannot be cruel enough to enforce such a command." He didn't seem to hear me. His feet continued their way to the door. My eyes narrowed, and a small bit of bitterness worked its way into my heart. Arcturus's family was no better than Leo's. He had no right. "How could you do this when you are the same as him?" The accusation in my voice left a sting in the air. Arcturus's steps came to a halt and his back stiffened, but he did not turn around.

"It was not your uncle's idea," he told me. Facing away from me as he was, I could not see his expression. "It was mine." Then, cloak sweeping out behind him, he left the room.

"Well that makes things complicated." Leo muttered, appearing suddenly from behind a bookshelf. "You didn't actually expect me to leave did you?" he asked when I stared at him. "I went out the door and came in through the back. I've been behind that shelf there the whole time." He laughed, and then suddenly was serious. "You don't think Master Sheridan really means what he said, does he?"

"I think he does. And I think he means to enforce it as well. But that doesn't mean I'm going to listen. We have until tomorrow, so let's not waste any time today." Deftly, I pulled a new book from my stack. "We can find a way around this, I'm sure. I'll figure something out, and he'll never be the wiser." I gave Leo a bitter smile and, adjusting the blue tasseled shawl around my shoulders, turned back to my books.

* * *

Dinner was over—a feast filled with too much food and too

much mirth—and I was ready to go upstairs. The Great Room seemed very empty tonight, a fact I could attribute to the Aviary being much too full. The feast of MidWinter night seemed to clash with dissonance against that. MidWinter was a night for celebrating the coming end of winter, and remembering we had made it this far through the winter illnesses and cold. Except we hadn't. Too many people were in the Aviary, under Lady Dubois's care—though a glance to my right showed me she was here tonight. Just today, I had heard news that many of the castle's servants had already lost their lives to the strange illness which had laid siege to the castle. And yet not a person at the feast seemed to remember any of that. My stomach felt sick.

I left the table, and made my way to my room. Ema would be waiting there, having left much earlier from dinner than I with the excuse that she needed a nap, and Leo would be up as soon as he could. I had been prepped by Arcturus at my lesson earlier of what MidWinter was all about, so I fully expected the little wrapped package she handed me as I entered the room.

"MidWinter is a time when we celebrate that winter will soon be over," Arcturus had told me. "It reminds the people to hope, and it reminds them that even winter cannot last forever. It is traditionally a time when we celebrate the relationships we have with people. When we thank and enjoy those who are still with us." Distractedly, I touched the ring that now hung by a chain around my neck. Several gold bands entangled like the branches of a nest and two little gold birds perched in flight around a tiny stone. "Do you accept this gift as a remembrance of what your life means to me?" Arcturus had asked, his caramel eyes suddenly soft.

"I accept your gift with honor," I had answered, ready with the reply he had prepped me with moments before. He had put a small package in my hand then, pressing my fingers around it. My cheeks flushed as I remembered how embarrassed I had been, and how I'd had no gift to offer myself. "When you have no gift prepared," Arcturus had told me, "it is customary to offer some small thing you carry on your person. It can be anything. A glove, a handkerchief—"

"Will this do?" Reaching back my hand, I had pulled from my hair the fine, blue silk ribbon I had used to tie it back. In response, Arcturus had nodded. "Do you accept this gift as a remembrance of what your life means to me?" I had asked slowly, working the words through my mouth to make sure I had gotten them right.

"I accept your gift with honor," he answered, his deep voice less rough than normal. I had pressed the gift into his hand then, just as he had shown me.

"Do you accept this gift as a remembrance of what your life means to me?" I jumped at Ema's question. It startled me from my thoughts. I smiled warmly at her, outstretching my palm to accept the little package she was reaching towards me.

"I accept your gift with honor," I told her. "Do you accept this gift as a remembrance of what your life means to me?" I'd had time to prepare a gift for Ema already. As soon as I had finished my lesson with Arcturus and before the feast, I had begged Uncle Alastair to let me go down to Caeyra. It had been a short trip with no one to accompany me but a young Guardian who had scraped and groveled so much—never mind he didn't even know I was the princess—I had considered ditching him. I'd picked up two gifts, one for Ema and one for Leo. Nothing big, though according to Arcturus, they weren't supposed to be. Just large enough to fit in the palm of your hand.

"I accept your gift with honor," she answered, her smile so warm that for a second, I wanted to hug her. I pressed the gift into her palm and watched her bright eyes light up. She opened the wrapper and giggled in delight at the tiny comb inside, made with silver and decorated with little mother of pearl roses, to hold back her hair. She threw her arms around me before I could even think about the package in my hands. I patted her back awkwardly.

"Thank you, Calli! It's perfect!" Her blue eyes were sparkling and her cherry red mouth parted into a big smile. Then her eyes darted down to the package in my hand, and grew even wider. "Open it, open it!" she pressed. I grinned and awkwardly undid the wrapping. A small silk handkerchief fell out into my hand. "I embroidered it myself," Ema told me proudly. On the edge, in very fine cursive print, was my name. It was surrounded by little embroidered lilies, and some leaves on a vine. "Leo said they were your favorite," Ema told me softly.

"Thank you Ema." I told her softly. "It's beautiful." I rubbed the silk fabric through my fingers, and then placed it ever so gently in my pocket.

"The servants brought up cider," Ema told me suddenly. "And peppermints! We can sit by the fireplace." Her face glowed and she grabbed my hand to tug me to the hearth. I didn't complain. Instead, I sat beside her, cross legged on the floor. The fire was warm.

Ema began talking, and as she did, I let my fingers stray once more to the ring around my neck. Arcturus's gift. I had memorized his words when I had opened it. I played them again and again in my mind. "This was your mother's," he had told me. "It was her wedding ring. I thought you would like to have it." *Her wedding ring.* A knock on the door jerked me from my thoughts.

"Calli? Can I come in?"

"Leo! You came!" The door opened a crack and the boy slid through it, grinning sheepishly.

"Of course I came. Do you think I want to sit in a room with Avery all night? He's as sour as a cat in the rain. I'm not sure what got his fur wet." Leo rolled his eyes, and sat down cross legged on the floor before me. Then he pulled something out of his pocket. I should have expected it, but I gave a little jump just the same. "Do you accept this gift as a remembrance of what your life means to me?" he asked solemnly. There was something particular in the way he said it, as if placing some sort of special meaning in the words.

"I accept your gift with honor," I murmured. I held out my hand as he pressed the little package into it, and then fished a wrapped bundle from my own pocket. He smiled as I repeated the required phrase.

"I accept your gift with honor," he whispered. There was nothing laughing in his eyes now. Instead, he only watched as I fiddled with the wrapping of the present in my palm. I peeled the paper aside, and found a small gold chain that glistened in the firelight.

"What is it?" I dangled the short gold thing in front of my eyes questioningly. Leo made a face.

"It's a bracelet. Gosh, sometimes I wish you were a *real* girl." The laughter was back. Open, mocking laughter. "You know... you put it on your wrist?" I held out my hand, and he fastened the little clasp around my wrist. I held it up, watching the light dance on its surface.

"It's so pretty," I sighed. Leo grinned, and demolished the wrapping on his package. His eyes widened. His fingers cupped around a small round watch the size of his palm. A long chain dangled from his hand like a golden thread.

"Calli..." he whispered quietly, looking rather entranced. "These are really rare. Where—?"

"In Caeyra. It was in one of the shops I went into today." I blushed and continued. "My father once said that every man should have a watch. He said...well—" my face grew redder and I began to stutter. In my mind, I pushed down the memory of a dream, one in which my father and mother were seated casually in the castle gardens with several friends I did not recognize. My stomach twisted at the way I spoke, as if something my father had told my mother in a dream were a memory I had witnessed with my own eyes. "If you already have one or whatever it's fine. You know I—"

Leo cut me off with a wicked grin. "Of course I don't have one! Avery's gonna be so jealous!" He continued to chatter for several minutes, making a show of winding up the watch and putting it in his pocket and attaching the chain. It made me smile to see him so happy. I hadn't seen him truly happy in a while.

Eventually his chatter wore out, and he turned with a suddenly serious face towards Ema. "I almost forgot," he said quickly. "Ema Chevalier, do you accept this gift as a remembrance of what your life means to me?" another small package came out of his pocket. He pressed it into Ema's gloved hand.

Ema gave a start and her face colored rapidly. For a moment, I thought she would say nothing. But then she opened her mouth and whispered her reply. "I accept this gift with honor, Leo Thurman." It was a slightly more formal version of the ritual, but she held the present as lightly as she would a bird, and there was pleasure in her eyes. Pleasure, and something I might have called shame.

It took her a moment to gather herself. When she did, she drew a small white kerchief from her pocket. "Will you accept this gift as a remembrance of what *your* life means to *me?*" Her lip trembled a bit and she bit down hastily on it with her small, white teeth.

"I accept your gift with honor," Leo breathed. And he meant it. He smiled at her gently, and watched as she tugged open the ends of the package he had given her. Her smile told me she liked it very much.

It was a little candle, carved with flowers and decorative scroll. The wax was an off-white, but the flowers had been infused with colorful ink. Ema stood, dainty as a bird, and walked over to her bedside table where she set it beside a glass of water and her book. "Thank you, Leo," she whispered as she sat back down. Then, taking a mug of cider in her hands, she buried her nose in it and was silent. I turned to Leo.

"So..." I began.

"So we have to work out this whole Arcturus thing?"

I loved how he knew exactly what I was about to say. I smiled and he grinned back. "Yes." I leaned against the armchair and eyed the fire. It was beginning to burn low. "Any ideas?"

"Not really. I've been thinking," he began thoughtfully. "I've had a lot of time to think today...and I think we should come up with a secret code or something."

"And...?"

"That's as far as I got."

I groaned and buried my head in a palm. This wasn't going

to be easy. Unless...I grinned and looked up at him. "I overheard a few young Guardians the other day talking about a country east of here—I don't remember what it was called—whose main form of language involves using only their hands. What if—"

"We develop a code using our hands?"

"Exactly."

Leo grinned. "Brilliant."

I stretched out on the floor, laying so I was propped up on my elbows. "We'll have to make it so nobody suspects anything," I told him in a conspiring whisper. "Ema, you can't tell anyone." She shook her head—seemingly consumed in her mug—and said nothing. I accepted that as an answer and turned back to Leo. "How are we going to do it?"

Leo shrugged. "Maybe if we used gestures that look like normal hand movements...you know scratching your head, rubbing your arm. Things like that. Nobody would have a clue."

"I like it. We can make gestures for certain words...words we think we'll use a lot and—"

"And we can come up with an alphabet, so we can sign out anything else that doesn't have a gesture of its own?" he offered.

"Perfect."

"When do we get started?" He grinned broadly, and I could tell he was excited. His eyes glinted mischievously.

I smiled back and moved so my hands were free. "Now."

27

Tea Party

"Calli..."

I ignored her. I was bent over a book which discussed the differences between one handed and two handed swordsmanship. Arcturus had given it to me. I grunted at her words.

"Calli!"

"Hmm...?" She sounded a bit urgent, so I looked up. It took a moment for my eyes to focus on her face. I had been reading for far too long. "Yes Ema?"

"Master McDunnon...he—" her voice cracked, and she stopped, seemingly unable to go on.

"What happened?" My brain seemed fuzzy suddenly. My stomach lurched, and suddenly I realized that Ema's face was streaked in tears.

"He's taken a turn for the worst. Lady Dubois doesn't think he's going to make it."

I closed my book and rubbed my temples with urgent fingertips. "Not going to make it?" My voice sounded thick. My throat felt dry and tight.

"Lady Dubois says..." Ema's voice shook, and I reached out my hand to rest on her silk covered shoulder. "She thinks he has a few days, at best." Tears were beginning to slip their way past her eyes, following the tracks that had already been carved. My own eyes felt heavy, whether from a lack of sleep or from stress, I wasn't sure. The effect was still the same.

"He'll be fine..." I whispered. "I'm sure he'll be fine. Lady Dubois is very good. The best in the kingdom, I've heard. He'll be okay, Ema..." My voice trailed off. "They'll *all* be okay." I wasn't doing a good job convincing even myself.

The clock in the west tower struck four, and I stood. I had to go to tea. I ground my teeth as I pushed my seat in, tucking my book under my arms. "I was invited to sit at tea with some of the older ladies," I told Ema quietly. She watched me go but didn't move, and didn't say a word. I cringed inwardly. A party of gossipy old women was the last thing I needed right now.

* * *

"Pray, Lady Rachel, have you heard of the newest trend in silk stockings?" tittered a younger lady I hadn't seen before. Doubtless from out of the area, and visiting.

"No cousin, I have not. Do tell. Have they gotten rid of those ridiculous ankle length things yet?"

"I believe so, Lady Rachel. Though I heard recently that Lady Elizabeth was spotted downtown in Caeyra with her dress hitched high enough that you could *see* her ankles! She had her stockings embroidered around the ankle in a most unusual fashion, so I've heard." The younger lady was leaning forward now, whispering in a way that suggested she was speaking something profound.

"Youth these days," muttered Lady Dubois from a corner. She was the oldest of the group. Her old hands worked at sewing embroidery into the edge of a skirt. She was not wearing her healer's blue. Instead she sat in green silk. Her hands were clean. "Seems like every time I turn around, little girls are galavanting in lower necklines and higher hemlines. Heaven knows, a year from now none of them will be wearing anything at all!"

"Trashy, that's what it is. Ankle embroidery. What will they think up next?" Beside me, Lady Rachel scowled disapprovingly, and took a long sip of her tea.

Back straight as a board, I stared at the embroidery in my lap and tried my best to ignore their idle chatter. It was no use. Like birds that could not stop their twitting, they rambled on and on. The subject changed to gold jewelry, and then to the up coming auction in Caeyra. They were meaning to raise more money so they could update the curtains in the castle—those "awful drab things." Stirring a lump of sugar into my tea, I frowned and turned back to my embroidery. After several moments of curling my stiff fingers into a knot, I managed a small scrawl in the fabric that looked like it might have been a rose.

My mind drifted, and I soon found I wasn't listening. *Master McDunnon might not make it. Lady Roselle and some of the Guardians are sick. Servants are dying. Master McDunnon...*My mind was spinning in a slow reel that would not stop. "Is that not right, dear?" I gave a start when I realized the comment was directed at me.

I opened my mouth, unsure of what to say. *Master McDunnon is dying.* Before my mind had registered what my body was doing, I found that I was on my feet. My embroidery fell crumpled to the ground. Beside me, I heard my teacup make a pathetic 'clink' as it dropped back to its plate. I could feel myself shaking. And suddenly, all the thoughts I hadn't known I had been thinking came flooding out of my mouth all at once.

"Shame on you. All of you! Sitting in here with your tea and your embroidery. People out there are dying! People in this castle are dying. And here you sit, talking about silk stockings and whether or not the new curtains should be in lavender or chartreuse! I—" and suddenly, I realized I had nothing else to say, "—I don't want to take part in this. In any of it. Good day." I turned stiffly, and stormed from the room. I left my embroidery on the floor. My just sweetened tea in its cup, grew cold.

* * *

I was in my spot in the library. Book after book was thrown aside. Books about dreams. I was done with them.

I left the table, only to come back. In my arms was a bundle of new books. I piled them in front of me and tore open the nearest. Desperately, my eyes raked the page. That was where Leo found me, hours later, eyes bloodshot and blurry from reading into the dark.

A knock on a shelf sounded. Three sharp raps. A signal Leo and I made to get the other's attention. I looked up.

Leo's hands flashed so fast that for a moment, I wondered if we hadn't always spoken to each other like this. "Calli, I found something interesting about dreams in a book," his hands told me. That phrase was common enough. It was one long motion, like sweeping a fly from your hair.

"I don't care," I answered silently. We had no motion for that one. I had to spell it out. My quick fingers scratched at the back of my palm.

"Why?" The look on Leo's face told me of the surprise his hands couldn't show.

I frowned, and glanced around the room. We had no signs for the conversation I wanted to have, and I wasn't about to spell it all out, letter by letter. No one was watching us, so I stood slowly and walked over to his desk. Leo waved me anxiously away, but I ignored him and shook my head.

"Let's go talk over there," I whispered, pointing to the corner of the room. With the curtains drawn back the way they were, nobody would be able to see us without us seeing them first. He followed, his shoulders hunched and his eyes scraping the room with hesitation. "No one's going to catch us Leo," I sighed. I pulled him behind the curtain and sat on the floor, spreading my skirts neatly on the ground around me. For a moment, I hesitated. But this was something I had to do. "I'm done worrying about a bunch of foolish dreams," I told him finally. "There are so many more important things to think about."

"These are more than just dreams—"

"But they *are*, Leo. They are. No matter how real they are... they are *just* dreams. They are a part of me, like my hair or my nose or my eyes. And just like my hair, I can't change it, so it's time I stop fussing over it. It's silly to complain about something you can't change. People are dying, Leo. And I have barely noticed because I've had my head buried in books, worrying about myself and my nightmares that won't let me sleep. But I'm done with that now." I took a long, slow breath, and continued. "I'm done. I'm going to start wearing gloves...I think. All the time. That way other people's memories will stay safe in their heads. I can't get memories if I don't touch anyone. I'll still have dreams... of course. Dreams of my own...and dreams of my mother. Those I can't get rid of. But gloves should help a bit. And with all the time I've spent in library being selfish and researching things to help myself—I'm going to use all that time to do my part to end this sickness. Maybe if I work as hard at researching this illness as I did my dreams, maybe then I can figure out a cure..." I trailed off uncertainly.

Leo smiled, his eyes catching mine and holding them. "You are one of the least selfish people I know," he whispered. "If this is what you want to do, then I'll back you a hundred percent. Maybe later, when we have free time and no one is about to die, maybe then we can figure out this dream thing." He chuckled slightly and leaned forward. Suddenly his arms were around my shoulders. "You're so brave, Calli. So much more brave than I could ever be."

I smiled at him, and then left to sit at the other side of the room. "Bye," he said silently, his fingers flickering. My fingers made their reply and I turned back to my pile of books. Out of the corner of my eye, I could see Leo starting a new pile of his own.

* * *

"Have you found anything yet?" His hands flashed to me from across the room.

"No. Nothing."

Days were beginning to pass in a blurry haze. Several more Novices had gotten sick, as well as a few of the ladies. Some were being sent to the Aviary...those who appeared in desperate condition. Apparently, Anderson had started a frenzy the other day after walking into lessons with a slight cough. Even Leo had been sniffling for a couple days. It was gone now, and he was as healthy as ever, but those few days had had my heart skipping beats. Daily, Leo and I researched—each sitting on opposite sides of the room with hands flashing like we had simultaneously caught an itch—and found nothing. Nothing in the histories—indeed, nothing quite like this had ever happened before—and nothing in books about cures or books about ailments. Nothing at all.

"Milady." Arcturus was approaching me from across the library. Leo's eyes snapped to his paper. I lifted my face from my book.

"Yes, sir?" His face looked tired, old almost. His eyes wouldn't quite meet mine. They were distant. I couldn't read them.

"Master McDunnon passed away early this morning," he said. "As I will be assisting in the burial, we won't be having lessons tonight."

My stomach dropped to my feet. Across the room, Leo had paled. "What? I—" I broke off. My voice didn't seem to be working right. "Can I come? To the burial, I mean?"

Arcturus shook his head, his eyes still distant. "We don't know if the body is still contagious. No one will be allowed to attend."

He turned to leave, and then stopped mid stride, his eyes darting for a second towards the book beneath my hands. "I do believe your research would be more efficient if you talked it out...verbally." With one sweeping movement, he left the room. Leo came over moments later, still pale.

"What do we do?" His voice was strained.

"Keep looking," I answered. Everything in me seemed numb. My mind was blank, filled with nothing but a dull buzzing sound located somewhere between my ears. "What else can we do?"

For a moment, Leo said nothing. Then, his brow creased and his eyes turned up to meet mine. "Why do you think he changed his mind?"

I didn't have an answer to that. Arcturus never changed his mind. Not that easily. "I don't know," I answered truthfully. "Maybe because McDunnon—" I broke off. I couldn't say it. "I'm not going to argue," I continued. "Now that we can talk things out, we should be able to research twice as fast. I'd like to get through another few books before it gets too much later. Now that I'm not practicing with Arcturus, we have extra time." It was better to keep busy. If I was busy, I wouldn't have time to think.

I turned my eyes back down to the book in front of me, reading a few lines before the text slid out from under my eyes.

"No," Leo said firmly. He was pulling the book towards him, tugging it from my fingers and shaking his head. "You have been pushing yourself too hard, and I know you are not sleeping well anyway. Use this extra time to rest. Please. I'll keep studying for a while, but you need to go upstairs and try to get some sleep."

I wanted to argue, but the soft tone of his voice wouldn't let me. Besides, I could hardly keep my eyes open. I let him push me from my chair and went upstairs to my bed. Sleep was quick in finding me. And just around the corner of sleep and wakefulness, waited the dreams.

Delicately, I pursed my lips and whistled, smiling as the bird whistled back. Her little claws gripped on my fingers. Her head bent towards me, and I stroked her small white face. "Jasmine," I cooed. She peered at me through intelligent eyes. Her coral beak clicked and whistled. Her bright white feathers glistened in the sun.

"Leslie? Leslie honey, can I speak with you for a moment?"

I turned to him and smiled. Then I turned back to the bird. "Later," I whispered to her. No one would ever believe me...but somehow, I knew the birds understood. Jasmine cocked her head, examining me with one bright eye. Then, making a gesture that looked to me just like a nod, she took wing and left through the open window. I turned back to the man beside me. "Yes?"

His hand found the small of my back and suddenly he was leaning towards me. He—

My eyes came open slowly, as if fighting the urge to awaken. I was still tired. Much too tired. Judging by the darkness outside, I had only been asleep a few hours. I yawned and pushed myself upright in bed.

Ever since I had taken to wearing gloves, I had dreamed about my mother more frequently. I smiled, thinking about the little bird that I could still feel, its claws scratching on my finger. My mother loved those birds, so I had been told. She kept them up in the Aviary, back when it was a real Aviary and not just a room for healing—I froze mid thought. *The Aviary.*

Leo was still in the library, as I expected. His head was bent over a book. He looked tired. "Leo," I hissed.

"Calli?" He seemed surprised. "I thought you went to bed."

"I did," I told him quickly, and then took a seat beside him. "But I had a dream."

"Calli..." his surprise seemed to be heightening. "I thought you were done with the dreams."

"That doesn't mean they are done with me," I snapped. "I had a dream about my mother and her birds."

"The caladrius birds?"

"I think that's what they are called. The white ones, right?" He nodded. "Do you know anything about them?"

His brow furrowed as he thought. "No...not really. No more than I've already told you. The queen—your mother—liked them a lot, supposedly. And she kept them up in the Aviary. And they all disappeared when she died."

I waved him away. "Not that. I mean, what do they do?"

"Look pretty? I dunno Calli, they're birds."

"It can't be a coincidence..." I muttered, half to myself. "It just can't be."

"What are you thinking?" He looked utterly confused.

I closed the book he was reading and pushed it aside. Then, leaning forward, I dropped my voice to a whisper. "I think they're the cure."

28

Caladrius Dreams

Book in hand, I took a seat at the table in front of him. I wasn't tired anymore. I was quivering with excitement. I flipped the book open, riffling through the pages until I had found the one I wanted. It was listed in the "C" section under "beasts of the air." I smoothed the page out on the desk. Leo scooted his chair closer and leaned in to read over my shoulder. With a shaking finger, I traced the lines as I read.

"The caladrius is a pure white bird, prized for its magical properties. Often found in the homes of kings, it is said that the caladrius bird has the power to heal any ailment. When placed by the bedside of a dying man, this bird will look into the face of the man and, drawing the illness upon itself, it takes off into the open sky where the illness is dispersed and rid of. In some instances, however, the bird will look away as if refusing to heal the ailment. Any man from which the caladrius has looked away, will surely die..." I trailed off slowly, staring at the page before me. "That's it, Leo," I hissed. "That's the answer."

Leo nodded slowly, but he didn't look convinced. "Even if it is, Calli, what are we going to do about it? There has to be another way. Those birds have been gone for fourteen years."

"We've been searching for almost a month now, Leo. You know as well as I that there is no other way. If there was, my uncle, Lady Dubois, someone would have found it by now."

Leo hesitated. "It's a long shot..." he muttered.

"It's a long shot, yes. But it may be the only shot we've got."

He sighed. His eyes were heavy. His face looked tired. "So what now?"

I glanced down at the open page before me. There was no other choice. "We find them," I said.

* * *

Three sharp raps from across the room. I looked up. Leo was making his way towards me, Ema trailing at his heels. Head low to the ground, Pan trotted after them, making a bee-line for the ground next to my feet. "I brought back-up," Leo's hands told me, flashing so fast no one but I would have noticed their movement.

"What do you want me to do?" Ema asked as she sat beside me.

"Has Leo filled you in on everything?" She nodded. "Take a book and start reading, I guess." I gestured to the pile beside me. Every book on magical creatures I could find. It teetered high above my head.

"What am I looking for?" Her eyes were wide. She reached forward cautiously and plucked a book from the top of the pile.

"Anything. Anything at all." I grinned again. "If you were a little white bird, where would you be? That's what I mean to find out. I'm looking for habitat...eating habits...anything that might give us a clue. Like this." I pulled the nearest book from the pile towards me, and flipped it open to a random page. I read the first line my eyes fell upon. "It is believed that the caladrius bird is not born with its abilities. Rather, it has been theorized that the young caladrius receives its magic capabilities from its parents by way of food. It is not yet known how the adult caladrius imparts these abilities to its offspring. Some think that perhaps something in the bile of the stomach, regurgitated..." I threw the book back in the pile. "Well, not like that," I said. "That doesn't help anyone. But anything else you can find."

"I will do my best," Ema whispered silently. And without a single complaint, she opened the book in her hands and began to read.

* * *

"Calli, we've been searching for well over a week. I don't think we are going to find anything. This is pointless." Leo groaned and rubbed his head. Ema was beside me, sleeping on top of her book. It was late.

"People are counting on us, Leo. We'll find something. I know it." I riffled through several more pages before closing the book and laying my head across my hands. "What if...?" I wondered aloud, and a sudden understanding seemed to pop into my head. I sat up straighter, brows furrowed in thought. "What if we've been searching for the wrong thing?"

"I think that's obvious..." he said. If he was going to continue being this grumpy, I'd chase him off to bed right this second.

I ignored his comment. "All this time I've been focusing on where the birds might have gone. Maybe the real question is, *why* have they gone? Why just leave?" I rubbed my forehead and stared blankly into space.

Leo rolled his eyes. "While you work on that thought," he sighed, "I'm going to go to sleep. There's no point sitting here staring at you when you get like this..." he scowled and stood. I nodded absentmindedly. My eyes were heavy, and my brain foggy. But this was a breakthrough. I could feel it. I wouldn't give up. Not when we were so close. Leo shook Ema's shoulder gently. She gave a little start and sat up, rubbing her eyes.

"I should get to bed too, I think Calli," she whispered quietly. I smiled weakly, my fingers curling into my hair. "Sorry," she whispered. Then they both left, one right after the other, until I was alone. The only light was the flickering of my candle on the desk. The only sound was the rhythmic ticking of a clock somewhere nearby in the dark, and Pan's steady breathing on the floor at my feet. I groaned and sank lower in my chair.

I don't know how long I sat there, staring out into black nothingness. At one point, I remembered half hearing the clock strike one, the single ominous tone resonating through the empty room. I didn't respond to it. Hours later and still I sat, frozen to the seat, my thoughts as empty as the long, cold plain of a tundra. I was about to give up and go to bed when a final stray thought drifted through the blankness of my mind. I gave a gasp, almost knocking over my candle as I straightened. What if...? Standing, I ran to another section of the library. A new section. Anxiously, I searched the shelves. My candle on the floor, I leaned cross-legged against the bookshelf, and began to read.

* * *

The morning sun had just begun to trickle across the floor when Leo found me. I hadn't moved an inch. My eyes stung from the strain of reading in the dark. I could feel the circles beneath them, deep and tight. My body felt stuffy—like it had been filled with cotton. I sat up slowly when he approached, trying to re-adjust my eyes to a form so large.

"I can't believe you're still here." He sat down beside me, smoothing back the wild hair from my forehead. The look I gave him must have been haunted. He cringed and muttered something about "needing more sleep." I bent my eyes towards him, and let my voice drop to a deadly whisper.

"I think somebody stole them."

"What?"

"The birds Leo. There was no good reason for them to just disappear. None. So I got to thinking...what if they didn't leave? What if someone took them away?"

"Calli...I think this is a lack of sleep talking. That's ridiculous." He pulled at me as if to drag me to bed. I swatted him away.

"Is it? I'm being perfectly serious, Leo, and I don't think it's ridiculous at all."

"Why would someone steal them? They're just birds."

"But they aren't *just* birds. Just look at what they can do." I waved my hand at a nearby book, opened to a picture of a caladrius, turning its face away from a dying man. "Look at these records." I turned his attention to the books I had been reading all night. They were census records. Records of deaths and illnesses over the past hundred years. "The rates of illness related deaths within the castle in the past hundred years are abnormally low, see here?"

"How do you know that's abnormal?" Leo asked thoughtfully, his eyes scanning the page.

"Because I compared it to the city." I drug another record in front of us, and pointed to the data, letting my finger trace the entries on the yellowed page. "To several cities, actually. Look at these. All of them, every last one, the deaths average around a few thousand or more per year from illness. But look at the castle. I know the population here is much lower, and we have better medicines...but that alone can't account for the differences. Only a couple of deaths every few years, Leo. Even including the servants. That's not normal." I pointed to another line in the records. "But look here," I glanced at him over my shoulder. His eyes were growing wide, I could tell he was catching on to what I was saying. "Starting fourteen years ago till now, the deaths in the castle have increased three-fold. Most of the deaths are in the servants, but sickness in general increases significantly too. And the dates—the change corresponds almost exactly with my parents' death, when the birds supposedly disappeared."

"So you think..."

"I think someone stole the birds. And that someone is probably Baldassarre...or one of his men."

"But why?"

"To weaken the kingdom. To make it more vulnerable...and probably more dependent too. When the sicknesses first happened, I had a theory. I thought maybe the sickness was seeded here by Baldassarre or one of his men. I've spent a lot of time in places where illness is the norm. I know how it works and I know that the patterns this illness has followed are not normal. My uncle convinced me to put the theory away, but what if I was right? What if this sickness was seeded here by Baldassarre? My uncle has always found a cure before...but maybe this year Baldassarre is trying harder. Because now he isn't just trying to weaken the kingdom. This time..."

"He has a target," Leo finished for me. A thick silence dropped over us. Leo ran his fingers through his hair nervously. I bit at my lip.

"The question is...where do you hide a giant flock of birds?" I asked aloud.

Leo shook his head slowly. I groaned and sank back against the bookshelf, losing myself again in thought.

* * *

"But uncle...I feel that the evidence is staggering. —"

"No more, child. Give it a rest. I am happy that you have come to me with your ideas, and I promise I will not overlook them, but I have more important matters to attend to. This thing you suggest, it is impossible. Ridiculous. Your time would be better spent practicing with your friend Miss Chevalier on more domestic tasks."

"I wouldn't come to you about something I thought unimportant."

Uncle Alastair stopped in his walk and turned to face me. "I don't want to hear anything more about this. These sicknesses, they are adults' business. Not yours." His blue eyes peered deep into my own, and for a moment all I could do was nod slowly. Then, with a curt bow, he left. I stood gaping after him, feeling more angry and frustrated than ever before.

Leo was waiting for me in the Great Room at dinner. His patient smile begged to be told everything. I groaned as I sat.

"How did it go?" His eyes peeked at me from behind his forkful of pork. He was trying to seem innocently disinterested, and was failing miserably.

I shook my head. "He wouldn't even listen to me, Leo. He thought it was ridiculous. Not worth the time. He told me I should forget about it." I toyed with the food on my plate and then discreetly slipped it beneath the table for Pan. I wasn't hungry.

"Are you going to? Forget about it I mean."

"No." I didn't even need to hesitate. "I know something's up. I can feel it. And I'm pretty sure that I'm right. If my uncle isn't willing to listen to me, then I'm at least going to keep working to figure it out."

"What is there to figure out, Calli? So what if Baldassarre stole the birds? That gets us nowhere if nobody will listen to us. And why would they? We're just kids..."

"I'm going to find those birds," I told him stubbornly. "The fact that someone stole them...maybe it doesn't matter if nobody will listen. But it does give us a better idea of where to look. And it means they can be found. They didn't just fly away to 'greener pastures'. If that were the case, they could be anywhere. But somebody hid them. There are only so many places and ways you can hide a flock of birds. All we have to do is figure it out. I'm going to find them Leo, whether my uncle helps or not."

"I'm sure the High Lord will find a cure soon..."

"That's exactly the point, Leo. I don't think he will. I really don't."

Leo opened his mouth as if to add something to my comment, but shut it again when a boy stepped up behind me, clearing his throat. "Milady?"

"Yes...?" I paused for a moment, giving him the chance to supply his name. When he failed to do so, I arched an eyebrow and prodded him to continue. "What do you want?"

"Lady Dubois has sent a message for you. Young Lady Ema has taken ill."

"Ema?" My voice cracked and the fork in my hand fell ringing to my plate. The boy nodded. "Tell Lady Dubois I'll come." I barely noticed the elegant bow the boy swept beside me, or the dull patter of his wood bottomed boots as he left the hall.

"Calli..." Leo's voice was cautious beside me. Cautious, and worried. "Calli, are you alright?" I ignored his question and stood, climbing over my bench and pushing my plate to the center of the table. "Calli?" His hand reached for my arm, but I pulled away.

"I have to go see her."

"You can't." He grabbed at my shoulders as if to hold me in place. I shook his arms off and all but ran from the hall. "Calli! Wait!" I ignored him. I could hear his feet ringing on the floor behind me. I knew he was following, and I broke into a run. He caught me when I reached the door. We were both panting.

"I have to see her," I repeated stubbornly.

He just kept shaking his head, his hands locked around my wrists, and tried to pull me away. "You can't go in there, Calli. You can't. Remember what your uncle said? No one is allowed in. You can't risk getting yourself sick."

Desperately I twisted against his fingers, like cuffs on my arms. Deep inside, I knew he was right. I didn't care. I was almost crying, but somehow I held the tears at bay. They were welling up inside me, filling my chest with a ferocious type of energy that made me want to scream. The world felt so far away, as if I were watching myself through someone else's eyes. My body acted without my consent. My heart thudded frantically, but my head felt numb. "Let go, let go..." I heard myself pleading. And then suddenly I was aware that there were tears on my face and that Leo's eyes were as wide and desperate as mine. "Let go..." I was sobbing now. I broke away from him, throwing myself at the tall doors in front of us and stumbling inside. Leo followed, still frantic and holding my arms like I needed some kind of support.

And suddenly, I was back inside my own body again, watching the scene unfold through my own eyes. Suddenly my head caught up to what my heart was feeling and I froze, teetering on my feet and uncertain of what to do.

"Calli..." Leo pleaded silently.

I turned to look at him and shook my head. I needed to see her. And I needed to be inside of this room too. The Aviary. Some part of the mystery was buried in here. I could feel it. "Ema." my voice came out of my throat like a croak. My lungs constricted. It was hard to breathe.

Lady Dubois was bent over a bed with her tools and potions. I recognized at once the glint of dark brown hair that tangled over the pillows. I hurried to the bed, ignoring Leo's quiet protests. He gave up after a moment, and followed silently. His eyes looked tight.

"Milady." Lady Dubois dropped a quick curtsy before turning back to Ema. I imitated her curtsy stiffly.

"How is she? It's just a cold, right? Just a little thing..." Even as the words left my mouth, I knew they were not the truth. Lady Dubois hesitated. Her eyes turned to Ema before answering. Ema's eyes were closed. Her breathing, labored. Sweat creased her brow, and her cheeks were flushed from a high fever. Her skin was pasty. I wrapped my fingers around one of Ema's small hands. Her skin felt cool through my gloves.

Before I could stop her, Lady Dubois had her palm against my cheek. I jumped a little at the contact. She turned my face up and looked at me with worried eyes. I wrapped gloved fingertips around her wrist, and slowly drew her hand from my face. I didn't drop it. I just held it under my gloves, my hands tightening over hers from uncertainty. For the first time, I noticed how unkempt her grey hair was. It fell out of its pins in a way that suggested she had not taken the time to do it up properly this morning. Her skin looked sallow. Her wrinkles, deeper. There were bags beneath her eyes.

"No, child," she whispered. She shook her head slowly, a twitch back and forth that seemed almost unconscious. "She has the same thing the others do."

I dropped her hand like it was a snake, and sat heavily in a lacquered chair which sat bedside. Leo stood behind me, silent. He was rocking back and forth awkwardly, as if uncertain what to do. Occasionally his hand reached towards my shoulder, and then dropped back to his side. "But she'll be okay, right? She's up here, with you, and you'll keep her safe. Someone will find a cure soon and then everything will be normal again..." I was rambling, and realized after several minutes that I had lost track of my words. Lady Dubois's head still twitched back and forth. My eyes turned back to Ema. She was trembling a little in her sleep. I smoothed the hair from her forehead and squeezed my eyes shut. Maybe...maybe if I stopped looking I would wake up and realize this had all been a dream. Maybe...I opened my eyes again, and nothing had changed. Beside me, Pan paced the floor.

"I'm sorry child. I promise I will do everything I can..." she trailed off, and for the first time, I looked around the room. The beds were filled. Little Emily...Lady Roselle...and a number of others I couldn't put names to. I didn't know them, and became suddenly worried that I never would. "I will do the same thing for her that I have done for the others," Lady Dubois continued. "I have put them all under a special warding. It slows down the progress of the illness. I cannot cure them, but I can give them more time."

"How much time?" Leo's voice from over my shoulder startled me. He hadn't spoken since we had entered the room. Lady Dubois turned her eyes up to him after a moment, and then sighed.

"I am not certain. It will vary on the individual, how strong they are initially. Master McDunnon and Lady Roselle were the first to become sick and I managed to keep the illness at bay for several months. Master McDunnon—" she broke off. "I am not sure how much longer I can hold it off. The others...they have a little more time."

"What will happen if no cure is found?" Leo asked, voicing the question I had been afraid to put forth. I thought I knew the answer, and I didn't want to hear it.

"The same thing that has been happening to the servants," Lady Dubois whispered. "Without my magic, once symptoms show, they've had two to three days at best." She turned her face from us and left, muttering about needing more potions. I shook my head numbly.

"They died..." I whispered. Then I closed my eyes again, and let Leo drag me from the room.

* * *

"Sleep. You need sleep."

"I am not tired," I told him stubbornly. He was dragging me to my room. The truth was, I didn't want to go up there. I didn't want to face how empty it was. "Bring me to the library." It was meant to be a command. He wasn't listening. "I said," and I tried to pull against his arms, "bring me to the library. I have things to do. I cannot afford to sleep."

His hands were clamped down on my shoulders, and I couldn't pull away. He just kept pushing me forward. "You can, and you will," he snapped. "You aren't going to do anyone any good like this. You need to sleep. To rest. You've been through a lot."

"What about you?" We were in front of my door now. I swung to face him, blocking the knob so he couldn't force me inside.

"I'll be fine. *My* best friend isn't up in the Aviary right now," he retorted slowly. His eyes crinkled into a small smile. "But she will be if she doesn't get some rest." Then he reached easily around me, and opened the door. I took a great shuddering breath, and tried very hard not to look at the bed. The comforter was pulled back, as if she had been found sick during a midday nap, and the bed had not been made yet after she was gone. The sheets were covered in blood. Leo helped me change them, and then closed the door as I undressed and climbed into bed. Once I was under the covers I called out to him and he opened the door just enough to come half into the room.

"Rest," he whispered.

Suddenly the emptiness of the room seemed to be choking me. "Leo," I said suddenly, my voice sounding strangled. He paused by the door, his hand resting in the action of closing it. "Stay."

I could have sworn I saw him roll his eyes. He sighed and shook his head. "I just can't get rid of you, can I?" he muttered sarcastically. But he turned around just the same and sat in the armchair by the fire. Pan, who had followed us to the room, curled up beside him. "I won't go anywhere, I promise."

I smiled then, and we were silent. It was easier to bear being in the room when it was not so empty. I closed my eyes and felt sleep begin to drug my senses. The room around me felt shimmery, as if it were fading away...

"But my Lord..."

"Do you not want to serve your people to the best of their ability, my Lady?"

"My Lord, I don't understand how such an action will serve anyone. Those birds...they mean the difference between the life or death of many, my Lord."

"There are many things you cannot expect to understand, Lady Dubois, but what I ask of you is to accept those things as necessity, and to trust me."

"What must I do?"

"Hide them. You are reputed to be very good at such things, is that not right, my Lady?"

"Yes but—"

"Then prove it."

"My Lord, it is impossible. Where could I ever expect to hide a giant flock of birds?"

He sat still for a moment, and then his eyes drifted slowly to the sky. A full moon hung like a great orb in its center. The shadows it cast on his face made him seem dark. "You know where." It came out as barely a whisper, tracing the wind in a way that almost made me doubt he had said a word at all. His eyes snapped back to my face—

"Milady." A knocking on the door made me climb from my sleep with a ragged gasp. A man came in, his servant's white adding a sudden harshness to the rich colors of the room. His eyes averted to the floor when he realized I was in my nightgown. I pulled my chemise straighter on my shoulders and my blankets close around my chin.

"Yes?"

"The Lady Rachel has sent her regards, and asks you to attend tea with her this afternoon."

"Tell her I decline."

"Milady?"

"I *said,* tell her I decline. I am not coming. Is that not clear?" My voice rose irritably and Leo, still in the armchair by the fire, woke suddenly mid-snore. He turned bleary eyes my direction, and then towards the servant. His lips twitched into a ridiculous smile.

"Yes, milady." The servant dropped a nervous bow, and scurried out the room before I could even think of anything else to say.

"What was that about?" Leo asked a moment after the servant had left.

"Quiet, I'm trying to think."

Leo rolled his eyes at me. "Forgive me your Highness, next time I'll ask permission before I speak," he said sarcastically. I ignored him. Something was flitting at the edge of my mind, threatening to slip away. Something important. Something that servant had interrupted with his unwanted arrival. The dreams. I stood suddenly, causing Leo to blush and stutter. He averted his eyes, and turned towards the wall. I gave him an irritated sigh.

"Lace it," I snapped to him after pulling a corset over top of the thick chemise. I turned my back to him and tapped my toe, waiting.

"Calli..."

"Lace it. I'm in a hurry and it takes too long to do myself."

"Calli, it's indecent—"

"I'm completely covered," I snapped, exasperated. "I won't tell anyone and you don't have to look if you don't want to. But I really need to leave. I have to talk to Lady Dubois. Now. It can't wait till tomorrow and I have to get to her before she goes down to tea if I want to talk today. She'll be heading down any minute." He groaned, but didn't argue. I heard him walk up behind me, and in a second his fingers were fumbling awkwardly to tighten the lacing. A quick glance over my shoulder showed him red faced, and staring stubbornly at the walls. I nodded when he finished the ties with untidy bow, and pulled a dress on over top. "The dress too," I told him. I sighed and added, "please." He nodded, and after a moment stepped away stiffly. "Thank you." It was meant to be gracious, but came out in a rush. Leo shrugged. I pulled on a pair of gloves, and stuffed my feet into two vaguely matching slippers. Then I bolted for the door. Leo followed.

"Calli, what are we doing?"

"I can't believe I didn't think of this before. The pieces fit so perfectly. Her family is neutral, so of course it makes sense that she could go either way. And she's certainly the gullible type—so she could probably be very easily convinced that doing this was good. And she's the healer, so of course she had access to the birds—" I was walking very fast, and talking even faster. Leo was almost trotting to keep up. His face was turned towards me blankly. I kept talking. "And the timing...it was so perfect. I had a dream at the beginning of winter about her. My uncle was asking her to come help out at the castle as a healer. He had a white bird on his shoulder, which means those birds were here when she came. And I'll bet you anything they disappeared within weeks of her arrival. In fact, if we looked in the census records I could prove it—"

"What are you talking about?"

"Lady Dubois—"

"Yes, child?" It was her. Lady Dubois was walking towards us. We had intercepted her on her way to tea. She wore her green silk and her hair was up in a braided bun. She didn't look tired anymore. The necklace around her neck fell deep beneath the edge of her gown. She dropped a polite curtsy, but her eyes never left my face.

"Milady," I greeted her, as cordially as I could. Leo bowed slightly beside me, murmuring a greeting so low I could barely make out his words. "I was hoping to speak to you."

"It is lucky I ran into you, then. On your way to tea, child? I was just headed there myself. Perhaps you can keep me company as I walk."

"Actually, I'm not attending tea today. I am on my way to the library to do some reading. It is good for a lady to have a well-read mind." I batted my eyes at her, and tried to look innocent. Leo's muffled laugh earned a sharp glance. He hid it in a cough.

"Of course, child. I understand. It is good you are so dedicated." I nodded vaguely, as if everything she was saying was of great importance. She continued talking for several minutes before trailing off and then giving a sudden giggle. "Silly me... running on like this. You said you had something to speak with me about, yes?"

Suddenly my stomach seemed in my throat. *Careful...* I cautioned myself. *You don't know whose side she's on, or what she's capable of yet. Caution is key.* I could feel her eyes on me. "I was researching magical creatures the other day," I told her off-handedly. "A lady once told me about their uses in different types of household magics and well, I thought that it would be a good thing to read up on."

"Of course," Lady Dubois replied kindly. She didn't seem to be paying much attention. She wasn't looking at me anymore.

"And well...I just sort of ran across a bird, the...caladrius bird, I think they were called?" I tipped my eyes up to gauge her reaction. She tripped. Tripped right in the middle of a perfectly smooth stretch of floor. Beside me, Leo's shoulders stiffened. "It said something about them being used for healing—and I thought since you were the healer you might know something about it," I ran on quickly. She let go of a breath, and I could feel the tension drop. "I was just thinking about it because of the sicknesses. A bird like that would be a lot of help." I smiled with what I hoped was naivety.

"It would...yes, it would. But I'm afraid I don't know much about them, child. I can't be of any help really. Not much help at all."

"I read somewhere that there used to be a few around the castle, but that they disappeared when the queen died." I glanced at her again. "Do you have any idea where they could be?" My heart was pounding in my ears. Leo looked sick. Beside me, she let out a sharp squeak.

"No child," and she looked like she was shaking. "I wish I did." I opened my mouth to question her further, but she stopped abruptly. "Here we are," she said, her eyes flickering to a door beside us. I had been so absorbed in the conversation that I had completely lost track of where we were going, or where we were, for that matter. For a moment I only stared at her blankly. The library. That's where we were. *Why on earth did I need to go to the library?* I blinked stupidly, and glanced at the door. Leo saved me.

"Thank you, milady for your help. It was nice talking to you. You have reading to do Calli. Remember?" The last word was said through gritted teeth.

"The pleasure was all mine." She turned and then spoke to me directly. "I *do* hope you find those birds, child. I really do." She curtsied, and left.

Leo drug me inside. I collapsed against the wall, breathless from a fit of giggles. "Are you mad?" He looked ready to snap my head off.

"Did you see her face?" I asked him, still grinning.

"I did," he said grouchily. "It's obvious she did it. But I don't think we will get her to talk." He scowled and drug me upright. His hands tightened over my elbows. "You're walking a thin line, Calli. Next time you try to interrogate someone, at least *try* to remember your lies. We are going to get ourselves killed."

"Oh, don't be sour Leo."

"How did you know it was her?"

"I dreamed it," I told him, throwing my arms wide and laughing. I turned, and wandered towards the shelves. He followed me, shaking his head.

"What are you doing? You don't actually mean to read do you?"

"Not about the things she thinks I am, no. I'm going to go through some more of the old census records. If I want to bring this new information to my uncle, I'd better have some proof. He won't be likely to listen to me without it."

Leo rolled his eyes, but followed. He didn't complain when I piled his arms with a stack of books, and sat across from me at our table in the back. "You're the craziest person I know, Calli," he muttered. I peeked at him around my pile of books, and grinned. He already had one opened and was scanning the pages.

"And you're my best friend so what does that make you?" He didn't seem to hear, but I could have sworn I saw him smile.

His eyes peered up at me after a moment, and I caught his gaze. "Crazier," he muttered, and turned his face back down to his book.

* * *

"Calli."

I didn't hear him. I was scanning yet another page of census records. I still hadn't found what I was looking for. Hopefully, I would find it soon. It was getting late, and Arcturus wouldn't be happy if I skipped practice.

"Calli." I heard him that time. I grunted.

"I'm busy."

"Calli, come look at this." He sounded excited, but I ignored him. He wasn't reading census records anymore, so it could wait. I needed proof now. I'd worry about specifics later. "Calli!"

"Please Leo, I'm busy. In a minute."

"Calli, come here. Whatever it is you're looking at, it's not this." Something in his tone made me look up.

He was sitting several tables away. When he had wandered so far, I couldn't remember. I probably had been buried so deep in my books, I hadn't noticed. His table was piled high, but his eyes were focused on the page in front of him. I stood and made my way over. He pointed to the page, and my eyes scanned the title. *"Magical Creatures—Theories and Untested Myths,"* I read aloud. "Leo, why are you reading this? It won't help us at all." I didn't mean to be rude, I was just frustrated. He cringed a bit though. Sighing, I sat down beside him.

"I didn't look at the title. It was in one of our old stacks. I just grabbed a book and opened it. I opened it to this page, and I was going to put it away, but I saw the picture so I thought I would read the article..." he trailed off and his eyes turned to watch my face. I looked at the picture. It was on the top left corner of the right-hand page; a bird sitting on the edge of a king's bed. Its face was turned towards the man. A sure sign that he would live.

"We've seen a dozen pictures just like that, Leo. Why did you decide to read this one?" I really didn't have time for this. I glanced back at my table, the census book open to where I had left off.

"I don't know. I just did." He sounded tired. "Don't judge yet, Calli. Just listen." He pulled the book towards himself, and began to read me a passage. "There are many theories about how and why the caladrius heals some men, and lets others die. One theory is that the phenomena is simply random. Another, more probable theory is that the bird somehow knows which men will heal, and which are destined to die. This theory has raised questions however. It undermines the very essence and purpose of the bird. If the caladrius simply determines who will heal and who dies, its abilities are only prophetic in nature—"

"I don't see what this has to do with anything."

"Shh. I haven't gotten there yet. Listen. Another, more recent theory—and more widely supported—is that the caladrius, when placing itself in contact or in near contact with the sick person, is able somehow to view said person's memories, and therefore the process and morality of their life, and thereby judge whether that person should live or die." He raised his eyes expectantly. I frowned.

"Leo, I don't see your point."

"Do you remember when you told me a story about the woman who raised you?"

"What about her?"

"You said she told you that one day she heard a knocking at the door, like the pecking of a woodpecker. She opened the door, and there you were, alone and barely walking on her doorstep. When she looked up, she saw a white bird flying away. You told me she used to think that bird brought you, Calli. You said she was crazy, but what if she wasn't? What if she was right?"

"Leo, that's insane."

"Is it really? How many stories have you heard like that, Calli? The wolf who raises two human babies; the bear that raises a child with its cubs? It might be insane...but what if it's possible? These birds are magical creatures. They are smarter than a wolf or a bear. Maybe as smart as you and I."

I nodded slowly. My whole body felt numb. Only my fingers were tingling, as if to remind me that this was all still real. I stood suddenly. "Wait here." It took me awhile to find what I was looking for. I scanned the magical creature section of the library, tearing titles from the shelves and dropping them onto the floor. And then I found it. I opened the pages, and there it was. A passage I had read long ago, one I had thrown away as useless. I brought the book back to the table. "I read this to Ema the day you brought her to help," I told him quickly, faltering a bit on Ema's name and running my eyes over the letters on the page. "Here." I pointed to the passage I was reading. "It is believed that the caladrius bird is not born with its abilities. Rather, it has been theorized that the young caladrius receives its magic capabilities from its parents by way of food. It is not yet known how the adult caladrius imparts these abilities to its offspring. Some think that perhaps something in the bile of the stomach, regurgitated up in feeding is the mode in which this bird transfers its abilities—that's it. It all makes sense."

Leo was leaning against the back of his chair now. His head was in his hands. "Regurgitated? That's disgusting."

"Leo!" I smacked him with the back of my hand.

"It is, Calli. It really is. That's the weirdest thing I've ever heard in my life. Just bizarre. But since when have you ever been *normal?*" He was laughing openly now. I smacked him again. His face sobered and he shrugged, gesturing awkwardly at the books in front of us. "Now what?"

I shook my head. "We have to find those birds. We have to." I stood slowly, and walked back to my book.

29

Quarantine

"Have you found anything yet?"

I groaned and ran a hand through my hair. "No. Nothing. Maybe we are looking at the wrong things. I can't find any records of names in here. Just numbers and dates. But where else could we look? There had to be an inventory somewhere of who was staying in the castle. All we have to do is find the date she arrived...and compare it with the date those birds disappeared."

Leo shook his head. "I don't think it will be that easy. Even if they both happened within the same week—within the same day even—we can't prove it's anything but coincidence."

I closed the book I had been scanning for what seemed like the hundredth time. "But it's something," I told him glumly. "And we need *something*." Leo nodded at the comment and stood to look for more books. I pulled a new book from our stack and kept reading.

The library door squeaked, and I the sound of heavy footsteps entered the room. "Lady Callista." I looked up, startled. That wasn't a voice I was used to hearing, in the library of all places. It was my uncle, wearing a quilted robe on top of a heavy pelt which made him look several times larger than he already was. I smiled at him weakly and stood, closing the book I was reading and moving to intercept him before he could realize what Leo and I were studying. He bowed, and I curtsied politely back.

"My lord?"

Alastair's brow furrowed and his eyes flickered to Leo. For a moment he looked as if he were about to say something, and then decided the comment wasn't worth his time. When his eyes returned to me, it seemed almost as though Leo had never existed at all. "Walk with me." His tone left no room for discussion. I nodded curtly, still too startled to say much of anything back. His attendants waited for us to pass, and then followed. One of them opened the door.

I glanced back at Leo. "Sorry," I mouthed. And then with my hands I told him, "I'll see you tonight."

His hands flickered back to me, scratching an itch to anyone who didn't know otherwise. Silently, he told me he understood. The door swung shut behind us, and Leo was out of sight.

"Three more people have been confirmed sick within the last hour," my uncle told me, after several long moments of silence.

"Who?"

"Two of my Guardians, and one of the younger Novices. The sickness is spreading faster. It's getting worse, and I still haven't found a cure." He sounded worried and looked very tired.

"Uncle—" he cut me off with a wave of his hand. I noticed suddenly that we were standing in front of my room.

"We can't afford to lose you, child. I addressed the issue with Master Sheridan and he agreed, albeit reluctantly." He grimaced and, taking my elbow, steered me into my room and sat me on the bed. "We have decided that it would be best for you to stay in your room for a while, until the sickness has passed. You will not lack for comfort. I will have food and tea brought to you at proper times by servants who have been well warded and checked for absence of illness."

"You're quarantining me?" I was enraged. Only his hand on my elbow kept me sitting on the bed.

"You could call it that, I suppose," he answered, sounding amused. "I have business to attend to. I will place guards on your door so no one can come in."

"But uncle—"

"I have to go, child." He stood, and before I could argue, he left the room. I checked the knob behind him. It was locked.

"This ruins everything..." I said to the empty room. Not a sound replied. With a strangled sob I threw myself on top of my bed, and cried.

* * *

She was older, well into her middle years, but beautiful in a rosy, plump sort of way. Her mousy brown hair was streaked with grey, and her cheeks dimpled with a smile that reached all the way to her gentle eyes. I hadn't moved since my uncle left; I was still laying face down on the bed when she came in. The tears on my face had only just begun to dry.

I lifted my face when the door squeaked open. She shuffled in sideways, and closed the door behind her. The lock clicked with a sickening thud, and I dropped my head back into the pillows. "Who are you?" I asked, my voice cracking from my recent sobs and sounding muffled through the pillow my face was buried in.

"Your uncle assigned me as your nurse," she replied cheerfully. There was the clunking of something heavy being set on my bedside table. Peeking an eye around my pillow I saw it was a stack of books—mostly on etiquette, sewing, and a couple on archery and swordplay that Arcturus must have snuck in. One about practical magic teetered on top. "For your studies," she told me, noticing my glance. I groaned and hid my head again. Those were not the kinds of books I wanted.

"I don't need a nurse," I told her sulkily.

"Of course you do," she answered. "Every young girl needs a nurse."

"No." I sobbed into my pillow stubbornly. I was being childish now, and I knew it. I didn't care. "Nurses are for sick people and babies," I choked. I scrunched myself into a ball on the bed. *Everything's ruined.* The thought repeated itself in my mind. *I can't do anything locked up in here.* I curled myself tighter, and squeezed my eyes shut.

"Nonsense," she cooed, and suddenly I realized the woman was sitting beside me in the bed, smoothing back the hair that had matted itself on my forehead. "Every girl who is somebody in the world has a nurse. Young Lady Ema has one, but she was too old to make the journey and stayed behind when Lady Ema came to the castle to join society. Most girls have had one since they were a baby, yes, but you did not because your mother wasn't there to give you one and have not until now because your uncle is a man, and did not realize that young girls need that kind of thing."

Vaguely, the thought ran through my head that somehow she knew my secret. My uncle must have told her, though why I did not know. I didn't comment further. It was clear she wouldn't leave no matter what I did, and right now I was just glad to have someone in the room to ease its emptiness.

"I want my dog," I sobbed into the pillows. It was a ridiculous statement, but I didn't care. I was desperate for any sort of familiarity.

"The big brown and white one that's out in the hall?"

I nodded mutely.

"I suppose that couldn't hurt," she said softly. The bed shifted as she stood, and her footsteps receded. I heard the door swing open, and then the click of toenails crossing the marble floor. Moments later, a warm, furry body had climbed into bed to nestle against me. Turning my face from the pillow, I buried it instead into Pan's soft fur. Next to me, the nurse hummed a simple tune until my tears slowed and I at last fell asleep.

* * *

"Clunk. Clunk, clunk." There was a strange noise coming from outside. I pushed myself upright and looked around. Beside me, Pan lifted his head, ears pricked and eyes alert. "Clunk. Clunk." It sounded as if it were coming from the window by the balcony. I stood, pulled a robe over my bed clothes, and glanced towards the nurse. She was sleeping in the armchair by the fire, an embroidery hoop in her lap. Every now and then she gave a little jump and let out a small snore. Turning to Pan, I placed a finger across my lips. "Shh." He dropped his head and remained motionless, but his eyes were watching. Then, as quietly as I could, I tiptoed towards the window, hurrying to undo the latch and glance outside.

"Took you long enough. I thought you'd never come." It was Leo, standing on the ground far below me. His arm was raised as if he had been stopped in the process of throwing something. A rock was in his hand. I could only just see him in the dark. His voice was hard to make out.

"I can't hear you," I told him, as loudly as I dared. The nurse gave a loud snort, and then settled back asleep.

"What?" He was shouting now, but I could still barely make out his words.

"I can't hear you," I said a little louder. Suddenly I heard him laughing, and an orb of light appeared around him. He motioned to my left, where the balcony was. I shut the window, took one glance at the nurse, and tiptoed out the door to the balcony. Then I ran to the edge, and leaned over until I could see him clearly. He could see me just fine, I was sure. There was a lot of light coming from the inside of the room. My hands flashed to him. "How did you do that?" I asked, meaning the orb of light. He laughed again, and his hands moved as quickly as mine.

"You forget I've been doing magic several years longer than you."

"Can you teach me?"

He paused. He was too far away for me to see his expression. "Maybe someday," his hands told me quickly. "But maybe I like knowing more than you." I could clearly imagine the smirk that was on his face. I laughed a little. "Are you okay?" I didn't have to see his face or hear his voice to know that he was concerned. I frowned and leaned further over the edge to free up my hands.

"As okay as I can be. This sucks."

"Yeah. I heard about your...imprisonment."

"How'd you find out?" I had been worried he wouldn't know where I had gone. My uncle wouldn't have told him, and how would he know to ask?

His reply was quick, his hands flashing like lightning and caus-ing shadows in the orb that surrounded him. "Master Sheridan told me." That was odd. I didn't answer, but glanced back over my shoulder to make sure no one was awake. When I looked back at him, his hands moved. "He is more than a little irritated."

"My uncle told me he agreed with this."

"Agreed is a strong word. I think he understands your uncle's reasonings. He thinks it's a good idea, but he doesn't like it."

"What do you think?"

He took a few seconds to reply. When he did, his hands moved slower, as if he were thinking. "It's a pain, yes...and it certainly puts a damper on our research..." and suddenly his hands were moving faster again, "How am I supposed to feel when my best friend is locked up in her room for who knows how long, and I'm not allowed to speak with her? Other than that..." he paused and I could have sworn I heard him sigh, though it might have been the wind. "I think it's a good idea too. This sickness is killing people. What would happen if you got it? This kingdom needs you, Calli. It's an unreasonable risk." His hands froze and dropped to his sides. I sighed and leaned heavily against the balcony edge.

Secretly, I agreed with him, though I had trouble admitting it to myself. This was terrible in every way imaginable. Would the sickness ever go away without those birds? I couldn't think of how to find them locked up in here.

Movement down below caught my attention. His hands were flashing again. "I found it."

"Found what?"

"What we were looking for in the books. You were right. Lady Dubois arrived barely a week before those birds disappeared. I found it right after you left. I went looking for you... that's when I ran into Master Sheridan."

I grinned suddenly and pushed myself a little straighter. There was hope left. "Are you going to keep looking, even though I can't help?"

"I will." The fear in my heart subsided substantially, and I smiled at him even though I knew he could not make out my face. Leo was my hope.

* * *

He came almost every night, at the same time after the nurse had fallen asleep, throwing rocks at the window till I came out. Most nights he had nothing and only shook his head. Sometimes he came with a tiny bit of news, but it was never substantial. More often than not, he simply came to talk.

It was midday, and I was sitting on my bed, reciting a bit of poetry again and again until I got the accent and vowels just right. The nurse said that all that time spent in the streets had wreaked havoc on my pronunciation and accent. As far as I was concerned, I sounded just like everyone else, but if she wanted to nitpick, I'd let her. It wasn't as if I had anything else to do. A lunch tray came in, interrupting her critique, and I stood so gracefully it surprised me. It is amazing how fast you improve when there is nothing to do but study etiquette all day long. I accepted the tray, and told her I was going outside to eat on the balcony. I tossed Pan the turkey from my plate, and turned to the door. I needed air.

I was halfway through a winter pear when a shout attracted my attention. I looked up. "Calli, over here!" Leo was clinging to the outer edge of the balcony.

"What are you doing?"

"I needed to talk to you. I was throwing rocks...but you didn't come. Then I saw it was because you were sitting out here, and I decided to try and climb up." His footing was precarious. This wasn't a good idea. I told him so. "I needed to talk to you," he repeated, as if whatever he had to say was worth breaking his neck for.

"You shouldn't be here, it's the middle of the day. I'm not sup-posed to have any visitors, remember? If my uncle sees you—"

"He won't. He's in a meeting right now."

"My nurse will hear us. And she'll tell him. I know she will." He shook his head, as if none of this mattered. "What is it then? What is it you have to say that's worth the risk?"

His eyes grew very wide, and his voice dropped to a low whis-per. "I found them," he said. "I know where they are hidden."

30

Circles

"Are you serious?"

"Yes."

"How did you find out?"

"It was logical really. I'm surprised I didn't think of it a long time ago."

"Are you sure?"

"As sure as I can be."

"Where?" I held my breath. My heart was pounding.

"In the Valley Shrouded in Mist." The name sounded familiar, though I couldn't quite remember where I had heard it before. I shook my head to tell him I didn't know what he was talking about. "It's somewhere in the mountains," he whispered, making me gasp as he took a hand off the rocks and waved vaguely towards the forest. He swayed a bit before grabbing onto the castle's stone siding again.

"Where in the mountains?"

He paused. "Nobody really knows."

I groaned aloud. "Nobody knows?" I chided him. "You are going to give me a heart attack, Leo, you had me thinking you figured it all out! We aren't any closer then when we started. Now we are just looking for a different thing."

"Yes...but we are looking for something easier to find."

"Calli!" A muffled cry came from inside. I had been sitting out on the balcony for a while. She probably wanted me to come in to recite more poetry to her. I wrinkled my nose.

"I'm coming Nurse, one minute!" I turned back to Leo. He was laughing openly. I glared at him. "I have to go," I told him shortly.

"Calli!" she called again. She was coming towards the door. Any second now she would see us. The doors were glass, though curtained. But the curtains were sheer. "Calli. Come here."

"I have to go, Leo. Can you come back tonight?"

He paused, and then nodded. "I'll come. I'll try to see if I can find anything else. Maybe if I get a few more hints, maybe then we can work it out together." He grinned at me and then to my horror, he let go. I gasped and leaned over the edge of the railing. He hit the ground in a tumbling roll, and sprung lightly to his feet. *Show off,* I thought irritably. His hands flashed me a good bye, and then he trotted out of sight.

"And who exactly, was that?" The nurse was standing in the doorway now, hands on hips. I hadn't heard the door open behind me. I had no idea how much she had seen.

"Nobody?" I answered weakly. She grabbed me by an elbow and drug me inside. My lunch was left forgotten on its tray.

"That was certainly somebody. Haven't I explained to you why you can't have visitors? If even one person who is sick comes in contact with you—"

"He wasn't sick, I swear it!"

"You don't know that. Maybe he is a carrier that doesn't shown symptoms—" she stiffened suddenly, as if she had realized something in me that was offensive. I cringed. She swelled like an angry hen and her face darkened. "He?"

I wasn't sure what to say, so I meekly muttered "yes?" It was the wrong thing to say. I should have lied. I should have told her it was a girl. But what girl would have been clinging to the side of my balcony? I didn't know a single girl who could climb that—save myself—and I wasn't sure even I was stupid enough to attempt it.

"A girl of your standing should not be having boys clinging to the side of her balcony. It is improper of one in your position. It is improper of anyone. But you! You do not have time for entertaining boys and your reputation cannot—"

Caladrius Dreams

"*Entertaining?* I am not *entertaining* anyone, Nurse. That boy was my friend. We were just talking, that's all. Really. Nothing more."

The nurse muttered something about that not changing the impropriety of the situation, but her face had softened considerably. She didn't approve of me keeping company with a boy... but I didn't think she was going to comment on it. "What is his name?" she asked at last. I mumbled something under my breath. "His name, child."

"Leo Thurman?"

Her anger was back, at least partially, though her voice was softer. Almost as if she was pitying me. As if she were about to tell me something I didn't already know. "Thurman..." she said slowly, chewing on the word. "That is not a good family. They were one of the first to cross over when Baldassarre left, and they are rather widely known to be very high up in his council." I couldn't stand the look she gave me. I wrinkled my nose, and stomped away from her.

"So I've heard," I snapped. "But Leo isn't like the rest of his family. He's not. Please just give him a chance."

She was softening. I could see it in her eyes. "Is he a young lord?" she asked quietly. I cringed.

"No..." Her eyes narrowed. "He's a Novice," I told her slowly. "In training to be a Guardian...he's quite good," I added quickly, as if that would help. "He might even enter Apprentice status someday."

"Fighting men are not the type of men you should be associating yourself with," she said sharply, almost on top of my last comment. "You are a princess...so of course you must associate with those of lower status—no one but the king and queen is higher or even equal—but a Guardian? They are lower than servants in the Court's eyes. You—"

I cut her off, throwing my hands up in the air. "I don't want to hear it," I told her roughly. "I've heard the same speech a million times." I sat down on my bed and stared at her, eyes pleading. "Please Nurse? Aren't I allowed to choose my friends?

It isn't as if I were picking husbands." My voice was softer now, and suddenly all I wanted was her approval. She didn't give it to me, but she sat down on the bed beside me and took my hand in her own.

"I will not say that I like such choices, but when you ask it like that..." she trailed off with a small chuckle. "You aren't nearly as bad when you aren't being headstrong with me, child. I may make a princess out of you yet." She smiled, and her hand stroked my hair as she spoke. "I have not met the boy...so I couldn't possibly know him as you do. But if he is as honorable as you say...well then I suppose being friends could not hurt."

"Thank you." I really was grateful. I smiled at her and stood, moving to the table so she could help me practice my letters.

* * *

I was sitting on the edge of my bed, waiting. Nurse had gone to sleep an hour ago, next to my bed on a little pallet that had been sent in by my uncle. I had tried to convince her to sleep in my bed with me, but she had refused. I swung my feet to the floor as quietly as I could, and whispered at Pan to stay put. Then, shuffling on a robe, I tiptoed to the window. *Where is he?* I peered outside anxiously. The boy was nowhere to be seen. He should be here by now. I sat down on the chair by the window, and rested my head against the wall.

The toll of a clock rung miserably through the cold air. It was midnight. My breath hitched and I pulled my robe closer for warmth. What if something happened? I couldn't allow myself to think it.

There was a sudden "clunk!" above my left ear, and I gave a start. "Clunk, clunk, clunk!" I stood and wheeled towards the window. I could see a light out on the ground. As quietly as I could, I ran outside to the balcony. The door squeaked as it opened and I stiffened, but Nurse just gave a small snore, and rolled over in bed. I hurried out the door, and clicked it shut behind me. Leo must have seen me, because the orb of light moved beneath the balcony. He shouted something, but I couldn't make out the words. "I can't hear you," I told him with my hands.

"Catch this!" he answered back, and then before I could work out what he was talking about, a rope weighted by a small rock came catapulting over the edge of the balcony. I caught it on impulse, silently thanking the months Arcturus had spent teaching me hand-eye coordination. I tied it to the edge, and flashed Leo an "OK." The rope swung a bit under his weight and a few minutes later a pair of hands appeared on the ledge, and then a face popped up. He was grinning broadly, as if immensely proud of himself. "Miss me?" he quipped. I would have smacked him, but I didn't want him to fall. Instead, I grabbed his arm and helped him up.

"Why are you up here?" I hissed at him.

"Because I brought a guest," he whispered back, and then his hands flashed and his face grinned. "He wouldn't understand if we spoke like this," his hands told me quickly, "and I didn't want him to feel left out." The rope swung madly, and suddenly someone else was climbing up over the rail. It was Tom Avery.

"I can't believe you convinced me to do this, Kitty."

"Watch your mouth."

Avery's face scrunched but he groaned and corrected himself. "Leo," he muttered quietly.

Leo seemed pleased with himself. "That's better." Then he turned to me. I was still gawking openly, and staring between the two boys. Avery's face bore the same malicious smirk, but to my surprise, there was a tightness about it. "I told him what we were doing," Leo whispered in my ear, "and he agreed to help. His little sister's in the Aviary right now. She's got it bad."

I smiled at the boy then, suddenly sorry that I had felt anything but grateful at Avery's appearance. I gave him a polite nod. He returned it with a scowl. "How do you know they are in this valley? What gave you the clue?"

Leo shrugged. "It was simple really. Granted, I didn't come up with the idea all by myself. One of the older Apprentices has stepped in for Master McDunnon, and we were talking about circle warding—"

"Circle warding?"

"Yeah. It's one of the simpler kinds of wards. Used to hide things, to keep them in, or something else out. They were used a lot in the First War, to hide people who were being targeted by Baldassarre."

"Like my parents," I whispered softly.

Leo nodded. "Like your parents."

"So...how do these wards work?"

"There are a few different kinds. We were practicing them on a small scale today." He gave me a quick grin. "Mine worked pretty well. Better than his," he said, jerking his head in Avery's direction. Avery's scowl deepened. "Anyway, I figure two types would be needed for the birds. One to hide them, and one to keep them from leaving. The first is easy."

Leo pulled a small contraption out of his pocket. A quill was attached to one end, and a point was on the other. It bent in the middle like two sides of a triangle. He sat on the ground, and I sat beside him. Avery hovered behind us, crossing his arms like we were wasting his time. Leo placed the contraption on a flat stone and pivoted it around one end to draw a perfect circle. He took a small round mirror from his pocket, "stole it from class," he told me, and placed it in the center. He closed his eyes. The circle, and the mirror inside, vanished. I gasped.

"How did you do that?"

"It doesn't matter," he answered quickly. He took something else from his pocket. A round piece of parchment. "This does." Slowly he waved it over the circle, and suddenly, the circle reappeared. "To hide something with a circle ward, you need a perfect circle and, in its exact center, a mirror. To find something hidden in a circle ward, you need another perfect circle. Everything reappears when that perfect circle is reflected in the center of the mirror."

I nodded slowly. "But what about the valley?"

"It took me a while to think of it. After class I realized that a circle ward was probably the simplest way to hide something so large. But you'd need a big circle to hide a flock of birds. It just sort of popped into my head then. The Valley Shrouded in Mist is in a lot of the old stories—we heard one at the Winterfest, remember?" I nodded. Suddenly, I did. "Nobody really knows where it is, but all the stories say that it is a great bowl shaped valley, and I'm willing to bet it's a perfect circle. In its center is Vision Lake, said to have certain magical properties. Vision Lake is perfectly round." He drew another circle in the dust, and then wiped it away with his hand.

"Are you sure that's where they are?"

"As sure as I can be. It's the only thing that makes sense and it's all we've got. There's a possibility we will get all the way out there, and find nothing. Maybe we will find the valley, and the birds won't be there. Maybe we won't find the valley at all."

"But we have to try," I whispered. "It's all we've got. But how do we find something nobody's seen?"

"That's where I come in." His voice startled me. I had forgotten the boy was there. Avery moved forward, and crouched beside Leo. His face was anxious.

"I remembered a few years ago, Avery went on for weeks, bragging about how he'd found the Valley Shrouded in Mist. It was the first year we had come to the castle. Nobody believed him. A few of the other boys and I followed him into the forest after a while, because we'd gotten sick of listening to him. We never found anything."

"So you are telling me that we are supposed to go trekking off into the forest with the hopes that he is right, *and* remembers how he got there? The forest is full of a million trees, and not much else. And trees have an uncanny ability of looking very similar."

"Do we have anything else?" Leo asked me. I glanced over at Avery. His face was pleading now.

"Right," I nodded. "So are you coming with us?" Avery shook his head.

"I'll try my best to explain everything I remember, but I can't come. If we were caught—it would just be bad news. I'd probably be dropped from the Guard. You too, Thurman."

"I know what I'm getting myself into, Tom." Leo replied harshly.

"So, you can tell us how you got there?" I asked.

"As best I can."

Leo held his hand up to stop us. "We don't need him to come with us, Calli. And we don't need to hear the story from him secondhand. We'd never find it that way. But we can do something just as good as bringing him along as our guide."

I frowned. "I don't follow you."

Leo's hands flickered, speaking to me quickly. Obviously he wanted to keep his words hidden from Avery. He was right. It was probably better that Avery didn't know about the dreams. "All he has to do is give you the memory, Calli. Then you will be able to lead us there, just as well as he."

"That will put us back an entire night." My hands flashed back to him, and I shook my head roughly.

Leo shrugged. "One night won't change much, and if it means less wandering through a forest with nothing but a few secondhand details as our guide, I say it's worth it."

Turning to Avery, I switched back to normal speech. "Very well. Avery, come here." When Avery gave me a confused sort of look, I realized suddenly that he had no idea what was going on. He hesitated.

"Do you want us to help you save your sister?" Leo asked brusquely. I could see the hesitation waver in his eyes. "Don't ask questions. Just do what she tells you." After a second Avery nodded, and scooted towards me. Slowly, I pulled the gloves off my hands.

"I want you to think very hard about the day you found the valley," I told him quietly. "Picture it as clearly as you can." I lifted my hands and cupped his face with my palms. It was hot under my touch. He shivered a bit, and closed his eyes. After a few moments he nodded, and I took my hands away. I drew the gloves back over my fingers, almost regretfully. I was beginning to miss the feeling of open air around them. The feeling of objects, directly beneath my touch.

"That's as good as I can do," Avery said silently. For a moment his face was almost vulnerable. The cruelness seemed to be gone.

"It will have to be good enough." I moved away from him and stood, wandering to the edge of the balcony. The wind was cold. I pulled my robe tighter, and peeked inside. Nurse was still asleep, snoring on her side. Pan was lying on the bed, watching us through the window. "Even if he does remember properly, that still doesn't answer the question of how to find it," I said. "Or how he found it. If the place is hidden, nobody should be able to find it at all. What are we going to do, go to the location and stumble around with a little round piece of paper until we fall into an invisible lake and drown? There has to be another way."

Leo frowned and stood as well, moving across the balcony to come stand by me at the edge. "I dunno," he answered honestly. "I hadn't figured that part out yet. As far as I know, there isn't any other way to break a circle ward, and if there is, it would involve magic that neither of us are capable of yet." He rubbed his forehead with a hand, and fell silent.

It was a pressing issue, and I stared out at the forest wordlessly. The trees seemed dark and ominous, covering the mountains in a black sheath. Who knew what was out there? The waters of the lake glistened gently, its ripples reflecting the moon above and—I froze. "Leo," I whispered breathlessly. "Leo, the moon." He turned his face to mine, brows furrowed. "It will be full in four days. That's how Avery found the valley, and that's why you couldn't find it again. He was simply in the right place at the right time. When the moon is full—"

"It will be a perfect circle," Leo finished for me. His eyes were wide. "Calli, you're brilliant." I laughed.

"You're the one who figured this all out," I reminded him.

He shrugged. "I was simply...in the right place, at the right time," he muttered. His face was glowing. "I may have come up with the idea, but it's you who will get us there." I was suddenly glad it was dark. I could feel my face redden.

"I didn't do anything really—" I began to protest. Avery cut me off, rising from his spot on the ground and joining us by the rail.

"You forget one thing," he said quietly. We both looked at him. "How will you free them when you get there?"

"Right," Leo said. "That's the more complicated part." I scowled at him, but he waved me away. "I said that there are probably two circle wards on the valley. I've covered how they are hidden. The other ward is what holds them there."

He crouched on the ground again and took that contraption back out of his pocket. He drew another circle and then folded a small square from his pocket into a little paper bird. He closed his eyes for a second and the bird began to flap its little paper wings. "A trick you learn when you're a bored little boy sitting in the back of a class you don't want to attend," Leo told me when he saw my look of surprise. He tore a piece of paper from the edge of one wing, and tossed it in the center of the circle. Where the piece of paper was, he took a pinch of dust and removed it. "Hold this," he muttered. I held out my hand, and he dropped the dust there in a tiny pile. Then he put the bird inside of the circle and held it there for several moments with his eyes closed. He let go. The paper bird flew in circles, beating vainly against invisible walls. Leo let out a cry of joy. "I couldn't get it to work in class," he told me proudly.

"So something was taken from the center of the circle?" I asked him slowly, uncertain if I had gotten it right. He nodded.

"And was replaced by something that belongs to what will be held in. Probably a feather, in our case. One feather would be enough. They are a flock of birds, so I'm sure you can treat them as a unit."

"So all we have to do, is find that feather and replace it with whatever was taken," I said slowly. "That sounds simple enough."

Leo frowned. "Maybe. But we don't know what was taken, and you are forgetting one very important thing."

"What?"

"The center of this circle, is at the bottom of a lake."

"Oh." That *was* a problem. Added to the fact that I absolutely could not swim, it was a major problem. I grimaced. "Before we worry about that, we have to figure out what was taken. Lady Dubois probably has whatever it is, so it's most likely in the Aviary or in her chambers. But what on earth would we be looking for?"

"Something you'd take from the bottom of a lake?" Leo suggested.

"A pebble or a stick," I said, working it out aloud. "Maybe some sort of plant—no. She'd want it to be something that wouldn't easily disintegrate. Something she could keep safe in case she needed to reverse the warding."

Leo nodded. "A rock or a stick then. In a safe place. That shouldn't be too hard."

"A safe place." I muttered. "The stone on her necklace," I said suddenly, and my eyes lit up. "She wears it all the time. I assumed it was something sentimental, but what safer a place is there?"

Leo's eyes were shining too. "Only a girl would notice something like that," he taunted. I sent him a glare, and he sighed. "That complicates matters significantly."

"Why? We know what it is now. All we have to do is get it."

"Exactly. All we have to do is get it. But I don't think she'd just give it to us, and before we were searching for an object in a room. Now we have to take a necklace off her neck."

"Our best bet is to look for it at night then," I whispered. "When she's taken it off and put it in a box." Leo nodded.

"Tomorrow night," he said affirmatively. My nurse gave a snorting jump in the room, and began muttering in her sleep. Leo gave her a worried glance. "I should go before she wakes up," he said. He moved towards the rope. Avery followed. "I'll be back tomorrow," he said quickly. "Same time. That will give us the night to get you out of here, and find that stone. Then three days to find the valley. And then the full moon."

"Two nights in the forest," I muttered, and suddenly the dark felt much darker. Leo swung himself over the balcony edge and began to shimmy down the rope. "You are a lot cleverer than you give yourself credit for," I told him before he had disappeared.

Leo shrugged. "In the end, it was all you." I opened my mouth to argue but before I could say a word, he was gone.

It was just Avery and I now. He stood awkwardly by the rope, waiting till Leo had reached the bottom so he could climb down. Then he reached for the rope and swung himself over the edge. "Tom?" I said suddenly, before he could start his descent. He paused and his eyes met mine. I was going to thank him, but I stopped myself. 'Thank you' wouldn't be the right words. He wasn't doing this for me. "I will do everything in my power to make sure your sister is okay," I told him firmly. He said nothing, but the look in his eyes said all that was needed. He disappeared over the rail.

I slipped back inside and crawled into my bed, curling close to Pan's warm body. I fell asleep quickly, soothed by the nurse's quiet snores. I dreamt of a forest.

31

Night Raid

"Clunk. Clunk." I slid out of bed and ran to the window. He was there. I could see his figure surrounded by an orb of light that he held aloft in a hand. I wrote a hasty note and left it on my pillow.

"Stay here," I whispered to Pan, who had risen to follow me. With a gesture that almost looked like a nod, the wolfhound lowered himself on the bed. I stole a quick glance at the nurse, and then slipped guiltily out the door. A rope was already waiting for me at the edge of the balcony. I tied it to the railing and swung myself over, whispering a silent prayer while trying not to think about how a small knot was the only thing between me and a broken neck. Halfway down, I slipped and let out a high pitched squeak. "Calli, careful!" Leo called. Like he could talk. He made being careless a profession. I wrinkled my nose and continued down. Leo caught me at the bottom.

"Do you think we should pull the rope down?" I asked him slowly. "You know...to hide the evidence?"

Leo laughed. "They'll know you're gone in the morning, rope or no. After that squeal you gave, we'll be lucky if they don't wake and find us in a few minutes."

I punched him lightly on the shoulder. "I don't squeal," I snapped. He rolled his eyes and shrugged.

"In any case, the rope will at least let them know you weren't kidnapped." It was a good point, and I nodded.

"I left a note," I whispered.

"Good." He gestured to me, and began to creep around the castle's side.

"How did you get by the guards?"

He stopped so quickly I almost ran right over him. He held out a hand, and peeked around the corner. "They go in shifts," he said. "If you time it just right, it's easy to get past them."

I frowned. "Remind me to tell my uncle we have an issue in castle security," I whispered sourly. Leo shushed me.

"Remember what I said about your whispering?" I did remember, though it seemed so long ago. He said I whispered like a bear. My frown deepened and I crossed my arms. "Go!" he said suddenly, grabbing me by the elbow. I copied his ducking scamper, and followed him through the castle gate. Just as we hid around the corner, I saw the guards pace by. They didn't look our way, and passed once more out of sight.

"That was close," I grumbled, rubbing my arm. Beside me, Leo was laughing silently.

"It wouldn't have been if you'd have run faster," he teased. "Come on. We're wasting time."

I nodded. "First Lady Dubois and the stone, then the forest," I whispered. We hurried together through a side entrance, and then paused in the dark hall to catch our breath. The only light was a single torch that hung on the wall above us. I hurried towards the stairs, and then leapt back as another set of guards passed by.

"Careful," Leo cautioned. I nodded, and continued forward.

Lady Dubois's room was on the castle's third story, next to the Aviary. We didn't see any more guards as we crept upstairs. I paused at the top of the third flight and pointed in the direction we were going. "I think her chambers are in there," I whispered, pointing to a door.

"The small door on the left, or the big one on the right?"

"The small one. The big one is a side door into the Aviary." I tiptoed down the hall and stopped, my hand resting on the door's brass handle. "We're lucky she doesn't keep guards," I said in Leo's ear when he was close. He agreed silently and pressed in close behind. I opened the door a crack, and then paused. "Leo?" I whispered. Suddenly my stomach felt sour. "What do you think would happen if we get caught?"

His face tightened, and his fingers moved up to rub at his neck. "At best? I expect we would be sent back to our rooms with a slap on the hand...and lose any chance we had at getting those birds." I nodded, and moved to open the door. His hand stopped me. "Don't forget who you are Calli. And don't forget who she is. If Lady Dubois does serve Baldassarre, this situation has the potential of becoming dangerous for you." I could see him hesitating, and I gave him my bravest smile.

"No matter the consequences, we have to try," I said quietly. Leo gave me a short nod. His hand released mine, and I let the door swing open slowly.

Her room was large and lavishly decorated. It was very dark, and I could barely see two feet in front of my face. On the far end was a curtain, hanging around the four posts of a bed. I could hear her snoring inside. Leo's hands flashed to me, barely visible in the dark. "I'll start at the table in the back," he said.

I replied with my hands as well, desperate to make as little noise as possible. "I'll look on the one next to her bed." I turned, and stole to her bedside table.

The moon outside poured just enough light through the window that I could make out the shapes in the room. There was a small jewelry box next to a candle stump and my heart jumped to my throat. This was it. I opened the box with care. It was empty.

A sudden noise came from the other side of the room. Several items were clattering to the floor. I could hear Leo mumbling curses. I froze and glanced at Lady Dubois. I could just see her behind the curtain. She grunted in her sleep at the noise, and rolled over. Something glistened around her neck.

"Leo," I hissed. A muffled grunt was his reply. "I found it."

"Good," he whispered. He wasn't bothering to speak to me with his hands anymore. I could hear paper rustling as he moved to my side of the room. "Let's get out of here."

I shook my head. "There," I whispered. It was clearly visible now, a dark pebble hanging on a thick chain draped around her neck.

Leo came to a stop beside me and his eyes followed my pointing hand. "Huh," he grunted. "That's not going to be easy." The jovial tone in his voice made me glare at him. Angrily I worked my hands, and switched back into silent communication.

"This isn't a joke." The gleam in his eyes didn't fade, but his face sobered. "How are we going to get it now? Can we just use magic to lift it off?"

Leo shook his head. "Probably not." He was using his hands again now too. "She'd probably sense it and wake up."

"She most certainly will if we just grab it from her." My fingers flashed quickly in the dark.

"It's our best option. I'm willing to bet there is something in place to keep us from stealing it with magic. She obviously isn't a stupid woman. She wouldn't go to all this work and then just leave the stone to be magicked away."

Unfortunately, I agreed. The better option was to take the stone manually, but that was an option I didn't particularly like.

I moved to the other side of the bed and stood directly in front of her. After a deep breath and several seconds of gritted teeth, I pulled back the curtains and hung them on their hook by the bedpost. The skin crawled on the back of my hands and down my legs. My chest felt heavy. I wondered suddenly how it was that she couldn't hear the racing of my heart. Leo crept to my side and his hands flickered. I felt my muscles twitch at the sudden movement. "How are we going to do this?" he asked.

It took me a moment to reply. "Lift it over her head?"

"Too risky. We might have to though."

"We can't just undo the clasp. It's behind her head. We'd never reach it." She snorted suddenly and I jumped, almost knocking over a glass lantern that stood bedside.

"We are going to have to take it off the chain," he said quickly, his hands flashing so fast I almost missed it. I had to cover my mouth to keep myself from groaning aloud.

That's impossible, was my mental thought, but I didn't share it. We both had known this would be difficult—near impossible—from the start. There was no point dwelling on the fact. I forced the tension spreading through my shoulders to release. I wasn't going to give up. I had made Avery a promise, and I meant to keep it. I also wanted my roommate back. I stopped myself from mentally going down the list of people. We had to try. There was simply too much at stake.

I took the lantern off its hook, and handed the post to him. "Lift the chain with the hook. I'll grab the stone and try to take it off."

Leo nodded once and took the lantern hook. As carefully as he could, he dropped the hook down towards her front where her chest dipped in and the chain lay an inch from her skin. She mumbled in her sleep, and I had to steady Leo's hand when he jumped. I had to remind myself to keep breathing.

"Careful," I whispered on an exhale. My hands were occupied, steadying Leo's, and the audible whisper slipped out automatically. I immediately regretted it. At the sound, Lady Dubois grunted and stirred in her sleep. With a little jingle, the stone pendant rolled from its place on her chest, and slid down the length of the chain till it was hidden beneath the crook of her neck. Air rushed into my lungs past my lips as I gasped. My hand reached forward to catch the stone. It grasped at empty air. Slowly, I let the hand drop back down to my side. I was shaking.

"I can't do it," I whispered aloud. A heaviness sank into my chest and I turned by back to Lady Dubois. Why had I thought I could? My feet hesitated. I glanced at the door.

My empty hand felt suddenly warm beside me. "Yes you can," Leo said. I glanced down. His fingers were around mine, holding me in place. "I promise you, together, we can do this." I smiled weakly at him. "We have to, remember? No matter the consequences, we have to try. Those are your words, and now I'm reminding you."

His words gave me the courage I needed. "Do you think you can lift the stone out with the hook?" I asked. I couldn't even see the stone where it was at, but the gap between her neck and her shoulder was large enough to slip the lantern hook through. Leo nodded and lifted the hook.

"Not too fast," I cautioned. Slowly, we lowered the hook into the gap between her neck and shoulder. A second of held breaths. "A little to the left," I whispered. It caught.

A few more seconds of gently wiggling the hook, and the stone slid into view. I caught it before it could slide back down the chain.

Taking the stone from the chain wasn't an easy prospect. It was hung by a jewelry loop drilled into the top of the stone. I tugged on the stone gently. It remained embedded. "You're going to have to untwist the loop," Leo whispered. My hands were shaking, and the loop was small. I fumbled at it, freezing several times when she twitched. Then, at last, the wire bent and the stone came loose in my hands. I took the chain off of the hook, and lowered it back down against her skin. Then I crept backwards and out the door. Leo followed. I collapsed against the wall, at last able to breath.

Leo stopped by my side. "Now for the hard part," he whispered cheerfully. He was grinning. I followed him down the steps, through the Main Hall, and out the side door that led to the training field. Once in the cover of the trees, we ran.

I stopped him when we reached the field, holding him back with a hand. I showed him the stone, and let myself smile a bit. Adrenaline made me shake. Leo let out a quiet whoop of joy. I wished he'd calm down. He had been right back in the castle. The hard part was yet to come. We still had to find the place. I closed my eyes, and remembered.

32

Into the Forest

It was dark and cold. The moon glowed faintly above, just visible through the clouds. It was almost full; in three nights it would be. I started wandering down the path, away from the training field and away from the castle. Towards the lake and into the mountains. My heart wanted to race but I steadied it. What was scary about a little forest and dark? Besides. It was a dare. I never backed down on dares. Just one walk around the lake, and I could tell the boys I had done it. Wandered in the forest after dark all alone. It really wasn't that big of a deal. I kept walking.

"Do you know where we are going?" Leo asked.

I cringed. "That's a long shot," I said, "and a risk I suppose we will have to be willing to take. In any case, he went that way." I pointed towards a trail on the far side of the training field. It disappeared into the forest, lost in the dark. Leo nodded uncertainly, and we started walking. We continued for a long time down the path. I had seen this path on maps before. It went all the way around the lake. The lake was large.

A long time had passed before I slowed to a stop. The sky was just beginning to lighten—it was the color of blue that comes just before black, like the embroidery on Leo's cloak. I smiled and glanced around. "What?" Leo asked. He sounded concerned.

"He left the trail around here somewhere," I answered. "Give me a second. I have to think." I closed my eyes.

The sky was just beginning to lighten. A sudden noise came from the bushes to my left and I yelled, running away from it and to the right. I tripped over a fallen log and fell on my face. I scrambled to my feet. I turned. The path was nowhere in sight. The forest pressed in, dark on all sides. I shivered. An old birch tree was ahead, the kind that grew on the edges of the lake. It looked promising, so I started after it.

A sudden shriek broke my concentration. Leo jumped sideways, trampling me and running to the edge of the path. A lizard hurried from the underbrush, and then vanished from sight. I rolled my eyes and left the trail, walking until my feet bumped up against a fallen log. It was older than the one in my memory, covered in moss and decaying, but it jutted from the ground just right and I paused in front of it, waiting for him to catch up. I turned until I saw an old birch. I kept walking, not giving him a chance to catch his breath. We had to stay on track. If I planned it just right, I could use the time of day as a guide. Leo hurried after me.

"It's seriously creepy when you do that," he muttered. We kept walking past the birch. Light was beginning to reach us through the trees.

"Do what?"

"Your face gets all stony like you've gone to sleep or something, and then you give a little jump and start walking in random directions."

I scrunched my face up at him. "I'll give you more warning next time," I muttered sarcastically. He laughed and hopped up on a small boulder, sliding down the other side. We continued walking.

* * *

We had been walking for hours, zig-zagging through the endless trees. I was following nothing. Bent twigs and funny stones that could have been misplaced moments earlier by a passing deer. The sun was climbing. It was midday, and then midday passed. We were gaining altitude, sometimes climbing steep cliffs. I was growing tired. I kept tripping, and beside me I noticed Leo was tripping too. In my mind, Avery was lost—stumbling around and wondering where he was and why he hadn't found the castle yet. In reality, we were lost too. I turned at a rock with a piece of moss that looked vaguely like a gryphon, and started in another direction entirely. Leo didn't complain. He just followed.

The rock I had chosen to put my weight on gave way. I slid, falling on my knees and tumbling down the slope until a tree caught my fall. I didn't get up. Instead I just lay there, looking into the sky and counting the stars that had begun to dot it. A few tears ran down my cheeks. Angrily, I brushed them away.

"Calli, are you okay?" Leo all but ran down the cliffside, tripping and sliding until he at last came to a halt in front of me. He heaved a sigh of relief when I turned to look at him. "I thought you were dead or something," he said with horror. "Don't do that again."

"I'll try not to," I said ruefully. Slowly I sat up. My dress and stockings had cushioned the blow for my knees and most of my body, but my hand stung. There was a hole in one of my gloves. I pulled it off, and looked at my hand. A small trickle of blood ran down one side.

"We should set up camp around here," I said, flexing my fingers to make sure nothing was sprained.

"Are you sure you're okay?"

"It's just a little blood, Leo. I'll be fine." I brushed myself off and pulled the glove back on. I stood. "In any case, Avery spent the night down there." I pointed to the base of the hill, where two fallen trees were leaning up against each other like the walls of an A-frame. Leo nodded, and followed me down the hill. At the base of the A-frame was a small circle of rocks—nearly hidden by fallen leaves and dirt. It was a fire ring. I breathed a sigh of relief. Proof that once, years ago, Avery had been here.

It didn't take long to set up camp. Leo gathered logs and dry brush to start a fire, and I turned over a couple of stumps to use as seats. Soon, we were warming ourselves by the crackling flames and eating strips of dried meat which Leo had packed in a knapsack for the journey.

The cold air made my nose run, and my hands were going numb, despite my fur-lined gloves. My boots were growing wet from sitting in snow. I pulled my hood closer around my ears, and jumped as a stick snapped somewhere nearby.

"Did you know an old wyvern lives in these mountains?" Leo joked.

"That's not funny."

"Don't worry. Wyverns aren't nearly as smart as dragons."

"Is that supposed to make me feel better?"

Leo's laughter was so loud, I felt certain any wyvern nearby would coming running for its next meal. Or crawling. Or whatever wyverns did. I scowled at him, hoping he'd quiet down, but my scowl only made him laugh harder. "You...should have...seen...your face," he choked between breaths. I wanted to slap him.

It was several minutes before he had calmed down enough to speak, and by then he was panting and holding his sides. "Really though, Calli, I was joking. The only wyvern around here lives several mountains away, and they don't travel very far from their territories. We are well out of his range."

I rolled my eyes. "Thanks for clearing that up," I snapped. Leo smiled at me, but said nothing. We sat in silence for a long while, listening to the sound of owls, of wind in the trees, and of the fire. Beside me, Leo appeared deep in thought.

"What's your greatest fear?" he asked suddenly.

I didn't hesitate. The answer fell right out of my mouth, even though I'd never given it much thought. "That my parents hate me," I said.

"What do you mean?"

I sighed. "My Aunt Margaret," I told him, "never spoke of my parents much. She wasn't really my aunt of course. She just had me call her that because she told me we were family, and that's what people say when they are family. She never once instructed me to call her 'mother' though, and I don't know why. Sometimes, I think that maybe it's because she realized that, wherever my parents were, they loved me and she didn't have the right to usurp that role. She never gave up on them. I did."

"Calli," Leo said gently, "you can't blame yourself for that. You were seven."

I shook my head. "I believed they had abandoned me right up until the day I met Arcturus. I can't help but wonder if they are out there somewhere, wherever people go after they die, and if they know the things I thought? The things I'd been thinking about them all those years. What if they know how much I hated them?" I paused and drew a ragged breath.

"And now, to learn that they gave their lives for mine, that they aren't here, not because they didn't love me, but because they loved me very much—it's almost more than I can bear. My mother loved me so much she *died* saving me, and my father died the same way. How can I ever forgive myself for that? How could they ever forgive me?" There were tears in my eyes, so much so that the fire in front of me was nothing more than a blurred mass of light. I coughed, and wiped the tears away.

"I'm sure," Leo said, "wherever your parents are, that they can see what's in your heart. They know what you've been through and the reasons for why you thought the things you did. I promise you Calli. I promise they love you. And I promise you they wouldn't blame you for a single thing you've ever thought."

"Thank you, Leo."

He gave me a consoling smile and wrapped an arm around my shoulder. I leaned my head against him, and closed my eyes. "I'll take the first watch," he said. "Go ahead and get some sleep."

* * *

"Maybe we should rest."

"We can't, Leo. We have to keep going." It was midday and, though the sun was bright, it did not offer any warmth. I could see my breath rising as mist from my mouth. The tips of my hair had frozen, and my face felt stiff. "If we stop, we won't be able to keep up with Avery's pace, and then I can't use the sun to keep track of where we are." Leo nodded, pausing to wait as I recalled a new memory. "Run," I said a few moments later. "Avery is running now."

Across the snow-covered slopes, dodging trees and sliding down sheer rock, we ran.

* * *

It was dark before we stopped to make camp. This time, as we sat in front of the fire, we were too tired to speak. Instead, we ate nuts and more dried meat in silence. I melted a bowlful of snow over the fire to share—we had run out of water earlier in the day. When we were done drinking, I stored the rest away for later.

"I'll take the first watch this time," I told Leo, standing and stretching my stiff limbs. Leo didn't argue and went to the dry bit of leaf matter we had warmed with magic for sleeping. He wrapped himself in his cloak, and almost immediately, he was asleep. I stoked the fire and settled in for a few hours of standing guard, trying very hard not think of what might be hiding in the dark.

* * *

I started coughing at midnight.

The moon was bright and directly overhead, causing the forest to look flat and depthless. I had removed my gloves earlier so I could warm my hands more easily on the fire. I used them to catch my cough. By the time my fit had ceased, they were covered in something warm and sticky. I held my hands out to the firelight.

It was blood.

My stomach turned in on itself, and I started on another fit of coughing. Soon, the snow was splattered with dark blood, nearly black in the night. I stood, panicking, and the world tilted sideways. Before I could catch myself, I fell onto the pot of water, spilling it into the flames and causing them to hiss out. The pot clanged loudly against the stones of our fire ring. Leo woke up.

"Calli?" Almost immediately, Leo was on his feet. "Calli, what's wrong?" I couldn't answer. It was too hard to breathe. When he noticed the blood on my hands and on the snow, he muttered an explicative I couldn't quite make out. He dropped to his knees beside me, wiping my hands on his cloak and then taking them in his own.

"I must have caught it when I went to see Ema," I said weakly. "I guess you were right when you told me not to go."

He didn't have time to respond. Something rustled in the brush nearby and a rat, probably drawn by the scent of blood, crept out of the bushes. Ten others followed behind. Eyes watched in the darkness all around us. There were hundreds of them. Using Leo's shoulder as a ladder, I staggered to my feet. Beside me, Leo stood as well.

The rats were the size of small dogs, and the moment I saw them, I knew something was wrong. They didn't move quite right, and as they came out into the light of the moon, their eyes glowed red. Something about them seemed sinister, unnatural, and dark. Beside me, Leo drew his sword. "I've never seen anything like this," Leo whispered. I reached for a nearby stick and held it in my fists the way I would a blade.

The rat closest to us was the first to lunge. It came at us like a banshee, shrieking and baring its fang-like teeth. From behind us, two more came. Back to back, Leo and I fought them off, slashing through them like thick underbrush. The wave seemed never-ending.

Leaping from the side, a single rat made it through Leo's sword. It launched itself at him and buried its teeth deep into the flesh of his forearm. Leo screamed. Turning towards him, I beat it off with my stick.

Five more attacked from behind, when I turned my back, climbing up my cloak and dress towards my face. Their claws scratched my skin. I flung them off, beating them with my stick until they had stopped moving.

Then, just when it seemed I could go on no longer, they were gone. Whether we had slain them all, or the rest had retreated, I didn't know. It didn't matter. Surrounded by the bodies of malformed rats, I fell to my knees. "It's over," I breathed. The thump of a body hitting the ground caused me to turn.

Leo had collapsed, his body contorted and his muscles corded tight. I drug myself across the ground to his side. His forehead was hot to the touch and beaded with sweat. The skin around his bite mark was angry and red. My heart lurched. The rats were poisonous.

"Leo, can you hear me?" He groaned, but said nothing.

I had no medicine and no training in healing. There was nothing I could do, but hope and wait it out. I wrapped him in both of our cloaks and restarted the fire. Then, with his hand clutched in mine, I settled down to wait. His groans turned to whimpers, and his whimpers to shrieks of pain.

He screamed until morning.

* * *

Somehow, I managed to stay conscious all night, despite the fever chills and exhaustion that wracked my body. Deep in the back of my mind, I was aware of the fact that I should have already succumbed. Master McDunnon, and all those who were sick, had fallen into unconsciousness within minutes of coughing up blood. It was a thought I didn't focus on. Whatever the reason, I'd be glad if I could hold off the sickness a little longer.

By daybreak, Leo had sweated out the last of the poison, and by breakfast he was feeling like himself, laughing like normal and making jokes. We set out once I was convinced he could walk, and put on a brave face. If Leo could walk, I could too.

"Are you sure you're okay?" he asked me after a while, slowing to a halt. I shook my head. There was no point in lying. What else would I say? I coughed and tried discreetly to wipe the blood on the folds of my dress. His eyes told me he noticed.

"We just have to find those birds," he said softly. "That's all. We just have to find them." A heavy silence fell. I didn't mention the thoughts that seemed to hang unspoken between us. *What if we don't find them? What if we find the valley, and they simply aren't there?*

The day passed and soon, it was night again. We were standing in the middle of a clearing. I kept turning in circles, around and around. Everything looked the same. I closed my eyes and ran through the memory one more time. Then I opened them and kept spinning.

"Calli, what's wrong?" I ignored him, staring into the dark and frowning until I was sure my face would stay that way forever. Leo shook me, and I stopped, glancing up into his face. "What is it?"

"There was a pine tree..." I said, waving a hand hopelessly in the air. "I don't see it."

"Calli...we are surrounded by pine trees."

"I know," I whispered. My voice cracked, and I sat down hard on the ground. "I know."

"How far are we?"

"Very close."

He grabbed my arm and pulled me to my feet. "Then we will keep going. Where do you think it was?"

"Over there?" I sighed, pointing vaguely. "But I can't be sure."

"Come on."

We stumbled on for quite awhile. Fifteen minutes, half an hour, an hour—I couldn't be sure. I coughed, blood splattering across the snow and front of my dress. I could feel my fever hiking up higher and higher. I stumbled and stopped. I knew this place.

"He sat down by a white boulder," I told Leo, pointing to a rock. "He just sat there, and it appeared."

Leo squinted through the darkness. "How did he know it was white? Is it white?" he asked, gesturing towards the rock. I shrugged. It was too dark to tell.

"I don't know." I threw myself down beside it anyway.

"How long did he sit there?"

"Not long."

We waited. Hours passed. There was nothing. I stood and stumbled off into the dark. Then I returned. I paced in circles until I could barely stand. Then I sat down again. "It should be here..." I whispered. "We should have seen it by now. It was right here. It was!" The night was very dark. Leo said nothing, and pulled me under his cloak. His arms wrapped around my shoulders. "It should be here..." he still made no reply, but when he bent his head to rest it on my shoulder, his face was wet.

"Maybe we calculated the time wrong," he said at last. "Maybe we were a few hours ahead of him. He only waited a few minutes, but that doesn't mean we will."

"No," I whispered. "I don't think so. In any case, it must be almost morning. Even if we *are* in the right place, it won't appear to us now. The moon has to shine in the exact center of that circle. That would mean the valley is visible for an hour, at the most." I shrugged helplessly. "If we don't find those birds..." I trailed off, not wanting to finish my sentence aloud. If we didn't find the birds, chances were, most of the people now sick in the castle, would die.

"It's not the others I'm worried about anymore," Leo said, his voice hardly a whisper. "Maybe your uncle will find a cure. We don't know. But without those birds, and without Lady Dubois, *you* won't last more than another day. I can't let that happen." Something in his voice made my stomach twist.

"It can't be helped." Defeated, I slid my back further down the rock we were leaning against and nestled my head into Leo's side. Somehow, death didn't seem quite as frightening as it should. The sickness had made me dizzy; maybe it had taken away my energy for emotion as well.

Leo shook his head, and I could feel him tensing. "This has to be the place. Maybe it was almost morning when Avery was here. It can't be the end— it's not..."

"Leo..."

"I'll carry you back. We will wait till morning and then I'll carry you back. I'll run if I have to. I will. I—"

"Even if you could run that far while carrying me, who knows how many miles we are away? We are in the middle of nowhere Leo. It's over."

"Calli..."

"No. Just accept it." He fell silent, and pulled me closer. The darkness of the forest was almost suffocating. I'd never seen a darker night. It was eery dark. *Too* dark. I froze and pushed myself away from him. "Leo..." he wasn't listening. "Leo, the clouds! The clouds are covering the moon!" I stood and looked up. He stood with me. His eyes panned the horizon, and then his face fell.

"What can we do?"

I sighed and sat back down. "Hope?" I muttered harshly. "Hope that the clouds disappear, and the moon is still in the right spot? They are clouds, Leo, what can we do?" He leaned against a tree, and watched the sky.

There was no point using magic. Changing the weather was beyond the capabilities of even the most experienced magic user. Something like that simply took too much energy—more energy than the human body could produce. So I copied Leo and turned my eyes to the clouds, tossing up a prayer and hoping beyond hope that maybe, just maybe, some small bit of wind would pick up and push the clouds away.

I'm not sure how long we sat there. It could have been minutes, it could have been hours. In all probability, it was probably only five minutes or so, but time felt exaggerated. The seconds drug on like days.

At first, all I felt was a strange tingling sensation running up my left arm and down my back. I figured it was just the last dregs of energy draining from my limbs. I let out a sigh, and focused on wishing harder. That was when the tingling evolved. It became a rushing.

Energy. Energy rushing through every pore of my body. My hair crackled with it. I felt alive, on fire. My blood burned, and a current consumed me. Raging, roaring rapids of white hot energy, threatening to drown me or sweep me away. It seemed to be coming from the ground, the air, even the trees, and I felt rooted, like the earth around me was just an extension of myself, or perhaps that I was an extension of it. Suddenly the image of the moon became crystal clear in my mind's eye. I could feel the wind I wished for passing through my body. And then, like a wind that comes and goes, all was still inside me.

"Calli? Are you okay?" Leo was looking at me strangely, and suddenly it was all I could do to sit up straight. I slumped down against the rock. "You were burning up a second ago."

From the corner of my eyes, I could see Leo holding up a hand in front of his face. His expression mirrored shock. "You gave me blisters," he whispered, still staring at his hand in disbelief. His voice seemed very far away. A small piece of my hair drifted past my face, caught in a breeze. "Are you okay?" He repeated. I didn't answer. "Is it from the sickness? I've never felt a fever like that before." I wasn't listening to him. Instead, my eyes were fixed on the sky.

"Leo, the clouds..."

He stopped fussing over me and his eyes followed mine. Slowly, his mouth dropped open. "They're vanishing," he said at last. The clouds *were* vanishing. A steady breeze had picked up, and the breeze was rapidly becoming a wind. The moon was growing brighter by the second, and then something in the air ahead of us seemed to shimmer. I glanced up to the sky. The clouds were gone. When I looked back, a giant bowl shaped valley stretched before us. Leo wasted no time. He grabbed my hand, and drug me forward.

"Impossible," I whispered breathlessly. "Absolutely impossible." It had to be coincidence. No magic could change the weather. "That wind was just in the right place at the right time. Just like us. Just like Avery."

"I think people are in the right place at the right time a lot less often than they think they are," Leo said vaguely.

"So you think——?"

He nodded. "I think those clouds disappeared because we needed them to."

I fell silent and stumbled forward. We both stumbled, exhausted, until we were inside of it. "The Valley Shrouded in Mist," I whispered.

"And Vision Lake." Leo nodded in front of us. A perfectly circular lake was in the middle of the bowl, the moon reflected flawlessly in the center of it. I looked around. The trees were not pine here. Instead, a forest of aspen and birch was stretched out before of us. The trees were leafy despite it being the dead of winter, and their golden leaves were blanketed in snow. I noticed with a start that there was no snow on the ground.

Then I realized that the white in the trees wasn't snow.

33

The Valley

Birds. Hundreds—maybe even thousands—of birds. They were singing all around us. I'd never heard a more beautiful sound. The trees shook with them. They bent under the weight. I pulled the stone from my pocket. "All we have to do is replace the feather with this?" I asked. He nodded.

"It should be in the middle. I say you take the left side, and I'll take the right. With both of us together it shouldn't take long. We can start in the middle and—" he stopped, noticing the look on my face. "What's wrong?"

"I can't swim," I whispered. He nodded and walked away from me for a few minutes. I could see his shoulders were tense. When he returned, his face was set with determination.

"You shouldn't be out there in your condition anyway," he said at last. "Go find a bird and see if you can get it to heal you, however that works. I'll be fine." He threw his cloak aside and pulled off his shirt. I could feel my face heat and I turned away. I stopped him when he was waist deep.

"Leo!" He turned back to look at me. "I'm sorry." Sitting on the shore like this, I felt useless.

"Don't worry about it. I've got this." His voice was hard, but he didn't complain. He never complained. He dove under the water, and disappeared.

Turning my back, I walked towards the trees. The birds were high above me, too distant for me to communicate with them.

I was several paces away from the lake when I felt it—a tingling sensation that ran down my spine. I was being watched. I looked around, but except for Leo and me, the valley was empty. I kept walking, moving towards the golden trees in hope that a bird would drift near enough that I could speak with it.

I was wandering through a patch of fallen leaves when a sound to my right made me turn around. Out of the corner of my eye, something dark disappeared into the trees. Something black. I hurried towards it, but it was already gone. I shook my head. Most likely, the fever was making me hallucinate. Whistling, I turned my attention back on the birds.

Near the edge of the valley, something caught my eye again, dark against the trees. This time, it didn't disappear when I looked at it, only shrunk back deeper into the foliage. A black cloaked figure, just like the one I had seen in Caeyra. Judging by the distinctive way it moved as it backed away from me, the two were the same.

Maybe it was the sickness, weakening my reasoning skills. Maybe it was my lessons with Arcturus which gave me confidence that I could defend myself. Most likely however, it was the feeling in my gut, some force that drew me to action, some strange connection that pulled me forward and towards the unknown figure at the edge of the trees. Before I knew what my legs were doing, I was running after it.

It became obvious after only a few steps of running just how weak I was. My feet stumbled into the action, and it took all of my strength to keep my legs following them. The figure darted through a thick cluster of trees and I followed, weaving through branches like a drunken deer. For a moment I was sure I couldn't keep up the chase, but then adrenaline kicked in and my legs steadied themselves. My heart drummed in my ears.

"Hey! Wait!" The figure took a sharp right, leaping over a fallen log. A thick blanket of golden leaves covered the ground, and they sprayed up when it landed, lacing the black cloak in gold. I clambered over the log, my dress catching on the rough bark, and slipped through those same leaves. Then I sprinted as fast as my legs could carry me, away from Leo and off towards the figure. Mud from a puddle splashed up on the edges of my skirts, and even as high as my cheeks. Branches wrapped themselves in my petticoats. Clutching my skirts in my fists, I ran faster. The distance between the figure and myself, steadily grew. It was getting away. I couldn't keep up.

"Wait! Why have you been following me?" I called out. My voice trembled of its own accord, and my legs began to forsake me. The distance between us kept growing. And then, just when I was sure I would never catch up, the figure stumbled over an exposed tree root, and fell. The hood toppled off its head—*his* head—and he turned to look at me in shock. My momentum carried me an arm's length away from him, and then my feet fastened themselves to the ground.

I stared. Light colored amber eyes stared back at me, covered by a head of honey hair. It was a face I recognized with startling clarity. A face I knew from my dreams. I didn't say a word and neither did he. We just stared as if something powerful rooted us place. Frozen. Something in my mind didn't seem to quite work. He was so familiar. His face—after a moment I realized with shock whose face it was. "Derek." My father. But my father was a man fourteen years dead, and this boy had the look of youth on his face. There was only one other conclusion left to me. A conclusion that made me numb to the bone. The boy. He was my brother.

The moment the thought crossed my mind, I knew it was true. I had my mother's memories, after all dancing around in the back of my head. I was a twin. Two of us had been born that night, not one. The hints had been everywhere, written all across my dreams. I hadn't noticed because I hadn't expected it, and often, the mind only sees what it expects. My heart pounded in my ears.

We were near the cliffs now. I opened my mouth to ask for his name when a loud sound stopped me. We broke eye contact then, looking up and towards the source of the noise. Something was moving, deep within a nearby cave. A head slithered out, followed by a pair of winged shoulders.

It was the wyvern.

He was as tall as a house and his grey-white scales rattled as he moved towards us. His head alone was the size of a horse, and as his lips curled back to bare his teeth, fangs the length of my arm glinted in the moonlight.

"Humans," he hissed, his voice piercing and deep. My brother had frozen behind me, and I backed up until we were standing side-by-side. *"Do you know what happened, last time I saw a human, little girl?"*

"No." My voice was hardly a whisper, but he heard it. His eyes narrowed.

"Come to the valley shaped like the moon, the man told me. All you have to do is defend it for a little while, and I will repay you with more food and riches than you have ever seen." The beast paused, so close to us now that I could feel his hot breath on my face. It smelled like gunpowder and rot. *"He lied."*

I could hear my heart, hammering out desperate beats in my ribcage. My lungs were tight. I couldn't breathe. Beside me, I could feel my brother shaking. "You can't know that," I said weakly. "Maybe he's still coming."

"He told me I could leave!" the wyvern snarled. His words roared inside my head, filling my skull with so much pressure I felt sure it would explode. *"But then he came at night and stole one of my scales, and dropped it in the bottom of the pond."*

"I'm not like that man. I would never betray you like that, I promise." I was pleading now.

"Lies," he hissed. *"More lies. I can smell him on you."*

Suddenly, I found myself wishing I had brought a sword with me. Then, my heart sank. Even armed, there was nothing I could do. Leo and I together could not defeat the creature that now stood before me. Even Arcturus would have struggled against him. My stomach felt sick.

"I haven't eaten for fourteen years," the wyvern said, his voice sending shivers down my spine. *"The only thing living in this valley are those birds, and I can't reach them."* He glanced up to the treetops, and then turned his eyes back to me. His wings were old and tattered, I realized, making it impossible for him to fly. *"I am hungry."*

My knees were weak. I wasn't ever sure I could run. I grabbed my brother's arm, pulling him with me as I slowly backed away. The wyvern reared back, his massive jaws snapping at the sky.

Just when I felt certain that it was all over, something shot like an arrow through the woods. It exploded from the underbrush, flying through the air and planting itself between the wyvern and me. It was Pan.

I barely recognized him. His form had grown as he launched through the air, and by the time he landed on the ground in front of me, he was the size of a large horse. His brindled fur was like fire in the moonlight, and his eyes like burning embers. Saliva dripped from his snarling jaws. *"Stand down, worm."*

The great worm lowered himself, stopping so that his curling lips were inches from Pan's snout. *"You are hardly a match for me, hellhound,"* he sneered. His breath blew ripples through the hound's coat, but Pan did not flinch.

"Do not use that term for me, worm," he said. *"My sire was a hellhound. I am only half. But half is enough to kill you."* His voice was guttural, like a snarl ripping from a throat. He paced in front of my brother and I, his hackles raised and his limbs coiled to spring. The grass beneath his feet shriveled and turned to dust.

When the wyvern hesitated, Pan took his chance. His snapping jaws closed around the wyvern's throat and he was lifted high in the air. He did not let go.

The wyvern screamed, a shriek that spouted fire into the sky. His thrashing shook the ground. Still, Pan did not release his grasp. The flesh beneath his jaws was turning black, withering in fast decay as the corrosive saliva from the hellhound's maw took effect. Moments later, the wyvern shook him off, throwing him through the air and into a tree, where he collapsed and remained motionless. The wyvern gave one last shriek before collapsing to the ground himself. I tensed, prepared to defend myself, but the wyvern did not move. He was already dead.

The moment I realized it was over, I ran to Pan's side and dropped to my knees beside him. He was small again, a wolfhound with long silky fur and soft brown eyes. *"I'll be okay,"* he said, and lifted himself to his feet.

There was a sudden rumble, and the ground shook. I looked up. We had made our way back to the lake, and something seemed to be shattering around me. Hundreds of birds burst into the sky and disappeared, flying beyond the invisible walls and continuing till they were out of sight. I glanced back towards the body of the wyvern, stretched out behind me, looking for the boy who had stood nearby. My brother was gone. Turning, I looked around the clearing. So were my birds. All but one.

She appeared just when I felt sure they were gone forever. Like a white jewel she glided from the sky, and landed on my shoulder. *"Let's go home,"* she told me, and her voice was as clear as a bell.

I gazed out across the bowl shaped valley. *Home.* What a perfect and wonderful thought. The sun was just beginning to rise, and I could see Leo staggering out of the circular lake. A white feather was clutched in his hand. He held it up triumphantly and grinned when he caught my eye. I turned back to look where my brother had vanished and shook my head. It didn't matter if he was gone. This wasn't the end. Not even close. It was just the beginning.

End of Caladrius Dreams
Book One of the Queenmaker Saga

Acknowledgments

I would like to send out a huge thank you to everyone who made this novel possible. I wouldn't have been able to do this without a single one of you.

First, I'd like to thank my wonderful husband, Brian, for sticking with me and offering so much support and encouragement. You kept me from going crazy when times got tough! I love you dear!

I'd also like to thank my parents, who never stopped believing in me, and have done so much to make this dream of mine come true. More than anyone else, I wouldn't have been able to do this without you both.

A big thanks to each person who helped me at one point or another during the painstaking editing process—my husband Brian, Dave Drollman, Alex Lasota, my uncle Steve Aranguren, and David Cates, author and faculty member of the 406 Writer's Workshop in Missoula, MT.

Thank you also to Mr. James Powers, who gallantly offered to help me out by creating the cover design for this book. It took a million pounds off my shoulders to not have to worry about doing that myself!

I am also eternally grateful to each of the people who have donated monetarily to help me get this far. I will never forget your kindness and generosity.

Thank you again, everyone! Wherever this book goes, you will forever be a part of making it a reality!

Erin Ann McCarter is a current student at Eastern Washington University. She will be graduating in 2017 with a Bachelor's degree in Journalism and a minor in web design. Erin is a copy editor for her school paper, and is a fashion and lifestyle blogger at her blog, Clothed in Sunlight. Her hobbies include riding horses, drawing, and adventuring through the wilderness. Erin lives in Cheney, Washington with her husband Brian and their dog Flash.